I0534157

DEAD BY THE HANDS OF OTHER MEN

A Jack McQueen Mystery Thriller

David P. Fraser

Ascent Aspirations Publishing

Copyright © 2024 by David P. Fraser
All rights reserved.

No part of this publication may be used or reproduced in any manner whatsoever, electronic, or mechanical, including photocopying, recording, or any form of browsing, storage, or retrieval system, without written permission except in the case of brief quotations embodied in critical articles and reviews. For information address Ascent Aspirations.
Email: ascentaspirations@gmail.com

This is a work of fiction. Names, characters, places, and incidents are products of the author's imaginations or are used fictitiously and are not to be construed as real. Any semblance to actual events, locales, organizations, or persons, living or dead is entirely coincidental.

Fraser, David P.
Dead by the hands of other men / David P. Fraser. — First Edition 2024
Cover Art by Patricia Carroll (www.patriciacarroll.ca)
1. Abduction—Fiction. 2. Detective Investigation—Fiction. 3. Identity—Fiction. 4. Memory Loss—Fiction. 5. Childhood Trauma—Fiction. 6. Human Trafficking—Fiction. 7. British Columbia—Fiction. 8. Organ Harvesting I Title.

Library and Archives Canada Cataloguing in Publication

Title: Dead by the hands of other men / David P. Fraser.
Names: Fraser, David, 1946- author.
Description: First edition. | Series statement: A Jack McQueen novel
Identifiers: Canadiana (print) 20240288017 | Canadiana (ebook) 20240288025 | ISBN 9781738240104
(softcover) | ISBN 9781738240111 (Kindle)
Subjects: LCGFT: Thrillers (Fiction) | LCGFT: Detective and mystery fiction. | LCGFT: Novels.
Classification: LCC PS8611.R38 D43 2024 | DDC C813/.6—dc23

For Patricia Carroll

Every day you inspire me with love, music, and art.

DEAD BY THE HANDS OF OTHER MEN

CHAPTER 1

I thought I'd put everything behind me until Murphy called.

"Help me," she said.

"What's up?"

"They've split up the Shaplow squad. Dispersed everyone who knew anything about what happened last year. I've been assigned to the mainland."

"I'll meet you. Tell me where?" Apprehension rose in my throat. I stared at the sealed Jameson bottle on the shelf.

"Brogans," she said. "You sound twitchy."

"Not much to do up here. I'm glad you called. You want to tell me what's up?"

"Just get your ass over. Call me when you land."

At the float house, nobody had called in four months. I drank only water and apple juice. Salvaged stuff for amusement or fired my Glock to scare a resident black bear. In solitude, I wrote poetry in a journal. One call and Murphy had dragged me back

The floatplane touched down in the estuary beside Vancouver airport and I looked down at a wide expanse of the delta, thought about Mark, and how his marina got torched, how I messed him up with the Russians, and now because of me, he lived on his offshore boat.

I thought about Shaplow Lake and how I'd almost recovered. The poetry scribbled in black notebooks helped me deal with the trauma.

I brought a lightweight duffle bag, a change of clothes, my notebooks and some cash, money left over from the Shaplow stash I'd shared with Tony, a flashlight, and the bottle of J. I had my Glock holstered on my belt and a Beretta on my ankle. I dropped down onto the dock, followed the check-out channels, caught the Skytrain in, and called Murphy for the meeting time at Brogans.

"What time?"

"Five o'clock."

Brogans was on Denman, so from the Vancouver City Center Station, I walked down Georgia. I noticed an unmarked behind me cruising the curb and without introduction two burly guys with thick necks and squinty eyes were on me. They knew I was back. Took my guns. Cuffed my hands. Welcome to Vancouver. I was stuffed into the back seat after a sarcastic "Watch your head." As if they care. I thought local precinct. Some bullshit excuse to roust me about a carry permit. But no. I was driven back toward downtown and across the Cambie Bridge to City Hall. Back door. Small room. Oval table. Built-in mics. This was a first-class interview room.

I sat at the table. The two coppers handed me off to a detective in a suit who guarded the door. The guy was long and skinny. At first, I didn't profile him. Been out of practice but when I did, I saw it was Reynolds.

"Whose ass have you been shoving your nose up these days?" I gave him a thin smile.

"Shut up, before I rearrange your face, McQueen."

I didn't get a chance to needle his butt. Someone knocked on the door. Reynolds opened it and stepped smartly to attention. Commissioner Machlan walked in and sat down across from me on the short side of the oval table. He waved Reynolds outside.

The prick. He stared at me. Not a word.

We went way back. He'd made the final decision to dump me from the RCMP. His words were "loose cannon" and a few others—PTSD, impulsivity, and insubordination. Excessive force was another word that came up. That's all after I'd stopped an abusive child killer dead in his tracks with a full clip of bullets.

Machlan started in with, "Last year was a good year for you in the press."

I opened my mouth. He didn't want a response.

"You tidied up the Island. I'm still dealing with the body count. I should've had you arrested for obstruction of justice, and abuse of police, but the media wouldn't let me get away with it."

"Obstruction of justice?" I almost said.

If the force cared about justice, I wouldn't need to do what I do, but for once I kept my cocky mouth shut.

"I'm not happy you're here, McQueen." Machlan stretched out the Queen part like it was a recalcitrant turd. I stayed quiet. Cautious.

"I'm keeping an eye on you. You won't mess with the way we deal out the law in this town. So don't get any ideas about investigations into issues that are none of your business."

"But how am I to know?"

"Look smart-ass, you'll know. Keep your nose clean."

Machlan got up and went to the door. He said to Reynolds, "Get this guy out of here. Check his permits first. Don't take him for a ride. He's got the message. If not, he'll find out soon enough."

My permits checked out, but I received a warning that I could only carry one gun at a time and only for assigned protective work. I was dumped out back, left to find a bus to Brogans and by the time I got there the sun was sinking into the Pacific.

Brogans was as close as it got to an Irish pub in Vancouver. Little cubbies or snugs where you could have a conversation with a friend or be left alone without a stranger starting a chat as if you were best buds. I couldn't stand that. Those conversations always ended in foul language and punch-ups.

The sentries nursed pints on either end of the bar. I couldn't swear to it, but they could be the guys who watched me leave six months ago before I got mauled and jacked outside. The regulars. I went to the bar. Apple juice? No. I'd done my time. I could handle it.

"A pint of Guinness and a double shot of J," I said, "and when a lady comes in for me, bring the same."

I found a booth at the back and faced the door. I watched the bartender do a slow pour and waited for it to settle before he came over. The first sip was a damn sight closer to paradise than the wilderness up north, but maybe more lethal. But I had it under control. My twitchiness began to fade.

The shot was gone, and I was halfway through the Guinness when Murphy came through the door. Both sentries swung their heads, and their eyes undressed her. I wanted to grab them both by the scruff and smack their heads together.

She was out of uniform and wore blue jeans, a wool shirt, and a fleece. She'd pulled down a 49er's cap over her eyes. She looked thinner and had a lean and hungry look about her. She had a pretty face, one that doesn't need a layer of makeup. She saw me at the back. I got up. We hugged. She was all muscle.

"You look good," she said.

"Liar."

"What about me?" she laughed.

"Go fish."

"Getting a compliment out of you isn't easy."

"I'm a man of few words. Besides I've lost what social skills I had up in the bush. Bears and wolves aren't much for conversation. Thought you'd always stay at Shaplow Lake with that tight-ass, Conner."

"Conner's gone. All those guys seem to move up the food chain. And like I said on the phone we've been shipped everywhere. Reilly's in another division and I'm here."

"Are you in charge?"

"I wish. Won't see that again. Once you mess with them, they have long memories."

She wasn't talking only about herself.

The bartender remembered the order. He set the Guinness down in front of Murphy and put the J in the center between us. Clever boy.

Murphy looked me in the eyes, and we raised our glasses.

"Welcome back," she said.

I sipped the Guinness and slid the J to my side and took half of it down. Paradise renewed.

"Good to be back."

"You're not heavy into that again, are you?"

"No. No. Just glad to see you. Nice to be seen."

Murphy looked at me hard. She'd heard this all before.

"Why me?" I asked.

Murphy reached into her purse, pulled out her cell, hit the screen a few times, and slid it across the table.

"The photos aren't pretty. Mutilation. You'll get the picture."

A set of thumbnails were on the screen. I stared at them.

"Just tap one. You can swipe sideways."

I moved through the photos to the end.

"Cut-off arms and legs." I said.

"Brutal."

I glanced over to the bar.

Murphy nodded. We got up. I threw down some bills to cover the tab, left a healthy tip, and we were out the door. All eyes followed us as if we were celebrities.

CHAPTER 2

When we left Brogans, it was dark. I hadn't realized we'd talked that long. It was a short walk to Murphy's late-model Corolla. Cheap and sensible. I didn't know why but I sniffed the air and checked the lanes between the buildings as we passed. Watched the traffic. Looked at faces behind the steering wheels. Questioned why someone stood at the window display for second-hand stuff two doors down from Brogans. Murphy's remote opened the car door, and we got inside.

She didn't turn on the ignition but faced me.

"What's the panic?" I said.

"You saw the pictures. Sensational."

"Sensational is an understatement."

In the next moment, she threw herself toward me and buried her face into my shoulder. Her body shook and she burst into deep sobs. I put my arm around her shoulders. And I thought I was the fragile one. I let her play it out before I said. "Okay. Murphy. Get a grip. Just talk to me."

I played the photos in my mind. Stayed quiet. Waited for her to speak.

Crime scenes are often messy. Without dignity. But these images were different. The scene was theatrical. A tableau.

Murphy pulled back, lifted my arm, and wiped her tears on my sleeve. She took a breath, put the key in the ignition, and fastened her seat belt.

"Buckle up." She put the car into gear and paused as she went into second. "Those pricks have hung me out to dry."

Murphy took a left toward Burrard Inlet and the docks on the east side. Where else would someone have the balls to create such a travesty? Commissioner Street is the main street that runs along the docks where the container yards sit with their cranes on the inlet. She cut one street deep and came in behind a narrow alley that runs parallel. She stopped beneath a dim light. I waited for her lead.

"Do you see that Crown Vic in the shadows and the alley across from it?"

I looked. Couldn't make out what kind of car it was. "I see it."

"He's one of us but I didn't assign him, and I don't know him. As I said, I'm on my own."

I looked at her. Not sure what to say.

"That smaller alley across from him opens to a square with loading bays. It's taped off where we found the body."

"So, the plan is?"

I was twitchy. I touched the Beretta Pico on my ankle, then felt the Glock holstered in the center of my back.

"I don't trust anyone right now. I will talk to him. He won't think anyone is with me. Everyone knows I got no partner, no backup. You go back down the street a bit, cross over and get down that alley and into the square. I'll distract him and block his view, so he won't see you. Take the phone. Look at the pictures, get oriented, and see what you can come up with."

"Sure boss," I said.

"Just do it."

Murphy was strung like piano wire. She eased out of the car and started to walk toward the Crown Vic. I slid from the passenger side and stayed in the shadows which was easy because where she'd parked was the only light. I crossed the street, slipped along the wall of the building, and slid into the alley. The air was warm with a strong diesel smell. It hadn't rained in a long while, but the pavement on the street and the alley's cracked concrete had a greasy texture—soiled and decayed.

I watched Murphy from the alley. She leaned on the driver's window. I heard a muffled conversation. I headed down to the end where the alley opened to the square. One feeble light was on over a loading bay and every other back entrance was dark. All the buildings were connected by brick walls ten or fifteen feet high, some with doors raised up a foot from the pavement.

I tapped on the phone and brought up the photos. The body was decapitated and without its limbs. I walked over to the widest brick wall. On the phone, I looked at the photo. A cross was propped up at an angle. That was where the torso was nailed by long spikes. The image jumped from the phone and onto the wall. No head. No arms below the elbow. No legs below the knee. In the blow-up image on the phone, the cuts looked surgical. Each cut was sewn together. The chest had a Y-incision as in an autopsy, sewn up like a rawhide jacket. No blood anywhere. A torso. A piece of meat.

I used the flashlight feature on the phone. I couldn't see anything. I could have taken my flashlight from my duffle but didn't think if it with Murphy being so energized. I ran the phone along the edge of the wall. Forensics would have gone over the site. But in a crevice in the concrete where the wind had blown a loose wrapper and a weather-soaked coffee cup, a round object flashed back in the dim light from the phone. I picked up a cream-colored button, larger than a shirt or suit jacket button. I slipped it into my pocket when I heard soft, furtive footsteps. The hairs on my neck stood at attention. I turned. I thought about how Murphy shook in my arms. It was so unlike her.

Three dark shapes with no definition came at me from different angles. I had no time to get to my Glock as the first shape came in high, arms raised holding a bat. I dropped and leaned into his momentum. Used my leg strength to brace myself, and he flipped over my shoulder. I stayed low and searched for the next shape. A swipe of another bat caught me across the shoulder, and another glanced off my shin. The pain set me back on my heels, but I regained balance and drove my elbow into the soft tissue below someone's neck, swung around and balanced with a raised leg, and drove my heel into the third shape's chest. The first shape was up, and the bat caught me across the back and his next swing crashed into the back of my knees. I went down. The shapes started to pummel my body with their bats. I curled into a ball and grabbed the Beretta from my ankle holster. All I could do as the bats pounded on my body was to fire low in a circle. I managed to hit two of them in their legs and heard them scream.

The bats became silent. I stood with the Beretta leveled but wobbled unsteadily and swayed the barrel in the air. It was enough for them to get the message. I wanted to blast them, but I didn't. One shape in the middle held the other two shapes up and they limped toward the street.

Jack. Stay calm. Take a moment. I didn't. I, too, hobbled to the entrance on the street. I heard a muffled noise beside the Crown Vic. No light to see. I'd been beaten up again. I'd been stupid, for not seeing them coming, and not being aware of what came next. I shined my cell phone light, caught a glimpse of a red star tattoo on the back of a hand coming toward me. Then I felt severe pain and a saw a flash of welding sparks.

I felt like a failure.

CHAPTER 3

If this was what hell smelled like, then I was dead. I opened my eyes to darkness and sensed a tight space. Rotten. Month-old-corpse rotten. A submerged floater rotten. I reached out and my arm sang to me in pain. Knuckles contacted metal and grime. The stench was overpowering. Dumpster. I was alive, but barely.

I stood and pushed on the lid. It swung open and slammed back revealing the early morning light. My whole body was bruised fruit. I had enough energy to push up on the edge of the dumpster and tilt over so that gravity took me to the concrete. This effort was all I had, and I lay there until I felt I could move again. I tried to put it all together, but the missing pieces slipped away. A low moan came from another dumpster. Murphy.

I was up. Flipped the lid back and stared down into the stinking waste. An arm reached out from soiled cardboard and rotting food. I wanted to say it's a fine mess you're in but grabbed the arm and hauled her body up into the light.

"Nice make-up," I said.

Murphy gave me the blank stare of a beaten animal. She tried to talk but her mouth was swollen. She had strength in her arms, and she swayed as she stood waist-deep in the garbage. I leaned her over my shoulder and let her weight fall over me and out of the dumpster. I thought I could hold her and lower her out of the dumpster but in the process, we both crumpled to the ground.

Murphy didn't speak. I looked around. No traffic. No one walked by. It was too early. The Crown Vic was up the street a hundred yards across from the entrance to the alley. I checked my ankle for the Beretta. Got it. The Glock was gone.

"Stay here," I said. "I'll walk over to the Crown Vic."

Murphy moaned. I was not sure if she thought it was a good idea or not. I stood and patted myself down. No bleeding. I felt like a bag of smashed spuds. Each step was an effort to balance and focus while I kept my stomach bile down. My cell phone was still in my jacket pocket. I investigated the passenger window of the Crown Vic. It was a wall of blood. I walked around to the other side. The driver's window was smashed.

The driver, missing the top of his head, was slumped over the steering wheel. The blood was congealed.

When I got back to Murphy, her eyes were more aware.

"Jack." She gagged.

"We have to get out of here."

I looked at Murphy. "Should I phone for a 'bus'?"

Her eyes got more intense. I read a no.

I slid the cell phone out of my jacket and called Stacie.

"It's Jack. I'm back in town. Don't ask. Yes, I'm in trouble. So's Murphy. We need medical. Somewhere to hide."

I gave her the location and hung up. That was all she needed.

We waited. Two bums beside a dumpster, hanging on to life.

CHAPTER 4

I stared up at rough concrete, rusted pipes, and air ducts. Around me, concrete support columns were pitted and patched with new cement. There were lights like in an operating room, but no windows. I was fragile, almost afraid to move, head heavy on a pillow, body encased in tight sheets on a narrow bed, oxygen tubes in my nostrils, a sensor on my finger. Another bed jutted out from behind the base of one column. A door swung open, but I didn't want to raise my head to look. Footsteps. Soft-soled shoes.

> I was back at the dumpster with Murphy. I was in the bunker in Helmand, blank details, underground, sandstone walls. I was in the tunnels with Tyler's dead body at Shaplow Lake, and in the basement of a reform school. All blends of incarceration. I wanted to remember rather than fight specters in the shadows of my mind.

"You're finally awake, Mr. McQueen. Can't stay here forever. We've got to make room. We will be signing you out."

Soft Soles was a nurse, or a doctor dressed in medical gear. Hard to tell. Maybe it was different colors pale-blue, surgical-green, white, deep crimson, or pink? Who knew?

"Where am I?" I asked.

"A doctor will be in soon."

"Murphy? Where's Murphy?"

"She's over there." Her head nodded toward the bed I'd seen behind the column.

"Is she okay?" I asked.

My jaw hurt to speak. My arm protested as I started to raise it. I lifted my right leg, and I could feel stiffness in the knee joint.

"She's dropped into a coma. When the doctor comes in you can ask all the questions you like."

I became numb. Hands flexed into fists. Eyes narrow. Teeth clenched. Couldn't speak.

Soft Soles left before I could frame a sentence. After a few minutes, another woman came up to my bed. She was tall and lean. Black hair tied into a bun. Stern look. Efficient. I tried to raise my head to speak.

"I am Dr. Mitchell," she said, "You're a lucky man, Mr. McQueen. Luckily you have a friend to bring you here. We've done x-rays, blood work, and palpitation tests. Nothing is broken that can jeopardize your life. You're stable. Someone doesn't like you, but not enough to kill you. Major bruising without any long-term damage."

"Good to know," I said. "They're going to wish they'd left me dead."

I got a blank look.

"How about Brigit Murphy?" I tilted my head toward the other bed.

"We'll have to wait and see."

There was movement behind Dr. Mitchell. From the background, Stacie walked toward the bed. Her short hair stuck out at odd angles in gelled spikes. She wore army surplus camouflage gear, loose baggy pants with numerous zippered pockets, a khaki tee, and a flak jacket. Brown boots. She slouched toward me as if she was on the street sidling up to potential conflict.

"I see they've taken good care of you. You don't deserve it. On the mainland, one day and you're a mess. What were you thinking?"

"Charming as ever, I see."

"She's your ride. Be nice," Dr. Mitchell said. "You will be discharged as soon as you get dressed." She turned, walked a few feet away, and said, "Good thing you're not on the street, or you'd be in jail." And she was gone.

I'd known Stacie for a long time. She was an independent investigator who I hired on contract to dig up information. She also owned AAA Consulting and Security and I worked for her on personal protection assignments. We'd become close friends as close as she allowed. Last year she'd encouraged me to keep writing when she discovered the stuff in my notebooks and heard what I dictated into the recorder. We worked well together although the relationship had always been complicated.

She slid a chair over to the bed near my head and looked me in the eyes.

"Oh, Jack, what is it now?"

"Where are we? This is not a regular hospital."

"It's not. Did you expect me to take the two of you into a city hospital after the mess you left?"

I thought back to the fight, the dumpster, then the unmarked police car's interior smothered in blood, bits of brain and bone.

"I guess not. What is this place?"

"It's Undertown, the good, the bad. This section's good. Let's call it an off-the-grid good Samaritan network. Here with the right connections and

17

if you are the right candidate, you can get fixed up. It happens you fit the bill, with my help and your reputation, shady in some circles as it is."

I wanted to ask who pays for this but didn't and let it slide.

"Get dressed," Stacie said. "I'll help you."

"What about Murphy?"

"They're taking good care of her. We'll be dropping back. Don't worry."

Together we got me dressed. I felt like I had lost some brain function because not all the muscles wanted to react properly. But I was up and at the elevator. Then we were at a steel door where, inside, a uniformed guard toted an automatic weapon and sprung a lock that released us into an alley.

Stacie pointed to a jacked-up Ranger truck that looked as if it had been in a paintball fight and lost. It was khaki and camouflaged in splotches and paint blasts in desert hues. We got in. Stacie started the engine. Said, "It's all the rage."

"Sure." I didn't question her fashion sense. I leaned back and decided to go with the flow.

"I thought I'd let you know," she said. "There are warrants for both of you. Homicide."

CHAPTER 5

I slept on and off for three days. Now I sat in a resin patio chair on Stacie's balcony that looked out onto English Bay. The sky was grey. Sun came over mountains that hugged the city in their arms and trapped its belch. Across the bay, international freighters huddled in groups at anchor, and grain ships floated high on their water lines. Their hulls reflected the first light that came over the eastern peaks of the coastal range. Stacie was still asleep on the couch inside. I'd recuperated in her only bedroom and today was the first day I'd got my butt outside into fresh air.

The bruises had begun to heal on my arms, my legs, and across my ribs. The skin had turned yellow. But I was still twitchy. I searched through my rage to pinpoint targets. I calculated how to crush their bones to dust. Those dark figures I couldn't remember. The therapist had told me to stay calm. Don't take it personally. Don't react to injustice. Don't retaliate. Let it go. Move on. Couldn't. Someone always had to pay. I heard a rustle of fabric at the open slider.

"Finally," Stacie said, "you're back."

"Eventually every beaten dog has to come out."

Stacie carried two cups, one in each hand. Bare legs, gym shorts, and orange T-shirt that said Just try it, buster! Short, black hair, five-seven, all muscle, as usual. She set the tea on the glass patio table beside me.

"Drink," she said. "You've lost weight. Not that you didn't need to."

"Thanks."

She was right. Shaplow months ago, had drained me. And life on the float house with no exercise hadn't helped. Now, this. I scratched at the bruises on my right leg. The ones on my arms were itchy too and had turned from purple to yellow.

"Who paid the bill in Undertown?" I asked.

"Don't worry about it. It's Undertown. What goes around comes around. You've probably paid your dues in other ways and didn't even know it."

I let a real explanation slide.

"And Murphy?"

"I see her every day. Still in a coma. Her bills are paid."

"I need to see her."

My mind raced, and I got twitchy at the thought of what happened to her.

"Nothing you can do," she said. "She's safe. You're not."

I looked at her, deep behind her eyes, and sipped my tea.

Stacie continued. "All the news feeds have you both on a most wanted. The story is about one of you executing an undercover cop. His log mentions that Murphy talked to him an hour before he died. Bullet casings on the street. Bullets inside the car from two guns, one registered to you, and one from Murphy's service Glock. Both guns were not found at the scene. Sounds like they want one of you for homicide and the other for questioning. I don't think you want to waltz around in public."

The sad bones in my hands clenched into fists. I was wasted by the thought of being set up and by Murphy lying in that bed barely breathing.

Stacie placed a hand on my forearm. Ran her fingers through the hair. I felt her power drag me from my darkness.

"I'm with you in this. So's Mark. He knows you're here."

"You have any alcohol in this place?" I asked.

"I don't. That's the last thing you need."

I knew she was right. But one drink would steady me. I saw the unopened Jameson bottle on the shelf in the float house, while I sipped apple juice. I saw the same bottle in the duffle bag I'd thrown into the trunk of Murphy's Corolla. I was twitchy.

"I need a strong coffee," I said. "Stronger the better."

Three coffees later I was wired.

"This is what we'll do. Are you with me, Stacie?"

"I am despite my better judgment."

"I found a button," I said. "Murphy said that Reilly could still be trusted, ornery as he is. I still got Becky with connections to the inside. You got Undertown. I need to know more about Undertown. Mark and you can do leg work. Maybe if we find out the name belonging to the sewn-up torso, it can lead us to what's going on and why they've set us up. Why didn't they just kill us? I should have seen this coming."

"Slow down. You'll give yourself a hernia."

"Funny girl. Do you have a gun?"

Stacie stood up and punched the air with a pull and thrust, then kick-boxed the space high above my head.

"Do you think I need one?"

"We both do."

CHAPTER 6

After two more days, I recovered enough to leave Stacie's place. I would miss the grain boats and the oil tankers as they crowded the harbor in English Bay. I would miss Stacie, but despite her protests, she figured I was better acting than sitting around. She'd said I was pudgy. Right. But that work at the oyster lease had kept me in shape.

Stacie bought me a change of clothes, blue jeans, a black T, a green shirt with short tails, and an Oregon State baseball cap. I wasn't much into caps. I liked the ability of a bare head and its element of surprise as a weapon for a Scottish kiss, but a PAC-12 Football Championship cap with my grizzled beard could work as a disguise.

Stacie pulled a holstered Baby Glock 26 from her wall safe. I attached it to my belt at the small of my back beneath the shirt that hung outside. She also gave me a burner phone, so I would not be traced.

I called Mark to let him know I was alive. He'd seen the news. Not much coverage of each day's regular violence, but it caught his eye. He told me he was back in the delta again, nowhere near the marina but on the river. I asked him if he had time to back me up if I needed. He said he would and hung up.

I remembered the cream-colored button which was larger than a shirt or suit jacket button. I checked the pockets of my old clothes. Thought, duffle bag? Thought, Murphy's Corolla? It would be in the pound and the duffle bag with it. Our guns were in evidence.

When I left Stacie's place, I took a bus downtown and found a window booth at Daffy's Diner. The street was busy. I sipped a coffee and looked at the scribbled map Stacie had given me to get through a portal into Undertown. All the years I'd worked the force on the Island and a few years back here on the mainland before the breakdown, I knew about Undertown, the seedy side: brothels, gambling joints, and smuggling enterprises. I did not know there was a network doing good connected to the place. A closely kept secret it seemed.

The diner was empty, so I risked a call with the burner phone.

Becky, who used to work central headquarters for the force, answered.

"Hey, Becky. It's Jack. I need a favor."

It was always my opening line. I'd known Becky for a long time on the force and later after she'd retired and set up a private insurance fraud team. She knew how to find stuff out related to the force as she had maintained connections and I paid her for her services. She wasn't cheap.

"Are you secure?" She said.

"Burner."

"You've stuck your finger in the hive this time."

"It's a frame, Becky, and you know it."

"Doesn't change a thing," she said. "I've raised my rates, so shoot."

"C'mon, don't be like that. We haven't spoken for a while. When have I ever got you into trouble?"

"All the time. I just shiver when I answer the phone and I get your Hey Becky. It's Jack."

"So, will you help me?"

"Said shoot, didn't I?"

"I can't get around in the open or get in anyone's face on the force or the VPD. I need to know what they've both got. I need the details on the autopsy on the torso that Corporal Murphy was left to investigate on her own. I need to know who calls the shots and why the details have been buried. I need information that can exonerate Murphy and me."

"You're optimistic. No guarantees. And it'll cost you."

"I'm good. Thanks, Becky. Oh, and you remember Reilly, Murphy's former partner? I need to contact him directly. Can you get me that today? Call Stacie at this number and later when you get the other stuff."

I gave her the burner number and then I hung up. I got a shiver. Hope this didn't shift Becky into someone's line of fire.

CHAPTER 7

That night I went to an Undertown soup shelter where Stacie had directed me. I sat at a round shaky table on a fold-out aluminum chair that was as comfortable as a razor-backed hog. The place was filled with people who sipped soup or coffee. My ears drooped listening to this guy across from me.

"In the olden days there were always three levels, but they weren't necessarily vertical like now. You had residential wealth, open, tree-lined streets, huge, two-hundred-year-old oaks, Douglas fir, cedar, parkland, ravines, and gentrified refurbished areas where the poor once resided. But they got pushed out by rising housing prices, yuppies moving in, then educated techno-skilled hipsters, and then you have the suburbs and pockets of subsidized housing for the poor.

"The landscape's changed. The suburbs are bedroom communities for the enslaved, chained to mortgages, car payments, and daycare. Suburban houses are in disrepair. People have no money for upkeep, and there's no government cash for infrastructure. Potholes. Crumbling bridges. Parks are a sea of weeds, and farmland is left fallow. Wild creatures have moved in."

It was not so much about what this guy said but there was no break, no way to wedge in a comment. My head spun. No one else put in a word. Not sure anyone listened either. He started up again.

"The destitute are freer than the working poor; they live off the grid, help each other steal, beg, and borrow survival stuff. We've gone underground to Undertown. But some live in the traditional haunts of the city's homeless, hang out in alleys on the lower east side, and deserted house basements. It's risky. We know about the random roundups where street people simply disappear. There are the rich and the super-rich who keep their money safe in unknown banks and don't pay taxes. They buy up all properties that are worth living in and never walk the street. Helicopters to mansions in the mountains or to beach houses by the sea. They live in their penthouse monuments. Walls of glass and steel. They see the city like a map, like from a plane's window. And these modern buildings are like castles, impregnable, and their shadows block out the sun for everyone else down on the streets where we work, in the parks where children play, and no one gets to see the sunrise or the sunset but the rich."

Finally, he took a breath. Maybe the day's wine had got him wound up. Two other guys rumpled in street clothes that either needed a wash or a cremation were slumped over, heads on their arms fast asleep. They'd heard it all.

I squeezed in a word. "Stop."

He kept on. "They control everything."

I cut in and walked over his words before he got to finish saying everything. "Been that way forever, buddy. Been that way forever."

"Doesn't have to be," he said.

His Doesn't have to be, was the most truthful sentence I'd heard in a long while and it put a huge lump in my throat.

My burner phone vibrated. This stopped the conversation, and the guy fell into a meditative silence.

"Yes," I said.

"I have a number for Reilly from Becky," Stacie said. I held it in memory, said it over and over, and created associations with the digits. "You find the shelter?"

"Yes."

"What's with you? You can't talk?"

"Yep."

"Got ya."

"Any other news?"

"Not yet. I'll call you." She hung up.

"You ain't so grimy as the rest of us," the constant talker said.

I watched him squint his eyes. They were dark brown. Matched his skin color which bordered on black. He'd listened to the few sentences I'd spoken to Stacie.

"Do you have a name?" I asked.

"Who's asking?"

"Oh, I see. It's Jack."

"Norton."

Norton had shocks of long matted hair, almost Rasta. A beard, mice could sleep in. Looked old but by the color of his hair, I knew he was younger than he looked.

I'd seen guys like this, maybe thirty, but looked sixty. War vets that got no help for their psychoses, men who'd made poor choices, lost everything, a job, a wife, and family, guys who'd hit the bottle hard or went overboard on drugs and settled on the bottom like sediment.

Norton wore bits and pieces—wool gloves without fingers, steel-toed boots with the leather skin ripped off, a once-white T-shirt and an army surplus, ballistic-nylon, flak jacket too large so it was bulky on him.

"Glad to know you, Norton." I reached out to shake his hand. He jerked back at first, then let me shake and he shook back with a grip that surprised me.

"You work out at the gym, Norton?"

He laughed. "Sure, you know I coulda been a contenda."

I laughed and saw a combination of a Robert De Niro/Richard Roundtree glint in his eye.

"What's your story?" he asked.

He got me. What story do I tell? My clothes looked like they'd come out of the wash. I didn't want to lie to him.

"Wife left town. Took my daughter. Took everything."

I rolled up my sleeves, so the bruises were exposed.

"Lived for a while on the Island's west coast. Oyster lease. Came here for work. Got beat up a week ago." A fair amount of truth in that.

Before he started probing me, I asked. "How about you? Do you have a story?"

I heard a groan from one of the two other guys with heads slumped in their forearms.

"Don't for Christ's sake get him started."

For some reason, my mind flipped to "Psalm of Repentance" by For Christ Sake—an extreme melodic death metal band that hailed from Belfast, Ireland. I could hear the music bash against my head.

"Shut up, Mitchell," Norton said, "You don't appreciate anything."

"Do you have a story, Mitchell?" I said.

"Depends on what one you want to hear," Mitchell said. He raised his head and looked at me straight on. "Are you undercover?"

"Would I tell you if I were?"

"Just asking. You look too neat to hang out here, that's all. Bruises. You on the run, then?"

"You might say," I said. "Like you, buddy. But that's my business."

I wanted to cut this, not become embroiled in details, too exposed. Who could be trusted here? But wasn't I trusting Norton? I wasn't, not yet. But I liked him.

"Okay," Mitchell said. "Okay. Got it."

Mitchell wore a soiled white shirt, one of those pullover sleeveless sweaters, and brown cotton pants tied up with a belt that hung like a six-inch tongue. A rumpled trench coat hung on his chair.

25

Norton started up. "I will tell you a story."

The main lights went out, leaving a few low-level lights to show people the way.

"What's this?" I asked.

"We must go to our bunks," Norton said. "They've locked us in for the night."

Bodies shuffled in the dark. People rousted the sleepers. I followed Norton and Mitchell. The other guy at our table followed us down a corridor that turned more times than a maze and emptied us out into what could be an underground high school gymnasium filled with cots.

Norton pointed to an empty one, and said, "Grab that one. We're only two over."

I did. I stripped down to my boxers, wrapped the Glock in my rolled-up jeans, switched off the burner phone, and lay down—and listened. The room was breathing, a giant beast the world had forgotten.

CHAPTER 8

The room groaned like a wooden ship at sea—a susurration of coughs, truncated gasps, a sonorant undulation of waves. The light was dim, enough to get up. Use the washrooms. I sensed it was almost dawn and I rose, dressed, concealed the Glock, wandered the labyrinth back to the soup shelter, sat in the dark, and waited for the beast's belly to belch out the sleepers into a new day. Cameras would be here for safety but hidden to not feed into an already paranoia about surveillance. Couldn't worry about it since I couldn't see where they were.

My eyes adjusted and started to take in the dark shapes on the grey background. Reminded me of the tunnels between Tyler's house and our homestead's cold cellar in Shaplow. I was back in that cold cellar, watching my father's fist flash, the wallop of a cast-iron frying pan against my mother's face. The room was dark with slaughter, the spray of teeth, and blood splatter on the kitchen wall. I saw the hatchet and I was in the middle of the room, hand on it, his chest heaving before me, fists like large, jagged rocks coming toward me, and I saw that hatchet move in the extension of my arm, and bury itself into that pumping chest, my father stumbling back, bouncing from the wall, out of balance and falling forward on the hatchet among the blood, teeth, and strands of my mother's hair.

Norton's voice came from the darkness.

"You aren't who you say you are."

Inside my body, I cattle-prod jumped like someone threw a concrete block at my back. I did not move. Norton sat two tables over against a wall.

"You scared me."

"I do this every day. Sit and wait. So, who are you?"

"Look, Norton, I told you the truth, just not all of it."

I expected him to come over to my table, but he stayed against the wall.

"You need help," he said. "I can smell a rat every time in here, and you aren't it. You've got a lotta baggage. Norton can always tell."

"You can tell all that over a couple of coffees?"

"You come in here. Brand new clothes. If you'd been a rat, you'd a stunk to high heaven, and the clothes. Well? What worries me is the piece you've got beneath your shirt. You aren't who you say you are."

"You got me. Neither are you. Where do we go from here, Norton?"

I got up and sat down beside him, back to the wall, and watched the entrance to the labyrinth.

"They'll be out soon," he said. "Soon as they put up the lights and play some music. Staff will be in here too, for breakfast, and then we'll all get turned out in small groups and we'll find ourselves in an alley. Not the same alley as yesterday or the day before or the day before that. Get my drift?"

"Seems organized."

"You ever heard about the Warsaw Ghetto? Ancient history, but this is it. Undertown. We might be hiding, but we have revolution roots."

"Okay, okay," I said. I got it. It was too early for a filibuster.

"As I said, you need help," Norton said.

"You're right, there, but why should I trust you?"

"No matter what, it's a leap of faith, no angel with feathered wings, just a belief, like falling in love, moving in together, opening a joint account, ripping out your heart, and handing it over."

"Let's not get carried away," I said. "Did someone kick your heart out in the gutter?"

"Hey, look where I was, bro."

Bro now isn't that an anachronism? But maybe bro is the right word now. Vietnam? No. Possibly Kuwait, the Gulf Wars? Iraq? Fallujah? Baghdad?

"Why do you want to help me?" I said.

"Because you got a story and that story ain't all about you. I can sense the good ones when they come."

"I wouldn't be so sure of that. Been on my best behavior here. Wait until the other side shows up."

I could say, road rage, fists, head butts, the hatchet that I used to try to save a life so long ago, emptying a full clip into Frederick Madson, a red surge, but I don't. Calm. Breathe. Count, so the therapist said when I was discharged, when they took me off the force, then in Birken Psychiatric Hospital when they tried to cure me, chase away the demons, unlock the memories. And I see Peter and Kat, brother, and sister, and me walk down a logging spur, rocks in our lunch boxes in the forest shadows, afraid of bears. And I see Peter and Kat at the Nanaimo ferry terminal, leaving for a foster home and I was headed toward my own private hell.

"You go places, Jack, between the dialogue."

He didn't miss much. For a guy like me with few friends here, maybe he could be a trusted asset.

"There's a lot you don't know," I said.

The main lights came on. Music. Someone with taste had chosen a Memphis blues song by Bessie Smith, "Nobody Knows You When You're Down and Out."

A solid woman came to the counter from the kitchen door. She had a large chest and hips, short stocky legs, and plain hair tucked beneath a hair net. She was not exactly beautiful. She smiled. Her teeth were a little crooked. The look was pleasant.

"What. You guys carved in stone?" she said. "Do you want some coffee?"

We both stood and got our coffee at the counter and returned to a table.

When she went back into the kitchen, Norton said, "She was on the streets when she was fourteen. She sold herself for survival, but she got out. Most don't. She cooked in logging camps when there were trees left and the market was good. She was a country girl lured by the city that ate her up. She helps people now. It's her life."

The belly of the beast woke up and came into the soup shelter. We had breakfast then they kicked us out onto the street. Norton stuck close to me, and we arrived in an alley.

I called Reilly's number.

"It's Jack."

"McQueen?" He said, almost as if he expected a call.

"Yep, it's me. We must talk. Can I trust you?"

"Someone wants you bad and you've got Murphy in a heap of trouble, too. Where is she?"

"In a coma."

"Where? Which hospital?"

"Meet me. The zoo. Baboon cage. Noon. Don't mess with me. Murphy needs you and so do I. Stand under the sign."

When I hung up, Mitchell came up behind us. I turned to Norton.

"Will Mitchell come?"

"He's good, but might be a liability, so let's just keep him for backup."

Norton thought we were on a mission, and we were, but I wondered if he thought more about tilting at windmills than at a darker reality.

CHAPTER 9

Across from me, the old-world monkeys were in a huge circular cage. Baboons hung out their pink asses. Smaller ones scampered about, and sprang at the wire mesh, while the older ones sat on their haunches. Two juveniles hurled their feces at one another until a male adult rolled his lips into a smile and charged at them with his jaws wide and his canine teeth exposed.

"Ancient Egyptians considered these hamadryas baboons to be sacred and associated with Thoth, the god of letters," Norton said.

"Sacred my ass," Mitchell said. "I had a friend with this beat-up sports car with a ragtop. We took it to one of those game parks. I warned him but he wouldn't listen. The monkeys swung on the antenna and then snapped it off and a pile of 'em chased the car when we sped up and they ripped the canvas right off. By the time we got out, the car was ruined. It was a wreck to start with, but the convertible top was gone, and the interior was in shreds. Sacred. My ass."

"You base your opinion on one incident."

"Well, all I know is to stay away from them rascals. They're dangerous."

I began to think I made a mistake about these guys.

It was ten-thirty. Norton knew a friend of a friend with a car. He managed to borrow it for the day. My idea. I drove out the Trans-Canada Highway East to Aldergrove. The zoo was practically deserted except for school groups and early risers. By noon it would be more crowded, and easier to escape if needed.

"The cop, Reilly, expects to meet me here," I said to Norton. "I'll be by the tiger compound." I pointed to the compound. "Hang out near the food concession and watch for a guy standing under the sign, he'll be the only guy waiting. Let him stew a bit then bring him over to me. Mitchell, hang about but further away. See that he hasn't brought anyone else along."

"Got it," Norton said. He looked at Mitchell. The chain of command was enforced. "You got it, Mitchell?"

"Sure boss."

I shook my head and wandered off. I heard Mitchell say in a low voice. "We're stuck here with these monkeys?"

"Watch them and learn," Norton said.

I had a clear view of Norton with Reilly walking along the pedestrian path toward me. I was mixed into a crowd up close to the tiger compound where it was feeding time. I was amazed at people's fascination, and their desire to watch carnivores with their meat. Like looking in the mirror.

It was a toss-up who had the best fashion sense, Norton in his Vietnam army surplus or Reilly in his off-the-rack suit pressed out at the seams, tie knotted in a hurry while he stuffed a piece of toast in his mouth. When he arrived and I turned, I resisted the urge to say, did you just wake up, Reilly?

I said, "Hello, Reilly. Wasn't sure you'd come."

"I'm here more for Murphy than anyone, so don't get smart with me. Tell me it's a set-up?"

"What do you think? Murphy's not a cold-blooded killer. You think I am?"

"I can vouch for Murphy. She's an arrow. Now, you? Don't tell me you haven't left a trail. Either in the city or on the Island."

We moved out of the crowd at the tiger cage to a tree with a bench and a wire wastebasket. We both leaned against the wastebasket that wasn't yet full. Norton had moved away but was observant and Mitchell further away watched us.

I rolled up my sleeves to show him my bruised yellowed skin. Reilly whistled and with a squint looked into my eyes.

"I was in bad shape for a while," I said. "But I'm the lucky one."

"Murphy?"

"It's bad. But we're hopeful."

"Tell me where she is."

"I can't."

"Won't, more like it."

"Look you have to trust me that she's cared for, safer where she is than if she were at General."

"Undertown, right."

"That's what you'd expect." I said.

He just looked at me. He was a good cop. He knew all about how the moral infrastructure had gradually broken down.

"I got no one on the ground inside. I need you to help me and Murphy get out of this. She was onto something that someone didn't want out in the open. The only way is to find out what she was onto and let's hope she wakes up soon."

"The guy who brought me to you. How do you know him? Do you trust him? He's a street guy."

"He's good. Met him yesterday," I laughed.

"You've sunk to an all-time low."

"You don't know the half of it. Will you help me?"

"I'm here to help Murphy. I'm not sure yet if I care about you. But yes, what do you want me to do?"

"That decapitation. No mention in social media or the regular web media and nothing on the front pages? Murphy assigned herself to it when no one on the force picked it up. She got no help with it like it has been swept under the carpet, or never happened."

"Right. So, what do you want?" Reilly said.

"I need details. Photos if there are any. The autopsy reports. Any record of evidence collected."

"When I heard about this," Reilly said, "I thought it was a hoax. Then I realized someone wanted this homicide to go away. I can't sniff around without raising the hairs on someone's neck. It'll be my life on the line."

"Reilly. Think about Murphy. We were beaten up and left in a dumpster at the crime scene."

I let the anger of my words drift over him. We both waited in silence.

"Murphy," Reilly said, "and a slaughtered cop. I'll see what I can do. Don't contact me. The station is monitored. Give me twenty-four hours after today. Say nine. Tomorrow night. There's an abandoned underground car park, beneath the old Victory Opera house. It's fenced for demolition. Bring a flashlight."

Reilly looked around, stepped back a few paces, turned, and headed back toward the baboon cage. I signaled Mitchell. Mitchell picked up on it and started to tail him. Norton came over and we sat down on the bench.

Somehow, even with some action in place, I still felt powerless and broken. Norton had enough sense to stay quiet. Perceptive son-of-a-bitch. Who was this guy?

CHAPTER 10

Norton and I sat on the bench in silence. I wasn't entirely sure about Reilly. Did he come alone? Was Reilly tailed? Always good to be careful. I trusted Norton despite the mystery, and Mitchell for me was what you see is what you get. He was harmless and naïve. In fifteen minutes, Mitchell came back. "He was alone. He got into an unmarked. No one trailed him as far as I could tell."

"Good work, Mitchell," I said. "You guys hungry?" I handed Norton a twenty. "Go get some hot dogs or whatever at the concession. Bring me back a coffee, double, double, large."

While they were gone, I called Stacie. Couldn't wait. She answered right away.

"Hey, Stacie."

"You were supposed to wait until I called you."

"Just met with Reilly. He will help."

"Becky called. Said she'd never had so much trouble finding information. That torso had an autopsy, but the files are sealed. Evidence is sealed to everyone. The only way you will get that info is if someone on the inside can break in."

"That's not what I wanted to hear."

"I know where Murphy's Corolla is. It's in an independent pound on contract to the force. Laskey Brothers."

"Any research on them?" I asked.

"Wait. Let me finish. The compound is on the East side near the abandoned Camden Fairgrounds. Huge area. Part junkyard, part pound. Do you know it?"

"I have a good idea. These Laskey's? What's their story? Mean and homicidal, right?"

"Let's say you're better off if you leave that car where it is," Stacie said.

"You know me. I'm a guy with common sense."

"That's why I mentioned it. You'll be back in Undertown again for more stitches, or worse."

"What's their story?"

"You won't go there, right?"

"Right," I said.

"They're ugly wrestlers, junk-dog tow-guys. A wrecking crew. Do snitch work for the force but stay on the seedy side involving drugs and disappearances. They know where bodies are buried. You know the type. Smart but throw their weight around like they got metal plates in their heads. And it's not only them. They have a battalion of guys on the payroll."

"Got it. I must run. But can you work with Becky to see if there is a way to see that autopsy file? I'll call later."

I called Mark on the phone, told him I'm in a hurry, and asked if he had a car now, which he did. So, I asked him if he wasn't busy and if he could meet me at the end of the bus line near the Camden Fairgrounds. Sure enough, he could. Said he'd be driving a '78 hatchback Pinto. I told him to bring heavy-duty bolt cutters.

A Pinto? Wonder what the horses think about that legacy.

Norton and Mitchell came back with hotdogs and a coffee.

Once we were done, I said, "Let's go back downtown. That friend of yours needs his car back. Then we will meet a guy with his Pinto."

Norton scrunched up his nose at Pinto. I ignored him.

"You guys up for some B and E?" I said.

It wasn't a question. I got up, walked away, and left them the choice. They followed.

When we got to the bus loop at Camden Fairground, we saw the Pinto. Two-door hatchback, speed green with green interior, a tad distressed like it had been in a fire and there was a big need for new cosmetics. Rust, ground-down to the bare metal, odd paint configurations different from the factory's original green.

Norton and Mitchell squeezed into the back. I climbed into the passenger side and closed the door with a heavy clunk.

Mark looked good. Trimmed down. The big doughboy belly he had almost a year ago was gone. You could see the definition in his shoulders and chest, and he had acquired abs. He sported a three-day growth that made him look more rugged than he was.

I still hid behind what had grown since the beating.

"Thanks," I said. "You're in good shape."

"Right," Mark said. "When did you ever give out compliments? How about the Pinto?"

"This antique is nearly forty years old," I said. "Does it have any power? Sorry, I'm kidding. It's good to see you."

"Sure, join the crowd and mock this baby," Mark said.

I could see I wasn't the only person to razz him about the new acquisition. But I couldn't help myself since he rarely left himself open to friendly abuse.

"Mark. It's not exactly mint and it's not a Mustang. Now there's a car that horses can be proud of."

Mark was up for it, and he shot back.

"The Model T, the Corvair, the Beetle. They've come back. So's the Pinto, sort of on its own terms."

"Why drive a car that is older than you are?" I said. "The interior looks good, but the outside?"

"Yes, well, I'm working on the outside. I started a little business too, fixing old cars. They're just like boats but a hell of a lot easier. I have a Quonset hut out on the delta where I dock Dulcinea, the Ranger Tug. I can't tell you where it is, because I don't want to get mixed up with people you poke with a stick who might burn it down."

"You still sore about that?"

"Damn right."

Norton and Mitchell had enough sense to stay quiet and listen, especially Norton who I knew didn't miss a thing. I trusted him, but I still wondered what his story was because right now he was under-employed.

"Mark," I said, "one day I'll make it up to you."

I believed what I said but I had no idea how.

Mark turned his neck around to look Norton and Mitchell over.

"So, who are you guys?"

"They work for me." Gave them the eye to stay quiet.

"I'm Norton. This is Mitchell. I work for Jack. Mitchell works for me."

"Sounds complicated," Mark said. "If I know Jack, there is bullshit mixed into it."

"Let's say we are associates for now," Norton said.

Mark turned back to me and said, "What's up? Stacie told me the fix you're in."

"You heard of the Laskey brothers? They have Murphy's car in the pound either compliments of the force or by a routine tow, since after the beating, the car was left. I need to get my duffle bag out of the trunk if it's still there, and I want to get her Corolla back."

35

"Aren't the Laskey's connected to organized crime?" Norton said. "You want us to mess with them?"

Norton seemed too well-informed. But he didn't seem nervous or too concerned about the task.

"What difference does it make? They have my duffle and Murphy's car. Bullies. They've been stealing other people's stuff since they were in kindergarten. Might seem stupid to take them on, but I can't help it."

> I see the hatchet in my hand. I see my finger on the Glock squeezing repeatedly. I see myself with a sniper rifle wrapped in rags, co-ordinates read, wind speed and direction judged, the slightest movement watched, the trigger squeezed so carefully, position moved, the process repeated, one sadistic, misogynistic, child-murderer at a time.

Everyone was silent. We didn't move. We sat in the Pinto along a road beyond where the bus looped. No sidewalks. Dirt shoulders. Tall grass in the ditches. Chain-linked fencing. Abandoned buildings with smashed windows, and boarded-up entrances. Parking lots with weeds and grass sprouted between the cracks. It was dusk and the evening quickly dropped into darkness. "Do you have the bolt cutters? Do you have a gun?" I asked Mark.

"Both. Got some pipe too if we need it."

"Let's hear how this baby sounds," I said,

Mark turned the ignition. The engine growled rather than purred. Before Mark put the Pinto into gear, I assumed it wouldn't handle well and was surprised when the power kicked right in. I gave him directions. He pulled away and headed toward the Laskey Brothers compound. I was convinced we were in for a long night. Maybe if I had planned better, it wouldn't have been so long.

CHAPTER 11

Mark stopped the Pinto a block from Laskey Brothers Wrecking in front of the entrance to the old fairgrounds. There were streetlights but the bulbs had been smashed. The only light was far off where the Laskey yard was lit up like a federal prison. Seemed they expected trouble all the time.

"Are you sure this is a good idea?" Mark said.

"I never said it was a good idea. I need to do this. I don't plan to walk up to the front gate if that's what you mean."

Before we jumped out of the Pinto to make a move, the only plan we had was an aerial GPS search on Mark's phone. Fuzzy images but clear enough to map the compound as to buildings, fence line, piles of wrecked automobiles, a metal compactor, a shredder, and cars lined up in rows on the dirt and gravel. Murphy's Corolla would be in the field. But from where we would enter through the fence, it looked like a trek across the continental divide, and through the high passes, the jagged metal of the rusted automobile. Long knives, dogs, guns, and mean and ugly men waited for us.

Mitchell took the heavy-duty bolt cutters, and Norton had the three-foot length of one-and-a-half-inch diameter pipe from the back of the hatch. Mitchell thumped the hatch closed and the heavy sound reverberated. All three of us swung around and glared at him. We hopped a five-foot temporary fence along the road to get cover so we could approach the twelve-foot compound enclosure with a curl of razor wire along the top. The plan was to go through, not over. Norton laid his pipe on the ground and gently nudged it up toward the chain link, then kicked it enough to make contact. There were no sparks.

"The cutters got electrical-proof handles," Mitchell said. "I could a handled it."

Mitchell weighed in on the bolt cutters and sliced through each chain-link one link at a time until he created a four-foot opening.

We entered easily but jammed against the fence was a rusted metal wall that stretched along the whole border. A barrier of crushed, rusted, dismembered cars, trucks, and obsolete machinery.

This place was the toilet of the industrial age. We squeezed through slot canyons, climbed, descended into pockets, crawled through bent and buckled front grills, and twisted doors like maws with sardonic smiles. The compound was brightly lit, and the light slanted through crevices in the jumbled carcasses. We followed as on an expedition: Norton, then me, followed by Mark and Mitchell. Occasionally, Norton with his pipe pushed against jagged edges that waited to slice us open.

For an hour we maneuvered through the wreckage wall, until Norton held up his hand.

"I'm through," he said. "Jack, can you see the stars?"

Even in the bright light, they filled the sky. This reminded me of Shaplow or the west coast float house where clear nights brought the universe into my lap.

"Hear that?" Norton said. The sound from the Laskey Brothers office, music full-on loud.

> The immensity of stars had triggered me to bring my sister back so vividly I spoke to her though not out loud. I wanted to flesh you out into this place, Kat, this time, now, you as you step down into the street, the river, lake, wet as I remember, you, the soft stone of innocence, stopped, sent, with our brother and me to foster care, lungs filled with tears, laughter and giggles gone, your fear of bears when we walked the woods, lost with our lunch pails full of stones, our wishes unanswered, voices stopped, and missed by me and my hunger for your words, self-splintered, high-cheeked and smiling through a horror never spoken by your lips. I need to find you, Kat. And Peter, too. Where you went. Where you are now. In the canyons I walk without you in shadow and in shame, here I regret not clinging to your slight frame, you who painted the raven with me and wept for our buried dog. These buried images are poetry I've yet to write. Poetry. A habit. Jotted down raw material in between detective notes, observations, phone numbers, and thoughts on leads. Like breathing. One-line obsessions, herding images like sheep and it was fun and pure magic. Now was not the time to scratch these thoughts and images on paper.

"You Really Got Me" started playing. I said, "Van Halen. I much prefer 'Eruption' as a guitar solo riff and how Eddie made that Stratocaster sing."

Norton nodded back and forth to the beat of the music, moved to the side and we each emerged from the wreckage and took refuge in shadow. I pointed to the cars, crushed flat, mingled with bumpers and grills, smashed windshields, and disembodied doors. Two cranes hovered in the air, long-necked predators. One trailed a wide set of jaws and the other a magnetic disc.

"Where do you figure the Corolla is?" Mitchell asked.

"On the other side of that mountain range," I said. "But we will not go over. We will go around."

The office was to the left of us, still blasting music. Back in the Saddle by Arrowsmith.

"We're going right," I said. "If I got it, that Corolla will be in a salvageable car lane."

Mark and Mitchell stuck to the fence side of the corridor around the twisted, broken steel, and Norton and I crossed to the other side and worked our way around its base. If anything happened, we could back each other up rather than have all of us caught together. It took a while before we circled the wreckage pile and came together as four. Before us was the dead-car parking lot beneath a clear sky punctuated with stars. The vague light spread out from the office building with the constant thump of Heavy Metal chords and licks. We broke up and walked among the cars in search of Murphy's Corolla. Norton alerted us with a short low whistle, and we came together again beside her car. This was too easy. No dogs. We hadn't attracted any attention. To myself, I spoke too soon.

CHAPTER 12

The driver's door was unlocked, and the keys were in the ignition.

"Thought we'd have to start it hot," I said.

"That would be too easy," Norton said. Now he was a wise guy. "Seems logical. Why have racks and racks of keys and tags then match them to the car you want?"

"At some point, they salvage the parts from a car so much, it won't go anywhere," Mark said.

"Do these guys keep spreadsheets on this stuff," I said. "Rack and pinion '87 Tercel pulled, sold, for sale? Someone must or their business would be a nightmare."

"This place is more than all these parts, isn't it, Jack?"

"Maybe so. But I just want to get the Corolla and get out."

I looked at Norton. I could kick my ass around the block. This Corolla couldn't go out a front gate that was chained shut.

Mitchell bent over the front seat and pressed the lever to open the trunk. Then he walked around to the back.

"This your duffle?" he asked.

"That's it."

I took it from him.

"Mark and Mitchell, you need to go back the way we came," I said. "Get out on the other side, follow the fence line to the gate, and if the gate's chained closed, and it will be, cut it loose with the bolt cutters, leave it loose so it still looks the same. Call me, ring, and hang up. Norton and I'll know. We'll start up the car and blast through the gate."

In the lowest parts of the yard, a mist had settled and diffused the light from the office buildings. Macabre. Surreal Heavy Metal and in between the shuffled playlist I heard screams of agony, followed by the chords of "God of Thunder" by Kiss.

Mark nodded. Both men turned, scraped their feet on the gravel and we all heard a low growl. I turned. A wolf stood on a truck beside the Corolla. A second growl rose from the ground at our feet into our bones. Don't move, it said. Behind us came another growl. In a wide circle a wolf choir, dark shapes, and faintly lit eyes.

Wolf pack. Their territory. Not ours.

The alpha male was on the truck.

I said to Mark and Mitchell, "Don't move until I tell you, then walk past the wolves, around the mountain where we came in."

They looked at each other, not sure if they should take my advice. I didn't blame them. I wasn't positive it would work either. But my idea was the best choice.

I moved toward the alpha. Stared into his eyes. I was triggered.

> Shaplow. Logging spurs. Kat and Peter. Lunch boxes filled with stones. Small fire beside a boulder where we sleep. Wolves in the thickets beneath the fir and cedar. A low growl. We are terrified. "Stay still," I say, "and they'll go away." I stare. Curl my lips. Low growl. Fingers grip the air as claws. Wait. Watch. I do not know if they will leave us or not. I watch the tails lower parallel to their backs. None of us move. I watch alpha's back curl lower, flattened ears, and piercing eyes. The long wait before they dissolve into the night. Forever after, I can talk to predators. Body language. The force of will. Fist and skull. Hatchet. Gun muzzle.

The alpha on the truck sat, then lay down, paws forward, muzzle low, eyes a-squint, ears back, tail down. He looked as if he planned to nap and wait me out. I nodded to Mark and Mitchell, and they began to walk. They passed the perimeter of their eyes. Each wolf relaxed. I heard Mark and Mitchell run and watched the wolves and they did not move. I motioned to Norton. He got into the Corolla's driver seat and released the passenger door. I walked around the car, kept an eye on the alpha wolf, and jumped in.

"Where did you learn that?" Norton said. "Are you some kind of wolf whisperer?"

"Long story. Let's say I've practiced it."

I kept an eye on the alpha. He'd not moved, and the others were still at ease. Now was not a time to hunt rats. Bigger things were about to happen in their world.

We waited.

"One of these days we'll have to trade stories," I said.

"Right. Let's get our asses out in one piece."

We waited in silence now, apart from the Heavy Metal. I traced Mark's and Mitchell's progress back in terms of time and pictured them at the gate where they would cut through the locks and chains. We waited some more. I looked at Norton. Watched Norton look at me. I checked my burner phone to make sure it was on vibrate. Decided to hold it in my hand. Waited. Nothing happened. I invented scenarios, expected gunshots, and saw Mark and Mitchell dead in the ditch beside the road. Saw them carried and put into the trunk of a car at a spot beneath the crane with the claw. Saw the crusher.

"It's been too long," Norton said.

I nodded. We waited some more.

"It's wrong," he said.

I nodded again. He started the ignition. We rolled down the windows. The alpha wolf watched but didn't move. The music was louder, grunge I couldn't identify.

"You heard those screams a while back between songs before the wolves showed up?" I said.

"Right. At the office. A party and not everyone is happy. Maybe Mark and Mitchell ran into trouble on their way out."

"Don't think so," I said. "More to it than that. Drive."

CHAPTER 13

The Corolla crept along the canyon walls, around the rusted-metal mountain toward the office buildings and the gate. Our lights were out. The office area was four attached double-wide trailer homes. It was connected to a series of Quonset huts with corrugated, steel roofs with huge garage doors, one for each hut.

"I wondered what's inside those?" I asked.

Norton abruptly stopped. The gate was still locked.

"Where are they?" he said.

I saw three loops of chains and two industrial locks still attached to the gate.

I touched the Glock wedged in the small of my back. I said, "Stay behind the wheel. Ready. Hand me the pipe."

Behind slanted Venetian blinds, shapes moved around the office.

"I'll get a closer look. Sit tight."

For the first time, I saw that Norton was nervous. His right eye twitched, and three fingers scratched at the steering wheel. His tell.

I stepped from the Corolla and left the door ajar so there would be no sound.

Looked around. I was in the forest once again.

The wolves sat hair triggered in a circle and watched.

But this was not the forest. Kat and Peter were not there and with each step toward the office, I felt loneliness deeper than the forest ever was. The music switched to a Swedish band, Dream Evil — The Book of Heavy Metal.

I slid beside the oxidized siding, took a few furtive steps onto a short deck beside the door, and peeked into the lower corner of the adjacent window. I was not prepared for what I saw. Part of me was in at least a ten-year-old combat zone, set to blow insurgents back to hell. These were memories that had never surfaced, not through shock and drugs at Birken rehab or in the Chief's house back on the Island in a mushroom-inspired walk-about.

Four guys: baseball caps, Caterpillar, Arco, John Deere, blue-grey overalls, greasy steel-toed boots. One guy had a heavy-duty vinyl apron and held a machete in his hand. Another guy rested with his chin on a butcher-block table, his arms outstretched with wrists tied to the table legs at the far end. One hand was missing a little finger. The finger lay on a white China plate. A gun was on the far end of the table. The air hummed with the music. One guy sat behind a desk flanked by two rows of beige filing cabinets, and another sat beside the missing-finger guy. He had a fist of the poor guy's hair. He pulled back his head and talked. I couldn't hear the words. A young girl sat against a wall, legs splayed, an elastic black skirt tucked around her waist, and no underwear. She was exposed, her blue blouse ripped open beneath her sagging head. Beside her, another girl, black, was ass-high bent over the arm of a battered couch and the fourth guy was engaged in fast-rough sex. He pounded into her from behind to the beat of Dream Evil. The two girls weren't there because they wanted to be, and the missing-finger guy looked like he needed salvation. I scanned the room to the far end and saw Mark and Mitchell trussed up on the floor with silver duct tape across their mouths and wrapped around their feet and hands. Fuck. Fuck. Fuck.

The soundtrack stopped, and I heard the machete guy yell, "Go, Bobby, go," and Bobby swung one arm in the air and pulled back on the hair of the girl's neck, and continued to pound himself into her. Another Dream Evil track came on. The sound blasted from the speakers. I heard Missing Finger wail, "No," and his other little finger appeared on the plate, a matched set.

The image of Mark and Mitchell made me gulp air, and gasp in silence. My hand sweated on Norton's metal pipe. Then I saw it. The crimson star tattooed on the machete guy's right hand. Same shape. Same color, only more vibrant in the light. These were the guys who beat Murphy and me. Explained the Corolla too. Didn't expect anyone to find us in the dumpster, or maybe they had planned to bring our bodies here and crush us up with the rusted automobiles. I heard the therapy words. Calm. Breathe. Let it go.

Fuck it.

I was through the door. Both hands on the pipe. I lined up, stayed balanced, sideways, left leg forward with all my weight moving forward. Home run across machete guy's windpipe. For a moment he hovered. His arms went limp at his side. He let the blade fall to the floor then he dropped like frozen beef.

The torture guy at the table reached for the gun that rested beside the finger plate. Down went with the pipe across his arm. He was in instant agony with an arm bone smashed to pieces. He tried to grab the gun with his left hand. The pipe took his head at the bridge of the nose and whipped him backward in his chair.

Across the room, Bobby in a daze moved to the beat of the music. Yet with panic, he looked at me, fumbled in his loose overalls for something more dangerous than a stick of gum. I pulled the trigger on the gun I'd picked up from the table, and he dropped from the girl's back and fell to the floor. A red dot bloomed on his forehead.

I dropped and rolled low behind the table. Again, I saw a red star on the back of a hand, not the machete guy who had run out of oxygen, but the guy behind the office desk who had grabbed an AK47. I rose and emptied two shots into his chest, his body lurched backward, his finger on the trigger and the room erupted—muzzle flashes, sprayed bullets, flying glass, girls screaming, and blinds dancing on a string. The girls hid behind the couch. I stepped up to him, fired one bullet into his temple, and kicked the Kalashnikov into the corner beside the filing cabinets.

Silence. The air was full of an acrid gunfire residue. Missing Finger was head-flat on the table, a bullet hole in the back of his skull. Calm. Breathe. Let it go.

Dream Evil was still running through the album tracks of The Book of Heavy Metal, the title song filling the room through static speakers. I said a line related to the lyrics out loud, "Don't think these guys are going to become immortal any time soon." It cut the tension.

Norton was through the door. Full-on action. No hesitation. He stripped duct tape from Mark and Mitchell, calmed down the girls, and got them tidied up in a washroom. He had taken the bolt cutters that he'd found in the dirt and cut the locks on the gate. He deposited everyone except Mark into the back of the Corolla. Mark, he put into the Pinto and told him to go home and call us in the morning.

All this time I stood with the pipe in one hand and the handgun in the other. The AK47 was on the floor beside the dead shooter.

The room is blood red, sun on eyelids on a hot day, farmhouse kitchen, hatchet in a chest, and broken teeth, Glock clip emptied into Frederick Madson, trigger squeeze, sniper bullet, a faint mist of blood where there was once someone's father's head. Room and head exploded like an IED.

I wiped the prints from the gun. Norton had been careful too. No shell casings that belonged to us.

I walked out the door with the pipe in my left hand and my Glock in its holster at the small of my back. Never fired. I left the door open to match the empty windows and twisted blinds. I got into the Corolla. The alpha wolf and his pack hovered close. Who knew if revenge could lurk in their hearts? But I knew that they would not let it go.

"Drive. Drive," I said to Norton. "Anywhere until morning comes."

CHAPTER 14

I contemplated dropping the ladies at a motel. They'd made it plain to us while in the car that they were working girls, whose recent ordeal wouldn't stop them from looking to seize an opportunity. They affectionately called themselves Mindy and Sugar. Original enough. I thought of asking Norton and Mitchell to get a room, too, so they could look after them. Give all four of them some money to lay low, off the radar. Safe. So, they all could recuperate from their trauma, but I thought better of it and kept driving. I deposited everyone in an alley at the soup kitchen door.

"You all know nothing happened last night." I looked the hookers straight in the eyes, gave them a hundred each.

They snatched up the cash like it was their last meal, but Sugar, the feisty one in her leather skirt, said, "We aren't charity cases, you know. A hundred to shut us up?"

"Sugar," I said. "I will say this once. You and Mindy are lucky to be alive. If you feel you want to blab about that scene, think again. A bigger situation than your next trick will crash down on both of your heads. And there is a good chance I won't be around to save you. So shut up."

I looked at Norton and pulled him close to the window and asked him, "Any way you can keep them off the street, do it."

I handed him five hundred.

"Find a safe motel. Get the girls a room. You and Mitchell get one beside them. I want you to protect them. Let them recover. Take them out for breakfast. Order lunch. Take them to a clinic. Get them some antibiotics. They'll need a lot of sleep. So will Mitchell. He's been affected by this."

Norton understood. Tapped the side of the car as he walked away and said, "To keep them in one place, won't be easy."

I left them in the alley at the soup kitchen door.

I phoned Mark. Found out where he was, although he was reluctant to tell me, and headed straight there.

A CD poked out of the player below Murphy's dash. I pushed it in. The interior was filled with Norah Jones, "Come Away with Me", "I waited 'til

47

the rising sun", and sad notes to complement my low ebb of adrenalin. The last two days felt like a month.

When "The Nearness of You" on Norah's album started, I arrived at Mark's Quonset hut. Mark leaned over the guts of the Pinto engine. I walked right up to him. He knew it was me, and said, "Heard you coming. That Corolla needs a tune-up."

"You're good," I said.

He didn't look up but said, "I need a tune-up for throwing in with you again."

"You're in one piece aren't you," I said.

I was sorry now. Like I'm a magnet for the sewage of the world. There are no happy lambs left in the barn.

"Stay away from me," he said.

"So, why'd you even tell me where you were?"

"Not too bright, am I?" he said. "What do you want?"

"I need to hide the Corolla here. Oh, and maybe borrow the Pinto."

Mark was silent. He stood up and wiped his hands on a greasy rag that he pulled from his overalls. He held a socket wrench with an extra-long extension. He walked around to the tool bench and put it down. He took another rag from a drawer and wiped his hands, then he looked me in the eye.

"Is that all? Thought you'd want me to sign on to sacrifice my beating heart one more time."

"You're a sarcastic prick. Do you have anything to drink?"

"You nearly get me killed and you want to sit down and drink with me?"

"It's better than pissing on each other."

He didn't respond. He walked into a small glassed-in office, one door, a solid wall halfway up with glass that looked out to the rest of Quonset hut. Inside there were two oak swivel chairs and a desk that looked like he'd picked up at the Sally Ann or a school district auction. Mark sat in one of the chairs, opened a drawer, and pulled out a bottle of Laphroaig along with two stubby glasses that he wiped with the rag from the bench. He poured two fingers into each.

I walked in and sat down. He picked up his glass. Left the other for me to reach over and before I could touch it, he grabbed my wrist.

"Promise me you'll never ask me again for any help. Because you know I'll come. And I know one of these days I won't come back. Promise me."

He let go of my wrist and I picked up the glass.

"I promise," I said and downed it. Peaty, mingled with the engine oil from the rag. Didn't matter. The single malt slid down my throat, burned, and then heated up in my stomach like the warm lips of a hot lover.

"I promise," I said again, and really meant it. I looked at the haggard fear in his eyes, a dead stare that floated in the current.

"Stacie called," he said. "She wanted to know where you were."

I should have called her but last night was frenetic.

Mark poured another two fingers, and I downed it fast. We'd been friends for a while, since I met Del, my ex, and he'd basically helped me through a lot of troughs when I was kicked off the RCMP. I knew he was overwhelmed. Tied up and taped at the Laskey Brothers office was serious.

I couldn't help myself, but I said, "Can I pull the Corolla in?"

The question seemed mundane, a change of topic. I was not handling this well. The switch. He let it slide.

"Sure. But you promised."

"I did. I'll hold myself to it, but right now I need to sleep."

I pulled the Corolla into the Quonset, opened the car door, and folded the driver's seat forward.

Mark said before I climbed into the back seat, "Stacie told me to tell you, there's been a change. You need to talk to Murphy."

"Thanks. I'll deal with it." Murphy in a coma had never been too far away from me despite the chaos.

I laid down across the back seat and fell asleep in twenty seconds among the hooker pheromones, sweat, fear, and a dead man's DNA.

I dreamed.

Fragile white neck in the jaws of a wolf. Freedom is blue, tastes of the morning air, is wet spring dew, a small bird's song cupped in wind, after-rain drips on a smoke-bush bough, an open road in a scarred sky. This is where Kat and Peter are not together, but somewhere close to the sharp teeth, and salivating jaws. I've not tried hard enough. I should have set out long ago in sturdy shoes, a backpack, binoculars, a few good books, an ice axe, and crampons. I should have watched the black sky stars for a sign. Instead, I'd dug holes, planted posts, and chained myself to them, while you have both gone missing, as I went missing in an era of anger, solving problems behind a fist or a gun barrel. Again, I had no energy to write it down, but the words stayed.

When we all go to Fran's for lunch. Mom. Kat. Peter. Me. No fear of arguments because our father was away making deals. Waitresses in pink uniforms, shorts, white aprons, and black practical shoes. They serve up hot roast beef sandwiches, French fries and gravy, and southern fried chicken, and the chicken comes crispy nestled in a woven, wooden basket with honey, and we all lick our lips together, laugh, and order banana cream pie or lemon meringue and the seats are deep red and stand out on the black and white tiles and the aroma of coffee in heavy white cups hangs in the air and chocolate malted milkshakes sit in aluminum containers and the time it takes to eat and drink and talk like grown-ups far away from silent conversations at the farmhouse with the click of knives and forks over stewed vegetables and grey, mashed potatoes, mystery meats as hard as hockey pucks.

I have the poem in my head, memorized.

Fran's Restaurant

Fran's Restaurant, after movies,
all the waitresses, dressed in pink,
short, white aprons, and black, practical shoes,
who served us banquet burgers,
southern-fried chicken in a basket,
French fries, gravy, that chicken, crispy,
real honey to drip on a drumstick or a wing
and we both licked our lips together,
talked like adults, ordered banana cream pie,
lemon meringue and I remember how
the seats were deep red, and they stood out
against the black and white floor tiles,
and how the coffee came in heavy white cups,
the chocolate shake in an aluminum container,
and I remember the time it took to eat
and drink and talk like grown-ups,
far away from the usual silent conversations,
the click of knives and forks over stewed vegetables
grey-white potatoes on brown-scratched plates
and mystery meats as hard as hockey pucks.

I woke in a sweat with my dreams and the taste of engine oil. The Corolla smelled as if I'd slept within a panting dog's breath and an all-night taxicab's backseat stench. I felt old because I couldn't sit up all night, drinking through a bottle of Scotch with Mark.

His washroom had a shower stall where you bang your elbows to get yourself soaped, but I was thankful and decided to wash my clothes at the same time while I was in the shower and put on the only other clean set, I had from the blue duffle bag. Jeans, T-shirt, and a loose dress shirt.

Mark cooked eggs on a hot plate as I hung my clothes to dry on a line outside. We drank coffee and ate the eggs in silence for a while until I said, "I'll take TransLink in and walk or take a cab to Stacie's. Can you drive me to the nearest station?"

He nodded.

"Mark, I'm sorry."

"Don't worry about it. It's me. Can't do it anymore. If you want, give me a safe job to do, fine but not like what went down the other night."

"Got it," I said. "So, you stay here most of the time?"

"Back and forth to the boat. Each place I can scrounge a little work."

"Are you serious about work that's safe?"

"Right."

He warmed both his hands wrapped around his coffee cup.

"Tracking down a trail?"

"Depends on who and what," he said.

"Honest, Mark, I'm overwhelmed. I need your help. Some memories have come back. First, the stuff back at Shaplow Lake, my childhood, my work with Murphy, and the force. I get glimpses of a reform school. I need to track down Kat and Peter. Find out if they're alive. I can't deal with it by myself right now with this manhunt and Murphy in a coma and the other night. It all might crash down on me. If we both search maybe, we can find them. Can you find them after they got shipped off the Island when they were kids?"

Mark didn't answer, so I said, "No leg work. Only phone calls and computer research. I'll get Stacie to help you too. It's important."

"I'll do that. No guns, knives, or duct tape, right? You promised."

On the way to the station, I filled him in on what I could remember and reassured him that Stacie would do any legwork if necessary.

On the train, I thought about Murphy in a coma and if it weren't for loyalty to her, I could walk away. I wondered if Norton and Mitchell had been sharp enough to keep the hookers safe. The money should be enough to make it work. And what was up with the concept of talking to Murphy? Then I thought about Reilly and remembered to bring a flashlight to our meeting at the Victory Opera house at nine o'clock. I phoned Stacie and left a message. Told her where I'd been and when and where I was going. I closed off. Could I trust Reilly, not to turn me in?

51

CHAPTER 15

The Victory Opera House was a grand building that once could stage a full orchestra opera to stand-up comedy and everything in between—rock concerts, classical guitar soloists, musicals, and even spoken-word poetry slams. But over time, technology had kicked its ass into the dark ages and left the old dame abandoned with a leaking roof too expensive to be repaired with its caved-in parts. The rats had got in and picked at the stuffing from the seats for their nests. With the elements inside, the stucco cracked, and plaster fell from the ceiling and the walls. Dust accumulated.

Reilly said to enter by the stage-right exit door. That it would be open. I came early with my duffle over my shoulder and a heavy-duty flashlight.

The Victory was still considered downtown but on the blighted east side. Here the storefronts sold mostly experienced merchandise among a competition of pawnshops and back-alley gold and diamond dealers who ran their businesses couched behind dry cleaner fronts that rarely entertained a shirt to be pressed, and other shadow trades that catered to anyone who wanted a deal. No questions asked. No consciences. No empathy for any blood spilled for what was lusted for.

Ambient streetlights seeped through holes in the ceiling and an oval skylight high above the balconies. Reilly said front row, center, so I went five rows back on the side and sat in a seat that still had stuffing. I didn't use the flashlight. I waited.

I had never been known to be a trusting soul. Experience had not convinced me otherwise. And Reilly, although he convinced me at the zoo, still left me wanting. I wished Murphy could be here. She'd give me a better perspective. The open exit door might mean Reilly was already ahead of me, or maybe it was always open and a portal to a favorite meeting spot. I heard movement across the broken plaster on the stage. Rats? Footsteps?

A figure came out of the backstage darkness into the muted light from the holes in the ceiling.

"Jack. I said front row center. Always a smart-ass."

"I'm not a six-feet-under smart-ass," I said. "I'm still pissing people off."

Reilly's head turned toward the sound of my voice. I could see his eyes squint. He wore a brown, wrinkled suit. A fedora. He looked pulp-fiction noir.

"Don't make me come over there and get you."

I rose from my seat, not because of his lame threat, but rather to get this over. If he had information and I was not being set up, I wanted it. Here I felt the presence of ghosts. I heard them mumble in iambic pentameter, chortle arias, slam out hip-hop rants. Reilly dropped down from the stage into the orchestra pit. I was surprised by his agility. He was hardened and fit. This gave me more respect. I met him and we leaned against the stage.

"Are you alone?" he said.

I nodded. "You?"

"No."

My hackles went up and I gripped the flashlight in my right hand, grabbed the lapels of Reilly's suit with my left, and said, "Is this a setup?"

"No. I could have lied. Said yes, couldn't I? A one-person backup. No threat. You know him."

"Bring him out."

Two hands clapped from the back of the theatre.

"Bravo. Bravo."

I knew the voice but couldn't believe it.

Turned to Reilly and said, "What are you up to?"

"Take it easy."

Calm. Breathe. Let it go. My right hand passed the flashlight to my left, and once empty I reached behind my back for the assurance of the Glock. Reilly's hand was on my wrist and his eyes were on mine. His head moved slowly from side to side. The moment was trapped in amber.

After I left the Island, I never thought I'd hear Connor's gravel-cluttered voice again.

Conner spoke from the dark at the back.

"You're in the headlines, McQueen. So is Murphy. And there is a dead agent with his brains splattered all over his vehicle's front seat. Do you want to tell me about it?"

I was a fish, and a voice I didn't trust mouthed words underwater. Reilly twitched beside me. We were out in the open. The dark hovered around us, and theatrical criminal ghosts moaned in my ears.

I remained silent.

"Where is she, Jack?"

I still didn't answer him. My mind raced for an exit. I wanted to reach for the Glock. My left hand gripped the flashlight like a club.

Conner's voice softened. "I'm not here to arrest you. If so, you'd be in custody now. Others may want to prosecute both of you."

I stepped back. My feet searched for more shadow.

"So why are you here, Conner? To hound me because of Shaplow? To get some satisfaction?"

"You did a good job there. Out of bounds as usual. There are many people on the Island better off."

"Don't patronize me. It's not your style. Tell me what you want."

"I want you on my team. I sent Murphy to headhunt you. Despite what you think, I'm not compromised."

"Your team." I looked over at Reilly. He looked like a guy who was genuinely sorry he brought me here. "What exactly is your team and why me?"

"Murphy, Reilly, Jack McQueen, and a couple of young kids out of the Academy who are not yet tainted. Are you interested?"

"Maybe, but, why me?"

"Because you can go wherever you want. You do what you like. No warrants, judge's signatures, no exposure."

"Sure. Who has my back if I join this team? Why would I want to get mixed up with this?"

"We need someone on the outside with a network that can do things we can't," Reilly said. "Someone who can take risks. There are not many of us left. They're all in the vaults of who runs this town, this country, and this world."

"Now you're getting melodramatic as you stand here in this raped goddess of a building, all chipped plaster, faded drapes, and fragmented murals."

"It's come to that," Conner said from the back. "No paranoia. It's all conspiratorial. Only the mad are sane. The keys are no longer in the locks. Look around you. Things fall apart."

"I'm listening," I said.

Part of me wanted to believe him and another said he would use me to get to Murphy. She never mentioned Conner when she called me over. Maybe she knew I'd never come. But maybe he saw an opportunity, brought Reilly in, and figured he'd find her.

"A John Doe in the morgue," Conner said. "Mutilated. Arms severed at the elbow, legs at the knees nailed to a cross. Decapitated. No dental records. No fingerprints. No DNA in the system. All his vital organs are gone. Surgically removed. All openings in the flesh are sewn up with precision. A travesty."

Reilly piped in. "No headlines. A report on the fourth page. DISMEMBERED BODY FOUND. No public police response. From the top it came down to cool all investigation. Now doesn't that smell."

"So, ask me, why bother? Simply mind my business and obey orders? Leave it alone?" Conner said.

A flutter of wings echoed, and particles of dust in a shaft of sunshine from the skylight rearranged themselves in the air as three pigeons flew across the theater from one side to the other. The Victory for a moment was transformed into a cathedral.

"You have me. I'll join," I said.

Conner continued. "The reporter who wrote about the fourth page article on the dismembered body, we found on the east side beneath the docks. A floater. Blunt force trauma to the head."

"We searched missing persons for the John Doe to find a match. No luck yet," Reilly said.

"We've had an increase in the number of dead gangsters connected to a Russian gang in the last few days," Connor said. "No ID. Seems odd, so there may be a connection."

"And now what?" I asked.

I was twitchy and had a strong desire to leave.

"Reilly will tell you about our safe house where we will operate. We'll set up a network. You can meet the rookies. For now—"

I heard a footstep behind me, soft and creeping and I was down. Conner's shape rose from his seat as a flash came from the balcony above him. A bullet whizzed past me, then more muzzle flashes light up the ceiling in a barrage of automatic fire, but no bullet hit me.

Behind me, someone fired a gun over my head toward the balcony.

"Jack!"

Stacie crouched behind me in army fatigues. She fired her handgun and yelled at Reilly and me who were both bent low and firing.

"Get out," Stacie yelled. "I've got your back."

She fired a couple more shots at the balcony. No return fire and Reilly and I ran into the darkness toward the exit door with Stacie just behind us firing her Glock into the opera house.

Outside, I saw Stacie's jacked-up Ranger. I guided Reilly to it, and we piled into the back. Stacie jumped into the driver's seat, turned over the engine, and squealed down the road. Reilly stared down at his hand and watched blood slide past his wrist and pool into his palm.

He said the obvious. "I've been shot."

CHAPTER 16

A bullet had sliced through Reilly's left triceps and missed the bone and the artery. A flesh wound. I sat on a bench in the Undertown hospital and waited for further information. Stacie brought us here. Murphy was still in a coma. Stacie didn't talk about Murphy.

Once Reilly was patched up and on painkillers, they let him go. Stacie drove him back to his car and I went to see Murphy. Stacie had visited her every day this week. Made me feel guilty. So, I crept in and sat beside her. Stacie was a good talker. Me, maybe not. So, for a while I sat there, silent as my gut churned inside out.

Murphy's eyelids were still. Once a top eyelid flickered as if her eyes beneath had woken up, but then they were still again. I started to talk.

"Conner's got his team. Not sure why he wants me. We met in the Victory. It's a wonder they haven't torn it down and built another tower to corporate finance, another sun-blocker for the super-rich. We talked, Reilly, Conner, and me. Then the shooting started, and Stacie saved our asses. Conner seemed to slip away. That made me wonder. Reilly picked up a flesh wound."

My voice seemed stilted without a reply. Murphy didn't probe for details. I could have recited a grocery list. Once I thought her eyes moved but they didn't.

"Conner mentioned that several guys connected to the Russians had turned up dead. He didn't mention the Laskey brothers, but then again you don't know about the Laskey brothers and Mindy and Sugar, do you? I'll save that for later, creating some suspense in your life so you have a reason to wake up. Murphy, you must come out of this.

"I got the autopsy dope from Reilly and Conner. The organ removal was news, but I hope Stacie can get forensic details from Becky. The body's still a John Doe. This is way bigger than a random killing. Why would someone do this? Why would the force make sure it was buried on the fourth page, one paper, one day, then nothing? And the reporter. He's dead. Turned up a floater near the docks on the east side."

Maybe Murphy heard me, and she realized it was real stuff to think about.

"Conner says our team, as he calls us, is working on this in secret at a safe house. Don't know where it is yet, but Reilly will fill me in. Got a couple of young kids just out of the academy siphoned off and not corrupted. Tech work. Maybe find a missing person link to John Doe. Until we make that connection, there's not much to go on.

"I found a button before I got whacked. In the dim light from the phone, it looked like it could have come from a cotton coat that workers put on to protect their clothing. You know the kind. Foremen on shop floors, scientists, butchers. Sort of old school. The button's gone now. And the Glock, of course. Evidence. They got warrants for our arrest. Homicide, if you can believe it. The guy in the unmarked who you talked to? He's dead. Plastered all over his car. Shot with our guns. So even if we could walk away from this investigation, we're screwed. They'll either gun us down or prosecute us with circumstantial evidence. We must carry on. Murphy, I'll see this through."

I had rambled, but I'd caught her up.

I felt a hand on my shoulder. Stacie stood behind me. I turned toward her, and she said, "Becky called. Here are her points. They found traces of anesthetic. I wrote down what she said. I won't try to read this."

The note that said (RS)-2-(2-Chlorophenyl)-2-(methylamino)cyclohexanone).

Stacie continued. "Ketamine for short. A needle mark in the right trapezius. Incisions made with a fine sharp blade. Likely a scalpel. Bone cuts consistent with an autopsy saw, I'd say a Stryker—"

"How do you—"

"Internal organs missing," Stacie said. "Process methodical. Evidence of suturing where the organs had been removed. Professional sutures."

"Stacie, thanks. What made you come to the Victory?"

I had told her I was meeting Reilly there.

"Brains and synapses are not always in the head. I got a gut feeling, and the criteria made me worry."

"Fair enough."

"Can you stay the night with Murphy?" she said. "I've hit the wall. I need to go home and make a cup of tea. Noodle a bit. Curl my feet up on the couch with a blanket. Mark called me and asked for that stuff I found at the library six months ago in Shaplow and I'm helping him find out about Kat and Peter and where they went. It might jog some more memories for you."

I felt weary now. The lights were dimmer, a flicker now and then.

"Sure. Is there a comfier chair?"

"I'll bring you pillows. In the morning come over to the apartment, I'll make you breakfast."

Once Stacie was gone, I settled in. I shuffled the chair with its pillows close to Murphy's bed. I held her hand. It was soft and warm. Murphy's skin was olive, her hair dark, and her figure good even under a sheet and blanket. No longer did she have that refined look she had as Staff Sergeant back in Shaplow, but she lacked the tension and the fragility she showed me in the Corolla before we went to the homicide dumpsite. She was calm.

"Murphy. I'm here for you."

I paused and looked around not knowing what more to say.

The emergency utility lights cast vague shadows and washed the floors in a yellow-green tint. I placed my chair sideways to Murphy's bed, sat up near her waist, and rested my hand on hers as it lay still on the outside of the sheet. Murphy was intubated with a tracheal tube. I settled into the chair with my head on one pillow with two others tucked in beside me. The lights had an odd hum and I heard footsteps with a purpose far in the distance.

"It's hard to see you like this. Stacie's been here every day and now you have me, and I don't know what to say. Your hand is soft, sweetheart. You'll come through this."

I left my hand in Murphy's hand and tried to sleep.

CHAPTER 17

I arrived at Stacie's apartment in the early morning after I'd spent the night with Murphy. My back was stiff like I'd lived on the street for a week. Stacie hummed while she poured the tea. I sat in my boxers and a T-shirt at her kitchen table, and she brought over a mug of clear, black tea.

"It helped didn't it," she said.

"With Murphy?" I asked. "It helped me. I sensed that she could hear me and feel my hand on hers."

"I don't know if there is any practical medical proof," Stacie said. "New-age articles say it makes a difference."

"You know how when your leg twitches for no reason? I felt her hand twitch but then it could have been me."

"You have Mark working to find Kat and Peter," Stacie said. "I mean when they shipped you off to foster homes. You can't remember?"

"I still draw blanks on many things that happened. I want to find them, more than I want to find myself. Mark's looking into it. He doesn't want any part of new investigations. He said it terrifies him. Figures one day he'll turn up a fatality. I can't blame him. He wouldn't let me have his Pinto. Someone could trace it back to him and he'd have a repeat of what happened at the marina last year. And you know how that turned out."

"He called me, so I scanned the files from the newspapers that I found last year in the Shaplow Library."

"I didn't get a chance to read them," I said. That wasn't the reason, and Stacie knew it. But we didn't have to put that into words.

Stacie leaned on the counter and tossed me a muffin. I caught it with one hand.

"Sign him up," she said, "Any more information for me?"

"I do. I still must be careful where I pop up. There was a reporter for The Record who did the story from the fourth page on the mutilation. The reporter turned up dead. Floater on the east side. I can't waltz into their offices. Maybe you can sniff around. Talk to a few people. Maybe he told a lot more to a colleague or a friend."

"I'm on it. I'll add another line on the invoice."

"Seriously?"

"Yes. And the fixer fees for saving your ass and the taxi charges. A girl must run her business."

She wasn't kidding.

"Okay. Give me the invoice at the end of the month. Can I spend the morning here? I want to read the articles from the library, then give Mark and Reilly a call."

"Fill your boots. I'll check on Murphy and then the newspaper office. Find out where they go to lunch."

Once Stacie left, I settled into another cup of tea and the printouts from the Shaplow Daily News, the twenty-five-year-old articles Stacie found in the Shaplow Public Library six months ago.

I looked at the headlines.

Missing kids return from the woods, Parents found murdered in homestead kitchen, Barn contains mysterious cages and a child's clothing, and Orphaned children sent to separate homes.

There were more, but my mind was on stones in lunch boxes. Our fear of bears. Silences at supper—be, but not be heard. Visits from policemen muffled words at the farmhouse door. My once beautiful mother with her broken teeth, and stifled sobs was in the kitchen on a pine floor that weekly she scrubbed with a bristle brush.

I read the article; *Orphaned children sent to separate homes.*

One line caught my attention in the second last paragraph.

Caseworker, Sarah McDonald, said, "It is necessary that we follow department policy. Child Services always tries to find a suitable placement suited to each child's needs."

I'd heard this kind of comment before in bureaucratic speech. Sarah McDonald had no choice but to uphold this policy despite what her heart might have told her.

I tapped on Mark's phone number.

It rang through to his voicemail. "Call me," I said.

Moments later he called me back. I got the sense his mode of operation was to lie low. He'd peek through curtains at the knock on the door, not answer the phone, take messages, and then ring back. He was too shook-up.

"That was quick," I said.

"One can't be too careful."

"I noticed. Listen, I read the articles Stacie sent you and I got the name of the caseworker. I remember her, young like she could have been our older sister. That young."

"I'm on it. Sarah McDonald. I made a few calls to Social Services. There's no office in Shaplow anymore. The remnants after the cuts are in Nanaimo. Got a lady to look back at the records twenty-five years ago. Not much, but there is an employee record for Sarah and an old emergency contact number. She didn't want to hand out the information, but I mentioned how the three of you were tragically orphaned and were sent in different directions. It either pulled at her heart or with the cutbacks over the years it played with her morale since she gave it up anyway. I told her the information would stay with me."

"Did that lead anywhere?" I asked.

"Contact is her sister. Still in Shaplow. I called her and got nowhere. Soon as I mentioned Sarah, she clammed up. Got nervous. I mentioned your name and she hung up.

"But I called around. I contacted Shaplow News and asked about the old article. Then I asked if anyone was still at the paper who was there twenty-five years ago. Turns out the owner then is still the owner. I talked to him. He wasn't sure but he thought Sarah moved up Island and lived on a small island north of Johnstone Strait."

"Did you ask at Social Services if there were any records for where we all were shipped?"

"I did. The records from the Shaplow office during that time are missing."

"I'll go over. Take a floatplane. Nail down where Sarah McDonald is by talking directly to her sister. Good work. I may need your help again. Are you up for that?"

"Yes. I can help."

"Thanks, buddy," I said and hung up.

I rolled all this around. Records missing. A nervous sister. Sarah moved away. When did she move away? Office closed after we got shipped off to foster homes. If so, that's interesting and scary.

CHAPTER 18

I rummaged in Stacie's refrigerator for another muffin. My phone rang. It was Reilly.

"Jack, where are you?"

"What's up?" I asked. He didn't need to know.

"I can't talk on the phone."

"I'll meet you at Daffy's Diner," I said. "Do you know it?"

He did. I changed out of my boxers and the T-shirt I slept in. Blue jeans, black T, cotton shirt, Oregon State baseball cap, small Glock.

I left Stacie's apartment within minutes and arrived at Daffy's in half an hour. I watched Reilly come in. He sat down and faced me in a booth beside the window. I had to find a place where he could get the wrinkles out or I would go crazy.

"Have you ever thought a suit and shirt could be pressed or left on a hanger while you take a shower?"

"Shut up. You ain't no fashion plate yourself. Where's my coffee?"

The waitress more worked off her feet than slim came over with a cup and poured as if she'd heard him.

"Happy?" I asked.

"Not really. We're set up off Powell near Pacific Elevators at the grain terminal, four blocks from the Victory. The rookies searched the missing persons' records that corresponded to the estimated day and time of death for John Doe. First, there were no matches. I thought that the one we wanted had been pulled, so they dug deeper into any written reports that would have been filed before they got scanned in. And they found about five potential reports and one I think is a hit.

"A Doctor Sokolov, a surgeon who works at Vancouver General. His spouse, Ekaterina Sokolov made the report. There is a child, Lana Sokolov. They live in a high-rise penthouse in town. I have the address. It wasn't easy but I have a warrant to search if no one's home. You want to take a ride?"

"Have you got my back?"

"Yes, I forgot."

First came the skyscrapers that cast long shadows across a booming economy. And over time every city needed office towers and monuments to commerce and then came these spawned condos and penthouse suites, mansions in the sky.

The address of Dr. Mikhail Sokolov was such a mansion in the sky that its shadow shortened every sunny day in the public park it overlooked.

Reilly took the lead. He flashed his badge at the security guards in the foyer. One guard scrutinized it carefully. The other squinted at me. He stood tense and alert. They let us through to the marble-floored entrance and the curved security station. Two other men sat behind computer monitors behind the granite counter. Reilly walked in as if he belonged. I followed.

"Detective Reilly, RCMP," Reilly said, as he produced his badge again and pulled an envelope from his coat pocket. "I'd like to speak with Ekaterina Sokolov in Penthouse D."

Both men's eyes widened. From the cut of their suits, they were armed with holstered handguns.

One of them hit a few keys, peered at a screen, and said, "I'm afraid Mrs. Sokolov is not at home."

"Dr. Sokolov?" I asked.

"It appears Dr. Sokolov is away on business."

"His daughter, Lana? Is she home from school?"

"Sir, The Sokolovs are not at home."

At this point, Reilly produced the search warrant. Security looked it over.

"Why do you need a search warrant, Detective Reilly?"

"Dr. Sokolov has been reported by his wife as missing. We have tried to get in touch with Mrs. Sokolov since she reported him missing and we haven't had success. There is a suspicion of foul play, and this warrant gives us permission to search the penthouse. It might very well help us to find Dr. Sokolov. How long have Mrs. Sokolov and Lana been absent from their home?"

"Sir, we are not at liberty to discuss private information about an owner's habits. It's security."

The sir was delivered with disdain. Reilly rose to the occasion. Next motion and he'd have the guy by the collar, but he didn't.

"I have a warrant that allows me to search the premises, and you can either answer this question now or after we have gone through the penthouse apartment. If not, then, you and I can take a trip down to detachment headquarters and I will sit you down on a chair in an interrogation room and you will answer this question and many more. Do you understand me?"

"I'll look it up."

The security guy looked as if he had been grabbed by the collar. He tapped the keyboard and read from a screen.

"Dr. Sokolov has been gone for three weeks since May the first. His wife and daughter have been gone for three days."

"Thank you. We'd like to see the apartment."

There were four elevators one for each quadrant of the building. Beside each elevator was a security attendant.

"What do those guys do?" I asked.

"They ride up with the owners and with any approved guests of the owners. There are four condo apartments on each floor, one for each quadrant. Owners have their own iris scans, and each elevator opens directly into the condo. Guests can only enter the elevator here and exit at the condo with an owner's iris scan. Double security."

"So how do we get up there and into the condo?" Reilly asked.

"We can override the system, detective."

At the top floor, we emerged under the scrutiny of the guard.

"Who has this much money?" I said to Reilly.

The expanse in front of us was huge, maybe nine thousand square feet. An entire security team, eye-scanners, probably bullet-proof windows, armored doors, cameras, magnetic sensors, panic buttons.

I scanned the paintings on the walls. Said, "Not your cats on velvet."

The place was spotless. Not a hair, a dust ball, a smudge on the glass, the granite, the stovetop, or the refrigerator handle. Your average person didn't have enough money or time to be this clean. In the bedroom, I saw what looked like a human-sized safe, but it was a panic room.

"Who needs this kind of sanctuary?" Reilly said.

"People who need to look over their shoulders every day," I said.

We walked into a storage room big enough to be someone's small bungalow. It too was neat and orderly, except there was a large box in the center. I saw a courier label and an invoice still in its taped-on plastic. I pulled it out. UPS. The guard had not let us out of his sight. I turned toward him.

"Do you know anything about this?"

"That box is a recent delivery that came three days ago. I brought it up here along with the driver and his hand truck. I informed Mrs. Sokolov when she came home. This is our standard practice."

The box was coated in wax much like the kind of boxes the fruit in grocery stores get shipped in, but bigger, two feet high, maybe three feet wide and three feet long. Reilly flipped open the top flaps. Inside was a large picnic cooler slightly smaller than the cardboard box.

"What do you think is in there?" I asked.

Reilly rolled his eyes. I knew he'd been here before, not a picnic cooler, but a freezer maybe or the trunk of an abandoned car. He hesitated then lifted the lid.

The room was transformed. The guard involuntarily pressed his back against the wall. Both Reilly and I gagged as air rose from the cooler.

"I think we found the rest of Dr. Sokolov," I said.

CHAPTER 19

The team office near Powell was on the top floor of an empty warehouse complex. Low rise, third floor.

The two rookies were busy with their computer screens. Nick Commisso was tall and lanky, with dark hair, Calabrese. He carried himself as he moved around the room like a testa dura. Not that there was anything wrong with that.

Davin Boyle was shorter than he looked when he sat down, but he was wiry. The guy you meet in an Irish pub and like right away then regret it later but you're not sure why. I should talk.

I sat in front of a computer at a desk assigned to me. I didn't know computers, other than to type a letter. Reilly put up photos on a corkboard on the far wall.

"What do you get if an Italian," I said, "two Irishmen and a demented Scot with PTSD are cooped up in a warehouse ready to solve a crime hardly anyone knows about or cares about and a hum comes from Jeffrey Dahmer's refrigerator?"

Reilly swung around after he posted a close-up of Sokolov's torso, beside shots of the body parts from the cooler.

"Don't be a smart-ass."

"It's hard enough to solve a murder with the full command of the force behind you. And why does Conner have a detective that's been bounced around, two rookies, and a guy the force wants to arrest on a trumped-up assassination? How is this clandestine little team going to do that? And there's Murphy."

The two rookies were quiet. Their eyes shifted back and forth, and they kept their heads down.

Back at the penthouse, Reilly had to think fast, so he'd called Conner. Conner came right away, sent me over to the Powell office out of the way, and kept Reilly with him.

Reilly filled me in later. Conner had called in the forensics team. He did it by the book not before he'd taken pictures, checked for prints on the cooler, and got the cooler's manufacturer written down. Asked the guard what he knew about Ekaterina Sokolov and the daughter. When they'd left.

What they were wearing. Whether they looked calm or upset. No prints on the lid of the cooler. It was made by Coleman. The day the UPS delivery was made, Mrs. Sokolov left shortly after she came home three evenings ago with Lana from school. 'Frantic' was the word the guard had used. Got picked up in a chauffeured, black Lincoln "L" Series.

"You know anything about Murphy?" Reilly said.

"Nope."

I couldn't tell him, not until she woke up. Not until I could confirm Conner's story. And I knew Reilly didn't buy it, but I'd deflected him for now.

"My assistant, she's looking into the reporter they found dead in the inlet on the east side," I said.

"The autopsy report said he was strangled," Davin Boyle said. "Ligature marks on the neck, no water in his lungs. He was dumped. Didn't drown."

I realized these guys were serious hackers.

"Well, my gal is Old School."

I didn't mean to come out snarky, but the Luddite in me made me do it. They both turned and looked at me as if I'd pissed on the floor.

"Hey, guys. I didn't mean it that way. I appreciate what you do here. I mean, you know, good old personal contact. Down in the gutter can still work, right?"

I could see them relax a little. Reilly waded in from the corkboard. "Jack, Boyle, Commisso. We all got our ways. Don't get me started on how to dig into horseshit. If we all dig in our own way, we're bound to find a pony."

I changed the subject. "How can Conner keep whoever's up the food chain from smothering this investigation and riding up his ass or worse?"

"He reported the find," Reilly said. "Followed up a lead on a missing person. As far as everyone is concerned no one's making any connections publicly. We put the scare on the guards. Let them know that two detectives, Conner, and Reilly, arrived with a warrant. They didn't get your name anyway, Jack."

"Well, that'll hold up," I said. "I suppose that's the best you got."

"Reality snapped into place with Conner," Reilly said. "When he was brought in over on the Island back when Shaplow erupted when Murphy should have got that promotion, he came in as a hard-ass. Toed the line. Played it out as one of the good old boys. Looked as corrupt as the rest of them. Then things changed. I don't know if it was the fact that everyone got shunted around who knew about the Strang empire and what Strang had done over there, or if he'd discovered deeper stuff than that, but he's changed. It's like he doesn't care about his own ass. He's on a mission and he wants to take someone down. It might be personal. He doesn't talk to me, like over whiskey in his private library with fancy oak wainscoting. He conscripted me just like the rest of you. And I'm on board for better or worse. So, let's get to work."

"Why did the body parts end up at the Solokov residence?" I asked. "Why did a mutilated John Doe get displayed in that alley?"

Both rookies slid their chairs back from the computer screens and were fully attentive.

"Why is the only reporter to do a story on the John Doe found dead in Burrard Inlet?" Nick Commisso said.

"Who would kill and dismember a prominent surgeon?" Reilly said. "And where are his major organs? Where are his eyes?" Reilly pointed to a photo of Dr. Sokolov's eyeless head. "No one gouged those eyes out with a spoon. They were, like every other organ in his body, surgically removed."

"A lot of questions. No answers," Boyle said.

"Well kid, this isn't a crime novel, where it all falls into your lap," I said. "It's easy when you read case studies at the academy, but life and death are messy, and there's always horseshit and there's always bullshit, and there's only us. What are the odds?"

The wind rattled the panels of single-pane glass on the warehouse windows. Then a hard rain hammered. The room grew darker, followed by thunder and a lightning flash. I was sleeping here tonight and thought about leaving.

"On that cheery note that's not a reason to stop trying," Reilly said.

"What motivates you, Reilly?" I wanted the right answer.

He said to Commisso and Boyle, "Give us a minute will you."

They both got up. Commisso sauntered off to the washroom. Boyle found a quiet corner and began to shuffle papers.

"You want to know?" Reilly said. "You want to know what's got under my skin that will make me risk my career? I'll tell you."

I waited. He paused.

"It's Murphy. I know you were beaten badly in that courtyard. I know you regained consciousness beside the dumpster where some assholes left Murphy for dead. I know both of you have been set up for the undercover cop's homicide. It is the cop they killed that bugs me. I know all this. I don't know where Murphy is. I worry she won't come back from this. I'm going to get who is behind this. That's what motivates me. Murphy motivates me because she was on to something, and she's paid for it. I won't let her down. Does that answer your question?"

I saw a numb sadness in his eyes. The loss. I saw a man driven to action so his soul could stay on this side of sanity.

"I believe you. I'm sorry I asked. You had me when you said it's Murphy."

CHAPTER 20

Undertown hospital's green lights bathed the walls in a hue of the lower depths. I sat beside Murphy and held her hand. It was midnight and I couldn't sleep. Just as well since I needed to talk. Keep her updated. I began to believe she could hear me and knew the details. But nothing was obvious behind her benign exterior. I felt her pulse while I held her hand and watched the faint flutter of her closed eyelids as I spoke to her. She was reacting.

"I haven't told Reilly where you are. I will wait until I can trust him. I think I can now, but I'm not ready to expose this sanctuary.

"Mark has tracked down the caseworker who shipped us off the Island when I was a kid. Images and my memories have come back. The three of us stayed at the Madson's house for a week or so, until it all blew over. Reporters stopped coming to the door. The police questioned us, over and over. They wanted to catch us in a lie, but we'd stuck together. Didn't tell them about the cages. I didn't say much. I rocked back and forth and held onto my knees tucked in front of me.

"Then we were taken away. Three kids huddled on the dock and waited for the ferry to take us to the mainland. That wasn't so bad, a boat trip and we were all together. But on the other side, three cars waited for us. They took Kat and Peter first. Kat had her face pressed up against the side window, Peter cried, and I stood by myself. The gulls screeched and flapped over a piece of bread. I watched the two cars pull away and then watched one gull descend and take the bread, and when I looked back, Kat and Peter were gone."

Murphy's eyes were closed. The eyelids static. I stared at our hands touching. I felt the warmth that flowed through her veins. I continued to watch her. Heard the constant rhythm of her breathing.

"A lot has happened since we last talked," I said. "Well, since you last listened, that is if you are listening, and I sense you are. Met with Reilly and Conner. They are worried about you. Told me that you got in touch with me to recruit me onto their team. Your team. Not sure even yet if it is all bullshit and I'll wake up and find myself in the slammer or if not, not wake up on a slab at the morgue. I wish you could tell me if I should trust them."

A clock on the wall had a twitchy minute hand that jerked around the face as the second hand passed the twelve.

"Anyway, tomorrow I meet Stacie and a reporter who knew the dead colleague who wrote the story on your John Doe. And we have a name. Dr. Mikhail Sokolov. Ring a bell? Found the rest of him. Eyes were surgically cut out. Makes me think one of two things."

I stared up at the ceiling. I followed the various color-coded pipes and lines along a girder.

"That this is an elaborate revenge perpetrated by a skilled surgeon himself, or a message, an example being made. But why the organs? Part of a ritual, a message, or an organ harvesting operation, and Sokolov was a convenient victim. The other body parts were at the Sokolov penthouse apartment."

I fell silent for a while and kept my thoughts to myself.

I pieced together the images of memory.

> The ferry docks. I wait with the family services social worker. She is anxious. She tries to talk to me. I am silent. A white panel van arrives. Two men in beige uniforms get out and leave the engine running. Exhaust drifts up into my lungs. One guy grabs me by the elbow and has me step up through the rear doors. The back is framed in plywood to form two benches. He sits me down, and straps on a seat belt. The seat is hard. He puts handcuffs on my wrists and attaches these to an eyebolt on the floor. He steps out. The social worker stands by herself. She reaches into her purse and hands him a file folder. She looks at me. Her eyes are soft and sad. She's worried. Why is she worried? The door closes. The van drives off. Her expression scares me more than the handcuffs.

I let go of Murphy's hand and adjusted my position in the chair. I grabbed hold again and entwined my fingers with hers. I wanted to hold on more for me. My eyes closed, so I could trace a thread. A brick wall, wrought-iron gate. A long driveway through the woods. An open meadow. A twenty-foot-high chain-link fence. Galvanized razor wire. A prison.

CHAPTER 21

In the Undertown hospital, I felt myself sliding sideways. Virtually homeless. Not much better off than Norton. Figure I'd go pay him a visit at the shelter. It felt like it had been weeks, but it was only a couple of days since I'd dropped off Norton, Mitchell, and the girls. I wanted to see how they dealt with their trauma. Who knows? I couldn't keep this up. I couldn't hold Murphy's hand forever or fall asleep wherever I landed at night. I didn't want to bother Stacie either. So, I thought first thing, I will rent a place. A one-bedroom with a sink, toilet, and shower. Small fridge and a hot plate. A place without a lease I could rent by the week. A place full of old tired men who smelled of aftershave and wandered around in white singlets like aging Kowalskis. I took a bus over to the east side near the inlet, closer to where that reporter was found. I was not too particular. Apartments are overrated. They're places to store food and a few clothes, quiet places to eat and park your body for the night, like a cardboard box or a pup tent beneath bushes in the park, but a little more substantial. Any more than that and a person was apt to collect junk, enough to drag him down.

I found The Painted Parrot Guesthouse. Fancy name but a hostel for the single and the lonely. It fit the bill on one count but not the other. Never really been lonely even when I was empty and alone. At a bargain outlet, I bought a small black gym bag, another pair of blue jeans, a flannel shirt in the thrift store, a couple of packs of boxers and a six-pack of grey socks, shampoo, and a bar of Irish Spring.

The landlady's name was Mrs. Sharpe. Short and stocky but as gentle as a tea cozy. Fussed as she showed me the room. I laid down cash for three weeks and immediately took a shower. Soaped my skin and the clothes I'd worn for the last two days. I opened the single-pane window and put the clothes over the back of the one wooden chair in the room. The only other furniture was a small round oak table that folded down on the sides, a bed, and a narrow armoire that leaned toward the window. No television. Just as well. Too much chatter, violence, wars, and capped-toothed celebrities engaged in mind-numbing survivor contests. Give me books. But books were not part of my childhood. Long ago a guy traded me a tattered copy of *Tao Te Ching* by Lao-Tzu for a pack of cigarettes after I'd quit. A thin book. I'd been hungry for a long time, so I ate thin poetry books. I formed a habit that changed the way I saw the world. I was born to write poetry, to search for discarded envelopes to write on among the trash, vague scratches from my mind etched out on clay, pencil marks that captured the day. I'd done this as a child, but I do not remember where the words went, or what I'd written down. I have a vague sense I hid them in the barn, the barn that burned.

With the shower, I felt purified at least for a while. Carried the black gym bag with me and left the duffle bag at the Painted Parrot, flattened between the box spring and the mattress.

I took the bus to the downtown east side and got off close to the shelter entrance, then went down the alley and knocked on the door. A window as wide as a set of eyes slid open. I asked for Norton and the guy told me I'd likely find him in Salsbury Park.

"Where's that?" I asked.

The eyes tilted to the right and a voice said, "Six blocks up and over one. On Adanac."

"Thanks," I said.

Salsbury Park was a small square of green with a clump of overgrown bushes in the center. The park was located at Adanac and Salsbury in a neighborhood that regarded this park as a gathering place on a Sunday for families, a place where kids could play ball and lovers could lay out a blanket and get hot and bothered. Not now. Here the local tribe hung out, slept off the afternoons, drank cheap booze, lit fires to keep warm in winter, and slept raw on warm nights in summer beside the bushes.

I spotted Norton in the middle of his tribe. He wore the same flak coat and from inside pockets, he pulled pamphlets and paperbacks and waved them in the air. He looked like a televangelist on a pulpit. He jived so hard he could've had backup gospel singers beating out a storm.

When he slowed down, I waved him over.

"You've worked up a lather," I said.

He smiled and knew I'd made fun of him.

"Seriously do those guys listen to you?"

"Doubt it." He stuffed a paperback into his coat. "I got it all. The Koran, Bible, Bhagavad Gita." He patted his inside chest pockets and a deep pocket on the side. I saw a thick paperback and a small silver flask.

"You're a walking philosophical library, Norton. You up for a ride?"

"Do you have a car now?" He looked around toward the bushes where the gang hung out. Several guys shouted over to us. "Don't mind them."

"I am about to buy one. Come on."

We took a bus to Main and W 7th. Here was where a few independent, used-car dealers sold the clunkers, cars destined for small scrap-iron dealers who did their greasy work behind huge twelve-foot fences, where tired cafes with four or five tables fronted for local, punk mob bosses.

Most of the car dealers, I wouldn't trust to sell me a piece of toast, but I knew a mechanic, Johnny Calabrese who'd see your granny got a deal. Even had his own name on the banner, Calabrese Motors. He was a hardhead, but he was honest.

Within an hour I was behind the wheel of a metallic blue '87 Tercel 4WD wagon with 250,000 miles on her. She was old with a lot of make-up, but she ran well through five gears as we drove her east on the Kingsway toward New Westminster to clean her out. Last words I heard Johnny say before I said I'll take it and handed him $900 was, "Don't worry about the miles. These engines are tough little buggers."

I got Norton to register the Tercel in his name on the way back to Brogans where Stacie said she would meet the reporter. We arrived at Brogans on Denman by noon. I had Norton watch the car. I wasn't sure Brogans was a good choice since I had a bad memory of the place. Its karma could send the day into a slide but figured Stacie knew what she was doing. I figured it wrong.

CHAPTER 22

Stacie was in a booth at the back dressed in a navy-blue business suit, and sensible high heels. Dressed to kill. She could be ready for combat in any outfit or maybe nothing at all.

I didn't sit down. Said, "Where do you want me?"

She motioned with her head to another booth, so I settled in with my baseball cap low over my eyes, ordered a Guinness, and nursed it. I knew the drill. If he saw two of us, he'd bolt. But once she lured him in, I could slide in beside him.

A couple of guys were at the bar as usual. Did they own the place? Were they bodyguards, or had they invested enough in the product that Brogans was their home?

Stacie said noon but he was a tad late. I spotted him as he entered. He scanned the room, lit on the two sentries at the bar, then on to me as I checked the menu. He found Stacie, hesitated, liked what he saw, and came forward.

He was young, in his late twenties, with short blonde hair. Casual. Everyone wore blue jeans, neat and tidy these days. He was no exception, black fleece, and a pale-blue wind jacket. Zipper front. He had a cell phone clipped to his belt. When he passed by, I could smell his cologne. Acqua Di Gio, Giorgio Armani. I recognized it because of a birthday gift my ex-wife, Del, gave me when a present went a long way toward a happy relationship. Now for me, it was Irish Spring in the shower. Less fuss. A lot cheaper. He breezed by me without a caution since Stacie's appearance drew him in.

I was within earshot even if they whispered, so I focused for an appropriate cue.

Stacie half stood up in the booth. I couldn't see, but I knew there was some intentional cleavage.

"You must be Robert," Stacie said.

"Robbie. Robert Mayne's for the by-line."

"Take a seat. Drink?"

"Coffee's fine."

I heard them shuffle around in their booth.

"Relax. It's safe here," Stacie said. "So, you're a friend of the reporter who broke the story of the mutilated body, four pages in. What was his name?"

"I worked with him. Wouldn't say I was his friend, but close enough. James Harris. Did stories together sometimes."

"And you did that story?"

"Not exactly. He was on the scene when the body was found. Took all the details. Photos. Notes. He showed me what he had. He thought it was weird. Not the scene and all that, but the fact it got buried on page four. Too much violence in this town, but this seems to me to be sensational. Front page material, don't you think?"

"So, the story sat there and went nowhere?" Stacie said. "Do you have any idea why?"

I heard Robbie Mayne twist and turn in the booth.

"Trust me," Stacie said. "I work for two friends who nearly died investigating the murder, so I need answers."

That was my cue. I hopped up and before you could down a shot at closing time, I slid in beside Robbie. He panicked. Couldn't talk. I could smell the sweat on his upper lip.

"Relax, pal." He didn't. I said, "Robbie calm down. I'm with her. We work together."

I flashed the badge that Reilly gave me to make it official. Stacie smiled.

"You're a cop?"

"Sort of. Consultant, you might say."

The guy became twitchy, and I feared he would leap from the booth and bolt. Stacie leaned forward. There was the cleavage. Better than I expected. She touched his wrist with her fingertips. Even I got excited, but her gesture seemed to calm him down.

"This is Jack." She swept her palm toward me, "Why the fourth page?"

"James had a big argument with our editor. Blamed him, but the editor's line was that someone higher on the food chain pushed it back. So, James asked me for a favor. Then he disappeared. Didn't answer his phone. I even went over to his apartment thinking he was sick. No one had seen him for several days. I did the favor. He told me to tell no one at the paper since he didn't trust anyone after the story went nowhere."

"What was the favor?" I asked.

Robbie paused, took a moment, looked me over, let out his breath, inhaled deeply, and lowered his voice to a whisper. He was struggling to keep it all together.

"James was on to something bigger than a murder, but he never told me. He asked me to stake out the murder scene and put a camera in the courtyard where the body was found. I positioned a camera to take a wide angle of the street in front. Each night I'd come by and change the batteries and the chips. I played them on my laptop. At first, there was nothing. Then one night it happened. Two people arrived, acting furtive, a guy and a girl. Then I saw that someone was in a car in the shadows. The guy went into the courtyard. He got roughed up."

"He comes out of the courtyard," I said. "He survives it. Then he gets his lights knocked out."

Robbie looked at me as if he'd been hit with a hammer.

"Don't say another word," I said. "I've got to see the video."

Stacie chimed in. "Did you get it all? The dumpster. The undercover cop who was murdered. Someone coming to the rescue."

Robbie started to fit the pieces together. His eyes vibrated in their sockets. His chest sucked air. He reached for a sip of coffee, but his cup was empty.

"You guys?" he said.

"Us guys," I said. I thought of Murphy, "One's still in a coma. Does the recording show who killed the cop? All the details?"

"It was dark. I had to play with the brightness and contrast with the raw digital. You might have a better idea about what it shows."

"I assume you have it on a stick," I said, "so, we can look at it?"

"You sure James didn't tell you about what he was following?" Stacie said. "He could have mentioned a word, slipped something we can follow up on?"

"No," he said.

The waitress came over. She tried to refill Robbie's coffee. She asked me, "Want another?"

I waved her off. Said, "No thanks. We're leaving. I'll get the tab."

I got up. Motioned with my eyes for Stacie to stick with Robbie who had suddenly got jumpy again.

Out on the street, I said to Robbie, "So when can we take a look at this?"

He looked at Stacie and not me and said, "Give me a few days. I have it in a safe place and need time."

"Maybe I could go with you?" Stacie said. "It might be quicker?"

Robbie looked at Stacie. He was sizing up his chances even in his state of anxiety. He was still a kid in his twenties.

Finally, after a good but subtle look over he said, "No, I'm better off alone. It's Thursday and I must pull a few all-nighters for some deadlines, so Stacie, why don't you call me Saturday afternoon. I'll have it then and you can have a look at it. Okay with you?"

He looked at me searching his memory.

"It's Jack," I said. "Fine with me." I started to walk a few steps toward the Tercel.

"Give me a minute with Robbie, here," I said to Stacie, put my arm over his shoulder, and led him to the edge of the entrance to Brogans.

"Robbie, I like you. You're honest. I like that. I think you're loyal too. I'm worried about you. You've got dangerous evidence in your possession. Evidence that someone who is not as nice as I am, will kill for."

Robbie nodded his head. He was panicking again.

"And another thing. See Stacie over there. She is my friend. Don't even think about making a pass at her. Because if she doesn't send your nuts to the hospital, I'll cut them off."

I left him there with his hands making comforting gestures toward his crotch. I went over to Norton who leaned on the Tercel's passenger door.

"You do drive, don't you?" I said.

"I can figure it out."

I looked at him and he smiled.

"Follow that guy. Follow him when he is in his car. Follow him on foot. Wait for him when he goes to work. Not just outside. I want you to lurk about. Know where he is all the time. His co-worker's dead and this guy's life may be in danger. I got another matter to attend to. Are you okay with that?"

Norton nodded.

I grabbed my gym bag from the back seat, opened the zipper and peeled off three hundred dollars.

Norton took it. He watched Robbie get into a late-model Ford Focus. When the Focus pulled out, Norton turned the ignition, jack-rabbited the clutch, and followed him. He could drive. He did that to get me going.

I walked over to Stacie and said, "Do you think he'll call?"

"If only to try to seduce me."

"This is business. Norton will tail him."

When Stacie got to her camouflaged Ranger, she said, "Want a lift?"

"Drive me to Sea-Air, I've got to see someone on the Island."

CHAPTER 23

The Sea-Air floatplane dropped me down at Northwest Bay and taxied to the government wharf where the shrimp boats unloaded their catch. Across the bay, the sea lions barked up a storm. With my gym bag, I hopped out onto a floating dock with a swing ramp to accommodate the tide. Tony, the First Nations chief of the Snuneymuxw leaned against his truck. I'd called him to take me into town.

Tony was built like Chief Bromden in One Flew Over the Cuckoo's Nest. When I'd first met him, I'd in my head, thought of him as The Sink because of his size, but later got to know his name.

"Thanks, Tony. I won't take long."

Tony produced a thin-lipped smile and hugged me with both arms. I'm not a hugger, but with Tony what could I say.

"Jump in. Tell me where you need to be."

Tony was a man who never said much. Someone you didn't want to mess with but high on a psyche evaluation for loyalty and a protective nature. I assumed he knew what had gone down with my obsession to find Peter and Kat.

He dropped me off in downtown Shaplow. One main street—The Duke Hotel, the library, a coffee shop, a gas station, a hardware store, and the newspaper office, Shaplow News.

I met the owners, Bob, and Betty Roland, who had run the mom-and-pop paper for twenty-five years. I told them why I'd come, and they gave me the name and address of Marilyn Townsend, sister of Sarah MacDonald, the case worker who handled the foster home situation for Kat, Peter, and me. Mr. and Mrs. Roland couldn't help me since there were no additional articles I hadn't already read, but Mrs. Townsend who had clammed up on Mark, could. I knew she could tell me where her sister lived.

Tony drove me to Sarah's sister's home and waited in the truck.

Mrs. Townsend lived in a bungalow on Backsaw Street, which ran off Main. Stucco siding, carport on the side with a five to ten-year-old Ford Taurus.

I knocked on the storm door beside the carport and listened. Crickets. I knocked again, but still nothing, so I walked back to the front door. A small window, the glass in the front door, and a picture window were all draped. I wondered if she lived alone, had agoraphobia, or was simply not home.

I went to try the front door. Before I reached it, I heard a voice.

"Whatever you're selling, we don't want it."

"Mrs. Townsend?"

"Who's asking?"

"I'm Jack McQueen. My family had a homestead that was burned down last year. I have a sister and a brother, and I'm looking for them."

"What makes you think I know about it?"

Her voice had an edge that told me maybe she was always feisty and suspicious. She opened the door and stepped out onto the concrete porch. She had been working in the garden. She wore rubber-palmed garden gloves, a sweatshirt, and jeans with dirt smudges at the knees.

"My friend who is helping me phoned you to find out where your sister lives now so that I can talk to her. Sarah MacDonald."

"I told him I didn't know. So, you can haul yourself off my property or I'll call the police."

Mrs. Townsend looked about sixty, lightweight and sinewy. Her face had seen sunshine and wind and maybe sorrow too. I couldn't blame her if she wanted to be left alone.

"Can I talk to your husband?"

"He hasn't been here for ten years. He's compost."

A sliver of pathos slipped into her voice. I took the liberty to sit down on the concrete steps at the front door.

"I'm sorry," I said.

She was not happy that I'd sat down. My presence looked permanent.

"What makes you think my sister knows anything?"

"When we three kids were orphaned, she handled our case, and she took us on the ferry to our new homes. I've lost some memories of where I went, and I never did know where my brother and sister went. That has haunted me all my life. I need your help. I only want her address so I can talk to her."

She looked at me long and hard.

"Come inside. You can sit at the kitchen table while I find it."

I waited a few minutes, and she handed me a strip of paper with Sarah MacDonald's address. I thanked her and met Tony back at his truck.

I asked Tony to drive me up to the family homestead while I waited for a Sea-Air float plane to be available to take me to Zabella Island three-quarters of the way off the northern tip of the Island on the sheltered east side. He sat in the truck while I strolled around the carnage from the fire.

Both of us had been here before. At the back where the barn had stood, I looked down at the charred earth and a memory came to me.

A black mass of ravens is smoke over the dark cedars behind the barn. They mock me. I have no choice. I have never had a choice. No escape from this place. He hands me the shovel. In his anger, he tells me to dig. I dig deeper than I need and wider than I need. I push back time. I stand in the long hole, two feet deep, to my skinny-kid waist and wonder, head turned to a dying sun. He hands me the dead painted raven and I lay it in the grave at one end. He pushes the dog to the edge with his foot. I was still in the grave. I won't let him kick my dog into the hole. I pick Max up and hold him across my biceps. Max is now limp again, not rigid as before with his broken teeth and his crushed skull. I lay him down on the grave's bottom. The moist earth glistens on his bloodstained muzzle. "Fill it in," he says as he walks away and I do, first with my tears and then the earth. I want not to forget, but I do. I want to forgive but I don't.

CHAPTER 24

The Sea-Air Beaver's pilot pointed the nose north then curved around into a light southeast wind and dropped me down on rippled water that went placid as we taxied toward a wide, wooden dock. A group of First Nations guys crowded around and guided the tail, so the plane pointed out into the cove. I stepped down from the back door, held on to the wing brace and stepped down two rungs to the pontoon, then took another step onto the dock.

"I told you it was the DHC-2 DeHavilland Beaver," One guy in a red knitted toque said to another.

"Is that what it is?" I asked.

"Could hear the Pratt and Whitney," he said.

"R-985 radial engine." Another guy said. "450 horsepower. I recognize it anywhere."

They both looked at me. The other guys smiled after they watched the white guy get off the plane.

I wanted to say something impolite, but I was the main event for the morning, and they were having fun at my expense.

"Morning guys. You almost got me."

They all started to laugh, even the pilot who had just stepped onto the dock.

"It's just a plane," I said.

"Only one of the most successful bush aircraft ever built," the pilot said. "So good when the planes got old no one ever came up with a replacement. So here we are. They're still in service."

"Good to know."

"Call when you want a pick-up," the pilot said.

The pilot strolled down the dock with the guys who'd come to see the show.

I took my gym bag and walked the dock and up the swing ramp to the island's solid ground. A boardwalk stretched along the cove above the tideline, and I climbed the wooden steps to the main street that ran parallel to the cove.

For me, it had been a long day—two flights, the interview with Sarah's sister, and a few involuntary moments where I delved into my past. The sun had gone behind the island, slid over the Big Island's mountainous spine, and sunk into the Pacific. It was twilight. I wandered past the Sea-Otter Hotel, the only place to bunk in town, it seemed. Decided to check in there a little later. Continued past a lean-to garage converted into a variety store and booze outlet with a pool table. The structure was open, and dark figures with pool cues moved about the table in the low incandescent light. First Nation's kids rode their two-wheeled bikes in and out and down the street. The town had a tattered tidiness to it like an all-purpose bedroom hastily straightened up with stuffed toys shoved into closets and beneath the bed.

I walked into the store's relaxed ambiance. A step back in time when regulations didn't apply. A haze of tobacco smoke and breathy alcohol mixed with kiddie bubble gum and half-digested potato chips. The air smelled like an old diet I might have had myself. The place made pizzas too, so I was sold. I ordered a large pepperoni mushroom and a six-pack of Coke Classic. Until the pizza was done, I hung around on the edge where there was still some daylight, and the smoke was not as strong.

After twenty minutes my order appeared. I carried the six-pack looped around a finger with the gym bag in one hand and the pizza box like a platter in the other and headed for the Sea-Otter Hotel. Too late to find Sarah today and I looked forward to being alone.

The room was adequate and over-priced but what the hell. The drywall ceiling showed its seams. The paneled walls were laminate. One window looked over the street and the cove. One double bed. A round table and a couple of straight-backed wooden chairs. A TV was on the cutting edge of the sixties. Two channels, the National and the local First Nation station. Not a problem. I was not on vacation.

I watched the light disappear as I scarfed up the pizza and washed it down with a coke. I leaned back on the chair with my feet up on the table. My Glock with one in the chamber and the clip beside it was on the bedside end table. I settled into the quiet, far from the mainland's grime, greed, and clutter. Someone knocked on the door.

I approached the door and asked the obvious, "Who's there?"

"Police. Open the door."

I was here an hour on an island in the middle of nowhere and the force was at the door. Did they have an APB out on me or what?

"Officer honest, I was only going forty."

"I've got a smart-ass. Now open the door."

"Seriously what's this about?"

I stood back from the door enough to avoid it flying into my face.

"If you don't want to pay for a smashed door latch, I'd open the door."

"Okay. Okay."

I opened the door and a burly uniformed police officer stepped into the room. He looked half First Nations. His eyes swept over the room. He didn't miss the Glock or the gym bag.

"Do you want some pizza?"

"Comedian, eh?"

"No, seriously. I got pizza and some coke, the beverage, right."

"Mr. McQueen, this is only routine. I saw you come in by plane earlier and I got your name at the desk. It's my job. We don't have too many loners who want to come up here. Mostly tourists in the summer. They come for the totem poles, our museum, and whale watching. You don't look like you're interested in any of that."

"I'm here for a night. I need to check on someone from my past."

"I'll need to know who this person is. I run a tight ship up here."

This was kind of weird. I knew I stood out in a native community, but this was the twenty-first century.

I moved back to my chair and sat down.

"Have a seat." I pulled the other chair away from the table. "Before we start, officer, I'd like to know your name and badge number. You're required to give them, right?"

He sat down and put his hat on the window ledge.

"Officer Douglas Walkus. Number 007. Walkus, Douglas Walkus."

"So, you have a sense of humor. I'm here to see Sarah McDonald, a retired social worker. She was the last person on the Big Island to see me and my sister and brother before we got shipped off to foster homes."

I didn't tell him details about where they sent me.

Douglas squinted and looked at my face closely.

"You're from down Island, right? Well, at least you were."

"Right. Do you know anyone down near Shaplow Lake?"

Douglas shook his head and smiled. His smile was delightful. Genuine, writ large.

"That's why you looked familiar. Jack McQueen. You worked with Bridget Murphy back in the day. You were in the news last year, took down the head of the Strang family, right?"

"I'm your guy. Although it wasn't me alone. I had help."

"We heard about it. We were lucky to be tucked up here."

I opened the pizza box and motioned for him to have a piece, and he did. I grabbed a coke and handed him one. Douglas snapped it open and smiled.

"It's not often I make a connection when I do these routine checks on visitors."

"Maybe you know big Tony, I said. He's chief now."

"I do. We're cousins from somewhere down the line. He's turned that band around."

"Sure has,"

Douglas stayed another hour and helped finish off the pizza and all the coke. He asked about Murphy, and I spilled much of the story, how she was in a coma now and how we were falsely accused of a murder. He hadn't heard about it and explained that mainland problems rarely got sent to Zabella Island and he liked it like that.

When he finally left, he offered to drive me over to Sarah MacDonald's house in the morning, but I said I could find it on my own and wanted to walk around anyway.

He waved as he went down the hall. I liked him. A stand-up guy. I felt I could trust him but wondered if he'd do some research that might come back to bite me.

CHAPTER 25

Morning came early after I tossed around in a murky sea of dreams. Inside my head, I wanted to know the missing pieces, what happened to us as kids, and all the violence that had gone down, in my childhood, in the Special Forces, the time spent on the force, and the recent stuff with Murphy. Depression's black dog gnawed on all those dusty bones. I had a priority. Get the fuckers who did this to Murphy and exact retribution on whoever is the kingpin who pulls the strings.

I hit the main street. The grey light washed across the cove. I walked south out of the town's center. The tide lapped against the shingle and the captured driftwood stumps. On my right stood the totem poles, grey sentinels of old carved crack-lined cedar. Hook-beaked eagles, killer whales, and black bears were carved into the thick trunks. They watched the sea, Douglas Walkus and his family, and the entire community. Maybe a poor wretch like me. Among these totem poles was a rough-chiseled stone cross, another kind of spiritual power that with its history did not deserve its place, but that's another alley for a different rant. Crosses erected and onward Christian soldiers sung on traditional, unceded land.

The Christian cross among the totem poles made me uncomfortable, as the muted light struck its face as well as the thunderbird carved at the top. A raven flapped heavily in the air. Its voice knocked, and gulls squawked among the driftwood and the washed-up crabs. I thought of old lines I'd written.

Ravens play haunting flutes.
Their watchful eyes
witness to our crimes.

Morning bloomed and the sun glinted from the boat's metal masts in the harbor. Every living thing scurried about with a purpose and was employed.

I slopped up my breakfast in the Rock Mountain Café. No mountains in sight on the island, but I liked the name, and it was the only place that served food. Bacon, two eggs, hash-browns, toast, jam in plastic containers, and coffee, cream, and sugar. After breakfast, I walked up Canmer Street to Sarah MacDonald's house. When I knocked on the door, she opened it.

"I'm Jack McQueen."

"I know. My sister called me. Come in."

Sarah led me into her living room. She looked about fifty, so she must have been twenty-five or so when she dealt with our case files. She had taken care of herself, or she had good genes—even in a pair of jeans and a bulky sweater her figure looked good. She had a warm genuine smile.

She studied me as if I were an old photograph.

"You want to talk to me about your brother and sister," she said. "I'd know you anywhere Mr. McQueen. Once my sister called, my first thought was to run. To hide somewhere. I didn't want to think about what happened back then. But I couldn't run. Yesterday after I'd stewed about your visit, I finally went to the attic and found the files and searched through them, found all the McQueen family references, and photocopied the files at the public library."

I was about to thank her when she got up and moved toward the kitchen.

"Coffee?"

"Yes, cream or milk and sugar," I said.

I observed the room. No photos of people in picture frames. A few small black and white photos of small boats. No knickknacks. A couple of brass animals—an armadillo and a deer.

She came back with two coffees, returned to the kitchen, and came back again this time with a brown manila folder. She handed it to me.

"I am not sure what you really need to know. I'll let you be the judge."

"Why did you take the files with you? Weren't they the property of social services?"

"They were but I didn't want people to know. They seem private for the Island, not a wider public."

This told me how protective she was. Even as young as she was then, she knew something smelled.

"You must have just begun your career when they closed the office?"

"Yes. What a shock. No reason for it, I thought. I didn't hang around. I needed a job, so I planted trees and found I was suited to the wild, and here I am."

"I'll look at the files. And thank you. But I want you to tell me what happened. What happened to Kat and Peter and what happened to me?"

"When your parents were found dead, that's when the police and social services stepped in. There were a lot of kids. Not only Katherine, Peter, and Jack. Do you remember the kids in the cages?"

I nodded. "Off and on, the three of us were in cages too. But the others who came and went, they were always in the cages."

"I read about the cages and what they found last year. What you did."

"I had help. What happened to us when we were kids?"

"Each of us took some of the kids and tried to find foster homes for them. They gave me you and your siblings, but I didn't get the opportunity to decide where you went. That's what has always bothered me."

"Who decided?"

"Someone high-up in social services. The signature was a scrawl. I was young, lowest seniority. How could I question a decision from above me?"

Sarah fell quiet and I could see the guilt creep into her facial expression. We sipped our tea.

"Different foster homes were chosen for your brother and sister. Each of them didn't know where they would go or where the other went. I was instructed to keep those facts secret. That policy bothered me, but I couldn't do a thing about it. It disturbs me today, how cruel that was." She paused and tilted her head down then looked up at me. "On the forms, you were to be sent to a separate foster home but when I researched the location, I couldn't find it. And when I inquired further, I was told not to worry about it because the kids would be picked up separately when the ferry arrived on the mainland. I was to get them there and deliver the forms which I did."

My chest tightened. My fingertips became numb.

I see the white panel truck where they put on the handcuffs. Through the open back doors of the panel truck, I see a young Sarah. She is not expressionless. She is sad and confused. She is lost.

"I remember the white panel truck," I said.

"CPRC. Crime Prevention Reform Commission."

"That's where I went? Not to a foster home, but I have huge gaps in my memory. Some came back. The handcuffs? Do you remember the handcuffs?"

"When I saw the CPRC truck I knew. Then the handcuffs. There was no need, you know. But then I suppose they followed the procedure. I was numb that day."

We continued to talk more about the time between when we left the Island and when the offices were shut down and if there was any follow-up or connections made as far as Kat and Peter and their placements. Sarah had periodically phoned the foster homes especially when their reports were late. It was a two-year period and then connections broke down once the decision was made to close the Island offices.

"By then I'd had enough, she said. "My doctor told me I was burned out. I didn't see it then, but I was in bad shape. So, when I was let go, I didn't keep in touch, came up here for a tree planting job, and after that I worked in the office for TimberWest."

I left Sarah MacDonald's home with the file folder under my arm and before I could step off the veranda she touched my wrist, leaned forward, kissed my cheek, and said, "People said you were an angry, messed-up boy. They've got it wrong. I know good character."

I called Sea-Air and booked an afternoon flight. I hung out at the café. Had a second breakfast since the menu was sketchy and what could they do to breakfast. I finished fast and didn't dwell on the past. But words such as when your parents were found dead, and there were a lot of kids, highlighted the enormity of what went down.

The dock was crowded with the same guys as when I'd arrived. There was always lightweight cargo to be expected. As I was about to step on the pontoon and hoist myself up into the back seat, I heard Officer Douglas Walkus' voice.

"Jack." He was right behind me as I swung around. "You take it easy on the mainland. And if you need help. I mean it. Call me."

Our eyes locked. He knew about the three orphaned kids, Kat, Peter, and Jack who were shipped off the island. His hand squeezed my hand like we were good friends.

CHAPTER 26

When the floatplane touched down, I was gone. I grabbed a cab and headed downtown. Since my stay on Zabella Island, I couldn't get the lyrics of "Summer Song" out of my head. I hear laughter from the "swimmin' hole/ Kids out fishin' with the willow pole." It sounds like the deep south but it's more the feeling I got back there. A peacefulness cut off from all that's wrong in other places.

So much for peace. My mind raced. I told the cabby to stop at Quick Copy. The first one he knew. He found one within three blocks since there seemed to be one on most corners. Didn't know why in the age of the internet, but there were holdouts who still liked paper or needed documents faxed as opposed to scanned and attached to an email. I was in that category a guy dragged kicking and screaming into the cutting edge of the nineties even though it was well into the twenty-first century.

I ran in with Sarah MacDonald's files. Got them photocopied. I dashed back to the cab and sent us off to find a post office where I mailed the works to Mark. I skimmed them on the plane but couldn't say I'd read every detail, but I was in a panic for him to follow up on them.

I was in the post office longer than it takes to make a Christmas dinner, but the cabbie waited especially with a couple of twenties in his fist. I hopped in and said. "Drop me at Powell and Woodland."

"Sure thing, buddy, but it will take a while since Cambie Bridge is down a lane. They're painting it."

"You're kidding me," I said.

"Don't get sore at me, I'm just the driver."

"No, I'm in shock because someone's requisitioned a repair on the infrastructure in this town.

"Don't get too excited. It is for appearances for the new developments down in False Creek. Fancy condos hardly anyone can afford. The ones that the fly-in's buy, just to say Oh, I got a place here or a chalet in Davos and a villa in Spain or Dubai. And the markets and the malls that go with all that. Who can afford to shop there? Don't get me going."

I could see I'd already lit him up, so I kept quiet. He was right. As soon as we got near the bridge over False Creek and I saw the hooked-nosed cranes like war machines out of H.G. Wells or for the younger crowd, Star Wars. We slowed down to a standstill.

I needed to call Stacie to find out if that reporter came up with the video recording. Also, to call Reilly to tip him off that I'd be coming in. I had forgotten to tell him about my trip to the Island. Bad move. I pulled out the burner cell and noticed I had turned it off.

Oops. I've had this off for two days.

I hit Messages. There were three from Reilly linked vertically down the screen. They were recently within the last hour. First said, "Jack, we need you at the office." Next said, "Where are you?" The third said, "Don't bother. If you get this in the next millennium, get your ass over to 4292 Parker Street. Someone named Norton. He's in bad shape."

I leaned over the cabby's right shoulder and said, "Change of plans. Can you get me to 4292 Parker Street as fast as you can?"

"Sure, but we still have to get through this and over the bridge."

I handed him a couple more twenties.

"I'll do my best," he said.

I called Stacie. It rang for a long time and then an automated voice said, "The number you are calling is unavailable."

Weird. Stacie always stayed connected. The timing made it likely that she was meeting Robbie Mayne to get the video stick. And Norton was in the mix after I'd asked him to tail Robbie in my car. That, along with Reilly's message, gave me a sinking feeling.

"Where's Parker Street?" I asked impatiently as our speed was inversely related to honked horns and frustrated gestures from the rest of the mutts on the bridge. The sky had become dark, and rain was on the way.

"Willingdon Heights on the other side of Boundary Road. Past the east side. Once we're through this on the bridge, I'll skirt the flow and we'll be faster."

I sank back in my seat. I'd got a good one who cared. Many cabbies wanted to stretch out the fare, and if you didn't know your way around, they'd run the labyrinth on you, and an hour later and a hundred bucks lighter, they'd delivered you ten blocks from where you started.

I called the Powell Street office. No one answered. I called Reilly. He didn't answer. I messaged him. Said, "On my way. On Cambie Bridge. Traffic jammed. Talk to me."

If he could talk, he'd call me back. If not, I'd get a text message.

Five minutes later I got a message. "The tough boys VPD in blue are here. Not my call. They beat me to it. Approach with caution or they'll take you down. VPD still wants Murphy and you for the homicide."

Once we were off the bridge, we took a turn. Back streets past boarded-up industrial relics, chain-link fencing with heavy-duty padlocks, and no trespassing signs. The scenery became more depressing as it started to rain. Nothing heavy, but persistent and with a sharp edge in a rising wind. The ride was one rolling stop after another at each intersection. Once we were on Parker near the address, I could see the scene. Multiple black and whites blocked the road. Yellow crime tape secured the scene. The usual neighborhood suspects milled about with hands in their pockets and talked amongst themselves about the unknown excitement that had descended on their otherwise drab lives. There were reporters. You could tell by the way they carried themselves. Confident. Pushy. Eager. Then I saw the '87 Tercel and my stomach took a heavy blow. I climbed from the cab. Went to give the cabbie more money, but he waved me off.

"I've got more than enough," he said. "Stay safe, buddy. Stay safe."

That was twice in one day, someone had wished me well. What did they see that I didn't?

Commisso and Boyle stood at the entrance to a six-plex apartment building, three floors with a sundeck on three around the upper level and a lit stairway to the ground on the right side. Two units to a floor. The tape ran up the walkway and along the road in a huge circle of pylons around the four cruisers on the street. No sign of Reilly. I mixed in among the neighbors bunched together on the sidewalk beside the apartment. I watched. The rain continued but didn't seem to bother the gawkers.

A woman about seventy with an umbrella, her hair in curlers shivered in the rain. "Heard someone got shot," she said.

A skinny guy beside her in grey track pants that were bagged at the butt said, "I heard several shots. I thought it was a muffler backfire. Like a firecracker. I thought gunfire sounds like on TV. If my window hadn't been open, I'd a missed it."

A siren broke their conversation. A few quick whoops got everyone's attention. Two coppers with thick cauliflower ears below their caps parted the tape and waved everyone to one side to let the ambulance through. Efficiency was at work. Two paramedics hopped out, opened the back doors, pulled out a gurney, wheeled it up the sidewalk, and disappeared inside.

They were not gone long. They came out with a zipped black bag on the gurney. It went into the back of the "bus" as reporters' cameras flashed from a distance and the neighbors rubbernecked to look at the gory detail.

Behind them, the forensic team emerged in their coveralls, booties, and rubber gloves. Then Reynolds stepped out, a hard-ass prick if ever I met one. Approach with caution. That's what Reilly had said. He must know him.

I messaged Reilly. "I'm outside in the crowd. Are you in there?"

He came back. "Yes. Stay put."

"Side steps to the deck?"

"No."

The rain came down harder. A black rain that was reserved for winter. It crept into me. Norton. I didn't send him off to get killed. Stupid. Should have told him to keep his distance.

Reynolds was all action. He pointed. Waved his hands but didn't look threatening in his blue plastic booties. Others descended the stairs from the upper deck. Reilly appeared, took off his booties, moved off to the side and leaned in close to Commisso and Boyle. The police sent everybody home. Reilly, Commisso, and Boyle crossed out of the yellow-taped area and disappeared into the shadows. I moved off in their general direction but not too close. The perimeter became smaller. Tape still circled the apartment but kept the entrance open. The stairway to the deck was taped off as I imagined the access to the apartment was on the third floor. All the excitement disappeared with the heavy rain and the forced exit of the crowd. Three of the four cruisers left, one with Reynolds who'd remembered to ditch the booties, and one cruiser remained beneath a huge maple across the road.

I watched Reilly and the boys move toward their cars, Reilly in his and the boys in another. Both cars moved off.

I waited a minute or two. The cars came down the street after they'd circled the block. I got the message and walked the other way, and they came around again, only this time I was far from the VPD cruiser. Reilly's door swung open, and I hopped in as his unmarked cruiser rolled past me.

"Coffee?" Reilly said.

"Later. I'll park the cruiser somewhere."

Reilly drove a couple of blocks with Commisso and Boyle behind him and then parked. They did the same. The rain hit the windscreen and ran down so hard that the view was a translucent blur.

"Norton," I said, "you said he's got it bad. Looked permanent in that body bag."

"That wasn't Norton. The guy's Russian or Eastern European. Two slugs in the head and from a distance. I'd say from across the room."

"And Norton?"

"Slow down, Jack. Let me start from the beginning. Stacie calls me when we are at the warehouse. She's in a panic. Says she tried to reach you but got an unavailable message. I sympathized with her since I tried to get you too."

"Is this a Russian novel?"

"Huh?"

"Forget it. Get to the point."

"Well, I'm trying to."

I scratched my head and blew steam out my nose.

"Stacie calls me. Says she's over at this Parker Street address. Robbie Mayne's apartment. Says Robbie wanted to give her a stick with a video that will let you and Murphy off the hook for homicide. Says Robbie's there but the place has been trashed. Then all hell breaks loose. I hear another voice and gunshots. Furniture being smashed, a door breaking, running footsteps, and then more gunfire. I figure the phone's still on, recording this. Then I hear two shots from further away, followed by two more, close together. I grab my jacket and motion to Commisso and Boyle to follow. I hightail it here. On the way, I get another panicked message from Stacie. She says Robbie Mayne's gone. She's tracking him. Says to phone for a "bus" since Norton's taken two in the chest and there's a dead guy in the hall. Then she hangs up."

I try to put the monologue of sound together to create the movie. Someone tossed Robbie Mayne's apartment looking for the digital file. Robbie and Stacie were in the apartment and when Stacie made the call the guy who ended up in the body bag came in with a gun. Knowing Stacie, she sprang into action. Robbie probably froze. Stacie fought her attacker, until Norton, valiant and naïve, showed up and busted the door. That was when the shooting started, and it was taken into the hall where Norton took two in the chest and Stacie sent the shooter into the next world.

I said as much to Reilly. His eyebrows went up.

"There's a catch," Reilly said. "You've got it right. But when we get there, Reynolds and the VPD are there first. Reynolds is curious as to why we're there. I tell him I heard the call, and it was close to a lead we were following, which is close enough to the truth. And he buys it. He's a hard-ass so I treat him gently and he lets me into the scene. He makes me leave the boys outside."

I got impatient. It was like the poison scene in The Princess Bride.

"Reilly. Tell me about Norton. He didn't come out on a gurney?"

"There was no Norton. Someone went through the hall window outside the apartment and onto the deck. Figured the first two shots hit someone and blew them through the window. Single pane. Maybe it was Norton."

"Stacie said Norton took two to the chest."

"Stacie wasn't there. Robbie wasn't there. The apartment was trashed and a dead guy with an automatic pistol was flat on his back in the hall with half his head blown away."

"Any blood near the smashed window?"

"Some on the glass and the deck but not enough if someone got two slugs in the chest."

"Let me out. I'll get my car; the one Norton came in."

As I got out and walked back toward the crime scene Reilly radioed Commisso and Boyle.

Boyle and Commisso ambled by the cruiser parked across the street from 4292 Parker Street. It was two am. I figured the cop would have nodded off by now, so I parked my butt behind a maple beside the Tercel. They approached, circled around the back of the cruiser, and tapped on the driver's window. I could imagine the copper jumping so far out of his shorts as to leave skid marks. Both Boyle and Commisso made sure they blocked the driver's view from his front and side windows and asked him if they could get into the apartment to retrieve a cell phone they'd left earlier. They didn't expect a Sure go ahead fill your boots, but rather a bleary-eyed response that would amount to a no that allowed me enough time with the Tercel out of view for me to take my second set of keys and get in, turn the ignition, put it into gear and drive off. It worked like a charm. I was gone. The Tercel was gone. I could imagine Commisso and Boyle walking away with a pretense of disappointment, and the copper guarding the murder scene wondering what had happened.

I headed straight downtown to the Powell Street warehouse where we'd planned to meet up. Boyle and Commisso were to get the donuts and coffees. I felt the grit in my eyes. It had been a long day that began on Zabella Island where now I wished I was. There was a sanity that remained unlike in the city in its cauldron that caught the rain and held onto its smog and haze even on sunny days. The rain pounded the windshield. I took the direct route downtown, but the scenery was bleak. Abandoned warehouses, and offices. Boarded-up storefronts. Empty housing developments were built and left unsold after the bottom fell out from the investment market and property prices dipped. This was a vast wasteland produced by greed and high ambitions. And behind all this lurked Undertown full of its rampant vice, its hedonistic pleasures, and its pulsing violence. And I thought of Murphy in her sanctuary amid the chaos and mayhem. And I thought of who put her there. The Laskey brothers, sure, but they were the pawns on a much larger board. I got angry. Wanted to punch walls, put the lights out on all the Laskeys, and those unknowns who pulled the strings with icy fingers and stone-cold hearts.

I was near the warehouse when I thought about Norton. How I got him shot. Of where he might be bleeding out in someone's shrubbery.

"Norton," I said, shaking my head and staring at the rain hitting the windscreen.

"Hello, Jack," came a voice from the back seat.

Norton swung up like a pendulum and I stared at his bristled face in my rear-view mirror. He didn't smile, but he didn't look like a guy who'd taken two bullets in the chest.

"Jack," he said.

"I summoned the dead, and the dead has arisen."

Norton opened his coat, the one with all the pockets stuffed with books.

"Didn't think a book would save me, but it did. Look."

He held out a thick dog-eared tome, Norman Mailer's The Executioner's Song, over a thousand pages. I could see where two slugs had burrowed through and out the back cover.

"Slowed them down, bruised my chest but didn't penetrate."

I could see dried blood on his right wrist.

"The blood?" I pointed to his hand.

"Oh, that. The impact blew me through the window onto the deck and I cut my arm on the way through. Wrecked the coat. I won't find one like it."

He held up a small silver flask. "Had this behind the book in my pocket."

All this while I drove and glanced back at Norton in the mirror, turning my head to talk when the road was clear. I got to the warehouse fast at this time of night and pulled in the back. We both got out and I buzzed the freight elevator. I heard it chug down toward us. I opened the horizontal doors, and we went in.

"Could have been Nietzsche," Norton said.

I looked at him as if he was from another planet. Thought of Murphy. Wondered where Stacie was and why she hadn't answered her phone.

"Norton, you're lucky to be alive."

"Don't I know it," he said as the freight elevator doors stopped.

I pulled on the strap, and they opened like two jaws. Then I raised the wooden slatted safety barrier and stepped into the warehouse, Conner's secret squad room for Reilly and the boys—Commisso, and Boyle. Reilly had his feet up on a battered desk and sipped coffee. Boyle and Commisso tapped at computers. The coffees had lost their steam.

Boyle looked up at me and Norton. Said, "So this is Norton?"

Reilly's eyes flickered. "Good work Boyle," he said. He motioned us both to a couple of chairs where a coffee sat on its own. I motioned to Norton to take it and he did. "Is Norton your real name?"

Norton glanced at me and smiled.

"Cut him some slack, Reilly. He's taken two in the chest."

"He doesn't look beat up to me."

The old Reilly exercised his bulldog broken-nosed tactics. It had been a long night for him, and with Reynolds on the scene, it hadn't been pleasant.

"Looks can be deceiving," I said.

"Let's have out with it."

"Thanks for the coffee," Norton said.

"Throw over your guardian angel," I said.

Norton did. Reilly looked at two small dents in the flask. He was quick on the uptake. "Wow."

We all looked at each other's exhausted faces. Commisso who uncharacteristically looked at Norton instead of his monitor, said, "So, what went down?"

CHAPTER 27

I woke up after a few hours in the early morning. Norton slept on the couch in the warehouse office. I convinced him to take a shower the night before. I slept with my head on the oak desk Reilly dragged from the Sally Ann. Reilly went home to earn some brownie points with his wife. Commisso and Boyle stayed.

So, where were Stacie and Robbie? And who was in Undertown to hold Murphy's hand last night? I called Stacie and left a message. "Call me."

I clicked on contacts and sent a message to Mark about his efforts to track down foster homes. Norton continued sleeping. I took a shower and came out in clean clothes from the gym bag I'd brought in from the Tercel last night. I met Reilly as he came through the gate on the service elevator.

He wore a black leather jacket, broken-in chinos, and deck shoes.

"Get your gear," he said.

I pointed to the shoes. "Are we sailing?"

"Smart-ass. Road trip. Geeks got us a lead on where Ekaterina Sokolov and Lana went after they left the penthouse. Surveillance got the plate on the chauffeured black Lincoln "L" Series. Registered to a Sergei Yasevich. He is connected to one of the Bratvas. He's Ekaterina's uncle. Got an address in China Heights, a gated, monster home. You up for this?"

"How far?"

"Fifty miles."

"What about backup?" I asked.

"No need. We're going to talk."

"I need to find Stacie."

I didn't want to be lumbered in the same car with Reilly and his total agenda. So, I said. "I'll take my car too. That way if I need to get to Stacie, I can, if you're tied up with this Yasevich."

"Suit yourself."

I stuffed five hundred dollars into Norton's coat and said, "Stay low. Find Mitchell, Sugar, and Mindy, and keep them safe."

I followed Reilly to the freight elevator, with my gym bag, burner phone, Glock, and Beretta. Once I was in the driver's seat, Reilly jumped in beside me.

"I called Boyle," he said. "I told him to get Commisso and get their asses down here, bring a black and white and meet us at the China Heights address."

I felt my head droop like a donkey with an extra load. The last thing I needed was being trapped with Reilly chewing on my ear.

Reilly directed me along a route to the main highway out of town, and within a half-hour, we were off at a cloverleaf. We then drove to higher elevations. The ocean view was behind us and in front, the mainland's snowy peaks loomed in the distance. I should know the hinterland and the cityscape but being from the Island, incarcerated in a foster home then boot camp and tours in the forces, I was disoriented. I let Reilly lead.

"You'll stay on this road for another twenty miles."

I nodded.

"I know you know Tarasov," he said. "From the Island."

Tarasov was a big-time reclusive oligarch who took his money and got out of Russia before Putin's shadow tainted the country. He'd helped me take down a local bully who had preyed on everyone on the Island since I was a kid. I hadn't thought of him since. I nodded at Reilly.

"He's not the only Russian mob boss in town," he said. "Yasevich is connected. Conner called with some details. There's a bigger picture here. When the sun sinks into the Pacific, the streets are dark, and it isn't because it's night. Yasevich is into owning properties like McDonald's is into beef. And it's cleanly laundered as a product. Prostitution is a client service. Drug trafficking is merely the purchase and sale of pharmaceuticals, security deployment's a protection racket designed to exploit small businesses. He's still small time, as is Tarasov who seems to keep his nose clean these days. And there are bigger sharks out there too."

Reilly looked at me closely. I felt his stare burn into my cheek. I turned my eyes from the road toward him for a moment. Got a sense of his look. He was not idly yammering away. This was calculated.

He started again. "You hear about the Laskey brothers. Three of them. Well, five, all about one and a half to two years apart. Their poor mother must have been ridden hard, kept barefoot in the kitchen, and put away wet."

He laughed.

I thought of all the poor women in Shaplow trapped and pregnant when I was a kid. I could smell the diaper pails and their desperation.

"I've heard of these Laskey brothers."

"Three have disappeared and a guy who works for them. No one seems to be bothered to check into any of the scant details. The whole family is connected to the Russians. Maybe not Yasevich or Tarasov. There are others."

Two more Laskeys. I see Mark and Mitchell on the dusty floor of the scrapyard office tied up like turkeys to be slaughtered.

"What do you mean disappeared?" I said.

"Boyle and Commisso stumbled on a rumor that there was a firefight at their yard. But they came up with nothing. The place was clean as a whistle. No one was home."

"Really. Like there was no firefight or like a clean-up team came in?"

"One or the other. You heard of Genrikh Yagoda, and Nikolai Yazhov?"

"Can't say that I have."

"No one knows much about them, but they live, breathe, and prey among us. You follow a chain of evidence, and it peters out in the lower depths that loosely casts a shadow on these two guys. But they're untouchable. Operations from the Laskey Brothers business connections lead to complications and the sewage trail flows out to sea murkier than it began and it taints several people who you might think are on the other side."

I looked at the odometer. We had only gone five of the twenty miles. My ears were ringing. I wanted to keep it simple. An eye for an eye. A bullet for a bullet. But Reilly talked like he was on a crusade like Conner who I sensed was too fanatical. I thought about Murphy, though. I thought of how long she had been in a coma. How long it had taken me to recover? How scared Mark was, that I had to give him the safe jobs, and even then, I wondered why I have him helping me dig into my past.

"Who do you and Conner figure for the torso killing?"

"Conner figures they all work together in the big picture. The usual stuff. Small to large. Pornography, prostitution, extortion, sex trafficking, murder."

"I'd forgotten the list," I said.

There was arson, bank robbery, motor vehicle theft, computer crime, and counterfeit credit cards. Narcotics. Bookmaking. Loan Sharking. But they didn't work together on the day-to-day stuff. There was fierce rivalry and within each group intense loyalty.

"The torso?" I asked again.

"It is different. Why go to all that bother? The staging. The box of body parts. The missing organs."

"It's a message," I said. I looked straight ahead and followed the road as it climbed around headlands along the mountainous coast, cut in around surge channels, and then emerged at a height above the sea.

"What makes you think that?"

"Sokolov was involved with whoever had him killed, why the theatrics? Just have him popped and buried in the woods. There are many bodies in the woods, and no one finds them. If it's extortion, they wouldn't kill him. They'd cut off a finger or an ear and send a package, wouldn't they? Revenge? Maybe a box of body parts serves a purpose. But the torso out in the open? The possibility of leaving traceable evidence, that's stupid. The stage is bigger and the message's writ large."

CHAPTER 28

I drove for another hour. The winding roads took longer than a straight run on the highway. Reilly was mostly talked out and maybe his silence was gearing him up to question Yasevich. I got a sense that he was a tad intimidated by Russians with power and money. I remained quiet but talk about the Laskey brothers played on my mind.

"You mentioned the Laskey brothers. A clean-up," I said.

"Reynolds mentioned it while I was over at Parker Street. His VPD city division got a call about strange activity over the last two days. Growling. Packs of fighting dogs. The place was empty like a business shut down. He said they were overworked and couldn't send anyone out for another two days. When they got there, they found nothing unusual. No dogs. No sign of a firefight. The Laskey brothers' offices were freshly painted. No dust anywhere. Nothing unusual except there were no Laskey brothers."

"And you figure what?" I asked.

"Either nothing happened, or a major event went down, and a team came in with cleanup skills and did a restoration. No one looked for the Laskeys and no one will shed any tears if they're gone."

The GPS chimed. "You have arrived at your destination."

The destination was a gravel road that headed straight into a forest. I turned and started down the road.

"We are expected, right?"

"Not exactly," Reilly said.

After about a half mile of forest road, I met a formidable gate. Two men smoked outside a square wooden guardhouse. They both carried shotguns crooked over their arms. They were dressed in baggy corduroys, white long-sleeved shirts, leather vests, and wool hats. One was slightly taller and had a mustache. The other wore glasses. They both looked more like characters out of The Godfather than Russians.

Reilly called Commisso and Boyle. Then he texted him.

"I told them when they arrive," Reilly said, "to park the car out on the main road and wait."

We both rolled our windows down when the two guards approached the Tercel.

"We're here to see Mr. Yasevich and his niece Ekaterina," I said. "Police business."

"Do you have a warrant?" the guard with the mustache asked.

"No, we don't have a warrant," Reilly snapped. "We are just visitors. We want to ask a few questions."

"Mr. Yasevich say you come."

"Smart man," I said.

Both guards motioned us from the car with their shotgun barrels. We found ourselves spread hands on the engine hood with our legs apart, waiting for them to get intimate and friendly. They took my Glock and Reilly's regulation issue. They missed the Beretta.

The forest road continued for another half mile and Reilly, and I walked side by side with the guards behind us. When the forest ended, the sky opened to a Garry Oak meadow full of tawny grass and wildflowers and beyond that was the house that overlooked the ocean. The large structure was built in the seventies as the clapboard siding betrayed her age. Small windows on the sides, a concrete entrance with faux pillars, and a new roof. The guards motioned us inside and we went through a series of paneled rooms with little furniture into a kitchen with laminated counters, black and white vinyl tile, and a refrigerator that could have been in an antique auction. They sat us down in a small living room adjacent to the kitchen where we could look out at a tired, rectangular swimming pool, the meadow, and the ocean beyond. One guard left and the other parked himself in the kitchen.

"You wait here," he said.

We waited for twenty minutes. Neither of us spoke. The building's austerity surprised me. I expected a modern monster home. Many other buildings constructed the same way were spread out over the property. Occasionally a guy toting a long gun walked across the meadow in the distance. This place was armed to the teeth.

"Welcome to my dacha. Not exactly the Palace on the Idokopas Cape but then I'm not as flamboyant as Mr. Putin." Yasevich was at the arched entrance behind us so that he appeared to suddenly arrive. He laughed at his joke and sat down on a threadbare couch across from us. He called into the kitchen. "Stepan, some tea."

"I am Detective Reilly, and this is Jack McQueen."

"Of course. I know how policemen work. It is good to know this."

Yasevich fit in with his surroundings. His grey, wool pants were stylish, but not recently. His pale-blue dress shirt had a high buttoned-down collar, and the cuffs sported gold cufflinks. Over the shirt, he had an open silk crimson vest. His hair was white, and his beard grizzled. His overall appearance was dated.

"I understand that you are the uncle of Ekaterina Sokolov?" Reilly said.

"You mean Katrin Yasevich. She is my brother-in-law's daughter. I was her godfather. We got our families out of Russia together. Putin. But I bore you with past, gentlemen."

I made a note to look up who was Ekaterina's father.

"We are investigating the murder of Dr. Mikhail Sokolov. What can you tell us about him?"

"Like what?"

"Did he have any enemies?" Reilly said. "Someone who'd want to make his death look dramatic?"

"I suppose he has many enemies. I did not like him. He was arrogant. He felt the world owed him. He was doctor. Big deal. Insisted everyone call him Doctor. Dr. Sokolov. He did not treat Katrin well. That is reason not to like him. But I did not have him killed."

"Names? Any names that might?" I asked.

He appeared to be thinking or rather postured the act of thinking.

"Not really."

He drew the words out slowly. Stepan from the kitchen came in with a small teapot and a container of hot water. Besides these were a sugar bowl, and jars of honey, jam, and wedges of lemon. He placed the platter on the coffee table between us. I recalled the teahouse the day Stacie and I met Anton Tarasov and how I was such an uninformed klutz in her opinion. So, I waited and watched for Yasevich to take the lead. Stepan brought four cups and saucers.

"Ekaterina told you about the box that was delivered to her home?" Reilly said.

"She did."

Yasevich picked up the teapot and poured his cup half-full. Then he poured in hot water and took one spoonful of honey. His hand had a slight tremor as it worked with the teapot, water, and honey. Not a tremor because the pots or the spoon were heavy or because he had an affliction. Rather beneath the surface, there was anger he couldn't disguise.

"The tea is strong?" I asked.

"Yes. If you like strong, pour full cup. If you like weak, then pour bit of tea and add hot water. It is traditional."

"Who would do that to Ekaterina? Why would they do that?" I proceeded to take the tea weak, and Reilly did the same.

"Take your pick. There are many sick people out there. I was glad little Lana did not have to see what was inside box."

"So, you can't give me a name?" I asked.

"Not really."

"Not even his associates?" Reilly said.

"He was Katrin's husband, not my friend. I really know nothing about him other than I did not like him."

I looked at Reilly. We were getting nowhere.

"Mr. Yasevich, I appreciate the visit to your home," I said. "We need to talk to Ekaterina. We need to know what Dr. Sokolov did with his time, what were his routines, who he associated with, and where he went. We hope Ekaterina can help us with this information. We need to talk to her."

"Gentlemen, she is recovering. She is fragile. I cannot risk you upsetting her."

"We understand that, but this is a murder investigation," Reilly said. "We don't want to have to take Ekaterina down to the station to make a statement. That's why we came here. So, she could do this in private."

Yasevich was struggling. He wanted to politely deny us an interview and wanted to maintain control, but also, I saw a practical side that said to go the route of least resistance.

"I call her. She is in another building."

Yasevich got up and walked to the kitchen. I heard him speak Russian, presumably on the telephone. He then sent Stepan to bring Ekaterina to the house. We had finished our tea when she showed up. I was stunned.

Ekaterina Yasevich/Sokolov stood in the opening between the kitchen and the living room. She was unreasonably beautiful. I was numb. Her face was oval, symmetrical, and smoothed to perfection with the slightest amount of makeup. Her eyes were a cross between a grey wolf and purple lilac. She stood in high heels, short white shorts with pleats in the front and a flat line that led up to a flash of skin at her abdomen, and above that a stylish, mauve halter. Her lips were cherry red. Her legs were long and sensuous. She did not look like a grieving widow or a traumatized spouse.

Reilly's jaw had dropped as much as mine. I saw Yasevich's thin smile.

"Ah, Katrin, my pet. Come sit down with us. Tea? I get Stepan to make some more."

"No. No. Not necessary," she said as she walked into the living room as if she was on a runway. She sat in an armchair beside the empty fireplace. We both stood up, but she waved us down.

Yasevich was amused and remained seated on his couch opposite us.

"Ekaterina, we're sorry for your loss," I said. "We want to get to the bottom of this. Can you tell us about your husband's schedule? We know he only worked at the hospital three days a week. What did he do for the other days?"

"He was often at his office downtown. At times each week, he would go out of town and come back late at night. He never told me where he went. I assumed it was work for hospital."

Ekaterina was young, maybe twenty-eight or thirty. Her husband was over sixty.

"Did he have any enemies?" Reilly said. "Did anyone threaten him? Any unhappy patients?"

Her gaze pierced into him. I figured Reilly's mouth was becoming dry.

"Not that I know. It was shock."

Ekaterina crossed her right leg over her left and the light caught the taut skin along the outside of her knee. My eyes followed the movement to the knee and up the outside of her thigh. I looked out the picture window past the pool to the meadow where I saw Lana run through the wildflowers with a butterfly net. The scene was an impressionist painting.

"Your husband has a car?" I asked.

"Yes, it should still be in underground parking. My uncle came for us, and we left city with him."

"We will need to impound the car. Let forensics go over it. Do you have the keys?"

"I can give them to you."

"Make and Model?"

"Mercedes. I'm not good with cars. New one."

I couldn't believe how calm she was.

"Do you have anything from the penthouse belonging to Dr. Sokolov that you brought with you?" Reilly said.

"No. We left in hurry when box—"

Ekaterina looked out the window, started to shake then put her head into her lap.

"Gentlemen, thank you," Yasevich said, "but we are done here. No more questions."

Yasevich stood up. Stepan appeared and the other bodyguard arrived in the kitchen. They escorted us to the door.

Katerina followed us out and said, "I get keys."

I watched her cross the back meadow to another smaller white clapwood building, and she returned as we walked toward the forest road with the two guards whom we'd first met. She was crying now and quite distraught. She came up close to me and put an arm around my shoulder for support and with a closed fist she handed me the keys and I placed them in my pocket. And then she pecked me on the cheek and was gone. Her perfume dizzied my head.

We walked the forest road in silence. The guards gave us back our guns. We got in the car, turned around, and drove off. I felt the keys in my front pants pocket and touched the edge of a business card.

A mile down the road, I pulled over. I watched Commisso and Boyle stop behind us.

"What did you think of that meeting?" I said to Reilly.

"A waste of time."

"Near enough. But it was worth the look. Untouchable, right?"

"Pretty much."

"Reilly. Can you go with them? I have thinking to do. I need to find Stacie. I will let you know."

I handed him the keys to Sokolov's car.

"We'll impound the Mercedes," Reilly said. "The GPS might tell us something."

I was running on empty. Wanted to stay here beside the road and have a long nap. Reilly got out.

"Stay in contact. Don't go AWOL," Reilly said.

"Who me?"

The last words I heard were strung together in a muttered sentence that contained the words "smart-ass."

Reilly motioned Commisso into the back of the patrol car and slid in beside Boyle who was the driver. They left me parked in a dusty haze.

I reached into my pocket and pulled out Katarina Sokolov's business card. On the back, she had written The Mephistopheles, Monday 7:30 p.m. Just You.

I started the Tercel and drifted down the highway until I found a pull-off lane that drivers of eighteen-wheelers used to let traffic pass or to take a rest. I couldn't drive any further. I stopped. Cut the engine. I'd been running on two hours' sleep from last night at the Powell Street office. I slid the seat back, tilted it to maximum, closed my eyes and I was gone. What was to be a fifteen-minute sleep stretched to a couple of hours, the day was done, and the sun was slinking over the headlands to the sea.

Today was Saturday.

CHAPTER 29

After two hours in a dream-sleep where my alter ego fell in love with Ekaterina's body, and where I worried about Murphy and the possibility that she'd never wake up and that Stacie was in trouble, my cell rang. It was Mark.

"Jack. How's it going?"

I didn't detect the fear and paranoia Mark displayed when I'd left him at his Quonset hideout before I met up with Reilly at the Victory.

"The usual," I said. Any extra details would freak him out more.

"I got some leads for you on the foster home your brother and sister went to when they took you from the Island. They went to the same place. It was more an orphanage than a foster home."

"Does the place still exist? I thought they went to two different homes?"

"Apparently not. It exists, although it's run more like an institution regulated by the government. Haven't gone there, but this is the initial research. It's called Hammer House and it's in the suburbs. Twenty-five years ago, it was out in the boonies. Secluded on a track of about fifty acres. The land's still there but the surroundings have been built up with the city's expansion."

"Do you plan to visit?" I was hesitant to get Mark too involved after our last conversation but asked anyway. Made it so he had a choice.

There was a pause from his end.

"Give me more time to research the contacts and any details I can from a distance, then I'll go in."

"Thanks for the update."

"There's more. I found where they sent you. But it no longer exists. The building is there but it's a different place. It was a reform school for boys too young to go into the prison system. They did away with it ten years ago. Do you remember?"

"Nothing jogs my memory." I said, "I can't remember much before I joined the armed forces."

"I'll do more work. Maybe sniff about before I get you involved. Maybe we can visit it together if that's possible. That might help you remember. Or if you can't, maybe Stacie can come."

"Right. Stay in touch." I felt disembodied. Scattered. Fragmented. Frustrated because I did not remember anything about where I went after I left Vancouver Island.

I was alert now. Not tired. I called Stacie's phone. Left a voice mail. Call me!

While I waited, I mulled over the visit with Ekaterina and Yasevich, and the trauma-scene cleanup at the Laskey brothers. Twenty minutes went by before my cell buzzed with a text message. Stacie.

"Followed Robbie. By transponder on his car. Put on back at Brogans. Taken a while. Now he's settled. I'm still not there yet. Follow me, Jack. Take Highway 1 east, trans-continental. Cut off #691 North to Hollinger. Take Lost Lake Road. I'm on that now. Keep you posted."

I typed. "Will do." I started the ignition and headed for Highway 1. Noted the time 6:45 p.m. and realized I hadn't eaten. No time now. I thought to call Reilly but didn't.

It took me a couple of hours to make it to Lost Lake Road, a gravel track cut into dense forest. I stopped and messaged Stacie that I was now on Lost Lake Road. She buzzed back immediately. Said, "Drive until you can't drive any further. Take the path to the right. Walk a few hundred yards until you come to a cabin."

I left it at that. Darkness had closed in. Headlights reflected from the trees and all shadows appeared menacing. Out here away from civilization's concrete and steel was a predator's landscape, the wolf, cougar, and dangerous creatures on two legs. The road narrowed until it was two tracks with a center median of grass and weeds and then suddenly the road ended. Through the trees, the headlights revealed open spaces and a pale grey sky. There were three cars. Robbie's, Stacie's, and a black BMW four-door.

I found a way by braille feeling for the roots, the needled floor, the curves, and the ups and downs that led me to the cabin from Stacie's message. I thought of ships and wishes. They were like the first stars that suddenly appear when the sky was still blue, as the sun's amber remnants still bathed us in that light the heart yearned for.

Headlights on a narrow road in a forest to a cabin that no one was supposed to know about were different things. Snapped twigs of dread. That prickly feeling when you first felt comfortable then knew you weren't. Not my headlights now cooling. Other headlights lights penetrated the spaces among the tree trunks and then winked out. In the darkness, my hearing heightened to a crescendo. The low hum of an engine in low gear.

Tires on pine needles. Car doors closed with four dull thumps as I got out and walked back toward the crime scene.

The heart took over. Hormones rushed to a rescue that I sensed was not about to happen. The cabin was dark, and I crouched low on the front porch that stretched its length. Shapes of furniture and a log railing. I waited, as the night's murmur descended in the space between those who wanted to be saved. Then I heard a low voice.

"Jack?" The cabin door opened a crack. No one was behind it except a dark shape in a clump on the floor where the door was ajar. I looked across the room. A candle flickered on a table at the back wall. With my knees bent and still in a crouch, I stepped inside and dropped to the floor as Stacie put her hands on my shoulders and pushed me down lower. She crawled across the floor and blew out the candle. I closed the door. She crawled back and hugged me. Her muscles were as tight as heavy springs. She moved over to the kitchen counter that faced the front window. No lights. The first stars were out. I wanted those first stars to be for us, so I could wish for an escape from here. But that was not going to happen, and I had a bad feeling that first wishes on boats or stars would not come to us tonight.

"What's out there is the cavalry. Back-up. I found Robbie." She pointed to an open space where there was no furniture except a toppled pressed-back wooden chair. Tied to it was a body.

"Robbie Maine?" I asked.

"They took their time before he died."

I saw the blood that had wept from his head in a pool on the pine floor.

"The Beamer?"

"It was beside Robbie's car when I got here. No sign of who did this to Robbie. Not a peep, but once I found Robbie, and the BMW still at the end of the road, I knew I was trapped."

"Reinforcements. At least four and whoever came in the BMW, right?" I said. "Between five and eight with artillery."

I clicked into combat. That place where your pores prickle and the trained body fights increased heart rate and excessive breathing. We both could not stay in the cabin like fish in the proverbial barrel. We'd be in the killing ground. The woods were safer.

"Stacie, we've got to leave. Windows?"

"There is this one in front and two back windows in the bedrooms."

I crawled over to each bedroom and released the latch and slid open each window. The ground was three feet below, flat and covered by bracken fern. I crawled back to Stacie.

"Help me with Robbie here," I said. "Let's get him near the counter and prop him up on the chair so the top of his head just appears at the kitchen window."

We did this and Stacie held him in place taped to the pressed-back chair, so his head was still below the window. I pushed a heavy upholstered lounge chair from near the fireplace behind Robbie's chair to brace it and keep him from tipping back.

"I want you to go out a bedroom window. Get clear and away from the cabin about ten feet. Watch for the first sign."

"And you?"

"I'm going out after I push the lounge chair forward against Robbie's chair so that his head starts to appear at the window. That'll only work if there's enough light left, or the window will be completely black."

As Stacie went out the window, I thought about the candle and scrambled to get it. Found matches beside it and brought them back to the counter. I lit the candle, then pushed the big chair against Robbie's wooden chair. I ran to the right window and jumped out. Then I moved through the ferns and into the trees adjacent to the cabin on the opposite side to Stacie. I waited.

I saw the first muzzle flash. Heard the bullet pock through the kitchen window. I heard Stacie's rebuttal and a guttural cry of pain. Maybe shock. Another flash and I fired. I used instinct, precision, and practice, and I knew a second bullet hit a target.

Automatic fire strafed the cabin. Too easy. We both fired our weapons, and all was quiet. Three were now gone.

I was worried Stacie wouldn't change her position. Worried they'd find her in their sights. I moved laterally in a counterclockwise sweep away from the cabin and close to a position where I suspected they would be. I moved in on the line where the muzzle flashes were, where the bush was silent. A low murmur of two voices speaking Russian.

The voices were between me and the cabin. I was moving fast ten yards behind them, Glock in one hand and the Beretta in the other. The embodiment that came with the voices turned toward me and I fired full face with the Glock. A bullet whined past my ear and my Beretta's bullet caught the second voice in the throat. I was beside them now. I lifted the second voice under his armpits with my arms at the elbows, held him in front of me as a shield, and gripped my weapons. His throat gurgled and pumped out a spray of blood. A third Russian crashed through the bush from my left. I turned the body toward him to protect myself. A muzzle flashed in the dark. Close. Personal. Angry. I returned fire and felt bullets thump into my shield. No result and the dark shape moved in closer. I caught him across the neck with the Glock's barrel. A sharp object glanced along my right side. Instant pain. I twisted and grabbed my assailant by the throat. Caught his nostrils in my two fingers below the trigger on the Glock. I curled those fingers into his nostrils' soft tissue and ripped my arm back. He was a gaffed fish.

One twist of his neck and he was gone. He dropped a sniper rifle as he fell. I picked it up and put the Beretta in my leg holster.

Silence. I waited. Then two clear deliberate hand-gun retorts. Silence. Then two more. Silence. I didn't move for a long time hidden in the leaf litter fifteen feet from the dead Russians. I waited way past a long time. My heart thumped out a staccato beat. Then I heard it.

An ignition started. Not seven but eight shooters. Tires tore at the gravel. Rubber twisted on pine needles. No headlights. One car raced down the narrow track away from the cabin.

Being cautious I started to worry that they had three passengers in the back of each car when they arrived. If so, then two were left. I couldn't be too careful, ever. So, I waited, one hand pressed down on the slice on my left side. No blood spurted from the wound. The blood's slow flow with pressure would congeal.

The silence was mind-numbing. Once I was engaged, I hadn't paid attention to how many shots were fired at Stacie's flank. I wasn't sure about the two sudden final bursts. Surely not, or there'd still be one Russian left. I waited.

The black night slowly conceded to the grey dawn light over the lake. A few birds announced the morning.

The leaf litter erupted with sound moving toward me. I started. A Russian. A bear. Cougar. In the pale grey light, a bush rat emerged with a few hops and moseyed around the dead bodies. I relaxed my heart. Breathe. Calm. Count. Calm. Breathe.

My burner cell vibrated. A message.

Marco.

I replied with, *Polo.*

Where are you?

You?

A shiver ran through me. What if Stacie was dead and a Russian was about to flush me out? Like that legionary Stalingrad sniper. A prompt to move. To reveal my location.

A message came back to me. *You go first.*

I texted. *Who taught Jessie how to shoot?*

The message came back. *Bi-Girl. Needs a hug. Got three. You?*

Four. Plus, one drove away. Meet?
You first, but don't creep up on me.

I went back the way I came. Climbed through the back bedroom window. Robbie was a mess. In the new light, I saw the blood smears where he had originally lain tied to the chair tilted on its side in his own blood.

Now propped up below the counter, the top of his head was no longer there.

I went. "Marco. Cabin."

The response was "Polo". Behind the carved log table. Porch.

I went. Creep in the door.

I heard nothing. Only the slow breathing through my nose. Slight creak. The door moved slowly. I heard Stacie's voice. "Marco."

I said, "Polo. Stay flat."

She crawled in unscathed and came to me behind the sofa chair that propped up Robbie's dead body.

"Not sure we're alone?" she said.

I pointed a finger at the kitchen window and then at the Russian sniper rifle I brought with me back to the cabin.

We waited half an hour. From the front window's edge, I scanned the forest around the cabin. Nothing. Nothing but paranoia.

I motioned Stacie to push the sofa chair against Robbie and his chair, so his head appeared above the counter and become visible at the window. Nothing. I motioned more and I scanned the forest with the sniper-rifle scope. I knew the action since I'd fired this gun before.

Stacie pushed Robbie's head higher and instantly pieces of his head were catapulted across the room. I saw the glint of a weapon's recoil. Calculated by nanosecond instinct and fired. The reflection disappeared.

Stacie moved Robbie higher into the view in the window and we waited. Nothing happened.

After a long wait, Stacie hugged me just to keep the shakes under her control. She ran her hand through my hair and drew me to her shoulder. She smelled of pine straw. With her touch on my cheek and my hand across her shoulder, our tears began to flow.

CHAPTER 30

It took a while for the relief and the adrenaline to come back into balance. Stacie and I lay on the floor in each other's arms. As normalcy returned, I knew what she would say. But she surprised me with her silence.

"Thought we were as good as dead," I said. "How did you know?"

"I didn't. That's just it. I didn't but my gut told me. Too easy."

"We've got to collect the weapons," I said. "Can't leave it like this."

Stacie nodded and we left the cabin. We surveyed the situation, checked that we were alone, found all the bodies, collected the weapons, and put them in a travel bag we found in a bedroom closet. I took pictures with my burner phone and went through their pockets but left it all with them— matches, wallets, and cigarette packages.

"What happened before I got here?"

"It was obvious someone beat me to Robbie. I followed the transponder's signal and when I saw Robbie's car and the BMW, I got worried. I stayed undercover and came up on the cabin then waited for a long while. Then I went in. I found Robbie the way you found him. I worried about the BMW and who was still around. They could have noticed me come down the road in the car or heard me as I approached the cabin. I wondered why they were still around and where they were. I concluded that Robbie didn't tell them where the storage stick was, or maybe he'd sent them off on a goose chase. I thought maybe they'd left him still alive, and he died while they were gone. All this went through my head and then as it got dark, I saw headlights. Thought, oh no. But it was you."

"You think the stick is here?"

"I'm sure of it." Stacie looked over at Robbie's wasted body.

We both looked over to the bloody carnage where Robbie had been initially. The floor looked like a huge finger painting in dark red blood. There were swirls and finger-length lines. I walked around in a wide circle twice before I saw them. Letters strung together from a spastic hand.

"Do you see that?" I said.

"Looks like an 'r' and an 'a'."

"Followed by a 'p' or an 'f' and a cross."

"rapx?" Stacie said.

"I think it's 'raft'."

Our eyes met and we both thought lake and raft and we came out the door and ran toward the lake. There was a grey, weathered half-submerged dock that was torqued and twisted. No raft.

I sat down on a rock beside the dock and looked at the water. Picked up a stone and pitched it. Then despondent, watched the ripples fade away.

"It was writing," Stacie said. "He tried to leave a message, right?"

"Looks that way. Are we imagining it?"

"Maybe he didn't get to finish."

We sat in silence.

"Like rafter," Stacie said.

She was on it and ran halfway back to the cabin before I could get up from the rock. When I reached the cabin, Stacie was standing on a chair. The rafters were open to the roof, and she was up above the crossbeams.

"Got it," she said.

CHAPTER 31

Later that afternoon, I followed Stacie in the Tercel. No cars passed us on Lost Lake Road. The drive back on Highway 1 was uneventful and we entered the city as the sun boiled down into the Pacific. Stacie parked in her apartment underground, and I nudged the Tercel beside a dumpster behind the building. I walked to the front and called her on the intercom. She buzzed me up. I hadn't slept since Saturday morning and neither had Stacie, but even after the long drive and what had gone down, we were wired and jumpy.

The air was a prickly liquid on my skin. Once I was inside, the apartment filled with our raw smell—Stacie's sweat, adrenalin, blood and bone, and gunshot residue. She touched my arm. I wanted to draw her to me and feel her flat belly against me. She was a pure rare perfume. I couldn't speak. She drew me close as if she knew these untamed thoughts. She raised herself on her tiptoes and kissed me, first lightly like feathers against my lips, then she moved back a touch before she came on hard, pushed her mouth onto my lips, and ground herself into my hips.

I shivered with her contact. I became drunk on her scent. Her dark eyes. My desire. Her short-cropped black hair. How the skull felt in my hands as she pushed her mouth into a connection.

I'd slept with her once before but slept and held her in her need for comfort and solace, but not this, not desire. I kissed her ear and her neck. I felt her hand caress my thigh.

"Will you sleep with me, Jack?"

"I should go."

"Not like before," she said. "Make love to me."

I wished this was not happening so soon after all the dead bodies and the carnage.

Her message was as primal as the violence we had endured.

Stacie clutched my hand, fingers mingled with fingers, and led me to her bedroom. I fell into her motion as she walked, full of desire and the knowledge that we both needed this and if it ended here, it would be a travesty.

When the wrestling through our clothes ended, Stacie took me on my back and played internal music that resonated with my soul. Three movements in a symphony. Maybe more, for in entangled after-sleep, slick and exhausted, there was no confusion, only memories.

Her pixie-cut head on the curled hair on my chest, one leg across my thigh, her breasts, pert and small like oranges but soft and forgiving against my skin, her voice murmur as her hand trailed across my collarbone.

CHAPTER 32

"I shouldn't have done that," Stacie said.

I came out of the shower with a white cotton towel around my waist. I wanted to say done what. The morning after now, but I stayed silent at first. Then I feared the worst, and said, "Done what?"

"Fall in love with you."

"These things never end well," I said. "Always tears."

Stacie moved toward me. She wore a white bathrobe. She released the towel from around my waist, unfolded the half-knotted belt on her bathrobe, and opened it to me. I couldn't speak. She spread her arms like angel wings. There was nothing to say.

The coffee was strong. The late morning summer sun hit the balcony. I was as giddy as a colt, first hooves on green wet grass.

Stacie came onto the balcony with two plates—mushroom and cheese omelets. Two bacon strips, toast, and a tomato slice.

"Did you send the photos?" Stacey said.

"I did. With a message."

"Reilly will be pissed you haven't called him."

"I'll fill him in once he's acted on the message. I told him how to get there. He'll put it all together. Commisso and Boyle will get to work on who these guys are."

"What about the memory stick? Wasn't that the point?"

"Well, we were occupied, right?"

"We can't make that a habit can we?" Stacie said.

I looked at her and she looked up from her plate. An omelet chunk hovered on her fork. I detected a glint in her eye, a secret message, but it was gone before I could decipher it.

"I suppose not." Then I smiled.

She wore black yoga pants, a pale mauve sports top, no bra, and a black Nike cap with a swoosh. It was all I could do to relax and not lean over and kiss her omelet-greased lips. Steady on. Calm. Breathe. Count. It was hard to believe we were outnumbered by professionally trained killers and survived.

I ate the second bacon strip, and said, "Murphy?"

"She's been on my mind. Been a few days since I visited her. Since I trailed Robbie. I will see her today. You?"

"Tonight." I felt the calling card in my pocket, and it dawned on me it was Monday. Ekaterina. Mephistopheles.

I must have had a strange vacant look because Stacie said, "What?"

"I have an appointment. Ekaterina Sokolov. Reilly and I didn't get much from our visit with her on Saturday. She slipped me a card. Obviously, she can't talk with her uncle around."

"Oh," Stacie said.

"What does that mean?"

"It's fine."

I knew that phrase, it's fine or just plain fine. Meant the opposite.

"I'm leaving now," Stacie said, "to see Murphy."

"What about the memory stick?"

"You look at it. Make a copy. There's an empty stick beside my desktop. Oh, before you go out, can you wash the dishes?"

"No problem. You don't want to see what's on the stick?"

"No. I've had enough for now."

"Can you check in with Mark? See if he needs you to do more research?"

"Sure. Bye."

The two words were short-clipped volleys back at me.

Stacie's footfalls were deliberate. With a stomp, the apartment door closed like a tomb.

One night and I got fine, heavy-footed-door-slamming and I was doing dishes. The relationship had gone domestic.

CHAPTER 33

The alpha wolf was close. A shadow inside me. A shadow on the wrecked truck's hood. The eyes that watched. In the dark, the video played on the computer screen in Stacie's apartment. Green outlines in the night vision camera. Three shapes moved toward one another. Gunshots, low to the ground. Ricochets from concrete and the wall. Three shapes limped toward the driveway and the entrance to the street. I hobbled and I was down like roadkill. Wolf shapes pummeled me. Murphy moved toward me and suddenly she was down. Three assailants in the ghostly outline beat her, then lifted her into the dumpster. Then they dragged me toward the dumpster, and I too was deposited. Crown Vic in the shadows. Car ignitions turned over. Multiple gunshots. The camera angle is closer now. More detailed. Still fuzzy. But I recognized a Laskey brother with a red star on his hand. The guy who tortured Missing Finger. Faint dialogue. I slid the time back on the video, watched it, and listened with the volume up.

Yagoda's gotta like this.

Shut up. You stupid fuck.

What? Nobody's listening. Machlan ordered this, right?

Are you stupid? Shut up. No one mentions names. Leave their guns. That's all.

I heard myself say to Reilly on the drive up to China Heights to interview Yasevich. Cleanup?

I heard him mention it. Yagoda, and Yazhov?

Murphy and I were left for dead and framed for the execution of an undercover cop. Yagoda. All this created a deadly chain—a floater on the east side who broke the story. His friend and colleague, Robbie was tortured and killed all for a name. Eight Russians dead in the woods outside Robbie Maine's cabin.

I attempted to fill in more details. Someone killed Sokolov and staged a tableau of the mutilation in an industrial courtyard that had gone to seed. Cut off his limbs and decapitated him. Froze the parts that were delivered later to his wife. Murphy investigated a case that no one was interested in, a case file that was deep-sixed in a bottom drawer, a case that someone higher up on the food chain needed to stay closed. I'd met with a silent Yasevich

119

and a scared Ekaterina. And Murphy was in a coma. And who was Yagoda and Yazhov?

I copied the original stick. Unscrewed a wall cover for the electrical socket in Stacie's bedroom and slid the stick between the wood frame and the galvanized, electrical box, then replaced the cover.

The Mephistopheles Monday 7:30 p.m. Just You.

I phoned Mark. He answered.

"Where are you?" I said.

"Home."

He was still cautious. He'd never change. Couldn't expect him to, could I?

"Progress?"

"Hammer House?"

"Hammer House," I said.

"I got through the door and met the woman who was in charge, but I got nowhere. The official response about sealed records."

"Maybe we should go over there together."

"Tell me when."

"The other place, the reform school?"

"I have gone there once. I stayed far away and looked through binoculars. The place is not approachable."

"I want you to take me there. To look around from a distance, right?"

"We can observe from cover, okay."

"I am a tad busy now. I'll give you a call in a few days. And Mark. Thanks. I appreciate this."

"Thanks. This I can handle."

When Mark hung up, I felt glad I'd given him a job that would keep him safe.

The phone went off. It was Reilly. He'd got the message and the photos. I answered it.

"Hello."

"Don't hello me, you son-of-a-bitch. What have you been doing?"

"Did you get the photos?"

"Damned right. What part of not being AWOL, didn't you get?"

I could see Reilly standing behind his desk snorting like a bull that's been jabbed too many times by picadors.

"When you get up there, you'll know I was not AWOL."

"It's tough keeping track of you."

"You knew that going in."

"I'll send Boyle and Commisso up there with forensics. They'll take your photos and their cameras to document the scene. Undercover."

"You mentioned Yagoda on the way up to China Heights. Who is this guy?"

"On the street, it's a nickname historically from Stalin's top-secret police," Reilly said. "No one knows him. No photographs. But he exists. He pulls strings and does nasty things."

"Nikolai Yazhov? Do you know any more about him?"

"Both men work for themselves but ultimately serve someone higher on the food chain."

"Why don't we know about these guys?"

"We do," Reilly said. "We see the results every day. Disappearances. Minor thugs were gunned down in the street. Drugs in schoolyards. Arms deals. Human trafficking. Prostitution. Bookmaking and gambling. We see the play each day. We can identify the minor actors. We can haul them in for petty offenses. But we do not know the director of the play."

"Reilly, what's this poetic metaphorical bullshit? Powerful people are sucked in and are stroked to let it slide."

"Are you coming in?" Reilly said.

"Not today. I'm seeing Murphy, and don't ask where she is. Later I got a date."

I closed the call. I could hear the wheels screech in Reilly's brain. Murphy? A date?

Reilly didn't ask me where I was. Figured he knew. Had a tail on me which meant he had a tail on Stacie, but then he'd have followed me Saturday after we'd separated in China Heights. Is he smart enough for that? To know I'd go AWOL? Hang back at the cabin? Watch? No. He is just so pissed with me that he forgot to ask.

CHAPTER 34

This morning looked to be a perfect day. But then all mornings started out that way. The late dawn. Light on the horizon even in a rain was still an illusion that the world was a wonderful place. It was later when the world woke and opened its eyes that the same old stuff became reality.

The cooler wet weather had left us. The sun was angry over the harbor. Tankers and grain boats lounged on the flat water like leviathans. An oily sheen tainted the water. Crude-by-rail cars snaked in long black curving lines down to the sea. Smokestacks belched their angry breath across the delta. The sky was pasted with jet exhaust trails. And the condos gleamed in the noonday sun and cast shadows on those who could not afford them.

I eased the Tercel from behind the dumpster, pulled out onto Beach Avenue, turned right to Denman, left at Georgia, and cut into the traffic toward Lions Gate Bridge. Once over the bridge, I headed toward the highway and the ferry terminal. Picked up speed, changed lanes frequently, and watched for a tail. A Dodge Magnum a hundred yards back drove in and out. I slowed down. The Dodge slowed down but not before I could make out the 2W start to the plate, and a dusty, red paint job that looked like chimps had been set loose with dripping brushes.

I got in the lane for the ferry then switched at the last second and took Highway 99 north to the mountains, exited at a turn-off near Lions Bay, a small community for the rich perched on the cliffs with individual homes cantilevered above Howe Sound. I twisted and turned in a loop beneath Highway 99 and returned south. I booted the Tercel as much as her four cylinders would handle back to Lions Gate Bridge and Georgia toward downtown. Took a straight line for a few blocks, then dropped down toward the docks on Burrard Inlet and the blighted industrial complexes.

This was a Vancouver area not talked about, a place that was left to its own devices where violence and crime were ignored by those in charge, and the dead were taken to common graves in secret places before sunrise. Here was where hope was lost at an early age.

I had lost the tail and headed back toward downtown. I parked on the street a block from Norton's hive in Salsbury Park. The usual suspects warmed up for the day beneath a large maple that provided relief from the summer heat. Norton and Mitchell were there, and Mindy and Sugar sat by themselves on a bench in the sun. They looked relaxed but were dressed for work. Short skirts, high heels, low-cut Tees, rouged faces, and red lips. In the adrenalin from that evening in the wrecking yard and even later when I dropped them off near the shelter, I hadn't really looked at them. They were younger than they looked, and beneath the costume and the make-up were far prettier. They were caricatures of themselves, made-up dolls with clown clothes and clown faces. They were sad for me, and like clowns and painted dolls, they scared me a little. They were broken toys that needed mending. But these toys didn't get mended. They got tossed.

I sat down on another bench next to them. It didn't take long.

"Hi," Sugar said. "Are you looking for a party?"

"Mister, you gotta smoke?" Mindy said.

They didn't recognize me. "Don't smoke," I said. "Used to."

"You know we're working here," Sugar said.

"Yes," I said. "But I'm not looking."

Both had short hair, Mindy's was bottled blonde, and Sugar's was jet-black. The hair looked like they'd shorn themselves with dull scissors and a cracked mirror.

"Guys are always lookin'," Mindy said. "You ain't no different. Everyone's lookin'."

"You got somewhere you can take us, and we can party," Sugar said.

"You've cut your hair," I lied. "Looks good."

This brought them up a tad short.

"Hey, you seen us before?" Sugar said.

"You ain't a cop are ya, Mindy said, "because we're just sitting here getting a sun tan minding our own business."

"You don't remember. Have Norton and Mitchell treated you, okay?"

"What do you know about them?" Sugar said.

Norton walked toward me. Mitchell was propped up against a tree trunk engaged in conversation with the hive. I waved Norton over.

"Jack." He still wore the jacket with all the pockets.

"Aren't you hot in that?"

"Saved my life. Now it's body armor."

He stepped up to me. I stood and he hugged me. As I said, I don't do hugs with guys too well, but I let him.

"Hey," Mindy said, pointing at me, "you're the guy."

"Yes, I'm the guy."

Mindy was tight and pert. Her short-cropped blonde hair. Her open blouse hinted at the petite package inside. A slim waist, and longish legs. No bruises. No tracks at the bend in her elbows. Looked about eighteen if I bypassed the make-up.

"We don't know nothin'," Sugar said.

She was a few paces ahead of me. Mindy stayed quiet now and slapped her jaws on bubble gum. I could smell the strawberry flavor from three feet away. Made my hands sticky to smell it.

"Those guys? At the wrecking yard? Are they regulars?" I asked.

Mindy piped up. "It was all Sugar. I told her we should have stuck to our beat. We had to fight for the new turf anyway and that's what happened. I told her it was a bad idea."

"Hey, shut up, Mindy."

"Ladies. Ladies," Norton said. He sat on the bench beside Sugar.

"I knew they were going to be trouble," Mindy said. "I've always said, don't get in cars."

"So, you never met those guys before?"

Both said in unison, "Nope."

"What about the guy they tortured? Cutting off fingers?"

"No," Mindy said. There was genuine fear in her voice like she didn't want to remember. "When I saw that guy with the rubber apron and that big knife, I peed myself. I thought we were goners."

"Do you remember what that big guy with the apron asked the guy he tortured?"

"I was giving Bobby what he wanted. I was so scared," Sugar said. "I blocked it out. I hoped they just dump us out down the road when they were finished."

"Can you think about it? Go back and listen to the words?"

Sugar shook her head, but Mindy tried. "Something about a shipment. A number. A time. But that guy only said a few words in a weird language."

"Was it Russian?"

"It could a been like a foreign language in movies with spies."

"Do you remember the car they drove and where they picked you up?"

"On the east side," Sugar said. "We walked at least five blocks to The Margot and hung outside and waited for johns. That's after we'd smacked several girls south when they hassled us."

I nodded to Norton and stepped away from the girls. He followed me over. I handed him four hundred dollars. Funds had dwindled in my account, but I still had enough cash left from last year's Shaplow investigation, so I wasn't destitute.

"Got a job." With the money was my burner cell number. "That number? Call me if you need to. Buy a burner. Take Sugar with you. Here."

I handed him the original stick with the video that Robbie hid in the cabin's rafters. "Give this to Reilly. No one else. Guard it with your life."

"Is that it? Why Sugar?"

"No. There's more. I also want you and Sugar to go to The Margot, like on a date. Buy convincing clothing. Use the money."

"The Margot?"

"It's near the industrial area. Sugar knows where it is. She's been there. That's where the Laskey brothers picked them up, so I figure maybe you can sniff about at The Margot to see if there are any connections. There are two more brothers, and they must wonder where the other three have gone. Stay under the radar. Keep Sugar on a string. Don't let her talk too much."

"Sure, boss," he said.

I liked it, but I knew he was being sarcastic.

"One day I'll crack you open. Find out who you really are. Listen. The wrecking yard had a total makeover. The trauma team came in and cleaned up the kill site. No bodies. No mess. Get my drift. Weird, right? So, nobody knows what went down. Talk, if any, will be all speculation."

I stepped back toward Mindy and Sugar.

"I've got a job for you. Good money. Easier than hustling all day and night. Sugar, I want you to go with Norton. He'll fill you in."

"How much are you paying us?"

"Five hundred each after you come back," I said.

"Rule One: Up front and tucked away, before I get on my back and sway."

"Clever. Another business, Sugar. Take the deal or leave it."

She looked at Norton who obviously she trusted, turned back to me, and said, "Okay, Jack."

I was surprised not because she accepted, but rather that she remembered my name, and this was the first time she had used it. I'd made progress.

Mindy who had crossed her legs, so her skirt rode up almost to her waist as she continued to smack on her gum said, "What about me?"

"I want you to meet someone. Maybe you can help me."

"I ain't goin' nowhere on my own with you without the details."

"The details? Getting fancy pants," I said.

What she said next blew me away.

"If we're working a job, we got to scope it out. Analyze the risk. Know all the back doors. Plan for blind spots. Or we're dead."

I wasn't sure if she was having me on, or all this while, she'd been playing the dumb Mindy role and there was more about her underneath.

"You're right." And then I told her about Murphy and the Undertown hospital and how I'd been helping her to wake up from her coma, and how maybe a female voice could help her too.

Mindy listened to the details. Sugar and Norton heard this too for the first time.

Then Mindy said, "I'm in, Jack. I'm in."

"Thanks, Mindy."

"Do I get some new clothes, too?"

CHAPTER 35

Norton drove the Tercel with Sugar in the front and Mindy and me in the back. He dropped us near the entrance alley for the Undertown hospital. In five minutes, Mindy and I walked down the corridor toward Murphy's bed.

Mindy held my hand so her high heels would not slip on the polished concrete. She wore a black cotton boat-neck top that covered her breasts completely but left her mid-drift bare. Complementing this was a pale green mini skirt respectfully longer than her normal street apparel. I wanted tasteful. She wanted clothes she could still work in. We compromised. Her shoes were basic black. Only the high heels threatened to give her away. She was happy.

When she slipped on the concrete and leaned into me for balance, I suggested she take the shoes off and walk in bare feet, which she did with the shoes slung over her shoulder like she was strolling down a beach. I liked the image. Could even see the sunset and feel the ocean brush against my toes.

Stacie was in the area where Murphy lay assisted by oxygen. She wore what she had on when she went out the door in a huff this morning. Tight slim-fit indigo jeans, and a sweatshirt. Her off-road, black-leather biker jacket hung over the chair. You could never say Stacie wasn't dressed in style. I paid attention.

"Murphy's the same." Stacie was despondent.

"We'll keep trying," I said. "This is—"

"Ekaterina?" She stretched the name out like she'd scraped a turd off her shoe on a curb.

Mindy sprung forward. "I'm Mindy. I'm here to help. You know, do what I can."

Mindy held out her hand to Stacie who stood up. Stacie looked at me as if I was crazy and then turned to look at Mindy.

"Nice to meet you, Mindy. So how did you find Jack?"

I jumped in quickly. "I met Mindy at the underground soup kitchen. She and I are good friends." I realized I sounded goofy, so I said, "She's here to help. End of story and she has the time to help which is more than we can say."

127

I expected Stacie to ask her what elementary school she attends, but she didn't.

"Well, in that case, welcome aboard."

She then said, "Everything is normal. No changes. I must go. I promised Mark, I'd help him out on that other thing. I'll write up an invoice for my hours on the job for you tonight and have it for the morning if you ever get back from your meeting." She emphasized meeting and I wondered why she was so high school about all this. First Ekaterina and now Mindy. I expected the invoice some time since she worked for me by the book.

She gave me a peck on the cheek and was gone. I motioned to Mindy to sit down, and I pulled up another chair beside Murphy.

"This is an entire hospital? Get out!"

I nodded.

"I mean like the soup kitchen and the underground bars and casinos?"

"There's the good and there's the bad."

"So, Murphy is not bad, so why's she here and not in a regular hospital?"

"Someone very bad tried to kill her and to kill me and they almost succeeded. If she were in a regular hospital, then someone would know where she is and there's no way we could defend against her from an attack. Can't trust anyone. Can't trust the police."

"Will she wake up?"

"I hope so. That's what you and I are here for. To talk to her. Stacie believes she can hear us and the more we talk to her, the greater the chance she'll wake up."

"Is Stacie your girlfriend?"

Mindy had asked a tough question. The way she had responded to me, I doubted it.

"She works for me."

"Oh, sure. There's plenty more going on."

"You saw that?"

"I'm not stupid."

I looked at Murphy. She had a placid look on her face, eyes closed. I held her hand.

"This is Mindy. I met her at the soup kitchen, and we will stay around for a while, and then I must go for a meeting about our case. Mindy will stay with you, and she will keep you company."

Mindy sat in the chair closer to Murphy's face. She leaned over and stroked Murphy's arm and whispered in her ear.

"It's alright hon. You will pull through this. One day you'll squeeze my hand, and your eyes will pop open and there you'll be. Like a brand-new penny."

I realized that time had moved on.

"Mindy, I'm leaving now. See you later tonight. If you want to sleep, you can put the two chairs together and I'll ask them for a blanket before I go."

"She will be okay with me. Don't worry. And patch it up with your girlfriend while you're at it."

I got a blanket and gave Mindy a hug before I turned down the corridor.

"She's not my girlfriend."

"Sure. You believe what you want."

CHAPTER 36

The Mephistopheles was a dance club that lurked in the lower depths with no fixed address. It was a legend and a closely guarded secret. Its existence was all about location, location, location, springing up somewhere one week or month and moving on. It had staying power by virtue of never staying still, in its theme and in its whereabouts. I knew about it by rumor and anecdote. No one ever had a picture. Photos were forbidden. The club never appeared on social media or news feeds. It was rumored that you could go one night, be lucky enough to get in, and go a second night and you'd find an empty space—a warehouse with its abandoned dust and detritus. No evidence to forensically tell of its former presence. Not an earring, a footprint in the dirt, a loose nail, or a pair of panties left in a washroom stall.

I did the research. Took time. Old school, unlike Stacie who would have found a fancy back door hack to track it down.

I found it. Arrived by cab. A narrow alley off Dundas among the abandoned warehouses on the east side. Thought 7:30 seemed a little early for dancing, but figured Ekaterina knew the culture. Maybe the time was not important since daylight wasn't the main attraction.

Cabbie pointed to a green steel door with a small slide-pull window that was shut. I was not the first ride he'd deposited here. Cabbies knew everything in this town. I was alone in an empty space. The evening was still hot and humid from the heat wave that had replaced the rain. The sun had dropped below the taller buildings on the west but had not yet fallen into the ocean. I knocked. I was not what they looked for with my basic black Levi's, solid pale teal shirt, button-down collar, my standard 'stuff', Glock and Beretta, sturdy shoes, and no jacket or baseball cap. I'd left the duffle bag beside Murphy's bed. I had enough cash for the night. I looked like a tourist, and I was sure tourists never got in.

The narrow window slit opened, the metal running painfully in its groove. The door opened and I followed a corridor to a room with a switchback weave of bodies that waited in a line to get in. At our destination were two more steel doors side by side. Acceptance and rejection. Two black guys in shiny silk suits stood at the doors. Dapper. Dwayne Douglas

Johnson-good-looking. That mixed look that everyone liked these days. Pink shirts, necks like rhinos. Bling. Scary hands like catchers' mitts. They stood before the line and let some people in and rejected others.

I knew I wouldn't cut it. I needed Ekaterina's smile and stunning body to get past them. I watched the dejected faces. That look lined up against the gym wall or the chain-link fence in the schoolyard while the popular people picked sides. The look that no one chose.

Ekaterina wasn't anywhere. The line moved faster now. The rejection door was busy. Only a few with the right look got through. I was not it.

I felt a warm hand brush and linger on my thigh. Smelled woodsy patchouli and sandalwood. Black Orchid perfume. Stacie had the same stuff. Smelled it once and it left an impression.

A pair of lips brushed my ear.

"Jack McQueen. I am your escort. Your ticket. Follow my lead."

My escort came up to my shoulder. She was Hubba, Hubba, drop-dead gorgeous. Olive-bronze skin. Short, ebony hair. Low-cut, sequined midi dress. All fur and leather draped over her shoulders. No jewelry. She didn't need it.

Foreign accent. Not Russian. I think Malaysian.

"Ekaterina?" I asked.

"She's inside. I am Meeko. No worries."

She clung to me, and I held her around the waist. We moved through the doors into a dark corridor lit by green overhead lights that created a surreal atmosphere. Two muscular silk-suited guards welcomed us to The Mephistopheles.

Everyone knew Meeko. She held my hand while we moved through the crowd while she greeted and kissed each person she met. She was formal like an heiress at a wedding. Meeko waved and jostled me through the maze of bodies with drinks in hand, where some danced, and others swayed and shouted above the music. After a climb up the stairs, we arrived at an open table that looked over the dance pit and three bars. We were high enough to be almost parallel to the suspended DJ station where against a brutal, mangled steel wall sculpture, the disc jockey blasted techno through a full-on capacity sound system. It wasn't blues or jazz or golden oldies, but I had to like it. Fortunately, the DJ was on a jag with Chillstep, slower and more melodic than a headache-generating Dubstep. I recognized "Free Yourself" a Liquid Drum & Bass Mix by Oskar Koch. It had a dreamy quality that maintained percussion and sustained its energy.

We ordered drinks. Meeko, a Bellini. Me a J and G. It had been a long time.

"When will Ekaterina arrive?"

"Soon. We will enjoy our drinks now."

"Sure. But I must visit the boys' room." I left money on the table. "For the drinks," I said.

I descended into the pit with its conversation, gyrations, and movements that could be cleverly disguised acts of total penetration. The unisex washrooms had low lighting with open stalls. There were dark rooms where couples straight and gay entered and emerged as I left the washroom. The scene was liberating and disturbing at the same time. Large abstract and realistic expressionist art was on the flat walls. Women and men naked on apocalyptic landscapes. Metal human sculptures in shiny honed steel created a titanic struggle on the wall behind the DJ and the bar. The room overwhelmed me with its mélange of perspiration, perfume, and pheromones.

When I returned, I noticed that Meeko had hardly touched her Bellini. Its long Y-shaped glass was beaded with condensation.

"To life," I said and toasted her Bellini and looked deep into her violet eyes.

She smiled and giggled which seemed out of place. Maybe a flash thought, clinking glasses with a man that could be her father. I downed the Jameson and then chased its burn with the Guinness. Then I saw Ekaterina walk through the dancing mob that parted for her in awe. I wiped the foam from my upper lip and straightened my posture.

Ekaterina ascended the stairs and Meeko stood up, moved to the side, took her Bellini with her, and said, "Nice to meet you, Mr. McQueen."

My tongue became numb. I needed to distract myself.

I stood and said, "Thank you, Meeko."

I wondered what other duties she had to attend to. I turned toward Ekaterina. She was more stunning than when I'd met her with her uncle Yasevich. She looked more mature, more self-assured. I offered her Meeko's chair, but she moved her body against me and whispered in my ear.

"Embrace me as a lover. Kiss me hard. Hold me close."

This was not a suggestion but a command. I did what she said, and she kissed me back with a lust that had waited a lifetime. We were a tableau, and everyone watched as the Dubstep music, less lyric, more beat hammered the interior like a racing heart. Then Ekaterina stepped back and stared into my eyes, sat down, and allowed me to push in her chair.

"Well played, Jack McQueen."

"Ekaterina. I didn't expect such a showy entrance."

"Call me Katrin. Out there I am Ekaterina Yasevich."

Gone was the fear and shyness I'd seen at China Heights. I had a sense that few got to call her Katrin and what I'd seen at the house was the show, and what I saw here was the real thing.

"You summoned me. So, let's talk," I said.

"Not here. I wanted you to see this but to talk here is not a good idea."

She noticed the rest of my Guinness, made a slight gesture with her hand, and a vodka martini materialized brought by a sweaty waiter who placed the drink before her, bowed, and quickly stepped away.

"Za lyo-bof."

Katrin raised her glass and we clinked. I looked deep into her eyes and wondered if I could trust her.

"To love," I said and swallowed more Guinness.

I drank as if I'd suffered drought and that worried me. I took Katrin's cue to rise and follow her down the stairs and across the dance floor. The mob parted like the Red Sea. We passed through a dark room where I sensed bodies heavily absorbed in each other. A door opened. Green light illuminated a carnal tableau for an instant and then the door closed the scene behind us.

Katrin wore a long black evening dress with pearls, classic, practical medium heels, and a sensible leather shoulder purse. I followed her swaying hips. The motion was a drug. Two bodyguards fell in behind us and another opened the door to the outside. A late model Bentley Mulsanne waited with the back doors open and a driver at attention. We were both invited into the back through separate doors. I sunk down into the fine duck-down cushions. This ride beat the Tercel. I thought about Norton, and why I hadn't heard from Reilly. I expected him to be screaming in my ear.

The driver spoke in Russian.

"Snax," Katrin said.

"Our destination?" I asked.

She nodded and switched off the intercom. We were sealed behind bullet-proof glass. The Bentley moved off as I sunk deep into the interior cushions.

"Katrin, are we on a date, or do you want to talk to me?"

I pointed to the driver and motioned with a finger to my ear.

"He cannot hear us without intercom."

"So, talk to me on the way to this place, Snax," I said.

"Club? It is mine. Place in China Heights? Mine. All muscle? Mine. My uncle? Let us say he is my caretaker and my employee. Got it?"

"I think I do. And Mikhail Sokolov, your husband?"

"He was convenient."

"As in convenient and dead?"

"No. No. That is tragedy. He is Lana's father. I loved him. Lana is so upset he is gone."

"Who would want to kill him? Make a display like that? Send you that box?"

"City is in chaos. New faces. Greedy faces with brutal appetites."

"Who killed him, Katrin?"

We sat in each corner against each door. We couldn't be further apart.

"I wish I knew. Mikhail was doctor. Surgeon. He saved people's lives."

"Did he know about anyone serious enough to kill to keep him quiet?"

"My husband was weak. Everyone with power could get him to do whatever they wanted."

"Like what?"

We had come to the edge. The point where she intended to force herself to open to me. That's why we were here. Not to dodge questions and make up phony answers. I could tell it in her eyes, a weight that had grown in her heart.

"Started small. Fake prescriptions. Few at first. Then larger quantities on regular basis. He could hide loss. Then they called him late at night. Would send car to penthouse. He would be gone until morning. He did surgeries and sewed people up. Extracted bullets. That too became regular."

"He told you all this?"

"I got that from him."

"He was not someone they'd want to lose," I said. "Kill the golden goose."

"Goose?"

"Never mind."

Katrin leaned forward and flipped open the bar. Took out a bottle of single malt. Lagavulin. Poured two glasses an inch and a half. Handed one to me.

"To health," she said.

"May those who love us, love us," I said.

I sipped. Katrin bolted half her glass.

"It's not vodka. Single malt needs to be savored."

"With all chaos, I am not sure there is time," she said.

"There's always time."

We were physically closer to each other now as we shared a drink. She leaned over and kissed my cheek. I felt her breath from her nose as it brushed past my ear.

"Mikhail cut his hours at hospital down to three days. But for other four he was gone from penthouse. Long hours. He would come home exhausted. Sleep with nightmares."

"You had no influence over him?"

Katrin smiled. I saw the sadness as she went into a room in her memory palace.

"You see how high employees jump. You see drunken rabble part for me. No one messes with me. But Mikhail? He did not believe in my power. He did not believe I could help him."

I fell silent with her pathos. I knew she hadn't finished.

"I had him abducted once. Drive by. Grabbed him from street. They took him into forest. Made him strip naked at gunpoint. Threatened him with bullet in eye. Threatened to smash hands. Those delicate surgeons' hands. They wanted names. I wanted names. They wanted to know locations. Where he went on those four days. They wanted to know what he did there. I wanted to know. He cried. He whimpered. He pleaded for his life but told nothing.

"Finally, they gave him shovel. They sat and smoked while he dug grave. Then they gave him one more chance, but he still refused to talk. They brought him back and dumped him on sidewalk outside penthouse."

"You called him weak. I don't think, Katrin, that Mikhail Sokolov was weak. More unfortunate than weak."

My Scotch was gone. Mikhail Sokolov was not weak. He was not a coward. He had protected something far more precious to him and I wondered why Katrin couldn't see it.

CHAPTER 37

After we crossed a bridge, the Bentley pulled off the main street. I hadn't paid attention to our whereabouts. The bridge looked like the Cambie. We headed northwest toward the sea and newly constructed condos, one unit per floor, with sunset windows and balconies, all less familiar, less in my wheelhouse. Local old money that competed with up-start foreign interlopers.

Katrin poured more Scotch. "Bottoms up," she said.

We clinked glasses. A big mistake? We downed the drinks. Now I paid attention. The Bentley glided past tree-lined streets with gentrified houses, came to a T-intersection, and turned south along the coast road. The condos stood above the winding highway and gazed out to sea. We passed bluffs and headlands, or sandy beaches. For each condo, there was a private thoroughfare beneath the coast road that led down to the ocean. These were the exclusive playgrounds of the wealthy. I then recognized the Lion's Gate Bridge.

Katrin clicked on the intercom. "1965 Marine. One mile ahead."

"Yes, ma'am," the driver said.

We arrived at a driveway and a roundabout with a portico. The doormen were in greatcoats even though the air was warm and humid. The driver stayed put and a doorman opened the door for Katrin, and she exited. Her long slender legs with her basic black and pearls and her stunning beauty were not wasted on them. I got out on my side by myself.

"Welcome home again, Ms. Yasevich. Will you be staying long this visit?" asked the other doorman.

"Not long, Richard. Maybe few hours. Maybe overnight."

"You own a unit here?" I said.

"Don't be silly, Jack. I own building."

"So why am I even here? I'm like a sidewalk shoe-shined boot. You're Prada."

She walked up the steps past the second doorman who held the door for her. He looked me over.

Katrin called back to me and said, "Let us say for moment, you amuse me."

She waved me to the elevator. Pressed the down button to P5.

"Jack," she said, "do not sulk. We are on date now. I make joke."

"This is Snax?" I said.

The doors opened to live jazz, slot machines, a piano bar, a stage with chorus girls, gambling tables, blackjack, Chemin de fer, roulette, craps, private areas cordoned off with velvet rope and brass stands, croupiers, dealers, hat check girls, waitresses in sequined jump-suits, men in tuxedos, women in long dresses with cigarettes in extended holders, ceiling mirrors and red plush carpets. Why was she trying so hard to impress me?

This was not Vegas. Not a home for the down-and-outs who chase dreams. Not for tourists in sandals, shorts, and Hawaiian shirts. But tuxedos, Hugo Boss, Ralph Lauren. A young wannabee crowd with expendable cash and an older well-heeled clientele that exuded confidence. Katrin breezed among the tables clutching my arm. I looked like riffraff but was getting away with it since I was ornamentation. No one looked up from their frenzied activity at the tables except the blackjack dealers whose eyes showed they knew Ekaterina. The Baccarat croupiers were more aloof. They saw her. A slight shift in their eyes. Nothing demonstrative.

"I want you to meet the Colonel?" Katrin said. "Let us see if we can win you some money."

I was at the point now where I decided to go with the flow but stay vigilant and worry about it later. She brought me to the roulette table. A game I despised. Roulette was among the worst bets in a casino. The house had a 5.26 percent advantage. There were strategies for increasing your chances but in the long run, no one ever came away a winner with any substantial cash.

"Easy game. Do you gamble?"

"My whole life's been a gamble," I said, "and I've never had good odds."

"Indulge me then."

Katrin nodded to the croupier who flashed Ekaterina recognition.

"Put a thousand on my account."

The croupier pushed a ten, green chip stack toward her.

"Go ahead."

I played along. Placed one green chip on black and one green chip on column three, which has eight red numbers. That way, I had twenty-six numbers to hit, four of that I covered twice. The croupier spun the wheel and sent the small white ball rolling on the rim in the opposite direction to the spin. The ball fell into the bottom with the numbered pockets in red and black, the green single zero, and the double green pocket.

It bounced a few times, slowed down, and rested on black six. Payout. I did this again. The balls fell on black thirty-three. Payout one to one on black and two to one on column three. Six hundred.

"Beginner's luck," I said even though the odds were still against me.

"Let me," Katrin said.

She took the thousand plus the six hundred in chips and pushed them over to red eighteen. A lesson in madness.

The wheel spun and the ball spun against the wheel, slowed, bobbled, and finally settled on red eighteen. Katrin jumped up and down like a schoolgirl at a rock concert.

How did she do that? Suddenly sixteen hundred had become fifty-six thousand.

"Let's stop, now," Katrin said.

The dealer cashed out the roulette chips and handed me five ten-thousand chips, and six one-thousand chips. I slid them into my pocket, and we walked on.

"Where's the Colonel?" I asked.

"He's at a blackjack table."

At the table, we stood back. I didn't need Katrin to point out the Colonel. He was a stereotype. Overweight. Short. Cream-white summer suit. String tie with a turquoise and silver slider. A red carnation in his lapel. Long hair with streaks tending toward white. I'd seen his face before but couldn't nail it down.

There was an empty seat. I walked up to it but did not sit. Katrin tried to grab my arm, but I was too fast. Jacinto with a name tag on his red silk vest was dealing. I watched and he busted twice. I put down a thousand. The cards went around. I had a queen up and a jack down. The Colonel showed a face card. Jacinto flipped over a four and a six, then a five followed by a ten. He was over twenty-one again.

Everyone won.

Katrin pleaded. "Let's go, Jack."

I dug all the chips from my pocket and added them to the two thousand. The amount was fifty-seven thousand.

"Sir, I need confirmation," Jacinto said.

His voice shook. Luck hadn't dealt with him very well and I knew he sensed a further bad streak. He pressed a button on the table. A pit boss arrived. He looked up at the mirrors in the ceiling. Then he nodded and looked over my shoulder toward Katrin who had stepped back a few paces as if she'd abandoned me.

The Colonel received his cards first as did the others before me. The Colonel took a card on a face-up two. A nine dropped. The others took cards or sat pat. Each hand looked as if they were eighteen to twenty.

I had been dealt an ace up and a queen down. Jacinto sweated. He looked at Katrin behind me. The pit boss looked as if he expected a beating. I looked back and Katrin had turned her head away from the table.

I flipped over the queen and said, "Blackjack."

Jacinto's hand showed a king. He flipped his down card and said, "Pay twenty-one."

The Colonel had a face card down that gave him twenty-one. I had it locked, too. The other players were losers. I put the chips in my pocket. Without ever sitting down, I walk away with one hundred and fourteen thousand. I walked past Katrin to the cash booth and converted the chips into large bills. The banker gave me a zippered pouch for the winnings.

I felt sorry for Jacinto. His black bow tie must be choking him. I turned to look for Katrin, but the Colonel was in my face as I turned.

"Say, son, that was fine work. Not even sitting down. Like you knew the Spanish guy was having a bad spell."

"Just being lucky."

"Join me for a drink," he said. "I think you threw him off or you got the magic with the cards because you sure made me some money although modest by your standards."

Katrin was beside me before I could answer.

"We're drinking single malt, Colonel. You remember me. Ekaterina Yasevich."

At the bar beside the chorus girls, the Colonel ordered Bowmore 25-Year-Old. Peaty. Mark's engine-oil-tainted glasses flashed by me. I felt Mark's anxiety about the unknown. I looked at the Colonel. He had that Colonel Sanders Kentucky Fried Chicken look without the facial hair.

"You're Jack McQueen, son?"

"Yes, I am, but you have me at a disadvantage, Colonel."

"You are an Island boy. Lost your parents. Reform school kid. Escapee. Special Forces. PTSD. Dismissed from the force. Private dick. Dangerous."

"And you?" I couldn't keep the edge out of my voice on you.

Katrin stepped in as referee, "Boys, boys. Let's enjoy our drinks."

As if in support of her request, chorus dancers leaped across the stage singing "Build Me Up Buttercup" written by d'Abo and Macaulay, but who'd care who'd jotted down the lyrics, when you watched the bare-chested guys and perky girls kick and spin.

The Colonel with effort swung his body around to admire the dancers. I stared at the flesh that hung from his jowls. I imagined him with short hair,

139

and fat rolls at the back of his head and I knew him from a nightmare I couldn't articulate. The complete memory wasn't coming back, only his younger face, the rage, demonic light, and a buzzed-down head. I wished at that moment that Katrin and I could get away from this guy.

When the song finished, as she'd heard my thoughts, Katrin said, "Drink up boys. I'm buying." She waved for the tab. "Let's go down one level."

I thought she was referring to tension, but she meant down in the elevator.

I thought it would be Ekaterina and me, but three of us descended. I didn't trust my guides to help me once we reached the underworld.

CHAPTER 38

When the elevator doors opened, the Colonel and I stepped back and let Katrin walk ahead. The room, as large as a small underground parking lot, was crammed with a mob that barked and lunged at a wire cage. Two men who looked like the silk-suited musclemen from The Mephistopheles escorted Katrin. Must be the uniform. The rabid crowd even though they were actively focused on the cage activities parted on either side of Katrin as we approached.

Inside was a ring made into a twelve-by-twelve-foot square, two hay bales high. Two bare-chested men in boxing shorts flailed at each other. One petit woman screamed, "Get your ass back in there. We need the money. For the kids."

Someone shouted, "Don't give up. You got family. Don't give up."

I got an indistinct memory flash.

My knuckles were cut and bruised.

One guy in the cage went down on the blood-smeared floor. He didn't get up. Many in the crowd went crazy with jubilation. Others swore with disappointment. This was all wrong for me. The Colonel smiled as we moved toward the promoter's table. A skinny guy with tattoos and lip rings handed me a folded paper scrap.

"Dude, you got the dot. You're in the ring."

"What is this?" I said to the Colonel. Katrin was nowhere. She'd evaporated into the crowd.

The Colonel still smiled. Said, "Jack McQueen. You aren't getting out this time. Do you remember me now?"

I didn't. His face was a quick flash like a strobe light on a dance floor. But this was not a dance floor. A faint white scar snaked across his cheek partially hidden by his facial hair.

I opened the folded paper. On it was a single black dot. The musclemen restrained me. Took the Glock. Found the Beretta. Discovered the money pouch in my pants pocket and the burner phone, plus the cash I'd brought with me.

I'm back in my head to a cold concrete floor. Teeth scattered beneath a kitchen table. My naked body on wet mosaic tiles. I am almost broken.

The musclemen opened the cage door and pushed me in. I heard the Colonel laugh, a familiar sound.

I knew this scene. Simple rules. No time limit. No rounds. No gloves. No doctors. No ambulances.

A bulldog bruiser entered the gate, and the crowd went rabid. I estimated six foot four, two hundred and seventy-five pounds. Bets were placed and I knew they weren't on me.

"Tonight, we have the home favorite by popular request, all the way from his last incarceration, The Slammer."

The crowd screamed and banged the chain-link fencing. Smart money rode on The Slammer.

"And tonight's lottery celebrity opponent, The Wanker."

Boos and whistles. The mind raced. Was it Katrin who set me up? The Colonel? She brought me here. Was it a coincidence she introduced me to the Colonel? I didn't have the time to figure it out.

The referee prowled the hay-bale ring. The Slammer and I stood on the outside of the ring, our backs to the chain link.

The Slammer jumped in and set up in a corner. He beat his chest. Stuck out his chin. Eyed me like *You're going to die*. I stepped over the hay bales and removed my shirt. Slammer wore green, boxing shorts with yellow trim and a shamrock on the thigh. A shamrock. The Irish didn't have enough sense to ever quit. He had on black high-top Pro USA boots with white laces. The guy was all togged out. He had a face even his mother wouldn't love. Ugly baby. That's why he ended up here. I had my street jeans and basic dress shoes. I had defined muscle and accumulated scars but looked like the skinny kid at the pool's shallow end. Irish with his bulk was formidable.

The referee waved us together. We touched knuckles. Mine were bare. His had standard white adhesive tape across the front. He looked down like a bird of prey. I was a potential explosion of feathers. I stared six inches up into his eyes.

We broke. I jumped to get a feel for moves in street shoes. Not well. The Slammer came at me. I threw a few jabs, bobbed, and weaved, forward, and back. He was a freight train on a single track for my head. Two roundhouse punches missed, and he slammed his body into me and sent me over the hay bales. I stood against the chain-link fence and felt the crowd's press. Their hot breathy taunts seeped into my back.

Outside the ring for a moment, I was safe. I removed my shoes and socks. The few movements I made to avoid Slammer were awkward. These shoes were a liability. There was no escape. No way to surrender. I either would exit near death or as a winner.

I leaped back into the ring over the hay bales. Slammer was ready and moved in for an easy kill. I threw a few jabs. Moved in close so his roundhouse punches couldn't connect. I dropped and pounded two into his solar plexus. Then stepped back to protect my head. Slammer staggered back. I had poked the bear and he salivated and snorted phlegm from his nostrils. We danced but he moved in with angry eyes determined to put me away. I weaved. Kept mobile, blocked his massive punches to my head and protected my body with my elbows but he slammed punches into my sides and connected with glancing blows to my head. Searing pain left me gasping.

He moved in with a long hard right-hand jab. I let it flow past as I stepped right and blocked with my left. Brought my right arm across his neck, bent his spine back, and blocked his base of support on his left ankle. Instinctively I'd done this before, but this required all my strength. I applied pressure to the neck, and he went down. Then he was on the way up. A bounced-back survivor. I was on him with a curved four-fingered punch to the lower chin where it met the neck. But rather than drop like a normal human being, he merely staggered back. I moved in again with the cupped four fingers of my right hand, full force to the solar plexus, and this time he went down a little longer before he rose. I was spent. Not in top condition. Not so practiced. But I could run on automatic.

The crowd was a contrast of silence and frenzy. They wanted him to kill me. They wanted him to win. They wanted to collect their money. I decided. Not today. Whatever it took, not today. I let him gather speed. I sensed bloody revenge pulse in his brain.

Calm. Breathe. Control.

His momentum was blind and vengeful. I was cold. As his first fists flailed at me, I braced myself, rotated my hips and shoulders into the attack, moved my body mass straight forward, dropped my body weight, and came in low. I struck Slammer with a knifed finger thrust to the neck. A devastating blow.

As he dropped, he got no more chances. I followed down across the main artery in his neck as he fell. Then I thrust my hands forward at nose level, so my fingers gripped his skull and my thumbs slid into his eye sockets. I pressured my fingers against his temples and sunk my thumbs into his eyes. I knew this was illegal, but it was survival. He slid back toward the floor. At first, he felt pain beyond his imagination, but then he was no longer aware. He felt no pain. He was beyond pain. He was unconscious. In the numb shocked silence from the crowd, I knew that he would not come back.

CHAPTER 39

I sat on a chrome chair behind a curtain far from the cage. The circus had continued without me. I could hear the crowd. Two more fighters grubbed out a living because they had no other alternative. The silk suits were with me. A short guy pressed a wet towel and a cold metal object on my skin near my eye. I felt adhesive tape binding my back ribs. My fingers were bruised but I still had my hands. I clenched them. No pain. No bones were broken. He finished and then took a thick, hooked needle and stitched up a cut below my right eye and to the side close to the ear. He'd only connected with glancing blows. I looked at the guy who sewed me up.

"You should see the other guy."

He looked at me and continued to clean up my wounds.

"You a doctor?"

"Don't talk." Then he laughed as if to say. Do I look like a doctor? "No one's ever beaten The Slammer. Always figured someone would need to kill him to win. Dammit, I shoulda bet on you. You're good to go."

A silk suit came toward me and threw me a short, tubular bag that looked like a cover for a bedroll.

"All your stuff's in there. This way."

The other silk suit parted the curtain, and we walked toward the elevator. People got lost as if wild predators had suddenly appeared. We rode the elevator up past the casino floor to where I had entered with Katrin.

When I exited, I heard Katrin's voice from the security lobby where she sat on a white leather sofa beside a blue-glass coffee table.

"Jack, you must be tired. Come sit with me."

I walked over. Sat across from her in a similar leather chair. Placed my hands in fists on my knees. Looked into her eyes.

"What were you thinking?"

"Don't be like that."

"I could be on a slab in a panel van where all the losers go."

"I want to hire you."

"One hell of a way to conduct an interview. If I'd lost, what would you have done? Offered The Slammer the job?"

"I had nothing to do with that. We went to watch fights."

"And the Colonel?"

"Suddenly, he had other ideas."

"Suddenly?"

"His number was on my husband's cell phone. When my husband never broke under torture, I checked up on him. But he never left a trail. But Colonel's number always came up. He recognized you."

I wanted to believe her, but I'd run out of gut feelings.

"Hire me for what?"

"To keep me safe."

Katrin leaned forward from the sofa. The light overhead caught her face perfectly.

"What's wrong with the muscle? The driver? Your uncle? Your organization?"

She crossed her legs and leaned further so that her breasts revealed themselves below the subtle white pearls around her neck.

"Find out who is behind husband's murder. Find out why husband would not reveal his activities even at point of death. Find out what is so precious to him that he would not talk."

"I am already paid to do this."

"Chicken soup. And that will not last."

I figured she meant Russian chicken feed. I hadn't moved my position, straight-backed fists on knees and I didn't intend to relax even if I could.

"How much?"

"One hundred thousand to start."

I didn't betray my surprise at the high figure.

"My terms. My timeline. My way," I said.

"Whatever you say. Make me safe."

"I know what is so precious that he wouldn't talk? And if you think about it, you know too. Lana. You need to protect her. Make her safe, so she is not a liability when I close in on your husband's killer."

Katrin smiled. I knew by that very smile she was still ahead of me.

"I like our arrangement already. I stay night. I have single malt upstairs and cotton sheets will feel good against your bruised body."

I could think about what would feel good against my bruised body. But tried not to let my mind go there. A hard thing to do when I looked at Katrin. It would be so easy.

"Your offer is very kind. But I have commitments. Promises."

Murphy and Mindy, Mark and Stacie, Norton and Sugar, Reilly. There'd be messages on my phone. It had been a long, unexpected night.

"It is up to you. Stay with me until morning. Or go in car back to city with Carlos, the driver. He can take you wherever you want. Wait for you and go to next commitment."

On commitment, I detected her disappointment. I was still wary. I needed to keep her off-balance.

She waved a hand to the silk suits. One pulled out a cell phone, punched in a number, and said, "Bring car around."

At the door to the Bentley Katrin leaned into me. The pain in my body overwhelmed me but I didn't flinch. She placed her lips off-center and trailed her palm across my upper leg. Her gambit had the effect she desired. I squeezed her arm gently. Then I slid carefully into the back seat, said, "I'll be in touch," and closed the door.

CHAPTER 40

At six in the morning, the city was asleep. The pawnshops and coffee houses still had their metal gates drawn down and locked. The Bentley moved through the greasy streets as alien as the Batmobile. Was Carlos, the driver, Italian? Over the last two hours, as we drove back to the city, we exchanged origin stories. I chose my segments wisely. Stuck to happier events. Mostly invented.

Even so early the outside world was a furnace at eighty degrees. When I saw the dial on the interior dash, I pressed the electronic window down. Air rushed in. Fire from the dragon's mouth. This was unusual for the coast, but occasionally El Nino would affect the weather.

The streets were deserted. A few hookers still strolled along the garbage-strewn sidewalks. A paper truck, almost a relic, dumped its bundles on corners on the fly. The sky was deep blue. No clouds were building over the distant sea. There would be no breeze today, only an angry eye that beat upon asphalt, concrete, and steel.

In a few hours, everyone with no work would sit in the shade. Doors would be wide open to the morning air.

We were on the way to Daffy's. Meeting with Reilly. His messages were clipped and short. I was in no mood to argue with his tone. I'd let him see the damage. See how stupid I could be if left unattended.

I received messages from Mark, Stacie, and Norton. I'd wait until I talked to Reilly.

The heat made the city hazy. Life was still. A languid longing that would never come. A lost hunger.

I was in the furnace where life's essence was rendered. Six o'clock? Too early to give up, to lose the hope I had when I was young, before the trauma. Some things I couldn't remember. Some with brief flashes like with the Colonel.

By the time the Bentley pulled up beside Daffy's Diner and I got out and thanked Carlos, I knew the tension had to break, but I was not prepared for the direction it would come.

A few booths in Daffy's were occupied but the place was far from full. Reilly sat far back in a booth with no window. He was in shadow and looked morose. I slid in and faced him. Held back a comment on how wrinkled he was. I chucked the tubular bag on the floor at my feet. It clunked and I remembered the guns.

A waitress came with coffee. I poured in the sugar and added cream. I waited for her to make her way back to the counter. Reilly was patient. He looked like tired.

"What happened?" I asked.

"Shouldn't I ask you that question?"

I'd forgotten about my face even though it still throbbed.

"Oh, that?"

"Did the doctor have the DTs when he sewed you up?"

"Sort of. Later. It's been a long few days and nights. I want to put my head down and go to sleep. But I can't."

Reilly looked me in the eyes. He was tired.

"Connor's dead."

"What? How?"

Reilly leaned forward and crossed his arms behind his coffee cup. "Gunshot to the temple. In his car. Driver seat. Underground parking lot in his apartment block."

"When?"

"Yesterday morning. A passerby spotted the blood splatter on the window. Called 911. That's not all. The unit is gone. I've been re-assigned. Commisso and Boyle have been re-assigned to internal affairs. It came down the same day as the call-in for Connor."

"Smells, doesn't it?"

"I checked your pay grade that Conner had set up. Appears it doesn't exist. Never did. Or it did, and now it's wiped. You're not there."

"I didn't ever count on it." Seemed sketchy I could be paid under the radar.

The waitress swung by and refilled our cups. I realized I was starving and couldn't remember the last time I ate. I ordered the two-egg breakfast with hash browns and bacon with sourdough toast. Reilly had the same but with sausages. I went with more sugar and added cream.

"That will kill you," Reilly said.

"The way this investigation is going, something else will beat out sugar. Right now, I need the hit."

"The office is gone. What little was at the warehouse got hauled off last night in a box truck from central."

"Did Norton drop off the memory stick?" I asked.

"I got that. It's safe. Watched it. Do you have another copy?"

"Yes. So, what you're saying is you can't dig into this?"

"On the surface, I've got no choice. I'll keep the memory stick safe. Now's not the time to make any sudden moves on guys above me."

"Really? That's it."

I felt lonelier than when I'd left the Bentley.

"I can't be seen investigating this," Reilly said. "I'm on the sidelines, no explanations. I push paper at central with old cases and files into worth-it or not worth-it. Boring. I need to be on the move. And you know who is supervising me? Reynolds."

"They moved him from homicide?"

"Apparently. This whole business is messed up. Everyone is stressed by budget cuts. Several guys have taken early retirements. There are staff shortages in the Homicide Bureau, the Medical Examiners' Office, and the courts. There's no space in our holding facilities. Transports for corrections are overworked and backlogged. With all the cuts, good men leave, and gaps appear in the ranks. Guess who gets promoted. All those folks who find themselves beyond their abilities. Guys are wide open to be tapped into corruption. It's so bad, I don't know who to trust and respect. I'm all alone."

Suddenly I was tired.

I switched back to Connor. "Autopsy said suicide. Single gunshot to the head?"

"You got it. Processed it lightning fast. And the funeral's tomorrow. Command performance. I'll be out there. Full dress."

"Some people want this investigation to go away," I said.

"Looks that way. And there's more. I sent out forensics to the cabin."

"Do you still have the photos?"

"I do. That's why I mentioned this. Forensics got to the cabin. Nada. Clean as a whistle."

A haunting shadow crept over my heart.

"What do you mean, clean as a whistle?"

"There was nothing there. No bodies. No indication that any violence had gone down."

I couldn't believe it.

"Sanitized is what I'd call it," I said. Like the Laskey's wrecking yard.

The breakfasts came and we ate in silence until I was down to my toast with jellied jam.

"Are you wondering about my face?"

"It crossed my mind. I was upset, I couldn't get you. Left messages. Thought you were dead what with all this other stuff."

"Really?"

I see a small light in Reilly's face.

"Don't flatter yourself. When have you ever responded to my calls in a timely fashion? And besides, I was too busy figuring out how to save my butt to worry about you."

I liked the edge. Showed there was some spunk still left after his previous comments. I should have called him.

"I was busy," I said.

I told him about the odyssey with Ekaterina Yasevich. I didn't leave much out either, except how physically excited she got me despite the mayhem. I glanced at the bag at my feet. Wondered if there was any money left in it.

"So where do you think Uncle Yasevich fits into all this?" Reilly said.

"He's an employee. Katrin's got the power in that syndicate. I don't trust her, but she's all she seems and not much more. Regular illegal stuff. There are some real villains, but she is not one of them."

I didn't tell him about her offer to hire me, or that I planned to take her up on it. With what went down, I'd decided this as I finished my coffee. Intuition.

"You said before there were no fingerprints on the box," I said, "or the cooler with Sokolov's head and limbs?"

"None. And his car was clean. But we did get a pattern on the GPS. Four days a week he took the car outside the city. We have a perimeter based on the mileage. Boyle was to check it out in detail but that's a wash."

"Send me the data. I'll do the leg work or get Stacie on it."

"This Colonel you talked about. How do you figure he knew you?"

"He's a character from before I joined Special Forces. I had flashes I couldn't pin down. I got a hunch there is a connection. I'll let you know if I figure it out." I wanted to tell him about the vague images from my reform school institution, the gut feelings but I let it slide. I stood up. "If I need help, I'll let you know."

"Can you tell me where Murphy is?"

Maybe he was having me tailed so I'd lead him to Murphy.

"Reilly, I can't. It's complicated."

"You are an asshole."

I decided to ask him about the Dodge Magnum.

"Have you had me tailed? Dodge Magnum with a dull-paint undercoat looked like monkeys attacked it with paint brushes?"

Reilly looked at me with a puzzled expression. He knew nothing about it.

"I will not even dignify your question with a response," he said. "And you're still an asshole. I worked with you because of Connor and Connor's gone, but there's Murphy and that's the only reason I'll stay tangled up with you."

Beneath his words was anger mixed with frustration, genuine empathy, and fear.

"That fills me with confidence," I said.

"I didn't tell you. Norton is now a person of interest for the Parker Street murder. He is in custody. We traced the Tercel. You had him registered as the owner, right?"

I ignored him. He was angry enough, so I didn't want to raise the ante.

"Was anyone with him when they picked him up?"

"A tired hooker. She went down for questioning, but they had nothing on her. They kept him and let her go."

"Did they have evidence to hold him?" I asked.

"Not really. He'll be out in twenty-four unless they come up with something to connect him to the scene more than his car on Parker."

"Thanks, Reilly. Can you message me when they release him?"

"Sure."

I walked away from Daffy's feeling empty and more worried about everyone I had ever encountered. My ex-wife Del was right to take Jessica and set up in Seattle. She was right to stay away from the poison and toxic waste that clung to me.

As I came out the door, I was surprised to see the Bentley across the street. I walked over to the car and Carlos held open the back passenger door.

CHAPTER 41

I switched on the intercom and said, "Carlos, I'm having a Scotch." He nodded his head. I poured two fingers

"Where to?" He said.

"Drive around the block a bit. I didn't expect you."

"You're on the payroll. I got my orders."

"Don't you think the Bentley is a tad conspicuous?"

"It is. For today. To get you home safe and sound."

"Oh, and getting shoved into a fight cage is considered safe and sound?"

"Don't know about that, Mr. McQueen."

"Carlos. Call me Jack."

The built-in phone rang.

"That's for you."

I picked it up. Waited for someone to talk.

"I hope you are not sulking," Ekaterina said. "And thanks for accepting my offer even if you were reluctant."

"Turns out I'm on the street as you predicted."

"Some men at some point just cannot handle pressure, Ekaterina said. "I assume you have looked in bag?"

I hadn't. I said, "Yes. Thanks. Have you dealt with Lana?"

"She is with Uncle Sergie. I pulled her from school."

"So, Katrin, I still have those commitments to deal with. Did you call for a reason or are you checking up on me? I'm not a dog that likes a collar."

"Relax. You passed interview, your words. You are hired. I will tend to family. It is all up to you."

"Thanks. I appreciate the ride."

I hung up and said to Carlos, "Have you worked for the family long?"

"For ten years. Ever since her father escaped Russia. I come with him. No other place for me. Grateful."

"Carlos sounds Italian or Spanish."

"Parents named me Yolya. I never liked name. Chose Carlos. Strong name."

"Head over to the east side. Take your time. Toward Parker Street."

Sadness sunk into my heart. Back on the mainland, the world seemed more like a puppet show. Behind the curtain, strings attached to puppets, attached to strings attached to other puppets, and on and on. And the most unfortunate puppets were the poor who had no strings to pull.

"Is there much poverty in Russia?" I asked.

"Mr. McQueen. People don't know about poverty here in North America. Poverty in Russia? It is where we find junk no one wants. We walked streets as children trying to sell junk for kopek. We find rusty bent nails on road. Bang them straight with rock and sell them. We find car part in ditch. Not know what it is. Sell it to bone man who pulls wagon behind bicycle."

He paused for a moment and then said, "My sister and I dig hole with sticks to bury our mother. We cannot dig deep. Ground too hard. Frozen. Dogs come at night and take her. I cannot talk about it, Mr. McQueen. We do not know poverty here."

We drove the east side streets, passed empty warehouses and industrial blocks, and passed dilapidated two-story row houses with slanting verandas, and weed-strewn patches that once were grass. People sat at windows and smoked; eyes glazed with despair. Many wandered the sidewalks and the streets as if a psychiatric ward had been purged. Some shouted and waved their arms in the air. Many women stumbled in the road lost inside their last hit. Vulnerable. Did they not sell junk that had no value? Were they not dead meat walking?

"Carlos. Take me back to the city center and drop me there. Pick me up at the same spot. Give me your number and I'll call you."

"Sure, Mr. McQueen. Why did we go to the east side?"

"I needed a fix that reminded me what I fight for. Maybe we can talk and share a drink."

Carlos dropped me off where I told him, and I watched him pull away before I headed toward the Undertown hospital. He'd got me wondering who Katrin's father was and where I currently fit into this bizarre landscape.

The morning was still early, and I found two hospital beds pulled together. Murphy's breathing gear was gone, and she appeared as if asleep. Mindy was on the other bed in blue flannel pajamas. She had curled into a fetal position facing Murphy, holding her hand as she slept.

I sat beside them and listened to their breathing. I was in the Wolf mother's warm breath cave. Stacie came up behind me. She had a coffee. She looked at my face and sadness fell across her eyes. She handed me the coffee.

"You need this more than I do." The cup's warmth enveloped me as did the breathing. Stacie got another chair, and we watched Mindy and Murphy for a while, then turned toward each other in silence and shared our coffee.

"Lots to tell," I said.

"I bet."

"Conner's dead. Suicide. Blew his head off in his own car."

Stacie didn't speak for about a minute. Looked at the wall and back to me.

"Reilly?"

"So-called task force is gone. Reilly has been shipped to central to do paperwork. The two other whizz kids have been sent to internal affairs. I don't exist."

"You're alive, and Murphy's coming back. I can sense it. You could both be dead and for what?"

Her soft hand was on my wrist, and I wanted to hold her in my arms. I wanted to cry. Jack McQueen wanted to cry.

"I could walk away."

"I know, but you can't, can you?"

"No, I can't. I've come from Daffy's and breakfast with Reilly. He will still do what he can. I phoned Becky at home. She wasn't pleased but she agreed to investigate the paperwork on Conner and the GPS information on the Sokolov car. Do you have anything?"

"Yes, but first do you want to tell me about the face?"

I reeled out the entire evening.

The emotion behind her eyes tried to shift into neutral without success.

"I don't trust her. She's playing you."

"I don't trust her either. I don't like her. But now that she's a client, I'll go with it and be wary. What have you got?"

"Mark found the foster place where Peter and Kat were taken. It's an institutional foster house, more like a large group home. It still exists. Mark and I decided after Mark couldn't get through the front door, we'd try a different strategy. B and E always worked just fine when face-to-face didn't."

She reached into an army-surplus shoulder satchel, a square pouch with a flap cover. She pulled out two folders.

"Haven't had a chance to look them over closely. See if you can find where they went from there."

"Where's Mark now?"

"He's on a roll. All fluffed up about breaking in with me. I think he's normal now. He's found the place you were taken to but is lying low. Observation only."

"I'll call him."

I heard sheets ruffle and looked at Mindy who had rolled over and rubbed her eyes.

"Morning, Sunshine," I said.

"What time is it?"

"Too early it seems for you. Thanks for the night with Murphy."

Mindy still held Murphy's hand.

"Oh my God. Oh my God, she's squeezing my hand. She's moving."

Murphy was tilted at an angle, so her head was higher than her torso. Her left hand, the one Mindy had been holding rose in the air. Her eyes fluttered and opened, and saliva ran from her mouth as she spoke, "Yes. Yag. Yes. Yag. Left hand."

Stacie was beside her.

"Murphy, can you hear me? Jack call someone. She is waking up. Murphy. Murphy. Can you hear me?"

Murphy nodded her head and blinked her eyes and raised her left hand up and down.

Three nurses appeared. They took control and we backed off. Mindy went to the bathroom and changed into her street clothes. Stacie and I waited. Once Murphy was calm, we were told we would have to leave. I bargained with the previous arrangement for Mindy to stay with her and talk to her, and they agreed.

We said goodbye to Murphy and Mindy. I bent over Murphy and kissed her on the forehead. Her eyes were closed, but she touched my arm with her fingers.

Outside in the alley, Stacie said, "Can you come back to my place?"

"I can't. I have something to do. I'll call you in the morning. I need space and sleep."

"You do that. Make sure it doesn't involve the Russian vamp."

"Do I detect jealousy?"

"Don't kid yourself. If you want to go off on your something to do, go right ahead, but don't come back tomorrow for me to sew you up. I can do a better job than they did, but I'm past all that. Do what you want. Get beat up all over again. I don't care."

She could have hit me with a sledgehammer, and I wouldn't have felt as much pain. I wanted a rebuttal but decided to let it slide. She stomped off down the alley to the street.

My burner rang. It was Becky.

"For some reason," she said, "there was no tox screen. Minimal information on the report. Dead by a gunshot to the right temple. Minimal gunshot residue on the opening."

"Is that it?"

"From what I could find. But I worked for Conner back in the day. He was left-handed—and shot himself in the right temple?

"Right. Thanks again, Becky. I'll send you my thanks in the mail."

"No worries."

"Oh, one more thing. Can you get as much as you can on detective Tad Reynolds? RCMP. He worked with Vancouver PD on a joint task force a year ago, then recently homicide. And did you get a chance to get the details on the GPS for the Sokolov car?"

"Not yet on the GPS and that better be a large package in the mail."

"Sweetheart, have I ever not come through?"

"No, but once in a while you've left a girl waiting."

"Trust me," I said and closed off.

Left hand. That's what Murphy tried to tell me.

I walked back to where the Bentley dropped me off, called Carlos and within minutes he was there. I got in the back seat and told Carlos where to drop me about four blocks from The Painted Parrot Guesthouse. Being careful about my own backyard was a good recipe for survival. I didn't want Carlos to drop me off at the house where I slept.

CHAPTER 42

I was up three flights at the top of the stairs. I held a knife I'd grabbed from the communal kitchen on the main floor when I came in. Slid it into the crack of the apartment door two feet down from the top. I felt the paper wedged there at the same height as I'd left it. Turned the key and was in. The sun hit the closed window and sent its light to the floor. Dust mites stirred up the world's sloughed-off debris. A bed never looked so good. I threw the tubular bag from the fight night on the floor and flopped down onto the mattress.

I resisted the Guinness in the fridge and the full bottle of J, I'd brought from the float house so many days ago, then I fell asleep.

The sleep was fitful, a trauma victim's nightmare. Car crash walk-away, blood dripping down a forehead. Body shakes and eyes so deep in sand-scrape I felt there would never be enough sleep to cleanse me.

The timeline was jumpy. I wanted even in sleep to nail it down, but that didn't happen.

I see the white panel truck. CPRC is on the side. The handcuffs. CPRC on a brass plaque on a brick pillar beside a wrought iron gate. Dark woods. A narrow driveway that goes on for miles. Chain-link twenty-foot fencing. A rolling gate. Razor wire.

> This is prison. Incarceration. The walk-in through gates and compound fencing. No grass. Gravel.
> Bleach smell. Beeps. Metal bars that slide open and shut. Uniformed men with unhappy faces.
> Shower heads in a row. Disinfectant. Nakedness.
> Fingers probe my anus. A hand cups my testicles and holds me in place. Paper slippers, clean underwear, and overalls. A cell.
> A guy in beige fatigues. Black steel-toed boots. A baton. Shiny.
> Two eyes stare straight into mine. Trooper hat and I can see

the bristle haircut, the flesh rolls on his neck. But it's the eyes. I've seen those eyes, without the facial hair, the age, and the extra weight. The Colonel stares at me and says, "Son. You're gonna be here a while. It can be an easy time, or it can be rough. You want it rough, just act as you did back on the farm, you fucker. Try anything and you will never get out here alive. Are you listening to me, boy?"

"You listening to me boy? You're not getting out this time. Remember me now?"

I was wide awake staring at the ceiling still in my clothes. Fuck. I saw the Jameson bottle on the table with a glass. I got up and poured one finger. Sat down on the bed and looked at the floor. Downed the glass in two gulps without savoring the whiskey. Poured another finger and sat in the wooden chair beside the battered oak table that was folded on hinges into a semicircle. This time I let a small sip slide down my throat and settle in my stomach. Outside it was still unusually hot. I stripped down to my boxers, and I was back in an institutional shower room.

Black and white mosaic tiles. My face presses against them. Black boots kick me. A baton cracks against my back. A bloody rivulet blends with the cold water running toward the drain. And I see the Colonel's smug smile morph back and forth from Colonel Sanders to the young buck with the shaved head and the fat rolls at his neck. "This little fucker's not getting out." And I see my stupid body hang on the razor wire. Two beige uniforms haul me down to earth. "This little fucker's never getting out."

"Wanna bet?" I say to myself. You wanna bet?"

I had slept less than two fitful hours. Should be sleeping now but I flipped open the folder that Stacie gave me before I left Undertown hospital.

There were two files. One was thick and one was thin. I opened the thin one first. Peter McQueen, ten years, six months, and the date of birth.

Thirty-four years old, now, three years younger than I. Like Kat who was his twin. I read the reports from the entry date into the foster home until seven years later. Incidents of bed-wetting, self-abuse—head bashing against a wall, holes punched in the drywall, small cuts on his arm with a fork, depression, memory loss, reclusiveness, low self-esteem, violence against others. The last file was a form that released him to a group home and an address, 177 Nichol Street dated eighteen years ago.

He'd been seventeen and a half. Six months from aging out.

The file for Katherine McQueen contained many psychiatric reports for suicidal attempts, theft, self-abuse, and eating disorders. No reports mentioned treatments. The last file was also a form dated at the same time as Peter's date. Same group home. 177 Nichol Street.

It was like they put out the garbage. Both, six months before their eighteenth birthdays when they'd be aged out. What could have gone wrong apart from being raised and abused by their parents? All three of us were damaged.

I poured another Jameson. Got a Guinness from the bar fridge. Slow poured. I almost hurled my stomach contents as I thought about Kat and Peter. I wondered if they were even alive.

I went back to the three of us in the forest after the abandonment. How we survived the woods. The wolves and our fear of bears, and how we returned home as if it never happened. But it had and we all knew it, especially me. And from that day I knew I'd lost what love I might have had for my father.

I remembered Sarah MacDonald told me that Kat and Peter went off in separate cars to separate foster homes. So how could they have ended up at the same home, and then when they were older found themselves at 177 Nichol Street?

It didn't make any sense unless plans had been made otherwise. I decided on a visit tomorrow to Nichol Street. Still not too hopeful since the last evidence about their whereabouts was seventeen years old. 177 Nichol could be totally different or not even there after seventeen years.

I found that I hadn't touched the last Jameson in my glass. I pushed it across the table toward the wall. I picked up the Guinness and placed it beside the J. I hunkered down with my thoughts. The phone rang. It was Reilly.

"Norton's out. I think they sweated him."

"Where is he now?"

"I suggested he go to a shelter and wait until you called, but I suspect he's asleep in the Tercel. Where are you?"

"I'm holed up until tomorrow. Licking my wounds."

"At least let me know where you are. You could also tell me where you've got Murphy. Why don't you trust me?"

"Reilly. I do trust you, but it's better I have somewhere safe that no one knows about."

"Screw you."

"Look Reilly, if they can get to Conner, they can get to anyone."

"What do you mean, get to Conner?"

"I made a call. An old informant. Got the autopsy information, skimpy as it was. Not much there, but did you know Conner was left-handed?"

Silence descended on the line. In the mechanical labyrinth's connections, I heard the gears of revelation grind.

"Yes, so you," I said, "and even the whizz kids, Commisso and Davin might be next. Watch your back. I have a personal issue to deal with tomorrow. I'll call. Maybe, meet at Daffy's later."

"Sure, you do that," Reilly said.

I could tell he was despondent. Not happy with me. And wrinkled-up Reilly was afraid.

"Reilly, hang in there. Keep a close watch on Reynolds."

I hung up. Called the burner I gave Norton. The tone rang almost long enough for voice mail then he picked up. He didn't speak.

"Are you there?"

"Shoot."

"Where are you?"

"Tercel."

"Figured. Were they rough on you at the station?"

"To be expected. Suffered worse. Kept my mouth shut."

Norton is more than he seems. Special Ops or maybe he's just quirky.

"Sugar?"

"I don't know. I swung by the park, but no one has seen her. When they picked me up, she was with me. They hauled her in, too, but let her go after a few hours."

"Are you saying that she's missing?"

"Not really. Maybe she's gone to ground. She's a big girl."

"Mitchell?"

"He is asleep in the park."

"Leave him there. Can you pick me up tomorrow morning at ten?"

I gave him the cross streets four blocks from The Painted Parrot.

"I'll be there."

He hung up.

I phoned Stacie to leave a message. Couldn't talk to her right now. Couldn't deal with the conflict she flung at me back at the hospital even though after I had time for it to settle, I knew she was right. She was always right.

I texted her.

Call Mark. Go to where he is staked out and see what you can find out. I don't want him all on his own out there. If it is any consolation, I'm on my own figuring things out.

I looked at the time. 2:00 a.m. I went to the window, an old wooden frame with sash cords on pulleys. I jerked it upward and managed to break the paint seal, so it opened halfway. Then I took the Jameson and the Guinness from the table and poured the two glasses into the eave trough. I switched off the lamp, lay down on the bed, and searched for sleep.

Everything came down to motivation. Even Mother Teresa had a motive. So did Superman. And I had a motive too. Characters came to mind—Katrin, Uncle Sergie Yasevich, the Colonel, Reilly, Connor, Reynolds, the Laskey brothers, Murphy, Mark, Norton, Mitchell, Mindy, and Sugar. All the images and thoughts were a surreal wash that sloshed around in my tired brain.

> I stand at a wooden fence in a neighbor's backyard. I look across a manicured lawn and through a sliding door. There are men on their knees with kneepads scrubbing the floor with brushes. They mop up black liquid that has spilled. They wear masks that look like well-worn brown paper bags, wrinkled, and tied tight around their necks like straw scarecrows. They look up and see me. I am vulnerable and afraid.

I awoke in a sweat. Thought guns. Thought about the bag from the fight. It lay on the floor untouched, unopened since they gave it to me. Katrin had asked me if I'd opened it. I'd lied.

I went for the guns. The Glock and the Beretta sat heavy with the cash. I eyeball counted it. I did the math. One hundred and fourteen thousand from the casino turned into, at 3 to 1 on the fight, three hundred and forty-two thousand, plus one hundred thousand from Katrin. It added up to four hundred and forty-two thousand. What was I to do with that?

CHAPTER 43

At 9:45 a.m. I stood at Colville and Brant, four blocks from The Painted Parrot. I hadn't eaten since Daffy's, over twenty-four hours ago and my stomach after it processed last night's J and G was in full rebellion. In the time it took to wait for Norton, I pulled out my notebook. The dedicated prose writers are always at their desks early and their butts are in the chair, and they write and re-write. Poets spend whole days living in the moment, letting the words and imagery swirl around inside them. Then words start to flow, and the poem beats them down the street. Some say the good poem, the lasting one, writes itself.

"Nature is a messy place.
When everyone is gone
who will be left to sweep?"

Norton arrived in his regular street gear on cue at exactly ten. He leaned over, released the door, and I hopped in. I threw the bag with the cash in the back on the floor.

"Breakfast first," I said. "There's a coffee shop up on the right."

Norton pulled away from the curb with a slight jackrabbit on the clutch and turned to me with a smile.

"Right, boss."

"Don't get me going."

He ran the gears smoothly through to fourth to cruising speed. Knows perfectly well how to drive. Didn't ask him what Sugar and he bought for their gig at The Margot.

The coffee shop had mostly cracked vinyl seats. Norton picked one that wasn't, and he used a napkin from the chrome dispenser to brush off the crumbs left by the previous occupants.

"Didn't know you were so picky."

"My mother was," he said.

"And you're living on the street, in the shelter, or in a dilapidated car? Give me a break."

"You're a little testy today," Norton said. "The face, right?"

"Leave my face out of it. How did they treat you down at the station?"

"Eventually I got the third degree. A duo. Bad cop and bad cop with cauliflower ears and dead meat between them. I could have dropped them even with the handcuffs, but where would that have got me. Not a smart move, right?"

"Right. Any more word on Sugar?"

"No, she's in the wind," he said. "No one's seen her."

We got coffee and I ordered a pancake breakfast with bacon. Norton got a traditional two-egg breakfast.

"Tell me about The Margot and the Laskey's," I said.

"We got all togged up. Don't ever make me shop with a woman again. Painful. Don't ask."

I left it alone and waited for him to continue.

"We walked into the place like we knew what we were doing. Ordered at the bar and then found a booth where we could see the whole place. Sugar made moves on me like that's how you act on a date, but I think she was too nervous to think about acting, so she fell back on what she knew felt natural."

Breakfast arrived, so he paused to eat and then started up after a few mouthfuls. I watched him. He was cautious. He always checked the room. He'd done that on the way in. Sized up the place. Noted details.

"The Margot. Fancy name," he said, "but it was a dive. Low-life, bottom feeders, and their squeezes for the week hang there. A few pool tables in the back. That's where we see the two other Laskey brothers. Laskey lookalikes. Limited gene pool. Prehistoric. Like sharks."

"What did you find?"

"We followed them when they left. Sugar almost peed her pants, but I figured she was safe with me, so I kept her quiet. Told her to slump down in the seat so no one could see her. The Laskey's drove a four-by-four truck. They went down to the docks on Burrard Inlet where the freighters come in."

"Make? Model? License plate?" Was he pulling my leg? I'd bet a thousand he got that.

Norton smiled. "It's all here." He patted his jacket.

I shook my head. Said, "One day I will strap you down on a chair and make you come clean on me."

He played dumb. Made a Scooby Doo "Huh." Cocked his head to the side and continued.

"Pier 31. Warehouse 204. Refrigerated freighter. The Santa Liberia. I tracked down the vehicle. Hummer. Plate T24976. Registered to William Laskey. The address is a condo on Marine."

"I know that neighborhood," I said. "What happens down at the Pier? I remember Sugar told me she overheard about a shipment, a dock number, and a time. Did she tell you about that?"

"She was too scared to talk."

"Okay. Okay."

"I watched." Norton said. "That's all. There was a covered gangway from the freighter down to an eighteen-wheeler with a container box on it. I didn't want to involve Sugar if there could be a conflict. Better to be off the radar until we know what's going on down there. I played it cool."

"True. So?"

"The Laskeys got out of the truck and went onto the freighter. It was dark except for a few bare bulbs on the ship. They were gone half an hour and came off the way they went in. No packages. Nada. Then they drove off and went to 2100 Marine. Underground parking. They stayed there for a while."

"How do you know they stayed there for a while?"

"I'd got a call back about the registration, so I knew where they were was home. Waited over an hour with Sugar snoring beside me. After all that time, I thought they'd be in for the night. Not so. The truck came out at about 3:14 a.m."

"About?"

"Yes. I tailed them to the wrecking yard and there they stayed. That's it. I went back to Salsbury Park. Let Sugar sleep. When it was light, I went to go to the shelter with Sugar and that's when I got pulled over."

"Norton, I know you are more than you seem. I meet you in the shelter waxing eloquent about the olden days and the infrastructure breakdown. No one listening. Pure bullshit, right?"

"Just for you, Jack. I spotted you right away."

"Right, my neat clothes. So out with it. You trust me now. Who trained you? Why the homeless act?"

"It's not an act. Figure it's the safest place to operate."

"And who are you operating for?"

"Myself."

I gave my head a shake. Said, "Why and who trained you?"

"Special Ops. Five years. But I'm done and on my own. No end to the causes I can sink my teeth into. Hell's corruption is all around us. Greed and mayhem. I do my small part to make a difference depending on who comes along. You happened to come along, and I had the nose on you from the get-go."

"Can I depend on you?"

"Have I ever let you down?"

"Nope." I threw down some bills for breakfast and a large tip even though I'd paid little attention to the waitress. "Let's see about 177 Nichol."

177 Nichol Street was as close to off-the-grid on the east side as you can get. The street was baking hot. Brown grass poked from the cracks in the asphalt.

The house was a two-story with a wide covered veranda that wrapped around the sides. The clapboard exterior was painted white, but peeled, exposing the grey wood beneath.

There was an ornamental foot-high fence that surrounded the front lawn and parched lilac bushes beside a concrete walkway that led to the steps. The steps and the veranda were covered with dilapidated green indoor/outdoor carpet. The front door was open and the screen door without a screen was ajar.

Norton followed me up the porch stairs and waited as I knocked.

On the first knock, I heard, "Hold your horses a minute."

Norton looked around for horses but found none and smiled at me.

The woman who came to the door looked fifty-five, a smoker. Grey-faced and wrinkled. She wore dated faded jeans and a loose white long-sleeved blouse with tails that hung out. On her head, she had a Grateful Dead bandana that concealed short-cropped hair or no hair at all.

"What do you boys want here?"

"Is this place still a group home? I asked.

"Who's asking?"

"I'm looking for my brother and sister. I have documentation that says they stayed here a few years ago. Can you help me find them?"

"Are you the police?"

"No ma'am," Norton said.

She looked at Norton sliding her eyes up from the shoes past his flak jacket to his hair.

"Guess not."

"I didn't get your name," I said.

"That's because I didn't give it. Most call me Molly, but it's Mary Skyler."

"Hi, Molly. I'm Jack McQueen. My younger sister and brother are Kat or Katherine, and Peter. Peter and Kat came here seventeen years ago. Were you here then?"

We still stood on the veranda. Molly stepped out past the door and motioned us to two old sofas against a curtained picture window. We sat. Norton first dusted off the surface. Totally OCD.

"Been here for thirty years. Seen them come and go. Seventeen years is a long time for memory, boys. Mind if I smoke?"

She didn't wait for an answer and pulled out a crumpled cigarette pack from the pocket in her blouse and dug out a zippo from her jeans, flicked it, and lit one. She blew out a short puff that hung around our faces. Norton waved his hand back and forth to disperse the smoke. I let it slide.

"They were in Hammer House when they were young," I said. "They would have come when they were seventeen and a half. Originally from the Island."

Molly looked at me as if she'd seen a distant nightmare. Eyes wide. Fag that hung on her lip and smoke that trailed into her hair.

"Jack. How could I forget a name they spoke every day?"

"Are they here?"

"You must be joking."

"Okay. Talk to me."

"Mr. McQueen."

I knew when I heard her start with Mr. McQueen, I wouldn't like what I was about to hear.

"You don't know how this system works, do you. 177 Nichol is a halfway house. When the kids are near to aging out, say, from Hammer House or any place where the government locks up kids with no parents, dodgy circumstances, suspicious backgrounds, or behavior problems, they're sent on to us.

"Government doesn't want them on the street until they're eighteen, so we get them. We are their last chance to get close to normal."

"Complete fuck-ups, right?" Norton said.

I gave a for-fuck's-sake look to Norton.

"First, I didn't make the connection that they were twins. But they talked about Jack like he was their salvation, because, God, they needed it. Don't know what went on in their childhood, but when they came to us, they were as you said—" She looked at Norton.

"Fuck-ups."

I didn't want the details. I knew enough already, and the blanks filled in would make it worse.

"I just want to find them, now," I said. "If you know where they are, you've got to help me."

Molly looked at me carefully.

"You sure you are Jack McQueen?"

"I'm their older brother."

"Prove it. Because if you ain't and you want them for the wrong reasons, I won't help anybody. They've got it bad enough."

"How can he prove it to you?" Norton said.

"Did they tell any stories? I can tell you one that no one would ever know?"

Molly took a long drag on her cigarette. Held the smoke a long time in her lungs. Then blew it out and talked at the same time.

"Tell me about the lunch pails, Jack."

The smoke punctuated each word.

Norton had a blank puzzled look on his face. He was silent.

I could hardly speak. The travel back was almost too much. I wanted a Jameson.

"He." I couldn't name him. "He filled the lunch boxes with stones. He drove us into the woods. From where he parked the truck, he walked us for hours and left us beneath a huge Douglas Fir that lightning struck. No one logged it since it had several crooked branches. I don't know how many weeks we spent in the forest with Kat and Peter frightened of the bears. I made traps. We fished. Caught small animals. We didn't want to eat them but did. We caught the water in cupped leaves overnight. Built fires from tiny sparks. I kept them safe and brought them home because at that age and at that time, we had nowhere else to go."

I let my head droop to disguise my emotion. To look into Molly's eyes and see her sympathy, would not have gone too well for me.

CHAPTER 44

In half an hour, we were in the neighborhood where Molly sent us. No street names. No streets but alleys, narrow routes only a small car could squeeze through, or narrow pedestrian paths were torn up by small motorbikes.

Molly gave us general directions.

I'd asked her how we'd know the house.

"You'll know when you find it, you'll know, Molly had said. "It's been a while. Information might be out of date."

Many core buildings were abandoned and now were settled by squatters. Houses were built upon houses. Attachments with found materials that sprouted up. Concrete blocks were salvaged or stolen. Corrugated sheeting served as roofs and siding. Wires for electricity and pipes for water and sewage were on the outside, joined and separated at junctions. On foot, we followed Molly's words from a paved street on the margins where we parked the Tercel, up an alley that we could have driven but decided against, then turned through labyrinth pathways where the earth was packed as hard as cement.

I recalled that the city council once voted to clean this area out but never got around to it. Once a portion was burned. Rumor had it that a developer had set the fire deliberately. The fire spread too close to homes with influence, so the fire departments from all the regions came.

In no time the squatters moved back.

Molly had said it would be a small house with a porch and a door. Four rooms. Wood. No paint. Salvaged lumber.

She was right. We knew it when we saw it, up in the hills with no vegetation.

I handed Norton my Beretta from my leg holster. He had a stern look. Took it. I kept the Glock in its holster beneath my loose shirt. Norton's signal was a can't-be-too-careful nod.

The porch was a crazy-paved wood sculpture, raised nails, bent screws, cross-pieces to hold rotten wood below, a surface that waited for an accident.

I motioned to Norton to cover the back and he moved around the side while I stepped up on the porch.

The door had a handle but there was no mechanism to open or close it. The jamb was wide around the door. As I pushed, it swung partially open, then stopped as it hit an object on the inside. I listened. Silence. I turned sideways and slipped through the opening. Newspaper stacks and filled green garbage bags were piled behind the door in the hall. Two rooms on either side. The inside stairs were in worse shape than the porch. An opening led to a small space at the back that looked like a kitchen. Hot plate and a naphtha camp stove. The rooms were corridors. Cardboard boxes, plastic bags, clothing, rags, and paper were piled as if someone took a full garbage truck and tipped it into two front rooms, and then people had made narrow paths through it all.

I walked through to the back, through rotten garbage. I found Norton poised at the back door.

"It's bad," I said. "All clear on the bottom."

He followed me in, Beretta in his hand.

At the bottom of the stairs to the second floor, I pulled out my Glock. Norton came up halfway. The stairs were a corridor with death-trap garbage piled on either side. Where did people get this stuff? It was worthless and it owned them.

I entered the room on the left but couldn't get further than two feet. Norton came up to the landing. I entered the room on the right. At the back among more paper stacks, stuffed toys, and garbage bags, was a single mattress. An emaciated woman lay there. Beside the bed on an overturned box were a used needle, a spoon, and a lighter. Medical rubber tubing lay on the floor beside the mattress. The woman was asleep in a cotton dress. Her hair stuck to her forehead in the heat. Track marks scarred her arms, and cuts and sores marred her face. Could this really be Kat? Could this be her? Could she ever have been that young girl I remembered?

From the left bedroom, a man emerged feral and protective. A baseball bat swung an arc at Norton who had his back to the wall on the top stair. Like a snake, Norton's hand flashed out, took the bat at the wrist and the guy was down—the bat tumbling down the stairs. I looked into the guy's eyes. I turned and looked at the woman lying on the mattress. I remembered them.

I didn't understand what hoarding was all about. How could anyone live in clutter? I didn't ever have many possessions. A dinky racing car with a bent wheel that I'd found in the gutter. I'd straightened the axle and it ran fine, but never was as good as a new one from a box. I never got new stuff from a box. Neither did Kat or Peter, so why did they turn out so differently? Some people said hoarding was OCD behavior. Addiction has so many causes and we had them all.

I phoned Stacie and she arranged an Undertown unmarked 'bus" for Kat and Peter. They didn't go easily. Who would after being evicted by strangers?

It must be something in the way she moved. Mindy connected with Murphy.

Murphy looked at me when I came in, and she sat up and smiled."

"She can slide her legs over the edge of the bed," Mindy said. "She's off the respirator and the catheter. She walks to the bathroom on her own, but she's not talking."

Kat and Peter were in another section. They were both sedated and restrained for now.

I called Mark to set up a visit at his stakeout. No response. Norton waited in the Tercel outside. I called Reilly.

"Do you have anything on the Sokolov GPS?"

"I was about to call. I got the coordinates within a mile for where he went each week." I jotted them down. "Jack, be careful. I can't get away, but rumor has it on the street, there are a few players gunning for you."

"No kidding."

"Reynolds wants you for the undercover cop's murder. He's playing the game. But that video will stop that. But others are searching for that video."

"Thanks."

"Be careful."

I closed off. None of this could happen without cooperation, collusion, and corruption at every level from the gutter to the penthouse. Flatfoots, to judges, to politicians. It had always been the same. Knock out one element and two heads grow back. Take out a dealer. Take out a supplier. Leave a space and in that empty space the weeds take over. Disturb the land and the invaders come in. Depressing. People preyed upon Kat and Peter all their lives. Good cops are manipulated and held hostage to real dark stains, or invented ones. Careers in the balance. What choices did anyone have?

I called Becky. Said, "Reynolds?"

"Been dirty for a long time. Machlan has got his number. That's all you need to know."

"Has he got a soft spot where we can open him up?"

"Let me dig some more." She hung up.

Commissioner Machlan. I shouldn't be surprised. If you wanted to keep cops in line, keep the head in line. If you wanted to keep the troops from rebelling against insane orders, put the colonels and the generals in your pocket. But it wasn't so black and white. There was always a motivation.

The passing of commander ranks in the forces takes me back.

I see the Colonel in full uniform lined up with the coffin tubes ready for their air-lift home. Men who trusted me. Men who trusted him. I see the faces. Feel the buzz in the air as the Chinook chops toward the ridge. Infrared sensors tell intel we're all clear. The summit is open to be taken. But the mountaintop is full of snow-covered caves, and the intel is wrong. And we are under fire in the dark, DshK 50 caliber Russian machine-gun fire. An RPG hits our tail, and we are down. Ten men with M4 light assault rifles. Pinned behind a rock ridge deep in snow. We return the fire, but we are no match. We're outgunned. We have no clear path. No answer. No air support. No bombers. No F16s. No medivac. But as well I have my sniper gun. I wasn't supposed to bring it, but I did. But what good is a sniper gun in close combat? What good are M4's against AK47s, Rocket Propelled Grenade launchers and a dug-in machine-gun placement? From the drop-down, after we are hit, three are wounded and the medic is operational but wounded. They stay with the chopper, while we scramble for cover behind the rocks under heavy fire. Six fighters remain against an unknown enemy who has been fortified for a long time. We wait for support that doesn't come. We are without radio contact, but they know where we are. The drones can tell them that. We know that if we stay where we are, we will die. If we retreat, we will also die. So, after four hours nailed to that ridge, we nod to each other and move forward on a run. We shoot and shoot and run. We take out the machine gun placement, we clean out the main cave, and we move together, aware only of the enemy and when the firing stops from the crevices and burrows in the mountainside, I stop. Hunker down with my M4 in my hands and the sniper rifle across my back. Silence. Deadly silence. The sun rises, but for now, I am alone. All my team is down. I do not know if anyone back at the Chinook is still alive. I see

172

all the faces when we first took off sitting in the chopper. I see the Colonel. His eyes are on me, as I see the Colonel in the casino, as I see him with his baton beating my naked body against the mosaic tiles in the showers at CPRC. Same man. Same eyes. Same menace. I know where I can place blame.

I went over to Murphy and gave her a kiss on the cheek. She smiled. I told her I had to go. That I would be back.

Mindy came over to me and said, "How about me?"

I hugged her close and kissed her on the forehead.

"Keep up the good work kid."

Before I left, I gave her some money for the cafeteria. The cafeteria down here in Undertown? People had to eat.

Norton drove me to the central train station. I made him go around the block, double back, and U-turn before he dropped me off. I told him to wait. I took the tubular bag with the money. Went to the long-term locker check. Paid with cash for a month. Stowed it and closed the automatic door. Kept the code card it spat out so I could claim it later. I copied the number onto a former client's business card and added extra numbers to the beginning and the end, then ripped the original into pieces and put them in the trash.

Norton drove me to the intersection where earlier he picked me up. The light had faded into evening. He handed me the Beretta. I stuck it in my ankle holster.

"Pick me up at 10:00 tomorrow. We'll do breakfast. Bring stuff."

"Sure boss. Bernardelli P-108." And although I didn't turn around, I saw his smile.

CHAPTER 45

Third floor. The Painted Parrot. I checked for the slip of paper in the doorjamb. It lay against the baseboard. The door had been opened. I backed away from the door and took one step down the stairs. Two muted shots passed through the door at chest height crossed the hall and entered the door on the other side. My Glock was out. I reached the three-way light beside the door, slid-bounced down the stairs into the darkness on the second-floor landing, and curled my body around the banister.

I heard a young woman's voice repeatedly from behind the door across the landing from my unit, saying, "Oh my god. Oh my god. Oh my god."

Below me, I heard a shoe pass across grit on the stair. Bannister pieces splintered beside me. I heard a dull pock of a silencer. At least two shots, one from above and one below. I was naïve to think I could hide in this city.

The door to my unit opened inward, so now back to the door, the guy peered with one eye down the stairs. I reached up with the Glock on the corner's edge with my left hand, took the Beretta from its holster with my right, and fired a shot with the Beretta down the staircase. A bullet snapped a baluster beside my head. I fired again then heard footsteps trundle down the stairs toward me. I aimed the Glock around the corner at knee height and fired three shots. No more footsteps, but rather a heavy weight tumbled toward the landing. I sprang forward and caught the guy mid-drop across the neck with the Glock's muzzle. His throat gurgled blood wept from his knees. I pushed him forward in a roll and let the body tumble step at a time down the stairs. I still held both guns. As his body in the darkness rolled awkwardly toward the bottom, the guy below came from the hall square onto the stairs and fired three times. I heard the dull pocks enter his partner. All sound, no sight, and I fired, no silencer, full reverberating echoes and I heard a body fall backward.

I ran down the stairs, stepped over the bodies and walked out the front door. Norton stood on the pavement before the steps. He motioned to a black H2 Hummer parked across the street.

"What?" I asked.

"I followed you back here. You can't keep me in the dark and it's a good thing."

"Right. So, where were you when they lit up my butt in there?"

"You'll see."

I pointed to the Hummer. "Is that vehicle available?"

Norton nodded.

"Then let's hurry and get these guys tucked in there for the night before the neighborhood gets curious. Neighbors will soon overcome their fear of gunshots and come out from their holes."

We acted quickly and hauled these guys across the street and dumped them into the Hummer.

Nobody knows how heavy bodies are until you must carry them. I drifted back to the wounded on the ridge before the airlift and how I hauled them from the chopper and prepared them for the rescue that eventually came.

"Lugging these men makes me realize what dead weight means," Norton said.

I looked inside the Hummer. A body was slumped over the steering wheel. I looked at Norton.

"I jumped in the back, and grabbed him from behind, but he went feral, pulled a gun, and fired it inside the car. My ears are still ringing. Can hardly hear you."

"And?"

"I broke his arm." I saw bullet holes in the side windows. "Then I asked him a few questions. Got the usual obscenities, and when the first few shots started, he jumped out on me, so I had to tackle him. I gave him a chance to tell me what was going on. He cooperated but it got crazy in there and he spat in my face. Let's say that was the last thing he did. What does The Slammer mean to you?"

By now the Oh-my-God girl was on the porch and so was Mrs. Sharpe, the landlady from the bottom floor.

I crossed the road while Norton got into the Hummer.

I said to Mrs. Sharpe, "I'm terribly sorry. Police business. We have some very bad men to take down to the station. I'll make sure the department covers this damage." I flashed her the standard police flip-out ID I keep for special occasions like this.

"Thank you, Mr. McQueen. If I'd known you were a policeman, well, I would have felt safer."

The young woman from across the landing from me moved toward Mrs. Sharpe and leaned her head on her shoulder. I turned and went back to the Hummer.

"Give me the keys to the Tercel and follow me."

I drove out to Laskey Brothers' Wrecking Yard. Parked in the dark close to the hole in the fence we'd made ten days ago. We carried the bodies to the fence, hauled them through the fence, and wedged them behind the rusting automobiles.

In convoy, we took the Hummer and the Tercel over the Lions Gate Bridge and up the Sea to Sky Highway. We stopped where there was a high point without a guardrail. Norton and I pushed the Hummer over the edge. It dropped a hundred feet into the gorge.

We got into the Tercel. I drove. "Shame we had to lose the Hummer," Norton said, "just so we can ride in this piece of junk."

He smiled. On the way back I told him about The Slammer but not about the money.

CHAPTER 46

Norton tried to sleep in the Tercel with me. I snored. He left. Then my phone woke me.

"The plate number you phoned me late last night," Becky said, "belongs to a guy called Jason Rivers. The documentation says Colonel Jason Rivers, retired Armed Forces."

"Thanks, Becky," I said, still half asleep.

"You sound chipper? Did you sleep in your car?"

"Now you're a mind reader?"

"You sound weary. No one sounds like that unless they've been beaten up or they've slept off a hangover in their car. Besides, you forget I know you too well."

"You're close to the truth."

"I'm still waiting on that package."

"It's all good. The money is in the vault so to speak. Just need to get my hands on it when the time is right."

"Sure. I will believe that when I see it arrive on my doorstep. I'll message you the details. Address. Vehicle registrations." She hung up.

I called Stacie.

"Are you still pissed at me?"

"Damned right."

"Where have you been?"

"I've got clients you know," she said. "You're not the center of the universe."

"Okay. Simmer down. I need a favor. Norton and I need to get cleaned up. Can we use your apartment?"

"Is that all? Sure. I'm not there. Knock yourselves out."

"Might need you later. You know, ready, right? I'm meeting Mark at his stake out. I can't reach him by phone."

"Right. I'll drop everything." She hung up.

Was that sarcasm? I'd have to wait and see.

I called Norton's burner and told him to get over to the car. We drove to Stacie's apartment. We entered the lobby with the key that Stacie gave me when she was in a better mood. The door was kicked in and the contents were tossed. We showered first, then I called the superintendent. He came up and fixed the lock so we could secure the place.

"If Stacie was pissed before," I said, "there's no telling what her mood would be in the future."

"They were looking for the video," Norton said. "You didn't see inside but I bet the Slammer guys had another reason to be in your room at The Parrot."

"The Painted Parrot."

"Right, as if the correct name makes a difference right now," he said. "It's all unraveling."

"Because we are getting too close for someone's comfort. Let's find Mark and we can check out the GPS coordinates for Sokolov's days off since they are both in the general area."

I sent Norton out to the Tercel and before I left, I took a kitchen knife and unscrewed the plate on the outlet where I'd stashed the video. It was still there. I called Stacie and left a brief message,

"Someone broke into your place and messed it up a bit. Super fixed the door. Don't go back there just yet."

We had breakfast and headed out using the GPS coordinates for the location that Sokolov visited four days a week. They took us to where the delta started as the river came from foothills in its journey from the interior mountains. Flat rolling land with peaks in the distance. As we climbed toward the foothills the cultivated land gave way to forest and meadow. The GPS took us from the highway onto roads that curved and wound into more rugged terrain. I phoned Mark. Still no answer. The GPS took us on a private, unpaved road a tad wider than the usual logging spur.

Norton suddenly applied the brakes. The Tercel tilted on its nose, wheels skidding on the gravel. I nearly smashed my face on the dash.

"Norton. What the hell."

"Do you see it?" he said.

Mark's Pinto was covered with bracken fern and spruce bows in a clearing beside the road. Norton jumped out, Bernardelli in hand. He ran toward the car. I struggled to keep up with him. He was tactical. Peered inside. Checked underneath. Slid the passenger door open. Popped the latch for the engine. Lifted the hood a fraction. Peered in. Then opened it all the way. I surveyed the interior. Didn't touch anything. The interior was clean. No Mark. The hatchback behind the back seats was clean too, except for a blanket.

Norton shrugged and looked at me. We both formed the same fearful question. Norton also looked in the hatchback.

We got back into the Tercel. Norton drove until I saw the forest open into a meadow. Across the meadow was a wrought-iron gate attached to a six-foot brick wall that stretched as far as we could see. Norton took the Tercel through a break in the trees in extra low gear over slightly uneven ground to get us off the road and out of view. I checked the GPS and we had arrived at where Sokolov spent those four days a week.

"Is it a coincidence that Mark was staking out a place where I was taken as a child, and it is connected to the current case?"

"Freaky," Norton said.

I remembered. We drove the road that crossed the meadow to the gate. Beside the gate was a pillar with a brass plaque, CPRC, Crime Prevention Recovery Center.

> I am in the van, handcuffed and I see the plaque for the first time. You're not listening to me boy? You aren't getting out.

> My memory flooded back. I knew this place for eight years. Manual labor. Solitude. Rebellion and reprisal. Defeat and manipulation. The Colonel and the beaten boys. The Colonel and the broken toys.

Norton looked at me. "Have you been here before?

I turned. I knew the angry face Norton saw, sullen eyes heavy in their sockets, tense and drawn into a single homicidal focus.

The gate was locked and wired for automatic opening and closure. Norton ran at the wall and was on top and over before I could react. He came to the gate and from the other side boosted me up and caught me as I went over. More meadow stretched toward another forest and the road lead through it. We walked until the forest opened to a clearing.

And there it was. A four-story brick building. The factory that enslaved me.

Around the outside was a twenty-foot chain link fence topped with razor wire.

"What goes on in there?" I asked.

"Whatever. That's where Sokolov spent his time."

"Do you figure Mark's in there?"

Norton nodded.

"Do you plan to climb a twenty-foot fence with razor wire?"

"Nope." From beneath his flak jacket, he pulled the bolt cutters that Mark brought to the Laskey Brothers wrecking yard.

"You carry everything in that jacket."

"No. The cutters were under the blanket in the Pinto. I helped myself and slipped them under my coat."

"And you leaped a brick wall with those? You could have died."

"I have carried more gear than that and had to move fast in tight spots."

While we bantered, Norton managed to cut through the fence. We ran across the open ground and pressed our backs to the building's wall. There was no one in sight. No towers. No guards. It was eerie. Nothing had changed. The concrete surface around the building where we marched was the same. I recognized the grassy field where they ran us and trained us for combat.

My heart thumped in my chest. Calm. Breathe. Count.

Norton was in a cocoon. We edged along the building. I tried the first door. Locked. Tried the second door and it swung outward.

No one was inside. There were corridors with bars and cells in the entire building. We went up three sets of stairs. The story was the same. On the fourth floor, windows let light into each corridor. We looked down. There was a container truck backed up against a loading door. We couldn't see much except its back doors were swung open wide and the container was pressed tight into the loading bay which I didn't see when we scoped out the bottom floor.

"Did you see a loading bay on the ground floor?" I asked.

"It must be separated from the cell area."

Norton tilted his head toward the stairs, and we descended. We approached the wall that separated the loading bay. We listened. Not a sound.

Norton said, "That truck? Could be the same one I saw at the pier."

"Too many trucks in this city. What would be the connection? We're chasing shadows."

"It was dark," Norton said. "The cab was white. I saw a red star on the cab door."

I got jumpy like we had been here far too long when we heard an engine start up outside.

"That's a PACCAR MX-13," Norton said.

I looked at him. "What?"

"The engine. It's how it resonates."

I got a déjà vu from Zabella Island and the stuff about Briggs and Stratton.

The truck passed the window on the right. White cab with a red star that hauled a rusty, brown container. The gates opened and it was gone.

"Let's see what's in that bay," Norton said.

We exited through the door, slid our backs against the wall, and kept below the windows. We came to the corner, and I looked around. The loading bay was flat with the ground and wide enough to accommodate the eighteen-wheeler's height, but the door was shut.

Norton cautioned me to wait. He went forward. I hung back and watched him work. From a deep pocket in his flak jacket, he pulled out a rectangular slab that looked like putty. I couldn't help myself.

"Now you're Inspector Gadget?"

Norton snorted at me which I interpreted as an attempt at laughter, and he pressed a detonator and timer into a C4 explosive. Who'd have thought?

"It's running."

We both ran around the building's corner and down its length until we heard the explosion. Once the debris stopped falling, we went back to the loading bay. The entire door was a fragmented metal mess. The room was empty space with an industrial elevator door at the back.

Norton nodded and said, "You ready to go down with Otis?"

We pressed the button. The doors opened. We went in, guns drawn. We descended in the elevator. When the elevator stopped at the bottom floor, the door opened to solid black darkness. The interior of the elevator was well-lit, so Norton and I pressed ourselves against the walls beside the open door.

We both sprang forward out of the elevator's bright overhead light into the void. Norton on the way out took out the light with a shot from his Bernardelli. I was in an empty space in a room. I let my eyes gather light, but nothing came. I always wanted reincarnation, not this. Norton hadn't moved. No sound. No light. The air was tinged with iron, and a smell fetid and stale. I sensed the room was large but cluttered. I listened to my heartbeat and my breathing. A gun discharged across the room. Muzzle flash, followed by a retort of chipped concrete behind me. Silence. I sensed Norton was no longer close. How many gunmen were in the room? Not too many or we'd be dead. Norton was so unpredictable. Where would they be? There was the lone muzzle flash without further movement. I imagined the room based on the distances from the muzzle flash and the bullet's contact point. Rectangular room based on what was above me. I predicted the positions if I were among the gunmen. They would have spread out. Covered the angles from the elevator. The muzzle flash was at ten o'clock, so I swung my focus to twelve and two.

The room lit up bright white with an explosion. Norton had detonated more C4. This ran through me in a nano-second, the echoing sound, the remaining light, muzzle flashes, and the crack of Norton's Bernardelli. I fired at twelve and two. Darkness. Dust. Debris rained down in arcs from the ceiling. Silence and then a shuffling sound, movement, then silence again. I waited. Darkness. The void. Maybe the void was what was really left out there for those not lucky enough to find peace in heaven, or maybe for the faithful, life's largest disappointment. I wanted to call out to Norton, but I didn't.

A hand touched my shoulder as Norton's lips whispered in my ear.

"Jack." And he walked off. A few seconds later the lights came on. The room was filled with hospital gurneys arranged in pairs with curtained partitions. In the center where the C4 exploded was a twisted hole. We walked the perimeter, Norton one way and me the other. I found two dead men dressed in security uniforms. Gunshot wounds. One more man bled from a wound in his abdomen.

Norton met me here. Said, "Two more back there. They're not talking. Something's wrong with their throats." He smiled. It was serious. He was more hysterical than funny. A smile like a nervous laugh. "We are alone now."

I bent down to the guy on the floor who was bleeding out. A sharp object had entered his gut several times and the main artery inside his upper thigh had been punctured. I grabbed his head and held it tight and looked into his eyes.

"Buddy. You're going to die. You are bleeding out. Nothing can be done. Do something you can be proud of before you go. Who runs all this?"

The guy's eyes were fading. I slapped him on the cheeks.

"Come on, son. Speak to me."

A gurgle came out with a blood trail that slid across his face towards his ear.

"I'm not going to see my mother, am I?"

The words were slurred but recognizable. I felt sad about his question. I said, "You've got a chance. Just tell us."

His eyes flickered, and his face changed from a person with a dead mother, maybe family somewhere, a woman who loved him, to worms' meat. He shuddered and said, "Colonel," as his face relaxed and his body settled into the floor.

"Do you know this particular Colonel?" Norton said.

"In many ways, Norton. In many ways."

I thought about this place. After I'd used the hatchet in my hand back on the Island, they sent me here. The Colonel was in charge. The Colonel replaced the man I thought was my father. The Colonel groomed me for the forces since there was nowhere else to go. The Colonel sent us to the ridge and to our doom. The Colonel waited for the bodies to be returned. And now again he is here in the middle.

"What is this place?" Norton said.

"We've stumbled on a factory while searching for something else."

Mark was in my mind.

"Factory? Looks more like a hospital."

"An organ factory," I said. "They're harvesting organs. Acquiring transplant material."

We wandered among the empty gurneys, smeared with dried blood. Did we arrive between shifts? So, Sokolov came here four days a week fearful that they'd take his daughter the only precious thing left to him. He came and took the organs from donors and placed them in recipients. But where were the donors? Where were they recovering? Where were the recipients being monitored?

It didn't completely add up. What did the eighteen-wheeler bring? What did it take away? And who was really behind all this? The Colonel? Or was he another guy in the system of corruption for everything that had gone bad in the city?

"I've heard there's big money in that," Norton said. "People go all over the world to get transplants they can't afford here or can't even get because the wait list is so long. I heard a stat that said most people who wait for a kidney die before their number comes up. People get desperate."

"We have to find Mark."

I looked for interior doors that led from the room. I opened one but it was a supply room. Tried another and it led to a corridor. The corridor was lined with cells. Not the kind with bars but solitary cells with steel doors with slits for a guard to peer in and a double slide compartment at the bottom to pass food through. And I remembered I'd been here before. Naked with one blanket and a steel slab for a bed and a hole in the floor for a toilet.

Norton followed me. We checked each cell, slid the narrow windows open, and looked in.

At the last cell in the corridor, I slid the metal shutter on the observation window. There was a body lying on a slab at the back. I turned the handle on the steel door. It opened. I slid the bars across and walked in.

Norton hung back at the door. Said, "Putrescine. Methanethiol, Cadaverine."

I choked back at him. "Stop it, Norton.

The body's chest had been opened from the neck to its lower abdomen. All the organs were gone. The eyes were empty sockets. There was surgery around the joints where ligaments had been removed. I bent down close to the face. The body belonged to Mark. I stopped numb, then bent closer and kissed him on the forehead, my tears falling on his cheeks. This was my best friend and I had sent him here.

I left this cell, but this cell would never leave me.

CHAPTER 47

Later that day, Norton dropped me off at The Painted Parrot. He wanted to stay with me, but I sent him away in the Tercel to wherever he went at night. He said he'd look for Sugar at The Margot. Told him to call me if he got a lead.

When I got through the front door, Mrs. Sharpe came right out into the hall before I had a chance to slip upstairs. She had near lost it with worry about the gunshots and the holes in the door and walls. I gave her money, more than enough to replace the doors and get a drywall guy in to patch up the walls. With the cash in her hand, she finally left me alone, but she'd let me know she still had a bone that had not yet been picked enough and she'd sort it out with me tomorrow.

The girl on the third floor behind the door opposite mine peeked out as I got to the landing. Asked if I was okay. I said I was. I lied. Gave her a smile.

I had never needed the Jameson more than tonight. Thought I'd go easy but the more I got to thinking, the lower the line got on the bottle.

Each J burned down my throat and hit my empty stomach like Norton's C4. I had a lot to sort through and I needed to be alone. I realized too that I'd had the burner cell off the whole time. First, I took the business card with the encrypted code for the locker at the station from my jacket and slid it between the drywall and the baseboard beneath the bed. No sense to carry it around and have someone find it and figure out what it was. Then I checked my messages.

I found the usual suspects—Reilly, Stacie, Katrin. I read them all first.

Reilly's said, "Call me." And again "Jack, call me." And the last one, "All hell is breaking loose. Get back to me."

Stacie's said, "You are bad news. Don't think I can keep doing this. The trashed apartment. You weren't kidding. And where are you?"

Katrin's text said, "It's been over two days. I thought we had an agreement. You're working for me, remember? Call me."

Was it me, or was everyone cranky? Right now, I didn't want to return anyone's message. I thought about Mark back in the day. How he helped me through the break-up with Del. How he was always there. Gave me a place to hang out. Understood the trauma I'd suffered without the details. Details I'd not known myself at the time. How eager he was to do work for me when I called him. I thought about the engine oil smell blended with Scotch we last drank together and the fear in his eyes and the anger and panic that came through, and my promise never to put him in harm's way again. And how I'd failed. I'd placed him right in the center and he had nowhere to turn and run.

I shot back the J and poured another. I wanted to pound my fist through a wall. But Mrs. Sharpe would have my nuts in a sling. And she was such a nice tea-cozy lady. I suspected though she had a darker back-up style as we all do.

We'd left Mark on the bed in the cell. Felt ashamed I did that. Couldn't risk it. Norton was right to call me on it. We left him. Inside the cell, nothing more could be done to him that would reduce his dignity. He was long gone, and his body was the shell that held him. Yes. I kept telling myself that one.

I took another sip of the Jameson. It helped. I found yellowed newsprint lining the armoire I'd never used. Ripped them into squares. I wrote down names from memory. Colonel Jason Rivers. The ballpoint pen scratched the dusty paper's surface. Yazhov. Yagoda. Commissioner Machlan. The last two Laskey Brothers. Reynolds. Conner. Reilly. Commisso. Boyle. Stacie. Kat. Peter. Ekaterina Yasevich. Lana. Uncle Sergie Yasevich. Brigit Murphy. Sugar. Mindy. Norton. Mitchell. Robbie Mayne. James Harris. Mark.

How did all these players fit together? What were their stories? I laid the names out on the floor beside the table.

What did I know? I knew that The Colonel was connected to me. He set me up at the fight club. He tortured and abused me at CPRC. He ordered the mission when I was in the forces. He was involved in whatever was happening at CPRC now, on the freighter at the pier and with the eighteen-wheeler with the red star on the door. And the red star was like the Laskey brother's tattoo.

The video soundtrack named Yagoda and Machlan and connected them to the beating laid on Murphy and me, and to the undercover cop's execution in the unmarked cruiser outside the mutilation crime scene.

Reilly mentioned Yazhov and Yagoda in the same sentence on the way to interview Ekaterina. Machlan as police commissioner was untouchable. Did he pull all the strings or was he, like many cops on the force compromised and acting under duress?

Where did the Laskey brothers and their wrecking yard figure in? Reynolds? Was he corrupt or merely a hard-nosed copper who tried to fit into corruption's culture, so his ass stayed safe?

Becky called Conner's suicide a murder. Murphy heard me. Murphy was more with it, as she came out from her coma and remembered Conner was left-handed. The button I no longer had that I found in the loading yard could be from an orderly's or a doctor's lab coat.

Reilly was being squeezed and forced to be obedient. Benched. I trusted him. And what was happening that he was in such a panic?

Commisso and Boyle. They came as a pair to Reilly. Didn't get re-assigned that way. Not sure where they were at. Were they merely young coppers feeling their way from the academy?

Stacie was too good for me. I shouldn't have left her in the dark and expected her to be there when I needed her. I'd screwed up.

Finding Kat and Peter addicted and living in a hoarder's house troubled me. It would take time for them to change. All three of us were broken toys.

Could I trust Katrin? Was she using me? Murphy made me weep. Mindy by helping her was helping herself. Sugar was missing and I wondered if she was in the same place as Mark, Robbie Mayne, and James Harris. Norton was deep water in a silent pool. I trusted him with my life.

I jotted all this down on the newsprint and thought about how this all started with Murphy's call to come over and help her solve Mikhail Sokolov's murder. I processed through writing. That's how I wrote poetry. Had hardly thought about writing these days despite Stacie pestering me to get my poems published. That all seemed so trivial. So out of context, but it wasn't. It was the way I saw the world. The way I coped.

I leafed through an old notebook that I still carried in the duffle bag. A poem from last year.

Angels for Missing Children

They have been left,
three shadows holding hands,
short, stunted stumps
along a logging road
deep in a wood that won't
be cut for many years.

Never has the forest been
so still, so dark.
Even the salal whispers
in the wind.
Night birds,

187

a spread of wings,
a comfort
as the children walk,
knapsacks with no food,
hearts weighted-
down with stones.

Before morning
it will rain, no time
to think of bears.

I called Stacie and I was sent to voice mail.

"Where are you? Call me back."

I rang Ekaterina. No answer.

I called Reilly. Said, "So, why are your shorts on fire?"

"You have been MIA for three days. You've obviously been away from the downtown, or you'd know what's happened."

I heard the stress in his voice. "What's the panic?"

"Four more mutilations. Bodies were left outside City Hall. Laid out flat and parts nailed into the lawn. Same M.O. as with Sokolov. All the organs were gone. The eyes. Even major ligaments. We crossed the John Does with missing person reports. We have matches, connected to four surgeons. Two prominent men at Vancouver General and two at St. Paul's."

"I haven't heard any details," I said. "There must have been some cover-up by the force?"

"Damn right, But the media are asking questions. We've got everyone working on this. The mayor's got a standby request for military deployment if this leaks out. It's a hushed-up state of emergency waiting to explode. No one is investigating. We are too busy keeping a lid on this."

"What can I do?"

"Stay safe. The official story is four bodies dismembered at City Hall. I'm afraid if fear runs high, we will have a control issue. We don't want vigilante groups targeting anyone suspicious on the streets. In the suburbs, people have bolted shut their homes and armed themselves. The complexes like the penthouse condos where the Sokolovs live are on emergency security. So, stay safe."

Immediately after I hung up from Reilly, the burner went off. I expected Stacie or Katrin, but it was a voice I didn't recognize.

"Jack. They are coming. You have two minutes. Get out. Back door. Across the lawn. Over the fence. Corbett Road. Look for a Dodge Ram. Stay safe."

I started to speak but the connection went dead.

CHAPTER 48

Once I heard the police sirens, it didn't take me long to trundle down the stairs to the main floor, run through the kitchen, out the back door, across the lawn, hop the low ivy-strewn, rusted fence, cross the back neighbor's yard, and emerge on Corbett Road.

I saw a black Dodge Ram with the monkey paint job at idle a hundred yards to my left. I called Norton. He didn't answer but the call went to voice mail.

"Listen. I am about to be picked up by a black Dodge Ram truck, a Laramie 2W on the plate."

I slipped the phone into my pocket still connected.

The truck approached and the back passenger door swung open. "Bang" by Gorky Park, a Metal Glam, a Russian band blasted through the cab. I entered hell. If I had to listen to the entire album, I would ask them to shoot me. I got in. Beside me was a guy bigger than a fridge. At me, he leveled a GSh-18, Russian, military, and KBG issue.

"Buckle up," he said in a thick accent.

I did, even though I didn't believe he cared.

In the front passenger seat was a smaller guy who weighed in like a side of beef labeled "Avoid me too." Behind the wheel was Carlos.

"It is pleasure to see you again, Mr. McQueen."

"Where's the Bentley?"

"That is another job."

"And this one?"

"You will see."

Carlos pulled away from the curb with a flourish. I sat in the dark and stared out from the tinted windows at the scenery. "Hit Me with the News" replaced "Bang" and I sunk into the lower depths. We left The Painted Parrot's blighted neighborhood, houses in disrepair carved into rooming houses for those who couldn't afford shelter bigger than eight by eight. Houses one step away from a shantytown or quiet corners in an alley beside a dumpster.

The truck cruised through the darkness. Warehouses sat abandoned but despite the heat homeless folk hung out in the shadows beside oil-can fires. Hollow eyes stared from lean faces with bodies draped in massive overcoats. We were still in the furnace. The weather hadn't broken. The rain seemed far away, too far away to wash off the grime, misfortune, and despair.

"Your boss lady, Mrs. Ekaterina, not happy, I hear," Carlos said.

"Seems that way. Don't work well with a watchdog," I said.

"Who does?"

I looked at the fridge guy beside me. Said, "Do you have to point that at me?"

He grunted.

"Small handgun," I said. "Bedside toy for a nervous householder."

Thought that would raise his hackles.

He grunted again. The disrespect went over his head. Carlos laughed.

"He got orders. I think you scare him."

"Sure," I said.

We crossed the Cambie Bridge and entered the city. From the bridge, the city looked deserted and lonely. We descended and passed a strip mall with smashed windows, and looters who rushed around in a parking lot dragging anything they could grab. The lost and deprived souls in these uncertain moments were getting their brief revenge.

"Cambie Bridge gives a good view," I said. "What's going on, Carlos?"

"You have not heard. Four bodies found dead at City Hall."

"And where are we headed?" I played to the open line on the cell phone, hoping Norton could hear this.

We cut off Cambie toward downtown but skirted the center. We headed for the docks where the freighters loaded in and out.

"Less violence here leading to the docks," I said.

And then Carlos became aware.

He applied the brakes hard and spoke Russian to the guy in the front seat beside him. The guy jumped from the passenger seat onto the sidewalk and opened the door beside me. The guy's fist came at me like a leg of frozen lamb, and I was out cold.

I gained consciousness with my head inside a black bag. A ship's horn blew in the near distance. My bound wrists and ankles restrained me to a chair. I knew intuitively that my Glock, my Beretta, and the burner phone were gone. My head attempted to keep up, but the pain still pulsed in my ears.

Whatever place I was in, swayed back and forth in the darkness. There were people here in the space, but no one moved.

"Mr. Jack McQueen."

I knew this voice. Smooth. Soft-spoken. Measured with untouchable confidence.

"You have me at a disadvantage," I said.

"Precautions. Carlos and boys, I trust they treated you well."

"You might say that, but I need something for this headache."

"You were foolish, that's all."

Why did I not feel assured by the tone and the words?

The cord around my neck was loosened and the black bag was removed. I was in a very small room with little furniture except for a bare wooden desk and a chair. Anton Tarasov sat dressed in baggy brown pants cinched at the waist with an oversized belt. Off-white shirt with sleeves rolled to the elbows. He was dressed wrinkled and looked like an immigrant laborer home from a sixteen-hour shift.

I remembered the Tea House in Campbell River back on the Island when Stacie and I had met him for the first and only time. He'd worn a designer, grey, silk suit, and stood tall and imposing. Here he looked more like the repair guy in a failing shoe store. But I was not fooled. This man had many faces. A man who lived and acted with impunity.

"That's what I do," I said. "Stay one step ahead of the villains."

I sensed the lamb-leg fist coming toward my neck. Watched Tarasov, who tilted his head enough to call off his watchdog.

"You ever consider, how you say, charm school?" Tarasov said.

"It's right up there with wing-suit base jumping and swimming with sharks. On my bucket list."

"Funny man. Can I trust you?"

"Look at me. I'm trussed up like a chicken, here. What do you want from me?"

"You and what was girl's name? Stacie. Yes, you and Stacie came to me for help last year. I want your help now."

"Mr. Tarasov, from what I know, you do not need anyone's help, so let's get to the point."

The room swayed again.

"Is this your boat?"

"Ship. Boats are toys."

"A ship. A freighter maybe? One that makes you money?"

"We must make living. All creatures must be employed, or they do not survive, even me." He paused. "What is it like to carry dead body around your neck?"

I felt the weight of all that had happened. He knew everything I'd done. He had the tail I tried to shake. I stared hard at him. Carlos and the two guys from the Dodge Ram leaned against the wall.

"He was friend. This Mark. I had friends, too. They float with fishes."

He didn't know. He suspected. That's all. No proof of my past crimes. He suspected and understood. But he didn't forgive. I didn't either and he knew this.

"Leave Mark out of this conversation," I said.

"Maybe we should dance? Dance now when no one is looking?"

I understood the riddle but not the larger picture about where Anton Tarasov fit in.

"Maybe we could dance," I said and looked down at my wrists and ankles.

Tarasov motioned to Carlos and Carlos flicked out a Kizlyar Hero 440C. He cut the duct tape that bound my wrists and ankles.

"Now I can shuffle," I said ripping off the attached tape with a quick but painful swipe.

"I am at war," he said. "I fired first shot. War on drugs is dead. So where do hardened criminals turn to make money? To projects far uglier and without morality or dignity."

"The first shot?"

"Mikhail Sokolov, my son-in-law." Tarasov got up from his chair with his arms folded and leaned against the desk.

"Katrin is your daughter, and you would kill her husband, leave him like that and deliver his body parts to her apartment? Only an animal would do that."

"You discovered where he went to work four days each week. You found place where transplants were done. Not just by Mikhail, but many others."

I was stunned.

"Thousands of donors," he said. "Thousands of recipients. Very lucrative."

Might as well take a stab at him.

"So why kill Sokolov?"

"He was bum. No morals. Same as other doctors who do this. He treated Katrin like dog. Marriage was nothing except for granddaughter,

Lana. So, you see he was display model. Attention getter. I made them pay attention."

His words came too easily for me to be sure he told me the truth. I stood up from the chair. The two huge guys were tense, and Carlos was alert. I paced from side to side. Looked down at the floor and then up straight into Tarasov's eyes.

"Your display nearly got me killed," I said, "and a best friend has just woken from a coma, and I don't know if she'll fully recover. That's an ugly piece of work."

"That was not me. Since then, I have watched you. Helped you."

"Really. I can think of places where I could have used some help and believe me you weren't there."

"You had long leash."

"Well, I'm not your trained dog."

"I cleaned up after you."

"You mean?"

"Yes. Cabin would have been traced back to you and Stacie. Wrecking yard even after wolves had their way with refuse that you left was still mess. So let us say we mopped up. No bodies. No stories."

I felt like a fool, like a puppet who danced for a master with a master plan.

"So where are they?" I asked.

"Bodies? In safe place, until I need them, but that is for later."

"I don't understand why you need me. Why I'm involved in your that's for later."

"Your friend Murphy. She is strong. Tenacious you say. Would not leave it alone. I knew police from top would keep Sokolov's murder off headlines, buried like missing body. But Murphy cut against all that and then brought you in. I could not predict they would try to kill her. I did not hear about what happened until story broke that they were hunting you both for homicide."

"You have had me followed since then?"

"Once you were out on street, but you have been slippery. We lost you a few times."

I paced. The ship tilted back and forth with the waves. I heard the anchor chain. We moved in one direction, stopped, and then moved in the other. We were anchored in the harbor.

"Why bother? You have this organization with its muscle. Why bother with me?"

"You are distraction for them."

"Them?"

"Yazhov and Yagoda."

Tarasov moved behind his desk and sat down. He motioned me to sit.

"Bring chair closer."

I pulled the chair toward the desk. Carlos left by the only door and the two huge guys stood at the exit with their hands crossed in front like bookends. Tarasov reached into a drawer and pulled out the vodka. Stolichnaya Elit.

"Now to business,"

Tarasov produced two old-fashioned glasses. Poured the vodka. Slid one across to me.

"Na zdorovie."

"Slàinte mhath."

Tarasov downed the glass and I followed.

He poured another for us. He let his sit on the desk and I followed suit.

"Yazhov and Yagoda? It is hashtag for Genrikh Grigoryevich Yagoda? Soviet secret police. Appointed by Stalin. Responsible for purges, arrests, and Bolshevik executions in olden days. He is symbol name. No one knows who he is. But he is boss. No one has photo. No one sees him. Nikolai Ivanovich Yazhov. NKVD from 1936 to 1938, during Stalin's Great Purge. Yazhov is hashtag too. Not real but another symbol. Both are what you call mob bosses, organized crime heads. They do not call themselves these names. But others do. They are rivals. Yazhov wants to be big man. Yagoda has everyone in pocket. Police Commissioner. Mayor. Provincial ministers."

"You?"

Tarasov's blue eyes turned to ice. His face dropped as if a mask had fallen from its place.

"I have higher standards, Mr. McQueen. No one owns Anton Tarasov, even if I was not big boss. Big fish in large sea."

"Higher standards? And yet you killed your daughter's husband, your granddaughter's father."

I took a sip of the vodka. Not my favorite choice. But I was sociable.

"Have you never killed someone, Jack?"

I stared at his glacial blue eyes.

"Thought so." He paused. "Remember riots in Frankenstein movie? Crowds formed in streets. Torches. It happens now. I started process. Four doctors were mutilated. Organs gone. Eyes gone. I admit it is sick display, but effective. Another distraction."

"And these doctors?"

"Scum. Predatory scum. They do transplants with organs delivered by serfs. Slaves without choice. That's not business. That is like back in olden days. Experiments in concentration camps. Calculated deaths in gulag. All this run by both Yazhov and Yagoda."

I let Tarasov talk.

"I am little under two hundred pounds. Blue eyes. Good teeth. No problems with my thyroid. All blood is pumping. I am tall. Good long bones. I stay fit. Work out three days each week. Go to steam baths every Monday. Eat proper food. I am habit creature. Addicted. Both kidneys are mint Ferraris. My heartbeat is regular. Many other organs, Jack, like you. On market, I could be worth a few million. Big money. Big temptation for greedy wrapped up in manageable package."

Tarasov finished his vodka and poured two more and threw his back. I did the same. My head was spinning. It was not the vodka. Carlos opened the door. He was panicked but tried to cover it up. Handed a cell phone to Tarasov who listened and didn't speak. Handed the phone back to Carlos. His jaw muscles tensed.

"Take Mr. McQueen to room for night."

Carlos nodded and jerked his head sideways for me to follow. I did as I was told. The disaster was about to erupt in this small room.

Once outside in the corridor with the door closed behind us, I heard the vodka bottle smash against the wall.

CHAPTER 49

There were no windows, and the room was dark. A blanket smaller than my body struggled to keep me warm.

Carlos entered at just past dawn and took me to the galley for potato soup and bread. Strong coffee. Then we climbed the stairs to the upper deck bridge wing beside the wheelhouse.

Since Carlos came to the door, I'd decided to stay quiet. He'd been pleasant and clued in when I didn't answer.

Moments later, I said. "What was the news?"

Carlos stared out toward the city's east side. The sun crept across cobbled-together structures. I felt a strong need to get to the Undertown hospital to check in on Kat and Peter and see what progress Murphy had made since she woke up. But I knew it would be a while before that happened.

"You will have to wait," Carlos said.

Tarasov and the two huge guys came up the stairs to join us on the bridge wing.

Tarasov wore black pants, a white shirt open three buttons down, and a sports jacket. He was no longer rumpled.

"Come into wheelhouse. We talk," he said.

Carlos and the two guys stayed on the bridge wing. I followed Tarasov up the stairs, and we settled in around a teak table. He brought two coffees. I waited for him to begin.

"This body we all live inside is only parts. Business is booming. In past they rob graves. China sacrifices prisoners. Brokers bully weak people to give up kidneys. So much demand. People who want transplants go on vacations to India for their new organs because if they do not go, they die. There is great sadness in this. But that is history."

"But that's not what's happened here."

"Three hundred and sixty-six million suffer from diabetes. Kidney failure's leading cause. Then there is liver disease, and needs for pancreas, heart, lungs, intestines, eyes, bones, hair, and ligaments. Legal hospital costs only rich can afford. Only insurance plans can pay into medical economy that supports doctors, nurses, administrators, suppliers, and transporters. They all have stakes in commodity. It is like oil, gas, or gold. Raw material to be mined. That is above table. Kidney. Seventy grand. Liver over half million. Pancreas nearly three hundred thousand. Intestines over million. That is huge money that above ground system bleeds from human suffering because of high demand, low supply."

"This is not you, Anton?"

"No. No. I import some legal, some not legal. Make some deals. Simple crime. Not this. I have humanity. I am not animal to prey on weak. As young man in Russia I saw gulag where there was nowhere to run. Freezing cold. Laying bricks and cement to make walls that went nowhere. I know cruelty. I promised if I did not die, I would not be like who sent me there."

"I have seen the organ factory where Dr. Sokolov worked," I said. "Not your business, then?"

"There are layers. There are some that want to be big boss. That factory is small stuff. Quick return. Ugly. But there are places. Big business. And Yagoda runs these. No face. Everything secret. No one wants to know where body parts are from. Yazhov. He is small fish but like shark. You met Colonel. He works with Yazhov. Laskey brothers too."

"And Uncle Yasevich?"

"Yasevich. He is Godfather to my daughter. We were in gulag together. We escaped together. We came here together. He good man."

"And are you a good man, Mr. Tarasov?"

Tarasov paused and looked out the window to the bridge and the mountains beyond.

"I prefer to stay away from city, but city comes to me. I must change what I have helped this world to become. I am no angel and I have no illusions I will go to heaven. And I know to fight is futile because you cannot win against men in fancy suits."

I thought about power. Commissioner Machlan. The mayor. Cabinet ministers. The puppet master or masters who pull their strings. And here was Tarasov, a multi-millionaire gangster not entirely in the loop, a vigilante who tears down the walls and exacts justice. He wants to cleanse and restore an ugly world. I saw the pain in his eyes as he spoke. Was he genuine?

"And you want me to help you? A washed-up former cop who hates the force. A trauma victim who can't even keep his own life together. A small fish."

"Uncle Yasevich and his household at China Heights are dead. Katrin and Lana are missing."

I was stunned. I thought they would be safe. "Hidden or taken?"

I thought about Stacie and Norton. Mindy and Murphy. Maybe no one was safe.

"This was message last night. I know Katrin has hired you. Too many dead Russians now. And if Yazhov has them, he has me. But I have put bodies from cabin—Yazhov's men—at China Heights. He is now tied to this, so there is chance to bargain. If you have something someone wants then there is hope and you, too, have something. Some things that Yazhov and Yagoda want."

"You know this?"

"I have pieced it together, Mr. McQueen. I dump Laskey brothers' bodies when I find out where Yagoda is."

"Look, Mr. Tarasov, I am flattered you want me to work for you and solve the world's dirty problems. But tell me why I'd bother. Katrin hired me to find out who killed her husband and why. I have the answers for her. She'll turn up. She is more clever and stronger than she looks. She would never let anyone get close to her. I know this from my gut. So, I have no obligation to her, except to find her and tell her who murdered her husband. So why do you think I will help you?"

I stood like I meant business to conceal the bluff.

"Remember Stacie?" Tarasov said. "We would not want anything to happen to her."

I jumped up from the chair and reached over the table to grab Tarasov by the collar, but he slid his chair back and I was staring at a Glock slimline G43, six shots.

"Do not be foolish. Sit down."

He got up and moved around behind me as I circled with him, keeping my distance like a dog herding a sheep. Still holding the gun on me, he tapped on the door's window. Carlos nodded and disappeared.

"Whether you like it or not, I need your help and you will give it to me."

Tarasov motioned me outside onto the bridge. Carlos was back. Beside him was Stacie, hands tied together. She looked up at me as if to say sorry. I, full of poison, turned to Tarasov.

"I see you understand."

"I more than understand. If she is hurt in any way, you will too."

I looked down, and Carlos and Stacie were gone.

Underneath my exterior, I had been head-butted across my nose and kicked in the balls with a steel-toed boot. Underneath, Jack McQueen was not a person who forgot.

"I need you to find Katrin and Lana and bring them to me. I need you to find out who Yagoda is and where he is. I want you to kill him. But I want you first to kill Yazhov."

"Yazhov? You think while I'm in the mood for executions, I might as well do him too?" My sarcasm was not lost in translation. "Piece of cake.

You and your organization can't find them. Can't kill them, or you'd have done that already, but you expect me to be able to do it. I'd have to be crazy to buy into this."

"Not crazy. You see, our friend Murphy, detective who came out of coma, and her attendant, hooker who you want to turn her life around by giving her purpose. So noble of you. Yagoda has them so my sources say."

First, I'd taken one on the nose and been dropped by a kick to the balls, but now I was face down on the concrete with my kidneys battered, and spleen ruptured.

The two huge guys took me by an arm each and lead me down the stairs to the main deck.

Before I was lowered into a zodiac for the trip to the shore, I heard Tarasov say, "I will stay in touch. I hope in time you are still among living, Jack, for as long as I am anyway."

CHAPTER 50

On the high point on the Cambie Bridge, Carlos stopped the Dodge Ram, and handed me a paper bag with my Glock, the Beretta, and my burner cell. I looked across from him through the open passenger window.

"It is my job," he said. "Not personal. You do the right thing by Mr. Tarasov. He will treat you fair. Stacie too."

"And what about Katrin and Lana?"

"Focus on Yagoda and Yazhov. I will focus on them. That is my job too."

The automatic window slid up. The tires screamed and he was in the traffic. I looked out across the skyline to the left where the city center cast its shadows then straight ahead where entire city blocks were smothered in yellow, muted light. I holstered the Glock at my back and the Beretta on my ankle. I leaned over the rail and watched two tugs pull a barge toward the sea. I hadn't a clue where to look for Yagoda or Yazhov. I called Katrin's phone. No answer, not even a voicemail. I called Reilly. Commisso answered. I asked for Reilly, but he was out. Commisso didn't volunteer any additional information. I called Becky and even her phone slid to voicemail.

I put the phone in my jacket and immediately I got an incoming call.

"Jack." It was Norton. "I've messed up. I am with Sugar at Laskey Brother's Wrecking. We're pinned down here. Need help. Come quick."

I went to speak but the connection was cut off. I wanted to ask him why he didn't pick up on my cell phone clues when I was with Carlos, but he must have been busy.

Norton would give me details. Not hang up. He was not pinned down. They had him. A gun was pressed into his ear.

A cab dropped me two blocks from the wrecking yard. They were waiting for me. I took a circular route that left me at the cut in the fence where we had all first entered. I covered my nose as a rotting flesh smell hung in the air.

The last thing Norton was going to do was sniff around The Margot to see if he'd find Sugar. Probably his search led him here.

I slipped through the fence. The four bodies that we'd dumped two nights ago were among the piled-up automobiles. They were not the way we'd left them but had been ripped apart and eviscerated. Wolves.

I crept along the rusted metal canyon and turned a corner. I saw a pancake compactor. A crane swung a claw over a smashed truck carcass. The arm lowered and the claw picked up its prey and deposited it into the compactor. Another crane worked the same way only its cargo was destined for a shredder that spits out small metal and plastic pieces to be sorted and then recycled. This was a working yard with employees staffing the cranes, the compactor, the shredder, and the sorting machines. A noisy place.

Where were they holding Norton? The office or the Quonset buildings? I decided he was in a Quonset building, so I gave the activity a wide berth. I wondered where the wolves went in the daytime with everyone around and figured they would lay low away from the noise in a den among the rusted automobiles. I looked at where the cranes drew their raw material and chose a debris pile where I could see the crew and the cranes with sight lines down toward the Quonset huts and the office. I decided this pile was where I'd hole up, be vigilant and wait out the day shift. They'd be expecting me. They'd get impatient and play their hand, but not before the shift knocked off for the evening.

It was a long wait and the twisted cavernous hideout I'd chosen heated up as time wound toward the late afternoon. I looked up at a high angle and saw each crane operator gather up the cars for destruction. Men in hard hats kept an eye on the compactor and the shredder. The assembly line workers picked through the plastic and metal. The noise was deafening.

I tried to play the information from Tarasov through my brain. Something was off kilter. Time passed. Four o'clock. Five. Six. Seven. Dusk. A whistle blew. The machines stopped. The cranes stopped. The ground workers moved like ants that came together into a stream that led to the office. I waited. The yard grew silent. The jagged metal silhouettes made a Dali tableau.

I heard a four-cylinder engine tick off the scrap-metal walls. My Tercel slowly moved through a clearing beside the Quonset huts and came up to the wrecking yard into the open where the cranes had been working. Two heavy-set guys emerged from the front seats. I could make out two people in the back. No details, but I knew who they were.

The two guys had to be the Laskeys. They looked the part. Their shoulders were each as wide as a Frigidaire. Their Hawaiian shirts were wide open at the neck. Black chest hair. Gold chains. Bullet-shaped shaved heads. One had a bushy walrus mustache. The other sported a bum-fluff pencil line across his upper lip. Bruisers like their dead brothers. Like the Slammer. Like every street bully in every city in the world.

They were both packing handguns in shoulder holsters. Walrus opened the back seat door and hauled out Sugar. She was in bare feet. Her blouse was ripped, and her face had been used as a punching bag. She staggered against the car. Bum-fluff pulled Norton out from the Tercel. No flak jacket. His trousers and his plain cream-colored shirt were splattered with blood. They'd worked him over worse than Sugar. I wanted to drop both Laskeys with two shots, but that was too easy, and when things were too easy, something was fishy. I glanced over to the crane that fed the shredder. A guy came down the ladder from the cab. He had a rifle. My heartbeat drummed faster as I looked up at the crane that loaded the cars into the compactor. I saw the reflected light from the scope above the sniper rifle's muzzle that stared at me in the dying light. He was close so his aim was easily targeting my heart. Here I was, hunkered down and they'd known where I was all that time.

A golf cart came over a small rise and pulled up beside the Tercel. The Colonel stepped off the cart. He wore a cream suit, three-button double-breasted with a matching waistcoat. Not wrinkled but a linen blend. On his head, he had a natural toquilla straw Panama hat.

I heard his voice. "Jack McQueen. Thank you for coming so soon. Now step out or your friends will die. And if you are stubborn, you're one trigger's squeeze from death yourself."

I slid behind a metal panel. I kept an eye on the Laskeys and the Colonel.

"Don't be stupid, Jack. My man has a weapon with armor-piercing bullets, so don't even think about it."

"I'm coming out."

I had no clue as to what to do except get up close and personal.

"Throw out your weapon first."

The guy who was descending the crane's ladder was on the ground. He came closer to me. The sniper in the other crane? I had his position nailed.

The Laskeys had drawn their guns. Bum-fluff had an automatic pistol shoved against Norton's head. Sugar was on her own slumped against the car. Her teeth were clenched, and her hands curled into fists. I threw out the Glock. Left the Beretta in the holster at my ankle. Stepped out. The light had faded. Floodlights came on in the distance by the fence and the office.

Beside the Tercel was a fifty-five-gallon drum. I watched the Walrus light a rag and throw it in the drum. Light flamed up casting the Colonel and the Laskeys in a glow against their silhouettes.

I walked up from the wreckage to the Tercel.

"Hands behind your head," Colonel said.

His ugly mug was so familiar to me now that he looked like a character from a book. Flash glimpses crept into my mind from CPRC and the

Armed Forces. Out of his jacket pocket, he pulled a Glock 42 Subcompact Defender .380.

The Colonel gave a head signal to the Walrus. The Walrus gave Sugar a crack across her head and knocked her to the ground. She stayed down. He then opened the hatch on the Tercel. He pulled out three flimsy aluminum folding chairs and set them up in a row. He hauled Sugar to her feet and taped her arms to the tubes that supported one folding chair. Bum-fluff gave Norton the same treatment. Sugar became conscious. Her expression wasn't cowed. I caught Norton's eye. He was silent and deadly. The Colonel took the remaining chair and handed it open to Walrus.

"Grab onto it so I can give it a good kick." They did it, but their expressions showed bewilderment. The Colonel then leaned back and kicked the aluminum seat, so it hung together by a few rivets. "Rip it out of there." And they did. I had an ugly memory flash from CPRC.

A dark room. Musty. Dripping pipes and a chair.

"Never could discipline you at CPRC. All the other boys. If you gave them a beating, they'd fall in line. No bad behavior at dinner. No anger. Sure, some tears at night. Same in the Armed Forces, Jack. You went to a different drummer. I should have killed you then. My big regret."

The Colonel motioned to the Laskeys, and they grabbed me by the arms.

"Pull his pants down, boys." And they did. They taped me in the same way, and I sat with my bare ass hanging through the chair's seat.

"Do you remember this? I want to lay one more on you after all these years." I looked at him. I knew I had been here before. My heart raced.

"Never could stand a father killer. A mother killer. Did you smash her teeth out with a hammer? Did you give her forty whacks? Did you Jack? Incorrigible, I'd say. I thought the Slammer would kill you and it would be done with, but no. Do you think I didn't know about these guys' brothers? Had your name all over it. The cleanup. The Laskeys disappeared. The minute I saw you at the blackjack table, I knew I had to kill you."

"Fuck you, Rivers. Where are Katrin and Lana? Where's Detective Murphy?"

"You don't need to bother about them. You need to worry about yourself and your two friends here. When you trespass in a dangerous environment, accidents happen."

"Where are they?"

"If I knew, I wouldn't tell you."

The Colonel paced beside me in his fancy suit, fanned his Panama hat across his face, and waved the Glock 42.

"You've got what's mine and I want it back. The money from the fight club. I have angry customers who figure it was a set-up they paid for. And I bet heavily on the Slammer, too."

"Is that all this is about? Your lost money?"

"That and I'm missing these guys' brothers, and the grief you've given me my whole life since you've been a stubborn little prick that wouldn't lay down and take what he deserved."

"The money's gone," I said.

"You think Sugar will find a date after we finish with her? Could carve up that pretty face. You think your guy here will be any better off with his eyes gouged out and his legs shattered?"

This guy was crazy. I knew it at CPRC. I knew it in the army when I couldn't do anything except bend orders, take missions in other directions, and ask forgiveness later. I knew he would have us killed whether I told him where the money was or not. This was his performance. His stage. His theatre. We were expendable.

"Leave them out of this. They are innocents. Deal with me." I meant it. I was prepared to die.

The guy who came down from the crane stood beside a pile of tires a hundred yards from us. He held an automatic pistol. The darkness lay outside where he stood as the fire from the barrel lit up a circle with its wavering flames.

The Colonel motioned the Laskeys. "Tip him over."

They bent me by the shoulders with the chair attached forward so that my face and shoulders smacked into the oily ground. My bare ass in the air protruded from the kicked-out seat. A memory flash and a younger Colonel was beating a young boy, and the young boy was me.

The Colonel walked over to the golf cart and placed the gun on the seat. He stripped off his belt and moved in behind me. The firelight flickered in the darkness and shadows moved outside the light.

The first buckle's crack stung. Another and another. Tears came. An automatic release. I heard the Laskeys laugh. The Colonel's shoes became dusty with his effort and blood ran across my hamstring muscles. My strength was rage. I clenched my teeth and fists and pulled at the tape that bound me with all the strength I had in my arms. Each blow increased my resolve. The shadows closed in. Blow after blow from the belt's buckle bit into my skin. I heard a snap. The aluminum shafts broke from the chair. I raked my taped wrists across the shattered metal pieces until my arms were free. At that point, I saw the alpha wolf lunge toward the Colonel's throat. I broke the chair's back from the seat, grabbed my pants, and hauled them to my waist so I could move. I took two steps toward Bum-fluff who fumbled with his pistol, and I drove the jagged tubing from the chair into his neck. I latched onto the arm that held his pistol and directed his hand. I swung him toward his brother, put my finger on the trigger, and fired twice. The Walrus dropped with two bullets lodged in his skull. I ripped the tape from Sugar's wrists and shoved her through the Tercel's open door.

"Stay down."

I started to worry about the third guy and looked up. Norton had managed to tip himself over to make a smaller target. The third guy fired round after round into the dark, but the wolf shapes came toward him until he was buried beneath a snarling, growling mass of fur. I hauled Norton, chair, and all, to the Tercel to protect him from the sniper bullets that came from the crane. Bullets pierced the car's body and blew out a tire.

I saw the Colonel reach the golf cart. The alpha wolf and three others snarled. He turned the key, stepped on the accelerator, and fired the Glock in all directions. I counted six shots and the cart disappeared into the darkness followed by the wolf horde. I belted up my pants and got the Beretta from the ankle holster. Norton looked at me. Pointed up to the crane then pointed to himself. I went to hand him the Beretta, but he shook his head. He pointed to me.

"Cover me," he said.

I nodded. He slipped into the darkness. I fired two shots from Bum-fluff's pistol. Norton climbed onto the treads, slid up the cockpit's body, moved to the back where there was no window, and appeared on the cab roof. I fired two more shots from the Glock and focused on the Beretta. I moved to the Tercel and fired again. Norton swung out onto the crane arm, swung back, and brought his booted feet through the cab's window. In an instant, the sniper was in free fall to the ground. Through the flames, the dust pitched up from the body's impact. The wolves moved in.

Norton met me on the ground beside the Tercel. He held the sniper rifle. I told Sugar to stay in the car. Norton and I headed toward where the Colonel set out in the golf cart. I looked back to the Tercel. The Laskeys had become dinner.

There was enough ambient light cast by the bright floodlights from the fence line and the office building for us to follow. We did not need to go very far. The golf cart was in the light near the office. The Colonel was in the seat. He was surrounded by wolves that had made a bubble around him. The alpha was slightly closer inside the circle. He stared down the Colonel.

I let out a low growl. Norton almost jumped out of his shorts. I growled again and the circle parted enough for us to walk closer to the golf cart. The Colonel waved the Glock 42.

"Out of bullets?"

He glared at me.

"Colonel Jason Rivers. What have you been up to? Norton, here, tells me you have quite a sophisticated smuggling ring, one that rivals Yagoda, so I am told."

He said nothing. His eyes were wary, and his body shook. He stared out at the wolf pack's glowing eyes.

"You work for Yazhov, right? You bring people from all over the world in freighters and house them at the old CPRC site and here. Promise them money for their organs, right? Colonel, you can do the right thing. Tell me where I can find Yazhov. Tell me who and where is Yagoda. I can save you."

"Fuck you, McQueen. Call these wolves off."

"What makes you think I can control them? They look rabid and very hungry. You have nothing now. Give me Yazhov, Yagoda, and Machlan."

"What will you give me?" For a moment I reveled in the Colonel's weakness. But he was a disappointment. He was no longer the cruel strong man who beat me, who put me in solitary confinement, who sent me on missions destined to fail. He was a thin shadow in the darkness.

"I can give you a bullet before the wolves move in. Yazhov? Yagoda? Katrin and Lana? Detective Murphy? Machlan?"

He was shaking. "You've got it all wrong. Katrin and Lana weren't at China Heights when we killed Yasevich and his men."

"Why the attack?"

"He worked for Yagoda. But no one knows who Yagoda is. Yazhov doesn't know. We tortured the old man, but he didn't know."

"And Murphy and her caretaker."

"Caretaker?"

"Where are they? Who has them?"

"I don't know," he said. "We didn't take them."

"And Yazhov? Your boss. Where can I find him?"

The Colonel paused as if he had a heavy weight pressed on his chest. He looked directly at me, scanned the circle of eyes, and looked back.

"A bullet? You don't have to kill me. I can give you what you want."

"One bullet. Where does Machlan fit into all this?"

"He takes money from anyone who will give it to him. It's the only way he can survive, like most cops. They got mortgages, families, and debts up the yin yang. What choices do they have? After a while, it becomes so easy to swim with the stream. Turn an eye. Cover up. Human nature. Gets them every time. Jack, you never went there. No one ever got to you."

I looked at him pathetically rationalizing practical choices for a life of crime. No, what had been laid before me, time and time again, had never turned me away from bashing bullies. I may be dark, but I didn't live on the dark side.

"And the guys who can be named but can't be seen?"

"In two days, they meet. The mayor's mansion. The annual party. Clowns and Dolls."

I hate clowns. It's the costumes and the make-up. Goes back a long way to my childhood.

"What good does that do me if no one knows who they are?"

Time was running out. I sensed the wolves were restless. Could the alpha be trusted to keep the pack in line for a few more minutes?

"Everyone who runs this city will be there. Each year once a year they meet. Yazhov and Yagoda but neither know who the other is beneath the masks."

"Masks?"

"It's always a costume party. No one knows anybody behind the masks."

"You have been there, then?"

"Many times."

"Does Yazhov have a tell, one that can be recognized even in costume?"

The Colonel was silent.

"You'll let me live?" the Colonel said.

"For what you've done in your miserable life, you deserve to die. What's his tell?"

The Colonel squirmed on the golf cart's seat. He looked from side to side at the wolves' glowing eyes and then back at me.

"When he's nervous on the phone, he stutters his w's."

"Thank you, Colonel Jason Rivers."

I stepped closer to the golf cart. The Glock still had two rounds in the magazine. I pointed the gun at the Colonel's head.

"Please. You don't have to do this," he said.

I didn't have to do this, but I thought about the beatings, the man's pure malice, and held onto the fact that I never surrendered despite the pain. I thought about the utter disrespect he had for his victims.

Our eyes met, mine narrow and determined to have justice, his eyes, pathetic and pleading.

He waited. I waited. I saw a quick and deadly shot that would end his pain. Also, I saw the one bullet I could fire into his gut. I saw the surprise on the Colonel's face. I saw the blood, crimson/black in the reflected light as it spread in a wide stain on his cream-colored vest. I saw him as he waited, not dapper anymore but tired, and wrinkled, a little man in a wrinkled suit.

"You said a quick bullet."

"Colonel. I said one bullet. I have your bullet. It has my friend's name on it, and it will kill you."

I heard Mark talk to me over the desk while we drank his Scotch. I didn't pull the trigger. I didn't send that one bullet into the Colonel's brain, or into his gut. I didn't get down to meet him, animal to animal on his pathetic turf.

I wiped off Bum-fluff's Glock and threw it to the ground.

"Just to be clear. I didn't kill my mother. I suggest you drive that golf cart as far away and fast as you can."

I turned and followed Norton passing the wolf circle.

"You fucker, Jack," the Colonel said. He stomped on the accelerator. The golf cart careened on the soft dirt beneath the tires.

The wolves came directly at him. Some bounced against the golf cart's windshield. Others leaped from the sides and tore at the frame and at his fancy summer suit. The Colonel swerved and spun the golf cart in a futile desperate frenzy until the cart tilted sideways on two wheels, lost its balance, and rolled. Out of the wreckage, I saw the Colonel start to crawl toward us, his eyes wide with terror. I saw the wolves move in.

CHAPTER 51

Norton changed the tire on the Tercel. I started it up and drove toward the Quonset huts. Sugar was asleep in the back. Norton shot the brass padlock from the first hut's door, and we looked inside. The interior was divided into detention cells. Each cell was packed with human beings who sat with their knees bent in a mass on the floor. They were silent.

Norton looked at me. We did not need to speak.

We went into the next two Quonset huts and found the same scene. Norton shot the padlock from the last hut, and we walked in expecting the same again but were hit with a vomit-provoking stench that bent us over and made us stagger for the door. We collected ourselves and re-entered. Bodies lay stacked in rows, no body bags. They lay on the concrete with their chests wide open and their eyes removed.

We knew what had been going on. These were the discarded remains. These were bodies destined for the crane and the shredder. Not the day shift, but the night. The people in the other Quonset huts were waiting for their turn. Expecting to give a kidney so their family could live another year or two on the money. They did not expect to have their vital organs harvested and die in the process.

We closed the door behind us when we left. Norton climbed behind the wheel, and we started to drive across the compound.

Norton paused for a moment at the clearing where the barrel still smoldered. He looked up at the cranes and across the compound to the compactor and the shredder.

"That's what awaits them," he said. "That could have been us. It was their intention."

I nodded a grimace. Pulled out my burner cell and called Reilly. Norton drove us out onto the street, and we headed back to the city.

"The Painted Parrot," I said. "We'll let Sugar recover there." Then I directed my attention to the cell phone that was still ringing.

"Reilly here."

"It's Jack."

The last time that I'd got through to Reilly he gave me the GPS coordinates for the Sokolov day visits that turned out to be CPRC. That was Thursday. This was early morning, not light yet, Saturday.

"Where have you been? I messaged you."

"Yes, and I got back to you, Friday, but I got Commisso. Didn't he tell you?"

"Commisso's dead. Friendly fire. I don't believe it. Parts of the city are ablaze. This was the second night. All hell has broken loose over these mutilations."

"What do you mean, you don't believe it?"

"I am running my sector all alone. I know what Murphy was up against. No one to trust. Commisso came to me. Came across some money transfers. They led to Reynolds, and they connected to Machlan. He'd signed off on them. Kept in touch. But these riots have us stretched to the max."

"Friendly fire?"

"A team was out on the line arresting looters and calling in fires. Gunfire was exchanged and when it was all done, Commisso was down. Bullet through the head. The autopsy came up with a police issue caliber. Boyle was there but he didn't see anything. Neither did anyone else and no one's talking. I could have used you for some support, pal."

I liked the pal even though it wasn't a compliment, but it conveyed trust and right now there wasn't much floating around.

"I'm going to add fuel to your problems," I said.

I told him the story at CPRC. Skipped the freighter and Tarasov and gave him all the details for the Laskey Brothers Wrecking Yard down to the wolves and the transplant donors and the bodies. During the entire narrative, Reilly was silent. I sensed a psychic numbing going on in his brain. For him, this was as big as the holocaust, and he was spot-on. When I was finished, I let him know I was safe without letting him know where I was.

There was silence on the line.

"Are you still there?"

"I have no one I can trust to take with me."

"Take yourself and the forensic team. Keep it low on the radar. Those forensic guys have not given us false reports. They've been on the up and up. No reason to distrust them."

"You're right. I'll do that. Let's stay in touch. Every four hours, right?"

"Right." I closed off. I meant it but couldn't imagine being able to live up to the request.

Norton pulled up across from The Painted Parrot. I carried Sugar inside and up the stairs and lay her on the bed. She was conscious but she needed rest. I'd been awake since a nightmare sleep on the freighter Friday morning. Almost twenty-four hours. Norton was in the Tercel outside.

I'd get Mrs. Sharpe to look in on Sugar when it was a more respectable hour.

I lay down on the floor beside the bed and let myself drop off. I thought about many things, and one was breakfast.

CHAPTER 52

Nothing like bare linoleum pressed against your backbone to foster thought, and my butt still talked to me with a mean ferocity. Sleep was the only option, and my twitchy mind was dominant. In dosing off, there was fur bristling on the wolves' necks, lips curled, and bloody mouths. The Laskeys were gone with the same wind that carried them through life. The Colonel with his long-drawn-out obsession for cruelty, to his surprise, got what he deserved. I forgot to ask him who sent me to him when I was a boy. I had my suspicions, but I felt I'd never know.

So many dead Russians. Now Yazhov and Yagoda remained, and a few others pulled strings for them as well as corrupt young men who started their lives with bright ideals.

Stacie was held hostage on Tarasov's freighter. I would not forget.

Murphy and Mindy were missing. Katrin and Lana were missing. Sugar lay on the bed across the room. Norton curled up in the Tercel. I had to check on Kat and Peter. Call Becky. Find a clown costume. Go to Katrin's penthouse. Create a plan.

Tarasov said that Yazhov's operation was small compared to Yagoda's. Transplant lists were long, the legal process slow, the operations expensive, and the need critical. No options but to travel abroad, but that was history. Now it was made in North America. Made in this city. No need to travel. Do it here. Save money, cut the waiting list. Bring in the raw materials—

"Send these, the homeless, tempest-tossed to me,
I lift my lamp beside the golden door!"

Lazarus, Emma. "The New Colossus." Statue of Liberty. 1883. New York, New York.

But the lamp was a scalpel and the door led not to life and liberty but to the grave.

How did one get justice when the game's inventors controlled the world? Designed the contracts for players? Held all the sanctions? Manipulated the old rules which we used to live by?

In my mind, I slept with scalpels, frightened children, mothers with babies, bodies decomposing in shipping containers, grease paint and clowns, mangled metal, and ground-up flesh and bones.

It was not my sleep that gave me rest.

The late morning light woke me. I left Sugar asleep and went downstairs to the main communal bathroom. I took a shower, and I washed the dirt away, but the water didn't cleanse me.

I knocked on the door across the hall. The girl who I'd never bothered to ask for a name opened the door a crack, saw who it was, and opened it wider.

"It's you."

"I'm Jack. Next door. Sorry about a few nights ago. I need help. I have a friend. Her name's Sugar. She's been beaten up. She's asleep. Can you keep an eye on her and make sure that she is okay?"

I reached into my pocket and rolled off two twenties and handed them to her before she could even answer.

She hesitated.

"I'm Roxy. Sure. Ain't doin' nothin' anyway. No bad guys comin' for you again, eh?"

"No, Roxy. Thanks. No bad guys coming. I've made sure of that. Maybe drop in later once I am gone. Keep her company."

"Sure," she said and closed the door.

I was certain she would do what she said and not look at the money as a ticket to a party.

I woke Sugar up for a moment. Told her I had to go, and that the girl, Roxy, across the hall would keep her company. Sugar got it but was still too groggy to be coherent, so I let her fall back to sleep and went down the stairs to the front steps. Norton was asleep in the driver seat, head tilted back. I sat down on the front steps and called Becky.

"Becky, I got a favor to ask."

"It's Saturday. The check has not arrived in the mail. Sorry."

"Funny. I got money but can't get at it now."

"You say that to all the girls."

"Tomorrow night there's a party at the mayor's mansion. Everybody who's anybody will be there. Can you get me two invitations?"

"What am I, Ticketmaster dot com? Do you know what's going on out there? The streets are chaos. The police can hardly contain the mobs."

"I know," I said. "I got bigger problems. Invitations?"

"I'm not somebody who gets invited to this dolls and clowns party."

"You've heard about it? You know someone, right? Find out what the ticket looks like and forge them for me. I'm desperate. I'm talking lives here."

"I suppose you want this by this afternoon?"

"Tomorrow morning would be fine."

"I'll do what I can. No promises. Names?"

"No names. It's all incognito."

"Swing by then tomorrow at 10:00 a.m."

"Right. I'll double what I've already given you."

"Right. Two times nothing. I've kept track and calculated hours at my highest rate."

"Thanks, Becky."

I searched the web for clown costumes on the phone. Came up with Clown Crazy. Scanned the photos. Made decisions. Phoned them. I ordered Killer Clown, a black and white baggy outfit with a mask that had a red scar across the forehead. The other was a Black Widow Avengers outfit, sleek leather and I could see a delicious Natasha Romanoff taking care of business with kicks, punches, and flips. With grease-paint makeup, the costume could be converted to incognito. I arranged to pick them up in the afternoon.

I had the newsprint notes I'd scribbled in my pocket. Dragged a sheet out, ripped off a blank section, and made a list for Norton. A few instructions and errands. I crossed the street. The day's heat was on the rise, and it didn't look like this southern air's tropical blast would let up. I nudged Norton to wake him, but he was not asleep. He'd been watching me. He was sharp and ready for combat. I handed him the list.

"It's going down tomorrow night at the mayor's party. I need you to drive me around a bit today. Then run some errands. Make some arrangements. Wait for me to call. Got it?"

Norton looked at the list and the few sentences at the end then looked up at me.

"Got it, boss."

I jumped into the passenger seat. "Drive me to the Undertown hospital. Wait for me at the park. I'll come and get you."

CHAPTER 53

I sat beside the bed that Peter occupied in the Undertown hospital. His arms were thin and scarred with slices from his biceps down to his wrists. How could his life have come down to this? An attempt to control the emotional pain. A way to cope with unhappiness? Who was to know what hell had passed his way? He was always the sensitive one. Kat as a child had been demonstrative and histrionic.

On Shaplow Lake I see us on the water skis with Tyler who drives the boat in the early morning with the black water flat and strewn with mist. Or in the hot afternoons when we are no longer in the cages and our father and mother are drinking at the Duke Hotel in town. Sun glints off the water and the spray off the boat and the slalom ski creates temporary rainbows.

Moments sandwiched between the pain.

I held his hand and he looked at me.

"I'm your brother, Jack. We've been through a lot, right?

You are," Peter said. "It's the eyes. You might say we've been through a lot."

I didn't really want to know. My imagination did a good job on its own.

"We're going to get you better. I gotta work hard. You gotta work hard, right? You will have to want to do it, buddy."

He looked at me as if to say he'd tried this all before.

"Nothing good ever comes easy," I said. "I'm messed up, but I try. Many memories have come back to me. They ain't pretty. We all need to pull together here. Are you up for that?"

"I suppose," Peter said.

"It's a start, right? I'm going to see Kat, now."

I squeezed his hand, and he squeezed back, and I waved as I went out the door, feeling uncomfortable and helpless with the unknown ahead.

I entered Kat's room after a tentative knock. She sat in bed reading a People magazine. She looked up as I entered, but her expression didn't change.

"I'm Jack McQueen, your brother. Do you remember how I saved you from the bears? Remember how we walked out of the forest?"

She stared at me as if I were from another galaxy.

I wanted to weep.

"Can I sit down and talk?"

Kat nodded and I took a seat in the corner near the bed. She didn't want me close.

"What do you want to talk about?"

Kat stared at the wall behind my head. Her face was ruined, gaunt, hollowed out with scabs on her cheeks and forehead where the crystal meth had caused her to scratch her skin. I could barely see her former beauty beneath this devastation. She didn't smile and her eyes were blank. Her wrists were cuffed by padded-leather straps that prevented her from scratching the delusional parasites beneath her skin. Crystal Meth. Classic.

"Do you know me, Kat? Remember the painted raven?"

I saw a tear well up in her eye. I watched it slide over the eye's lower lip and meander through the crevices on her face.

"Like yesterday," I said. "I, too, have scars. Nothing will change that. I've been to therapy, and I remember."

"Hi, Jack," she said.

"Well, that's a start, kiddo."

"A start."

She leaned forward from the pillow and patted the blanket with her cuffed left hand. I moved forward and sat beside her outstretched legs beneath the blanket, and she bent at the waist and leaned her head on my shoulder.

"That's all I can ask for," she said. "But I need help 'cause I've fallen back every time I've tried. Believe me, I've tried."

"I believe you, Kat. I believe in you. So. Together. We will try."

"Yes, but people are creatures of habit. Even in a crisis, they have rituals. Things they must do."

We remained like this in silence for a while, as Kat gently rocked back and forth. She pulled me into her lower depths. Kat like Peter was a stranger to me after all these years. Finding them like this, not like when we were kids, left me sad and empty. I'd need to work at changing that.

CHAPTER 54

I found Norton in the park as arranged and he drove me to Clown Crazy. He had Mitchell in the back. A good sign he was at work on the list. I gave him money from what was left in my pocket and had him go in and pay for the costumes and a grease-paint kit.

Norton drove me to Katrin's penthouse. He let me out holding onto the costumes encased in black plastic bags. To cut the tension Norton jack-rabbited the clutch on the Tercel when he pulled out into traffic.

He knows how to pull my chain.

I called Reilly.

"Yes," he said.

"Where are you?"

"Apart from looting at night, things have calmed down. It's a mess at the wrecking yard, but we've kept that under the radar."

"Good."

"Forensics is here at the wrecking yard. They're bagging everything. I am keeping this under wraps until I find out who I can trust."

"Listen. I'm doing something risky soon that will either get me killed or tie everything together, but I can't tell you."

"Not this again."

"I'm serious," I said. "It's for your own protection."

"Protection my ass."

Reilly hung up.

Even though it was late afternoon, the sun burned the landscape.

I walked into the Sokolov condo complex through the triple-glazed glass doors into the security glass rectangle with the automatic door lock. The air-conditioning was immediate. Security sat behind a semi-circular mahogany, console desk. The same two guys as when Reilly and I first visited were on duty. The intercom clicked alive and one of them said, "Name and who do you want to see?"

"Ekaterina Sokolov."

"Your name?"

"Lieutenant Jack McQueen." I flashed the fake badge from my pocket at the glass in their direction.

"Mrs. Sokolov is not available. I suggest you call her."

I waited in the glass rectangle. She could be in the condo above the casino and the fight club, or she could be here. I figured here was the best bet, but as far as getting her to answer her phone, the odds were low. But I tried. The call rang off into voice mail.

I left a message.

"Katrin. I know you are there in the family condo. I'm downstairs. I know you are hiding out. Let me come up and I will explain. I've got the information that you wanted. You know. To earn my retainer, right?"

I waited. Nothing. Then I heard a phone go off in the lobby behind the glass, but it wasn't a phone at the console.

I saw Carlos come out into the lobby with a cell phone to his ear. He closed off and put the phone in his chest pocket and motioned to the security guys who moved toward me. The door was released automatically, and I was in. The guy went to pat me down, but Carlos waved him off.

"Come with me," Carlos said.

We didn't speak in the elevator. The doors opened directly into the penthouse condo.

Carlos motioned toward a black leather couch. He took a matching leather chair across from me. The room was huge with not much in it but the couch, a chair, and a polished, marble coffee table. Looked like green Swiss marble from the Alps. Must have been here when Reilly and I last visited but I couldn't remember.

"So, tell me what you want."

"Katrin. I need to talk to her."

"She's not here."

"So, why am I up here?"

I was trying to figure out Carlos. He worked for Tarasov. Drove Katrin's Bentley. The last time I saw him he dropped me on the Cambie Bridge in the Dodge Ram that had followed me for Tarasov's amusement. Whose side was he on? Whose side was Katrin on?

"What has Tarasov got you doing?" Carlos said.

It was not Mr. Tarasov, but simply Tarasov spat out in a disrespectful tone.

"Thought you'd know," I said.

"Hey, I'm just the driver."

"Sure, you are."

"What's in the plastic bags?"

I had laid them on the couch beside me.

"You want to know? You tell me where Katrin is. You tell me what you know about Tarasov then maybe I'll tell you what he's got me doing."

I looked into Carlos' eyes. Watched his face for a tell. He was not getting nervous. He was not worried.

"She's not here."

His eyes slid involuntarily to the side and across the room. A nano-second. There was a mirror slightly larger than a door. I swung my eyes around the room. Pin-point cameras were cleverly concealed within a picture frame, on the fireplace mantle, and built into the bookcase used for knick-knacks. Why would there be cameras inside the room?

I stood up and walked toward the mirror. It was solidly connected to the wall. But as I stood before the mirror, the steel wall it was attached to, swung open, and Katrin walked out dressed in tight blue jeans and a loose casual Piqué raglan pullover. Lana held an iPad. Behind her through the opening was a complete apartment. Her panic rooms.

"Maybe I should have stayed with you after all," I said, "then I would have been in touch."

"You will never know what you missed." As before she was stunning, lithe, yet muscular with a face that was hard to turn your eyes away from.

"I called. You never answered."

"Do you blame me? You know about China Heights?"

I nodded. "Who did it?"

Carlos rose from the chair and went into the kitchen. I heard him pour liquid into glasses and he came back with a tray. Three single malts in old-fashioned glasses and a lemonade in a tall glass with ice, and a woven placemat under his arm. He set the placemat on the marble coffee table and placed the tray on top.

Katrin sat in another matching leather chair and Lana bounced onto the couch, where I sat. Lara wore fleece leggings and a long-sleeved tee shirt. On her feet were fuzzy slippers. She reminded me of Jessica, my daughter in her bunny slippers before she grew up so suddenly. I drifted off to seeing Del, my Ex, and her off on the plane and wondered how Jessie had adjusted to Seattle. It had been a while since we'd been in contact. A thin curtain of remorse slid over me.

"Yazhov did it," Katrin said, taking a sip from the single malt. No worries, cold and calm.

"Not the Colonel?"

"They are all connected."

"And how does your father fit into these connections?"

"He is stepfather. I have nothing to do with him anymore."

I looked across at Carlos. His face was expressionless.

Lana sat with her iPad on her lap wearing her earbuds.

"So why would the Colonel and Yazhov come after you and your uncle at China Heights?"

"In army, collateral damage. One way to get at stepfather. No matter. If Lana and I had been there, we would be dead, so we hid."

"You know about this business?" I said.

"I run dance club, casino. Fight arena. No big deal. Small potatoes. No drugs."

I wanted to believe her but wasn't totally convinced. Everything about her spelled class. I wanted to tell her who killed her husband, but I was not sure how she'd react. So, I stalled.

"You came to tell who killed Mikhail? You came for something else, too, didn't you?"

I looked over at Carlos.

"Carlos," I said. "Who are you really working for? Where are your loyalties?"

I'd taken him by surprise. An abrupt jerk of his neck. A vacant stare at the curtains on the picture window, then he was calm.

"I am driver. I work for Mrs. Sokolov."

"Carlos," Katrin said. "You work for me. You drive Bentley. You look after me. Me. You stay close to my stepfather so I know what he is doing as far as he will let you know. You are loyal to me, not him, right."

The right was not a question, but a confirmation. I heard conviction in Katrin's voice.

"Yes, Katrin. I work for you. I do not work for Tarasov."

Again, no Mr. meant no respect.

Katrin looked at the black plastic bags containing the costumes. I decided to tell her about Stacie's captivity and Tarasov's instruction to me.

"Tarasov holds my partner, Stacie, captive on a freighter in the harbor." Katrin's eyes shifted toward Carlos then back to me. "Let's say the key men who work for Yazhov have been taken care of. Let's say no one knows who Yazhov is. He's a mystery. Let's say your stepfather wants me to find Yazhov and kill him, or he will harm Stacie, my partner. My answer is in those black bags."

"You know all this? This Yazhov without face?"

"I knew the Colonel most of my life," I said. "Took some time to remember everything. Let's say it was still difficult to put him down. And the other guys who worked for him? Well, let's say our histories crossed paths. Yazhov? He's just a name. And Yagoda? He's just a name. A nickname."

"You do not know this Yazhov?" Katrin said. "This Yagoda? Nobody knows these names except in my country's history in olden days. Carlos?"

"Nobody knows them," Carlos said, "but everybody fears them."

"There is a costume party at the mayor's mansion tomorrow. A clown and doll party. Seems they have one every year. I convinced the Colonel to tell me. He'd been many times. You ever hear about this?"

"No."

"I thought you'd like to come with me to the party. I got you a costume. Carlos can drive us. I have a plan."

A plan? Show up and see what happens. Norton's got a plan. My plan has as much chance as a picked scab of healing.

"It's okay. But who killed Mikhail?" She was not distracted by my omissions.

I looked again at Carlos. His expression was still blank, but he was not covering anything up. He didn't know.

"You are not going to like the answer. Your stepfather."

I waited. Watched for it to sink in. Carlos' eyes were slightly wider. Katrin's mouth broke into a thin smile, but she started to shake.

"Why would he do that?"

I glanced over to Lana who was still engaged with the game on the iPad. I told Katrin and Carlos what Tarasov had said to me on the freighter. The transplants that Sokolov did and the example he created would be a start to undermine Yazhov's and Yagoda's sick exploitation of the human condition. When I finished, Katrin got up from the chair and went into the panic room. She retched into the toilet bowl.

When she returned, Katrin signaled to Carlos, and he left.

She said when he was gone, "He has own room in building. He is my security. You are staying this time."

Her eyes were red, and her neck was flushed. She moved over to me and sat beside me on the couch. I looked over toward Lana and thought about Jessica again. Katrin leaned close and kissed me on the cheek, curled her feet up on the couch, put her head on my shoulder, and closed her eyes. At this moment I sensed she felt safer than all the days she had spent inside her panic room.

CHAPTER 55

I wanted to believe her when we came together again in the morning. The light caught its long journey of wanting down to the shadow her ankle made beside the cream sheets we mingled in. I wanted to believe her like a sensitive guy who strayed upon a young girl who looked fourteen, hung out at a laundromat, and looked for anyone to give her somewhere for the night. I wanted to believe her need. Her vulnerability within the niche she'd carved out for herself. I knew it could be lust. Her soft skin. Her eagerness. Her package. Her survival. But it was like the hairs on my neck when I'd entered a dark room when I thought I was alone, and I suddenly knew I was not.

"Sleep, Katrin. This is what we need to do. Sleep."

In the morning Katrin was drowsy. Her body was still insatiable in her want to touch me. I resisted and thought about Stacie. I was twitchy and felt the day's electricity ahead seep into my pores. I stood up and left Katrin unsatisfied. I pulled on my pants and walked out to smell brewed coffee. Carlos sat at a breakfast nook with its own wall-to-ceiling window that overlooked the city. He drank coffee from a tall white porcelain cup and read a soccer magazine. On the cover, a striker mid-air drove a curving ball into the net, the goalkeeper horizontal like a porpoise doing tricks but failing.

"I work for Katrin," Carlos said. "The other is surveillance. Undercover."

It was hard to pick out who played for what team without a program. I wanted to believe Carlos.

"I need to be somewhere for ten o'clock," I said. "Can you drive me and bring me back?"

He looked out the window as if the answer was out there. I wondered that too. City chaos on the east side. Reilly's strategy. Containment. Stand back and let it simmer down. Burn itself out. Small potatoes as Katrin said. While bigger matters far below the surface drove this world.

"Sure." He turned back to me.

After I had coffee and got fully dressed, I left Katrin still rumpled in her sheets, wrote her a note, and Carlos and I went to pick up the tickets for the

Clown and Doll Party from Becky. It was a short trip. Becky opened the door to her bungalow in a well-treed middle-class west side neighborhood surrounded by main streets where big box malls had not yet invaded. However, the area slid away as the gap widened between the haves and the have-nots. Her door opened a crack where chain locks were taut across the narrow opening. I saw one eye. A hand passed the tickets to me in a narrow beige envelope. I thanked her and she told me to be careful. She rubbed an index finger and her thumb together to indicate money. I didn't want our relationship any other way.

Two blocks from Becky's place we slipped into a diner. Rosie's. We grabbed some breakfast. I'd forgotten when it was the last time I ate. I ordered a two-egg breakfast. Carlos did the same. We sat in a booth. The place was almost empty with lunchtime only an hour ahead. The creatures of habit had not arrived. Or maybe with the recent news people had hunkered down.

"Do you know Tarasov's plans for Stacie?" I did not expect him to know.

"He is not into hurting women, but he wants Yazhov dead."

"Will he be at this party?"

"Not that I know of. Too risky. Not his thing."

He did a shift with his head and looked out the window as his sentence wound down. That gesture didn't instill confidence. I was not sure I could find Yazhov in a haystack of clowns let alone kill him in a public place like the mayor's mansion. But Tarasov if it fit his worldview was capable of anything.

"Tell me what you know about the Colonel and the Laskey brothers," I said.

Carlos was a neat eater. He moved his food into special sections on his plate. He tucked the toast underneath the eggs so that when he cut into the sunny-side yolks, they bled into the bread rather than ran all over the plate. The hash browns and the bacon had their own sections far away from the egg yolks.

After he finished a mouthful, he looked up.

"Arch-rivals. Tarasov said Yazhov and the Colonel with the Laskey punks are a small operation, but they're not. Yazhov? Ruthless."

"And Yagoda?"

"He is smoke, like vampire. Whole war is because of him. I am sick of Russians being scraped off sidewalk."

"Katrin and Tarasov?"

"Stepdaughters always hate their fathers. No difference. She does not tell me stories, but I know."

I weighed his words. So many players are caught in a greedy violent web. Yazhov. Yagoda. Machlan. Politicians. Katrin.

We finished. I bought Carlos his breakfast. On the way back to the penthouse I began to think more about my fear of clowns. What lay beneath? What dwelt inside of me?

That night, Carlos was dressed in livery, but with a clown face. He drove the Bentley inland to the city's breadbasket. Here beside huge factory farms, this neighborhood was populated by oilmen, corporate CEOs, film stars, multi-millionaire sports figures, and media celebrities. This was not the suburbs, but a collection of estates whose mansions were the domain of those that moved and shook the local world. We were a long way from The Painted Parrot and the shelter where I first met Norton. Great structures loomed in the distance from the road, surrounded by wrought-iron fencing, privacy gates with cobblestoned driveways, mown grass, sculptured fountains, and landscape lighting. We passed security cars that patrolled the streets.

As we went deeper into the neighborhood, the lots got bigger, and the mansions became grander until the paved road lit up like it was the fourth of July. We left all these dwellings in the dust like so many small potatoes as Katrin would say, and we were alone on a private drive that led to the mayor's mansion. I'd googled it. Twenty-nine thousand square feet on two hundred acres surrounded by a rounded river rock wall. I thought that they had laws for harvesting river and ocean rock. Maybe the laws were only for the rabble and not the elite.

Katrin was stunning in her leather Avenger suit that fit her like a glove. My mind saw her in the mirror with the soft leather tracing all the sensuous parts. No underclothing. She didn't want to spoil it. She planned to enter with a flourish.

I was the killer clown. Black and white. Not grotesque, but scary in the mirror. A mask with exaggerated teeth. Red mouth like a wolf salivating after a kill. Baggy folds in the costume with deep pockets. My Beretta was in its ankle holster. I left the Glock in the car with Carlos. Katrin had a whip to go with her outfit and a concealed carry Kimber Micro in a black leather sling purse. Carlos in his uniform was packing.

The sedate grounds were frenzied with gaudy, eight-foot ceramic clown statues placed on the lawns that led to the entrance. Clowns and circus entertainers on stilts prowled around blowing fire from their mouths. Acrobats leaped and somersaulted in all directions. Clown bands competed on the front lawn. I wanted to call it a yard, but mansions don't have yards. Unicycles and horns. Pranks and banana slips. We drove through this as if it were the surreal rocket scene from Coppola's Apocalypse Now. For tonight this was the mansion's mansion, and this was the infamous Clown and Doll Gala.

Carlos pulled up to the front where the columns loomed above us. There were hunky footmen dressed in red-suit jackets with long tails, black waistcoats with white buttons, and black pants. Their physiques told me they could have come from an Abercrombie & Fitch catalog except for the white-face clown make-up.

Katrin stepped from the Bentley like she'd done this before at a Russian palace or summer dacha in the olden days. I climbed out the other side, still hurting from the pain suffered at the Laskey's wrecking yard. I was not elegant but then I never was. This place scared me. I sweated and became itchy.

I hesitated outside the Bentley, took a deep breath, and tried to stay calm.

"Park it," I said to Carlos. "See if you can nose around. I'll call you if we need help."

He pulled the Bentley away smoothly. I thought about where Norton was and if he was ready.

Katrin held my arm, and we walked past the footmen who were more than footmen for the evening. I felt her body's seductive sway as we entered.

Through the foyer we were ushered by the last two footmen, past two drawing rooms on either side and entered a stately ballroom, its span supported by plaster columns.

She moved around the outside, clowns and dolls parted as she approached. I tagged along. A clown band, saxophones, lead and bass guitar, and Los Payasos scribed on the bass drum kit, played "I, Who Have Nothing" with the lead singer, a Puddles look-alike. The song was slow and depressing. The dolls and clowns groped each other on the dance floor. The guy did a good job with a vibrant voice. I motioned Katrin to a marble-topped bar in the corner farthest from the band. As she approached heads turned involuntarily from some animal desire they couldn't control. She was a trophy who mingled toward me, a sad pathetic clown.

I ordered a vodka martini for her and a double J to clear my head. Katrin seemed too calm. Like she'd been here before.

I worked on the Jameson and surveyed the room. You had your white-faced clowns with traditional red noses, colored hair, basic black and white, red lips. Pink-faced comedic Auguste clowns. Sad hobo clowns. Rodeo clowns with baggy pants, suspenders, and crumpled cowboy hats. There were Bozo and Ronald MacDonald variations. Evil and killer clowns from Pennywise to Pogo, The Joker to Zeebo. Enough to make you afraid of the dark. There were girl clowns. French Maids, Spanky Stripers, Giggles, Polka Dots, Harlequins, Naughty Ringleaders, and Sexy Lion Tamers.

I finished the J and noticed that Katrin was on the dance floor with Emmett Kelly's "Weary Willy". It could be me. I grabbed another J at the bar where a couple of Krusty the Clowns held court and chugged their beers. I looked back at Katrin, and she and her partner had blended into the crowd. When the music stopped, they'd disappeared. The band broke and the spotlight swung across to a stage in the ballroom. A single spotlight lit an empty space.

Techno music. From the shadows, a hobo clown in a baggy canary-yellow costume trundled an oversized suitcase across the stage. He paused. Weary. Head down. Back bent. Small shuffling steps. Turned. Faced the audience. He panted from exertion. Bent to open the suitcase. He pulled out a black coat on a stand and a hat that he placed on top. Techno music. He brushed the coat, his back to the dance floor. Looked around wearily full of suspicion. Put one hand on the coat arm and the hand-animated the coat. The hand touched the clown. Took the brush and brushed the clown. The coat and the clown tenderly embraced. The coat brushed the clown's hair and then dropped the brush. They cuddled and swayed as in a dance. The coat hand pulled out a note and stuffed it into the clown's other hand and he put it in his deep pocket. Then the clown pulled out the note. Ripped the note into pieces. Threw the pieces in the air. More pieces fell from the sky. It snowed pieces of paper. He raised his throat to the sky and howled like a wolf. The blizzard came. The stage and the ballroom were filled with blowing paper snow and the floodlights filled the room with celestial light. With a musical crescendo, blasting snow covered the audience in the ballroom mingled with applause. This was a Slava Polunin performance.

The lights went up and I saw Katrin go through the doors behind the bar. I followed and moved through a wide corridor into a larger drawing-room than the ones we'd passed as we entered. A bookcase swung open, and I saw Katrin's costume cape trail through the opening before it closed beside a fireplace. I moved across the room and heard a voice behind me.

"Excuse me, sir. This room is not available for the party." A footman approached me clown-faced in his red and black uniform. His hand grabbed me by the bicep to escort me back to the ballroom.

I mumbled words about being sorry then caught him with a curved-fingered jab to the throat that took him down.

The bookcase had not clicked shut. I pulled on it and it opened. I squeezed through. A landing with stairs led down three levels. At the door on the bottom level, I hit the panic bar and entered an area larger than a small parking level on a high rise. Blue security lights washed the walls and floor in a garish light. There was a den for collector cars that slept in a night-light blue-haze silence. Lamborghini Aventador, Bugatti Veyron 16.4, Ferrari 458, Porsche 918 Spyder, McLaren 650S and a Pagani Zonda Revolucion. Who had that much money to spend on these toys? Old corrupt men who looked in the mirror and saw the slick-backed black hair, the tight-fit Italian leather jacket, and the runway walk from Milan, Paris, London, and New York. Sorry, I was a rumpled, wrinkled rusted Toyota guy. I heard a boot scrape at the far end and once again Katrin disappeared through a door.

Through the door, I entered a bar-lit room where an inside circus played. The clowns were lascivious. The dolls were inviting. I couldn't distinguish the players. Both sides were on offense pounding at the scrimmage line. But I knew who was behind the masks. Some had entitled faces. Others had the blank pages of subservience and survival. All faked relish. A repeated dull mantra, pathetic, sad counterfeit moans of excitement.

And in the corner, I saw Katrin in her black leather Avenger suit. The zipper from her neck was down to her navel and her breasts were being fondled by a Krusty Clown's pale hand. Grease-paint lips slobbered her face. I heard leather ripping on her suit. I heard a desperate moan. A punch. A stammered gurgle from a windpipe. My feet were cemented to the floor. Then a pipe crashed into the back of my knees, and I was down among the smells of carnal vice. I heard Katrin again—a brief smothered scream. But the scream was mine that covered over Katrin's strangled sound. Then a single gunshot. A raspy throat let out the sounds. Runjack. Runjack.

I pushed up from the floor. My hands moved but my knees hummed with pain that came in waves until I was deep in a clown-leg sea, oversized shoes, and sweat dripping from my forehead. The pipe came down on my shoulders and I was flat, mind and body full of black pain.

CHAPTER 56

I woke with my face on the carpet in the same room. Smelt the dirt, tobacco, semen, and spilled booze. Sensed the clowns who stood in the shadows. The room was no longer crowded with writhing sex-doped doll hookers. I wondered who was left. I saw six clown feet. I heard Katrin in the distance. A muffled plea for me to run. To get out of here. It was too slim a chance that she had called me. She had a reason for being here. She knew what she was doing. There was a plan.

I heard a clown laugh. The sound twisted in my gut, and I thought about Katrin, but also Murphy, Mark, and Stacie. How they all got sucked into this unspeakable vortex. And I was here, a pathetic clown who had followed his instincts but had not thought far enough down the road to avoid disaster.

"Are you with us, pal?" one said.

I didn't give them the satisfaction of a groan.

"Waiting for Yagoda," another said. "You'll need to have something left for when he gets here."

I detected the Irish. My twisted mind heard Waiting for Godot. My chances of escape were as futile. Bloody Irish. Not Italian like Commisso who was dead, but Boyle.

Two clowns picked me up and tossed me into a leather lounge chair with a curved padded back with brass studs. I surveyed the room. The hookers were gone. Three clowns with benign faces stared at me. Red hair, red lips, clowns you'd want at a birthday party to blow up balloons and make animals for the kids. But these clowns had guns and they were out and pointed at me.

Beside me in the corner was the Krusty Clown slumped in a lounge chair. In the dim light, I saw blood seep into his green pants. He had one hand on his gut. Smoke from his cigarette mingled with his green hair. Beside him, I saw Katrin's, Kimber Micro Carry.

I heard someone scream. I heard someone cry. Then I realized it was me.

One clown switched on the big-screen TV on the wall. They drank the booze left at the bar and watched a Seahawks game. They waited for Yagoda.

"Sound-proof. No one can hear you, McQueen," the Irish guy said.

Somehow, he knew I was McQueen. I was only six feet from Krusty where I'd last seen Katrin.

"I'm not goin' out like this," Krusty said. "What do you want with me?"

He stuttered on his w's. That was his tell.

"Shut up," said a clown who had stepped behind the bar. "Yagoda's waited a long time for you."

And in a flash, Krusty grabbed the Kimber, leveled it up to his eye, aimed, and fired. The bullet caught one clown in the chest. Not Irish. Irish placed a reply directly into Krusty's forehead. It was that quick. With impact, the lounge chair and Krusty both went backward. Katrin was in the corner, half across a table, face sideways. Her stare was vacant. A shadow lay across her jaw.

There was a scream inside my head when my arms were pushed to rise and propel my body toward her. I stumbled as my knees gave out in pain and I heard feet move toward me across the carpet. On the way down I grabbed the Kimber in the dead Krusty's slack hand. I swung around and fired a bullet into Irish's neck. Blood spurted like a fountain in pulses across the room. I fired two shots across the bar. Smashed the mirror and destroyed some bottles. The last clown had taken cover behind the counter. He kept his head and body down, but he reached up and fired in my direction. I pulled Katrin down onto the floor. She was warm and breathing. I tipped over the table, so we had cover behind Krusty's chair, the table, and the clown's dead body.

Rapid shots ripped through the room, perforated the back wall, and took out the TV and the Seahawks. No loss. But the shooter was out the door and into the showroom.

I felt Katrin for a pulse and it beat onto my thumb and forefinger. A thin wire was twisted around her neck. I loosened the wire, lay her flat, and breathed into her mouth, pumped her chest, and breathed and pumped and breathed. I felt her warm body beside me from last night and in the morning. Her failure at revenge. My failure to protect her. I breathed and pumped some more. Felt a darkness fall over my shoulder and then she choked up bubbles on her lips and with one huge gasp vomited on the carpet. I hugged her close, wiped the cold sweat from her forehead, and turned back to face the bar. I took cover behind the overturned table.

I ripped off Krusty's mask. The face was old and tired. Bald with thin tufts combed back across his head. Wrinkled skin. Glasses beneath the mask. He looked like a tailor or a cobbler, not a monster mastermind. I took stock. He was Yazhov, a man Katrin tonight had decided she would kill. I pulled the mask off the clown with the bullet in his chest. He was dead. Detective Reynolds. Irish lay still weakly pumping out blood. His gun was on the carpet. I kicked it away and looked into his eyes. He was all grease paint, no mask.

"Fuck you, Jack," he gurgled.

"Fuck you, Boyle." Then I put a slug into his forehead. "That's for Commisso."

Three shots out of eight were still in the Kimber. I checked my ankle for the Beretta. It was gone. Why did I bother to carry a gun? But it was on the bar's counter. I put the Beretta in the ankle holster and put Boyle's regulation issue in my pocket.

So, Yagoda was coming. I had my suspicions about Boyle and Reynolds, but the other guy was either extra muscle or maybe a mystery.

With my wrist, I swung the door open to the showroom with the fancy cars. I stayed concealed beside the wall. The opening took rapid fire. I slammed the door closed. With motion, my knees started to function as I ignored the pain. I picked up Reynolds. Dragged him to the door. Propped him up with my right hand and grabbed the door with my left and swung it open again. At the same time, I pushed him forward. His dead body took the bullets. I dropped and crawled out through the threshold and stayed low across the concrete toward the closest vehicle. Two bullets ricocheted off the polished concrete wall beside the door. I was behind the Porsche 918 Spyder, GT silver metallic. Who cared, right? Here and now, I wanted a Hummer. Not a gentrified street version but one that had been to Baghdad or Kosovo. I'd take the heat and drive out alive. That's what I wanted. And I wanted people to stop shooting at me.

Beneath the surface, I put it all together now. Yazhov, Yagoda's rival. Yazhov with the Colonel and the Laskeys went after Uncle Yasevich and Katrin at China Heights. Yazhov must also be Tarasov's rival, or at least an arch-enemy. Boyle and Reynolds, small potatoes in a syndicate run by Yagoda. And the missing piece tonight might be right here in the showroom. And Katrin? Was she here simply for revenge for what happened at China Heights? And if so, what about her revenge for Lana's father's murder?

I peeked over the Porsche. Saw a muzzle flash from beside the Lamborghini. Heard another deflection off the wall. Part of me wanted to hold back and not fire any bullets into this artistic machinery. The mind tallied the price tags and thought about all the food that could be bought to feed the hungry. I fired the three bullets from the Kimber into the Lamborghini and then threw the gun across the floor. It clattered against the Bugatti. I moved laterally the other way. I'd seen this in movies. Always worked.

I circled with Boyle's regulation issue Glock held out in front. Watched the last clown edge toward where I'd thrown the gun. I came up two cars behind him. He'd crouched both hands on his gun like in the manual but not as steady as a seasoned shooter who wasn't practiced. I waited until he showed a full profile, with arms extended, pointing the gun. I aimed the Glock, not quite a sniper rifle but accurate with a careful hand. I fired and hit both wrists with one shot. I drove my knees as much as the pain would let me and I fought through the pain and ran. Gained momentum and tackled him to the ground. One fist hit his neck and he gasped. I ripped the mask from his face. It was Machlan. What a line-up. The force's top dog. The guy who could control and manipulate just about everyone. And those he couldn't control or manipulate became disposable. He'd warned me, hadn't he, Conner? Commisso. Murphy.

"Commissioner. Fancy meeting you down here," I said.

"You're a dead man," Machlan managed to choke.

"Don't think you are in a position to predict that."

"I'm waiting for Yagoda. And so are you."

"No one knows him," I said. "Maybe he isn't real, and you've been working for a phantom all this time?"

"No one does something for nothing. Everyone has an angle. Everyone is motivated. What's your angle, Jack?"

It was a good question that went way back. Never did like anyone telling me what to do. I never did anything that wasn't justified. Maybe that was an angle. Maybe that was a reason to kill a man and not think too much about it after.

"Angle? Maybe I don't like bad people who take advantage of good people. Maybe I got a gene that wants to help the vulnerable. Maybe that gene got mutated along the line. Maybe it went viral on scum like you. Maybe that's my angle."

I heard hydraulics and looked up. The wall moved out and slid back. A Dodge Ram truck peeled out from the freight elevator and side-slipped on the showroom's polished floor. A clown drove with three clown-faced footmen with him. Suddenly I was tired of clowns and guns and cars.

The doors to the Dodge opened and they all jumped out and used the open doors as shields facing us crouched behind the Bugatti. I had Machlan in front of me with my Glock to his head. The clown from the driver's seat was white-faced, red-nosed, with shocks of purple hair. The driver had a red star on his face like the stars on the Laskey brothers' hands, like the stars on the trucks that delivered transplant victims to CPRC. Yagoda had arrived. No more waiting. The footmen, on cue, fired and both Machlan and I dropped lower behind the Bugatti. Windows pocked with bullets and the Bugatti's body splintered into the air.

"Kill him. Kill him," Machlan shouted.

I wanted to put a bullet in his mouth but didn't. I dragged him about with me. One footman on the right passenger side moved into sight. My first bullet destroyed his knee. The second stopped him cold. The next few seconds happened fast. Machlan and I got backed up behind the Bugatti and the last two footmen blitzed us, one from each side. I released Machlan but put a bullet in his leg. Then I dropped down and popped up with the Beretta and the Glock, sighted them both, and took both footmen down with two shots. All adrenalin. Machlan pulled himself up beside the car and started to scream.

"Take him down. Take him down."

I was eye-to-eye with Yagoda. The mythical Yagoda had finally arrived.

"Shoot him. Shoot him," Machlan said.

Yagoda crouched between the open door and the Dodge Ram and fired one bullet. I fired one bullet aimed at the Y-crevice of the open door where Yagoda was concealed. Machlan dropped like a stone with Yagoda's bullet, a small round hole in his head. The rear exit exploded into metal and bone fragments, and a fine red mist. My bullet clipped across Yagoda's ear. The Dodge Ram door slammed, and the tires screeched in their spinning toward the open elevator. I rushed out firing what was left in the Glock as the doors slid closed.

I slumped down beside the Bugatti and replayed the echoing sounds of gunfire. I went into the room to look for Katrin. I wanted to hold her warm body in my arms, to carry her back to Carlos and bring her home to Lana. I bent down again and felt her pulse and she grabbed my arm and squeezed.

"Don't leave me, Jack. Don't leave me."

CHAPTER 57

Carlos waited for us near the main doors. When I came out with Katrin on my shoulder and her feet above the ground, he was in shock. He bundled us into the Bentley, Katrin in the back seat and me in the front. He drove fast with a focused crazy look in his eye. He asked the obvious and I answered, "Later."

Later while he drove, I told him everything. As the story and his driving got more intense his knuckles became white on the steering wheel and his foot pressed heavily on the accelerator.

We headed for the docks and the freighter on the east side, toward Stacie and Tarasov.

"How did you get Katrin out?" Carlos asked.

"I retraced my steps up the stairs, through the bookcase opening and back to the ballroom carrying Katrin over my shoulder. The party was still going strong as a clown band blasted out heavy metal and the guests bounced and ground their bodies together on the floor. No one noticed a clown dragging his inebriated girlfriend outside for air."

Carlos didn't speak. Didn't turn his head toward me. He drove the Bentley as if it were a low-center-of-gravity sports car. I felt the car's mass, not hugging but shifting laterally with every curve.

"Slow down. We'll get there soon enough."

Instead, he gunned the accelerator. I screamed, dry-mouthed, inside my sweaty clown suit.

We passed where Norton and I dumped the Hummer. I made a connection. This time the memory was photographic.

"Pier 31?" I asked. "Warehouse 204. Refrigerated freighter. The Santa Liberia. Hummer. Plate T24976. Does that mean anything to you?"

That was Norton's story when he followed the Laskeys from The Margot.

Carlos gave me a quick glance with one eye. Then he was all focused again. I started to wonder if I'd got it all wrong.

We moved into the city toward plans that had been set. As we crossed the Cambie Bridge I saw the city's high point. There were a few fires in the distance. The center core and the more gentrified areas were in darkness. Decisions had been made. Certain areas had priority for containment, others were left to let the rabble loot and run amok.

Carlos cut off Cambie at the bridge and headed east toward the inlet where Tarasov's freighter sat in the harbor. After several twists and turns among warehouses, we turned down Pier 31. A small sign over a loading bay lit by a dusty orange light said No. 204.

"Drive on to the end."

When he got there, Carlos stopped, did a three-point turn, and pointed the Bentley back away from the water. Apart from a few dim lights on the pier and out on the water, we were in total darkness. We both got out. The harbor had developed a heavy chop. I heard the waves slap against the barnacled posts. The wind picked up in gusts. Felt like a blow and the warm air smelled like a storm would come. Gone was the furnace. The tide had turned.

I leaned on the car's open door. Carlos did the same. He looked jumpy. I saw the Tercel in the distance closer to Warehouse No. 204. I looked across the harbor at Tarasov's freighter. A dark wall cut across the inlet toward us. An apocalyptic beast began to howl. The first drops hit the Bentley. A tin drumbeat. Then the storm was upon us with vengeance. The wind was gale force. The rain in huge drops sideways.

Norton walked through the darkness as if he'd slipped past a curtain from another dimension. The water around the pier boiled around him. He carried heavy heat. A M16A2 5.56mm rifle. Although I expected him, I still jumped. Carlos looked like he'd need a defibrillator.

"Did you get them?" I asked.

"Waited for you, boss. No one's gone on or off the freighter."

"Mitchell?"

"He's with the Zodiac."

I swung around to Carlos. He looked pale.

"Carlos. Wait for us. Keep her safe."

"How long will you be? I must be somewhere in the morning."

"Where do you have to be that's more important than right here?"

I could pop him right then and there.

"Nowhere. I'll wait. I'll wait."

He looked a little panicked. Somehow the repetition didn't convince me, but I let it slide.

Norton and I moved toward the end of the pier. The waves lapped over the surface, and the Zodiac rose and fell. Mitchell held on in terror and tried to keep the bumpers as cushions between the Zodiac and the pier's concrete. I glanced back. Carlos sat in the Bentley with Katrin. The rain hammered.

Norton motioned with his head and as the Zodiac rose, he grabbed me, and we both jumped in. I heard the motor as we broke away into open water. White waves crested around us, and the boat rose and dropped, with propeller cavitation in the open air.

Norton had another M16A2 for me. Mitchell packed a handgun and wore a Kevlar vest. Norton watched me look at Mitchell.

"Got one for you too," he said.

As Norton plowed up and down over the waves and maneuvered toward the freighter, I put the vest over the clown suit that made me look even more ridiculous. Once we were in the lee of the freighter Norton cut the engine to an idle. Here the wave action died down to manageable. I knew why I'd never had a love affair with the sea. Through the grease paint, the salt spray tingled on my skin like tiny knives.

We tied up at the freighter's stern and Norton threw a rope ladder with grappling hooks over the railing. His motion was effortless. He'd done this before. Mitchell stayed with the Zodiac.

"If anyone but Jack or I come to this railing, shoot them. Don't hesitate."

He kept the same chain of command he demonstrated in the Pinto when Mark had asked him who they were. I could hear it now, "I'm Norton. This is Mitchell. I work for Jack. Mitchell works for me."

I followed Norton up the ladder. He wore Kevlar too and his pockets looked weighted down. We both took the M16A2s.

I retrace my steps when they held me here since they might have Stacie there too. I recognized a familiar door in reference to its position to the wheelhouse and the galley where Carlos had given me the soup for breakfast.

"Galley." And pointed, then jerked my thumb toward a corridor.

Norton held his position in that direction. I worked along the corridor. I heard a struggle in a room ahead, bodies bounced against walls. Grunts. Gurgling noises and then silence. I crept up to the window but couldn't see through the scratched translucent glass. I tried the latch and the door slid open. Silence. I held my breath. I stepped over the raised threshold and put one foot inside the dark cabin. Then I pull the door back. I remembered two Russian sayings and said, "Na zdorovie." Then, "Za lyo-bof." I stepped into the cabin dressed in a clown suit with Kevlar.

Mindy and Murphy were tied to chairs. Duct tape across their mouths. My eyes swung around the room. They both motioned with their heads to a corner. An obvious ruse if Stacie was tied up there.

I swung to the other corner. Mindy and Murphy did not know me in a clown suit. On the floor were two unconscious or dead Russians.

I took a chance and said, "Stacie?"

Silence.

I'd pushed all the chips into the center. "Stacie. It's Jack."

"You think I am a maiden who needs to be saved from wolves? I'm Loba, she-wolf."

Stacie came into the dim light from the opposite corner. Her face was lined with blood and dust mixed with sweat. I knew the two Russians on the floor were never getting up again.

"Those guys on the floor got a little lax." She held a handgun in each hand. "Thought you'd never get back here."

"Busy night," I said. "Doesn't look like you need any help right now."

She looked at me as if to say, "Jack. I'll take you down right here and now." I'd forgotten that she might still be pissed with me.

Stacie untied Mindy and Murphy.

"This is the last place I thought I'd see them," I said.

"This guy's a piece of work," Stacie said.

I tilted my head to the door.

"Norton's by the galley. How many different guys did you see?"

"Seven."

She followed me out the door. She told Mindy and Murphy to stay put for now. They didn't look roughed up.

"They asked me about the video and the money," Stacie said. "What money?"

"Later."

I looked through the galley window. Norton sat on a butcher-block table, legs dangling. The M16A2 was across his lap. Five guys were propped up on the floor against the far wall. Each one had a welt across his forehead and his hands were tied behind his back. I knocked on the window and Norton swung the rifle around, saw my clown face, and motioned with his head. We went in.

"Five guys?" I asked.

"Who's going to mess with this baby?" He shook the M16A2 slightly up and down. "They zip-tied each other and I tied up the last one."

Then he spoke in Russian to the men. First a calm sentence, then he jumped from the butcher block and moved right into their faces and shouted at them. One guy replied. Then another. Norton asked another question in Russian. A few more answers. Who knew? Who was this guy?

"What are they saying?"

"He is not here. The helicopter left this afternoon with two other guys. More than likely his muscle. These men here are all that's on the ship."

"Cargo?"

"We'll find what they've been trafficking. It won't be pretty."

"Did you ask them about the warehouse? 204?"

Norton spoke more Russian. One guy answered.

"Said, they know nothing about warehouse 204. Only what happens on the ship."

Norton spoke more Russian then turned to me.

"There are smuggled people in containers down below. I don't think these guys know the whole operation."

"You made all the contacts," I said.

"Reilly's waiting on my call."

"Let's do it."

Stacie and I helped get Mindy and Murphy into the Zodiac that pitched like a bronco with Mitchell wedged into the bow. Norton came to the ladder after he dragged the seamen to different rooms and braced the doors with metal bars so they couldn't help each other escape. They wouldn't have much time anyway, but it was his idea to be careful.

The harbor roiled as if it were the open sea. Waves came from all directions, collided on wharves and freighters, and rebounded back upon each other. The low-level sky was lashed with biblical rain. The city was dark. The fires on the east side were either out or obscured by the purple cloud cover. The zodiac bucked toward Pier 31. I heard the helicopters and through the darkness made out an erratic searchlight and a coastguard vessel's running lights. I'd called Reilly and knew he wasn't short-staffed anymore. Reilly had someone he could trust provided he was willing to do an end run. We did the blocking. The coast guard with its connection to higher powers was the cavalry. They'd find what was in the containers. They'd find what happened in Warehouse 204.

When we got to Pier 31, there was no time except to dash for the Tercel. Norton left the Zodiac as collateral damage. The Bentley with Carlos and Katrin was gone.

I let Norton drive. Stacie, Mindy, and Murphy were in the back seat and Mitchell curled himself like a wet mutt behind the back seat and the hatchback door. It was crowded and despite the heater, we steamed up the interior.

"Did Reilly bite on the rest?' I asked.

"That guy was so far out on a limb, worrying," Norton said, "he was willing to take extreme measures to get the chaos under control."

"And?"

"I assume he sent the video clip and all the reports from the Laskey's wrecking yard. The photos you sent him from the shoot-out at the cabin. I know he called up to that Zabella Island for the guy, Douglas Walkus, so if he isn't tainted, he's got your six."

Norton was serious behind the wheel. No one was on the road, but we were driving through the stormy broth. He got us to the Undertown shelter, where he'd had pre-arranged for us to get in no matter what time it was. It was three am. We were traumatized. I still had things to do, but I wasn't sure how I wanted to proceed.

CHAPTER 58

The rain still beat down hard on the greasy sidewalks, crumbling streets, and alleys beside the shelter. I lay back on a beat-up sofa that had found its next-to-last resting place here. Norton was wedged into a corner on the floor. The others were in the sleeping area on cots among the snorers and hackers. I ditched the clown suit and had a shower. Tried to sleep but was twitchy.

So many hydra heads—five Laskey brothers, the Colonel, Machlan, Yazhov. The heads that won't grow back. Reynolds. Boyle. All the muscle. Yagoda was the only one left. Something was poisonous and virulent. A body trail led back to the cave, but I was missing something.

Tarasov held Stacie to get me to go after Yazhov and Yagoda. Had me believe Yagoda had Murphy and Mindy. Told me Yazhov took down China Heights. Appealed to me to take both down.

But Mindy and Murphy showed up on the freighter. Katrin and Lana were not with Yagoda, but in their panic room. Yagoda didn't stick around to kill me in the showroom. Reynolds, Boyle, and Machlan worked with Yagoda.

The wall clock said six. It was light outside. Behind the blank wall, I could see in my mind the city waking up, the morning purged by fire and rain, and left to smolder in ruin. The cracks would be there, only wider. The dust, now a muck residue coated the ground. The ashes and soaked soot were pounded into the blackened earth by incessant rain. And yet joint ad hoc task forces came together to mop up, to quell the last looting and the fires. The looters had long slouched home to their meager beds.

I thought about Carlos and why he left. To get Katrin to a hospital or a safe house? Where did he have to go that was so important this morning that he didn't hang around at the pier? And then I heard Kat's voice. "Yes, but people are creatures of habit. Even in a crisis, they have rituals. Things they must do.

Who had something they must do?

"I will walk in," I said. "Tarasov is a creature of habit. Carlos has brought him here. It's Monday morning. Every Monday morning Carlos drives Tarasov to the Banya. So here he is."

Stacie and Norton were with me in the Tercel. They were packing, along with the M16A2 5.56mm rifles. For backup.

I looked across the road at an old-world hand-painted sign that said Slabada Banya—Russian Steam Baths. The square building was two stories with a concrete block exterior. The one entrance was an arch with a wrought-iron gate.

"If they let me in, it will be a long process," I said. "So, give me time. There will be no contact but after an hour, then. The muscle will be inside, but not in the actual steam baths. Got it?"

"Take in some heat at least," Norton said. 'A small gat. The Beretta."

"That's not how it works. It's not the way it's going down. I must be sure. I must be close."

"Jack. Please," Stacie said. "You can walk away from this. Hasn't it been enough?"

"That's the point. For the greedy, when is enough, enough?"

"And what's motivating you? What's your enough? A bullet in your brain? A knife slash across your throat?"

"No, Stacie. Enough is the truth and I'm going to get it and I won't be polite about it."

Norton was quiet. He knew. He'd been there.

"You're a stubborn idiot, Jack McQueen," Stacie said, "and I don't care about you. So go in there and do what your macho brain tells you, you gotta do."

I jumped from the car into the pouring rain, turned, and looked at Stacie. She was near to tears.

"See, I knew you were still pissed at me."

I crossed the street, rain splashing on my face and shoulders.

I passed through the black wrought-iron gate into a tiled corridor. At the end of the stucco sidewall was a two-by-three-foot opening with a glass front, iron bars, and a counter. Above was another hand-painted sign with a price list for Admission, Massage, Platza, Oil Rub, Salt Scrub, and Mud Treatment. As I reached the opening, Carlos came through the door.

"You have been paid for."

I walked up to him, and he handed me a key.

"Your locker," he said.

"Last night?"

"Took Katrin to penthouse to check on Lana. She is recovering fine. I called someone I can trust to look at her. Make sure. This morning, as usual, I picked up Tarasov for his ritual at Banya."

I nodded and said nothing.

We passed through the unlocked door to an interior lounge. The walls were lined with pine siding. The ceiling was fifteen feet high and in pine. The room was warm, and a wood-burning fireplace belted out heat. I recognized the muscle, two guys from the freighter who sat cross-legged reading magazines. They didn't look up but knew who I was. We entered then exited through double doors at the other end, passed through the treatment area, and into the locker room.

"Everything is set out," Carlos said. "I will meet you through that door."

He pointed to towels beside a locker and to the door that had a sign above it that said, "Thanks for the hot steam bath, the bundle of birch rods, the cold spring."—N.A. Nekrasov from *Who Can Be Happy and Free in Russia?*

I put my clothes in the locker and turned on the key. Palmed it, wrapped a thick white towel securely around my waist, and took another in my hand. Passed through the door into a cool pool area with showers to one side and a single door that I assumed was the bathhouse steam room. I went through this door. Carlos and Tarasov sat apart from each other on the lower benches. There were three levels rising from a mosaic tile floor. The ceiling was aged worn cedar. Two clouded mirrors hung on the walls. This was all new to me. A few buckets contained water and a dipper, and one bucket contained branches with leaves bound together soaking in water. The ends had been cut with a sharp hatchet on an angle.

Tarasov waved me closer to him and I sat down. He was naked and a towel was draped over his lap. His muscular upper body sported several tattoos. Two eyes on his chest. Money. Skyscrapers. A shadow gangster with a submachine gun. A double-headed eagle and the Statue of Liberty.

"This is bathhouse equation—steam room, oven, and plaitza bench. Welcome. My ritual, Mr. McQueen."

A massive brick oven four by four by five sat in one corner. Two iron doors. Gas jets. Granite boulders were like soccer balls.

"Good morning." I looked across at Carlos. No reaction.

"We work our way up. We talk later. Purify first. Use loofah and soap, steam here." He pointed to the lower benches. "Then we shower. Cold water on head. Dive into pool. Move up." He pointed to the next level. "Do this again. Then we go up to top for plaitza."

I pointed to the branches soaking in a bucket.

"Besoms," Carlos said. "Different branches. Birch, oak, linden, pine needles, maple, currant, juniper, oregano, and many other things. Good for health."

I smelt the aroma in the steam.

"We Russians stay strong," Tarasov said. "Good-looking huh? Steam bath makes me young again. Takes away evil through pores."

We all fell silent. We went through the process until we were each lying naked on our stomachs on the top level, Tarasov, and me. Carlos soaped us and brought the besoms and applied powerful strokes to our bodies, but his technique did not graze or stroke us lightly. He did not beat us either. His methods worked.

My body was opened to the steam, massaged, and invigorated. Infused with the essences in the besom. My lungs inhaled the steam and its fragrance. The heat was overpowering at this level and my head was dizzy. Eventually, we both got down to the lower level where Carlos poured cold water over us to wash off the soap and close our pores. Then he lifted the besom bucket where the branches had been soaking and heaved the hot tea onto the oven rocks. Hot steam rushed from the oven, the room temperature increased, and the air was filled with a heavy forest scent.

I am back with Kat and Peter and the lunch buckets that were filled with stones. Back in survival mode. Back with the wolves and the fear of bears.

"And now we talk," Tarasov said.

"And now we talk."

"When I am in city, I always come here. I find peace. I cleanse body. My soul. How you feel?"

I couldn't say that he was wrong. I felt more alert and stronger than I'd felt since I'd stepped off the floatplane weeks ago.

"It's good. Takes me back."

"I thank you, Mr. McQueen. You get Yazhov."

"But not Yagoda, right?"

I see Tarasov's eyes on mine. "But not Yagoda, is true."

"And the others? You know about the others, as you seem to know about everything?"

"Others? Commissioner Machlan?" he said. "Yes. And some muscle? Yes."

"And Katrin, your stepdaughter?"

Tarasov's muscles flex involuntarily. His tattoos seem to grow larger through the steam.

"Sergie asked me to look after her. I did. I was sad, but things happen."

"And Lana?"

"Hot steam will untie tongue. She is nothing to me. She is bastard. Sokolov, not her father." Tarasov pointed to the two eyes tattooed on his chest. "I know everything."

"Who is her father, then?"

"Not important." He changed the subject. "You know Stalin was a pallbearer at Lenin's funeral. He helped carry body to first wooden mausoleum. He was pallbearer survivor. He was last pallbearer. I am last pallbearer."

"And you are going to change the world? This city?"

"I am businessman. I know power. In gulag I survive. I know power."

I was frustrated with the attitude. The lofty arrogance. "You said you wanted nothing to do with trafficking people for transplants. So why are there victims in containers on your freighter?"

"Not my freighter. I hold meetings there." He started to laugh. The steam heat was intense.

"You took my friends and tortured them."

"Mr. McQueen. You are safe. I hear they are safe. It was planned. Now there will be no more Russians killed. No more squabbling over power."

I stared at Tarasov's face.

"You worry over few women," he said. "You worry over peasants donating their organs. The world is overpopulated. They are expendable."

"Mr. Tarasov. Wipe off the mirror. Look at yourself."

He had a puzzled look on his face. He turned to the wall beside him and wiped the mirror with his hand and looked deeply into the reflection. Then turned back to me.

A red star was emerging from the pores around his left eye. The same red star on the clown who shot Machlan in the showroom. The same clown everyone was waiting for. Waiting for Yagoda. And there was a fresh wound marring his ear.

I rushed him in a rage, driving for his throat, but my knees did not react as fast as they would if I hadn't been clubbed across my calves. Tarasov smashed his heel into my leg. I fell sideways and managed to punch him in the throat, but it was not enough, and he had me in a chokehold with both hands. My eyes began to pop. One hand flailed and found the empty water bucket. I grabbed it and swung it into his head. I picked up the besom and held the thick sharp end like a dagger. Tarasov's strength still held me by the neck with one hand and I drove the longer sharp birch branch into his right eye. He released me but kicked back and drove the air from my lungs, and I was down gasping on the concrete floor.

"Finish him off," he shouted to Carlos.

244

Carlos came between us. I saw the Kizlyar Hero 440C that cut the ties on my wrists back on the freighter. Three-inch, satin-finish, plain blade. His eyes were all business.

Tarasov sopped up his eye with a bloody towel.

He spoke in Russian. Sounded like an obscene command to kill me.

Carlos hovered the knife above my face and looked me in the eye.

"I told you I had to be somewhere this morning."

Then he swung around to Tarasov and drove the Kizlyar into the eye with the red star. Then Tarasov screamed when the blade plunged into his right internal carotid artery. In the steam, his blood was a red vapor that filled the air surrounding his head. Then Carlos sliced the femoral artery in Tarasov's leg and drove the knife time and again into his lower abdomen until Tarasov collapsed to the floor.

Carlos shook so much that he had to sit down.

"Lana is my daughter," he said in a low voice.

I watched him in silence.

"We are no longer waiting for Yagoda," he said.

On the way out through the lounge, we saw the muscle sitting in their chairs.

"These guys will be asleep," Carlos said, "for a long time."

CHAPTER 59

The big news that hit the media was the trafficking—the people who were crammed into containers on the freighter and in the warehouse at Pier 31. Once the story broke individuals came forward and told little details that had made them suspicious—dock workers, warehouse employees, nurses, and orderlies in hospitals. Several surgeons were rounded up. In warehouse 204 they discovered operating rooms for transplants. National Security tracked down leads to donors and recipients. Yagoda's and Yazhov's operations were exposed, and anyone remotely connected was charged. Appointments were made and positions were filled on the force that brought about investigations in cover-ups and individuals who were on the take. The riots were seen as having served a purpose since they made the politicians clean up their acts. The mayor and several cabinet ministers, though compromised, emerged from the muck unscathed and moved on, tarnished underneath but shiny on the outside. Small heads were made to roll. Scapegoats were found. Properties were seized. Bank accounts were frozen. On the surface, the dirty house had been swept clean.

Beneath all the public knowledge, the hydra that existed was dead. But the future hydra had seeds in the buried dragon's teeth that waited to be born.

Detective Murphy received a commendation for her efforts to uncover the truth and was promoted to the CO position at the Nanaimo detachment on Vancouver Island. Reilly was promoted for his work during the riots. He got Conner's position as superintendent in Vancouver. I let Mindy come back to the Painted Parrot to share my room with Sugar while I asked Mrs. Sharpe if I could sleep on the couch in the living room. Mrs. Sharpe didn't like that idea, so she offered me a back room with a closet and a bed just large enough for a medium-sized Bernese Mountain dog to curl up.

All this happened quickly over a week before the funerals. During that week I'd spent time again with Murphy. She was lucid after her coma and her condition improved every day.

One day I asked, "Did you hear me talking to you when you were in the coma?"

"I'm grateful you were there," Murphy said. "I'm grateful you sent me Mindy. She's such a delight. You both saved my life."

"But did you hear me talking?"

"You went on and on, Jack. Some nights I prayed for silence."

"You're kidding me?"

"Blah, blah, blah." Then she laughed and squeezed my hand. The light in her eyes told me she'd heard every word I'd said.

For the funeral, I shared the limo with Stacie and Jessica, my daughter, and Del who had flown in from Seattle. I hadn't seen them since they'd left a year ago. Jessica was excited to see Stacie since they had become close back on Vancouver Island, so she was a regular chatterbox. Del was glad to see me in a formal way but let me know she'd made the right choice about sole custody and about the move to Seattle so she and Jessica could stay safe from my toxicity.

It was the second funeral. Back-to-back. Katrin's father's funeral was first. Everyone bowed at his casket. Kissed the ribbon on his forehead. Placed a flower on the coffin lid. Watched him being lowered into the grave. Spilled dirt on top. Carlos was stern and strong for Katrin and Lana as he held Lana's hand while she placed the flower on the coffin. It was a ritual. Saving face within a family. An image to project to the outer world.

Funerals turned me into stone.

Everyone hung onto tissues. Wiped noses. Dried eyes.

The staff from Mephistopheles stood in a group all by themselves but they were there for Katrin. Only Meeko came over and spoke to me and Carlos, then hugged Katrin and bent down, and gave Lana a cuddle.

In the limo over to Mark's service, Del said, "I had a secret wish that you would change."

"I wish I had."

I meant it. I stared at the blinking light on the window as if this surreal reflection could take me back in time. All the bullets, shots of J, and punch-ups scattered on the trail I'd left. They'd carved out who I was. Del reached over and brushed my cheek with her fingers, and I felt for an instant that maybe I could be reborn, then the feeling like drifting smoke vanished.

Mark's service was short. A minister that no one knew mumbled a few words about stuff that no one knew. He took a segue toward the religious side. He talked about sacrifice and lambs. Burning bushes. And how Mark would be welcomed into heaven. I had trouble with that stuff, so the words drifted into blah-blah land. I could have made a speech but that had never been my strong suit. I could recite a poem about Mark, but that was it, and only inside my own head far away from the light. I was still too torn up inside with how he died, working for me on something he thought was safe.

I was a stone. We moved on to Brogans for the wake. We had the place to ourselves. Mark would have liked that. The sentries who were always nursing beers were absent. Both parties came together. Not everyone. Meeko kept close to Carlos and Katrin.

I'd been in touch with Bella from Nanaimo on Vancouver Island. All her life, she'd been saving young girls as a madam. She left that life and now ran a sex workers' outreach program, Step Out Sisters, for and by former sex workers. I thought I'd ask her for help. I even donated money to her cause.

So, I chatted with Sugar and Mindy wondering where all this left them, a small blip in their lives, now back to usual.

"How'd you gals like to make a fresh start?"

"What makes you think we need a fresh start?" Sugar, always feisty, said. "We're just fine. Ain't we, Mindy?"

"Well, there are opportunities, and if you're standing still." I wanted to say trotting around some corner in a short skirt and high heels, but I didn't.

They got the message.

"What are you sayin'?" Mindy said.

"I have a friend on the Island called Bella. She can help you out. A partnership. A paying job helping women, you know, who want out. Or even women and men who need help managing their profession, so to speak."

They both looked at me carefully and I saw they took me seriously and were mulling it over.

"Murphy is posted over there. I'll be coming over off and on," I said to Mindy.

I handed Mindy a card with Bella's name and number.

"Talk it over," I said. "Just saying, it's an opportunity."

I left them drinking rum punches and wandered over to Norton and Stacie. Norton was drinking a coke and Stacie had a Scotch. I hadn't gone to the bar. Might not. Murphy and Reilly sat at the counter in animated conversation. Both were laughing. Murphy wore a navy dress suit. She was back. I saw my hand holding hers in the Undertown hospital. All the talk in the darkness. Her darkness and mine. Hard to believe. I was numb thinking about it but looking at her now put me in a peaceful place. I turned to Norton.

"One day we'll have to have that long drink together," I said. "Heart to heart. All the details. Didn't know you spoke Russian. How many other languages have you got stuffed inside that head?"

"Maybe one day," he said.

"Can Stacie and I count on you on a regular basis."

"Regular? Count me out, but I'll be around."

Stacie chimed in, "Wait until you get my bill. You won't have a pot to piss in.

She put her hand on my bicep and in the other, she shook her glass in my face.

"So, you're still angry," I said.

She gripped my arm, firm but sensuous, not angry. She glanced over toward Katrin who had her veil down and was clinging to Carlos. Then she came back to me. Met my eyes.

"I don't care, Jack. That steam bath stunt was stupid, and I want my money."

Norton drifted away and I didn't blame him. I'd learned that he had his own methods for de-constructing.

I looked around and was glad Del and Jessica had flown back right after the funerals, or by now I'd be tag-teamed, on the mat and crying uncle.

I told Stacie about the cash that came from the gambling and how I'd taken it from the locker and deposited it temporarily in a safety deposit box. I told her, too, that to my surprise, Mark had named me, in his will for the Quonset property and the Ranger boat.

I didn't tell her that I had plans for the Ranger in the future after I had put some space between me and what went down. I didn't tell her about Kat and Peter. How I felt they needed to get away. How Peter wasn't sure, but how Kat was happy to go back to the Island to get away from bad habits. It all seemed so hopeful, talking to Kat. Telling her how Chief Tony was running a small-business incubator in Shaplow that was helping everyone who needed it in town get on their feet, not just the First Nations but everyone. I didn't tell Stacie that he was keen on helping them and would watch out that they didn't fall off the rails. I didn't tell her about the money I gave to the Undertown hospital, and that I'd paid Becky way more than she'd expected. I didn't tell her that the tattoos on Tarasov reminded me to go down to Lobelia's to get a small wolf's head put on my ankle to go with the butterfly on the other leg. But eventually, I will.

"Maybe, we could start a business together," I said. We could share the work. Get an office."

Stacie rolled her eyes at me. I knew then that not much would change. She'd have Triple AAA Security and Consulting and I'd be a PI who would work from whatever shelter I could find.

Then she said. "Let's stick to cat rescues, missing pets, and who lifted the cookies from the cookie jar." She laughed. I had not heard her laugh for a long time. She gave me a hug, and lingered on my hip, "Let's find somewhere else to be. Maybe you can write some poetry?"

"I know where we can find paradise."

Within an hour we were both looking out of a Sea-Air Beaver's windows. The Pratt and Whitney R-985 radial, 450 horsepower, engine hummed in our ears, as it headed for the Sea-Otter Hotel on Zabella Island.

Acknowledgements

Patricia Carroll for inspiring me and for beta-reading early drafts she
has been a keen developmental and line editor.
Renni Browne, founder of The Editorial Department, former senior
editor at William Morrow and coauthor of the bestselling Self-Editing for
Fiction Writers, for her help with this manuscript. Her encouragement and
advice have been invaluable.
Heather Scott, Brett Scott, Jillian Scott and Isabella Scott for their
encouragement and inspiration.

David P. Fraser

About the Author

David P. Fraser has lived in the UK, Canada, the United States and Mexico. He now lives on an island in the Pacific. His poetry and short stories have appeared in many journals and anthologies. He has also published six poetry collections but focuses now on writing mystery thrillers featuring Jack McQueen and Stacie Machado.

Dead By the Hands of Other Men is the second novel in the Jack McQueen series. His first novel is Dead or Disappeared. His third novel in the series, Respect the Dead will be available later in 2024.

Contact: ascentaspirations@gmail.com

www.ingramcontent.com/pod-product-compliance
Lightning Source LLC
Chambersburg PA
CBHW022159170626
46807CB00005B/2277